Collected Stories

Lily Brett was born in Germany and came to Melbourne with her parents in 1948. Her first book, *The Auschwitz Poems*, won the 1987 Victorian Premier's Award for poetry, and was shortlisted for the *Age* Book of the Year. Her second book, *Poland and Other Poems*, was published in 1987, and her third, *After the War*, was shortlisted for the 1990 Victorian Premier's Award for Poetry. Her first collection of fiction, *Things Could Be Worse*, published in 1990, was shortlisted for the NSW Premier's Award for fiction. It was followed by *What God Wants*, first published by UQP in 1991. In 1994 she published *Just Like That* which won the 1995 NSW Premier's Award for Fiction. Her most recent book of essays, *In Full View*, has received wide critical acclaim. Lily Brett is married to David Rankin and they currently live in New York.

David Rankin is a prominent Australian painter, represented in most major collections, and has won many Australian art prizes, including the 1983 Wynne Prize. He was born in the UK and came to Australia with his family in 1948.

Other books by Lily Brett

Things Could Be Worse
What God Wants
Just Like That
Too Many Men

In Full View

The Auschwitz Poems
Poland and Other Poems
After the War
Unintended Consequences
In Her Strapless Dresses
Mud In My Tears

Lily Brett

COLLECTED STORIES

UNIVERSITY OF QUEENSLAND PRESS

First published 1999 by University of Queensland Press
Box 42, St Lucia, Queensland 4067 Australia

Typeset by University of Queensland Press
Printed in Australia by McPherson's Printing Group

Cataloguing in Publication Data
National Library of Australia

Brett, Lily, 1946– .
Collected stories.

I. Rankin, David, 1946– . II. Title.

A823.3

ISBN 0 7022 3087 1

Contents

For David on the eve of
our twentieth year together

Acknowledgments

The stories from *Things Could Be Worse* were initially published together by Melbourne University Press (1990) and later by UQP (1992); some have appeared in various forms in the following publications: *Overland*, the *Canberra Times*, *Meanjin*, *Island*, *Australian Short Stories*, *The Australian Short Story*, 2nd ed., (UQP 1992) and *Neighbours: Multicultural Writing of the 1980s* (UQP 1991). The story collection *What God Wants* was first published by UQP in 1991.

Things Could Be Worse

It Was After The War

It was only after the war that Renia Bensky became obsessed with death.

In Germany in 1945, Renia had contemplated suicide. Her baby son was dead. Her mother and father were dead. Her grandparents were dead. Her brothers and sisters were dead. Her aunts and uncles and nephews and nieces were dead. Everybody she had belonged to was dead.

Her girlfriend, Basia, after surviving Stuthof and Auschwitz, had thrown herself off the top of a five-storey building. But Renia Bensky was too tired to die.

She sat in the barracks of the displaced persons camp and sewed. A British soldier had given her part of an old parachute. Renia was making a blouse for herself and a skirt for Rooshka, the young girl in the next bunk.

Rooshka screamed for her mother every night. As soon as Rooshka began, Renia would run out of the barracks with her hands clamped over her mouth. She was frightened her own screams would fly out.

The rhythm of the stitching reassured Renia. The skirt was taking shape. Some things were still predictable.

Renia didn't know where her husband was. She had been separated from Josl when they arrived in Auschwitz. She learnt later that he had been sent to a labour camp. Lists of the dead and the living were posted up regularly in the DP camp. Every day, Renia read the lists. But Josl's name had not yet appeared. Renia didn't know if Josl was alive. She didn't know if she was alive.

* *

Renia was suffering from a bad cold the day she found out that Josl had survived. She hadn't had a cold in her whole year in Auschwitz. Nobody had had a cold. There had been plenty of typhoid, and the Gestapo recorded diseases among the prisoners that had previously been seen by the SS doctors only in medical textbooks. But there were no cases of the common cold. Now Renia's nose dripped, her voice was hoarse and she had a harsh cough.

She could hardly look at Josl when they met. She felt separated from him by what she had seen, and what she had breathed. She felt poisoned. She could hardly accept who she was now. Her new knowledge was embedded in her. It seeped through her every thought. Sometimes it attacked her in her sleep and she would wake up crying. She knew it would always be like this.

How could she embrace Josl? How could she let him embrace her? She was not Renia Bensky, wife of Josl Bensky. She was someone else. She was a stranger to Josl. She was a stranger to herself.

Josl looked almost the same as when she had last seen him. He was much thinner, but he had the same childlike, optimistic smile that used to make her want to cry. He looked at her quietly for a few minutes. Renia now saw that he looked exhausted. He kissed her on the cheek.

In Auschwitz the prisoners were pressed so closely together on the bunks that they could only turn over if the whole row turned together. Often prisoners' vomit or diarrhoea dripped through the bunks.

In Germany after the war, when Renia watched Jewish girls flirting with soldiers, she wondered how they could think that there was any comfort to be had from somebody else's body.

When Renia kissed Josl, he wept. She knew that he understood something. She didn't know what. She went to her barracks and vomited and vomited. Josl sat silently and watched her vomit.

* *

When she arrived in Australia in 1948, Renia Bensky hated it. Melbourne was so empty. And the food! The cheese tasted like wax, and the bread was like cotton wool. The people at the Jewish Welfare Agency were kind. They found the Benskys a room in Brunswick, and gave them a bed, four blankets and two pillows. But Renia felt so alone. More alone than she'd felt in Auschwitz. More alone than she'd felt in the ghetto.

Renia and Josl were taken out by Josl's cousin, Max Borg, who had come to Australia in 1933. Max's friends, who were mostly assimilated Jews, looked at Josl and Renia strangely. Renia felt that she was an embarrassment to Max's wife, Esther.

Max and Esther were lesser lights in the Jewish social life of Melbourne. Renia could see that Esther looked down on her. One of the first things Esther had said to Renia was: "You should buy yourself an Australian dress. Here it is called a sunfrock. It will help you look like an Australian. We Jews are just beginning to be accepted, and you shouldn't cause trouble for us. Last week the bank manager did come to us, to our house, for a cup of coffee. He had coffee and a piece of cake, and he saw that we are normal, just like everybody else. It is important to be normal."

Josl tried to tell Max what had happened to Max's niece in Poland, but Max stopped him. "I know, Josl, she had a terrible time. You know, Josl, we didn't have it so easy here in Melbourne during the war. We couldn't get any herring. It wasn't so easy."

Renia tried once to talk to Frieda. Frieda was the nicest of Esther's friends. Frieda had taught Renia to make gefilte fish, and she always talked to Renia with tenderness in her voice. "Frieda, do you know that I saw some terrible things in Poland," Renia said one day. "In concentration camp, I wanted to keep living so I could tell somebody what I saw." Frieda interrupted her. "Renia darling, it is over now. You are here, safe in Australia. It is best to put those things out of your mind. It is best not to disturb yourself with those thoughts."

Esther's daughter, twelve-year-old Rivka, once asked Josl why he had big holes in his back. Renia and Josl were at St Kilda beach with the Borg family. Josl began to answer. "It was ..." he began. Esther grabbed Rivka by the arm with such ferocity that the girl began to cry. She dragged Rivka away. Fragments of Esther's conversation with Rivka floated over the tea-trees. "He could have a heart attack if he talks about such things. You should know better." Rivka returned red-faced and swollen-eyed.

After one month in Australia, Renia wanted to leave. But she had nowhere to go to. She remembered how she had begged Josl to get them out of Germany. From the moment Josl and Renia were reunited, all Renia's thoughts were focused on leaving Europe. She hated Germany. Every German sounded like a Kommandant. Josl gave her ten American dollars for her twenty-third birthday. With her birthday money, Renia bought four extra locks for the door of the room they were renting in Bayreuth. When Renia found out that she was pregnant, she bought another two locks.

One morning Renia was alone in the room. She was stitching the edges of a square of woollen material to make a blanket for the baby. The baby was due in one month. At a quarter past ten there was a soft knock at the door. Renia silently walked to the cupboard next to the bed. She got in and closed the cupboard door behind her. When Josl came home at half past six, Renia was still sitting in the bottom of the cupboard.

Josl would have been happy to stay in Germany. For a while, at least. He was doing business on the black market and making a little money. With his first bit of profit he bought Renia a black leather jacket. He felt so proud when he looked at Renia in her new jacket. It was a moment of pure joy. Josl thought that there couldn't be many higher levels of happiness than the happiness he felt looking at Renia in her leather jacket.

The rations that Josl and Renia received in Germany were enough to keep them from starving, but not enough to stop them being hungry. Josl began looking for ways to make more money.

He felt alive. He was no longer tired. He had a beautiful wife, and a child on the way. He had something to live for. God had given him a second chance. Nothing could stop him now.

Josl discovered a supply of extra food. The US army base. Josl waited outside the mess hall. When the soldiers had finished their meals, they scraped their plates into a large rubbish bin. Josl took the best scraps from the bin. He took potatoes, carrots, sausages. Sometimes he was lucky enough to find eggs. The food was so tasty. He carried it home, trimmed some of the chewed edges, and arranged the food nicely on plates. Josl never told Renia where this bounty came from.

Josl's business dealings with the US base expanded. He began buying cigarettes from the soldiers. He sold the cigarettes at a substantial profit. Josl used this profit to buy more cigarettes, and then some tea and coffee and chocolates.

He decided to branch out further. He hid himself on a freight train going to Pilsen in Czechoslovakia. There he did some shopping. He invested the bulk of his money in small electric hotplates.

Josl sold the hotplates to the Americans for cigarettes. He sold the cigarettes to Germans, who paid for them in Allied Marks. Josl sold the Allied Marks to the Americans for US dollars.

He bought an Opel Kadet. It was black, snub-nosed and very shiny. Josl hadn't driven a car for six years. He thought he would burst with pride when he first drove Renia around Bayreuth.

He bought a small white fur coat for baby Lola. This coat would keep her warm in the coldest winter. And he bought a small diamond for Renia. A new engagement ring. A new engagement with the future.

One day Josl was stopped by an American military policeman. The military police, Josl always told Renia, were gangsters, not normal people. "You just have to look at them and you can see they are not normal," he would say. "What normal person wants to be a military police? And they are all so big. Big gangsters. Big criminals. That's what they are."

The military policeman accused Josl of driving over the speed limit. The Kadet didn't go over sixty kilometres an hour, but Josl didn't argue. He was wondering what he would have to pay this giant to avoid being charged with speeding when the MP ordered him out of the car.

Josl knew he was done for. It took the MP two minutes to find the kilo and a half of butter that Josl had hidden in a box of old papers. Grinning with delight, the MP said "Today I am in a particularly good mood. If you eat this butter up now, in front of me, you can go home a free man. I will not report you for trading on the black market." Josl ate the butter. He was sick for a week afterwards.

Every day Renia asked Josl when they could leave Germany. She begged him not to do business on the black market. Each time Josl travelled to Czechoslovakia, Renia prepared herself for news of his death.

Finally, Josl couldn't bear to keep Renia in Germany any longer. They packed up. Josl gave his business tips to his old friend Moishe Mittelman, and Renia, Josl and Lola set off for Australia.

Moishe Mittelman remained in Bayreuth for another three years. In 1951 he migrated to America. He arrived in New York with $50,000.

Soon Renia Bensky became acclimatised to Australia. She no longer felt blinded by the harsh light. She owned sunfrocks and sunglasses. In the summer of 1948 she bought a pair of bathers.

Renia's next-door neighbour, Mrs Brown, taught her how to make an apple pie, and soon Renia's apple pies were the toast of many Sunday card evenings.

Renia became patriotically Australian. She hummed "God Save The King", and wouldn't let anyone voice any criticism of the country or its people.

Renia began to feel happy. At the same time, a new feeling edged its way to her consciousness. She felt that she was going to die.

In bed at night, Renia began to feel small pains in her chest. She went to see Dr Johnson. He examined her and sent her to the Women's Hospital for tests. "There is nothing wrong with you," he told Renia. "I think, Mrs Bensky, it's your nerves. It is definitely not your heart. Why don't you relax a bit? Do you have a dog? I find that taking the dog for a walk takes my mind off things. Why don't you get a dog?"

Then Renia's periods became irregular. In Auschwitz, Renia had been grateful that her periods had stopped. Her first and only period there had left her with blood-streaked legs and feet. Now, Renia was sure that this irregularity was a symptom of something terminal. Dr Horowitz was kind to her. "Mrs Bensky," he said, "we usually only worry when women bleed too much. Irregular and slight periods are nothing to worry about." Renia's next period was so heavy and painful that it reminded her of her adolescence.

Renia began to diagnose and prescribe remedies for herself. Her bathroom cupboards contained antibiotics, antihistamines, diuretics, tranquillisers and sedatives. She lectured friends on the difference between a viral and a bacterial infection, and sometimes dispensed medicines to them.

"I won't live long. You won't have me forever," Renia used to say to Lola. Sometimes she screamed at Lola: "You are killing me. Hitler didn't manage to kill me, so you want to finish me off. You will cry on my grave."

Renia went to a lot of funerals. She went to the funerals of people she hardly knew. She went to the minyans. She looked after the bereaved. But it was not enough. Renia couldn't feel as though she had buried her dead.

During the day, Renia was not alone. She carried the cries of orphans in the ghetto, and demented mothers, and lost fathers. At night when she went to bed all the dead came to visit her. The dead were all unburied. They were all in limbo. Renia often screamed in her sleep. Her screams were the screams of dying Jews. The screams had left the bodies of the dead and lodged themselves in Renia Bensky.

* *

At lunchtime at the Renee of Rome factory, the machinists ate in the staff kitchen. They shared cups of tea, sandwiches, sadnesses and happiness. Renia liked the women. All the sewing machines were pushed together in one corner of the factory, and Renia felt snug sewing in the middle of that crowd of machines. But at lunchtime Renia stood out in the hallway, in the dark corridor on the fourth floor, in Flinders Lane, Melbourne, Australia, and talked to her mother.

"Where are you, Mama? Are you in the air here in Australia? Or did you stay in Poland? I am frightened, Mama, that one day I won't be able to remember your face. Mama, there are no photographs. No photographs of you and Papa. No photographs of Shimek and Abramek, Jacob or Felek. No photographs of Bluma or Fela or Marilla. I tried to go with you, Mama, but somebody knocked me on the head and pushed me into the other line. The line of life, Mama. I don't know if you saw, Mama, I don't know if you knew that I didn't want to leave you. Oh, Mama, I am so lonely."

Sometimes some of the younger girls at Renee of Rome complained about their mothers. This one's mother didn't understand her, and that one's mother was unfair. Renia used to block her ears and plan what she would cook for dinner.

Renia often said to Lola, "You don't know how lucky you are to have parents." And Lola didn't know.

After a few years in Australia, Josl had his own small clothing business. Josl and Renia also had another daughter, Lina. Lina was born with one leg shorter than the other. Renia felt responsible for this. She thought that it could have been due to the fact that she had been bent over a sewing machine eighteen hours a day through the pregnancy. She felt consumed with guilt. She stopped working and stayed at home with Lina. At home, Renia washed and cooked and cleaned and looked after Lina.

She had a beautiful garden. A garden with rose trees and apple trees and lemon trees. Renia loved her garden. Early every morning Renia went outside and fed the birds in the garden. There had been no birds in Auschwitz, and no birds in the ghetto. For six years Renia hadn't seen a bird. Now, about a hundred birds waited for Renia every morning. There were seagulls, sparrows, starlings, willy wagtails and sometimes pigeons.

Renia never went shopping with her friends. She never went to charity luncheons or to fashion parades. She didn't play cards or bridge. She belonged to no clubs. Renia sunbaked.

On sunny days, Renia did her housework faster than usual. She then took the telephone off the hook. She rubbed Nivea cream over her face and her shoulders, and she lay down in the garden in the sun.

Even if it had been raining and the grass was damp, Renia didn't lie on a towel or a beach mat. She lay on the grass.

She loved to feel the earth on her legs, on her hair, on her scalp, on her hands. Lying there, blended into the earth, Renia Bensky felt happy.

Loti Luftman's Daughter

When she arrived in Australia, ten-year-old Michelle Luftman was put into grade one. "When her English improves we will move her up," the headmaster said to Esther Borg, Michelle's guardian.

"Mister Herbert," said Esther Borg, "Herr Professor, this girl is very clever. She can speak French. She travelled on a boat by herself for eleven weeks to come to Australia. She sat at the captain's table every night. She organised it herself. She had no-one else to organise anything for her. You know that she is an orphan. Herr Professor, if a girl is so clever that she sits at the captain's table, don't you think she doesn't deserve to be in a class with five-year-olds? Don't you think you could put her with children of her own age?" "All in good time, Mrs Borg. All in good time," said Mr Herbert.

"It's lucky my Rivka learns French at school," Esther Borg said to Ada Small, who could speak French, "and it's lucky I have got you, Ada, to help me, because, to tell you the truth, I don't know what I would do with Michelle otherwise. At least she eats everything that I give her. That you can say about her for sure, she is a very good eater, but she is a bit wild. I am used to my Rivka. She is such a good girl. She studies hard. She doesn't give me any trouble. This one, this Michelle, if I ask her not to dip her bread into her milk, she says 'Why?' I tell her it's not nice. But she doesn't care to be nice. She just keeps on putting her bread into her milk. And I know she can understand what I am saying. Oy, Ada, what am I going to do? You think God thought I didn't have enough troubles already?"

* *

Michelle Luftman was the daughter of Esther's third cousin, Loti Luftman. "I wonder if she has got some of her father's bad blood," Esther said to Ada Small. "You know, Ada, Loti married a bad type. He was a gambler with a big eye for the girls. Loti's parents didn't give their blessings to the marriage. This did upset Loti, but she was so madly in love with this gambler that nothing else mattered. They left Lodz in 1937 to live in Paris. I heard that Loti's mother was never the same after her daughter left."

When Esther was asked by the Jewish Welfare Agency whether she was willing to take in her cousin's daughter, she was horrified. She'd hardly known Loti, so why would they ask her to take in Loti's child? Mrs Silberman from the Jewish Welfare Agency had explained to Esther that welfare agencies in Paris were looking for orphaned Jewish children who had been in hiding during the war or who had lived as Christians in Christian families. They were reclaiming these children and placing them with Jewish families.

Esther was superstitious. She was frightened of not doing the right thing. She reminded herself that it was the greatest honour, in God's eyes, to look after an orphan. And so Esther had said yes, she would take Michelle into her home.

Sometimes, at night, Esther wondered how Loti had died. She knew that she had died in Auschwitz. She knew that by the time Michelle was born the gambler had already left Loti for a wealthy French woman. Esther had heard this news from her cousin in Lodz. Esther had also heard that in 1939 Loti had wanted to come home to Lodz with the baby, but her father had told her that things were very bad in Poland and that she and the baby would be safer in Paris.

Loti was making arrangements to leave for Grenoble when the Gestapo began rounding up the Jews in Paris. Loti knew that the Gestapo were making surprise raids on Jewish homes. Each time Loti returned to her apartment she left the baby in her pram in the street while she checked the apartment. Inside the pram Loti kept a note. It read: "This baby is not to be moved until I return. I have only gone inside for a short while."

The day that the Gestapo were waiting for Loti, she had parked Michelle outside Monsieur Renard's bakery. Monsieur Renard knew Loti and always kept an eye on the pram. Monsieur Renard watched the Gestapo take Loti away. She didn't even glance in the direction of the pram. When Loti hadn't returned by the time it was dark, Monsieur Renard wheeled the pram to his sister's house. He asked his sister to look after the baby until Loti's return. Monsieur Renard's sister kept Michelle for a few days before giving her back to Monsieur Renard. "She looks too Jewish," she said to her brother. "I'm not going to be killed or run the risk of my family being killed for one small Jewish child."

Monsieur Renard, a middle-aged bachelor, was heartbroken. Michelle was such a sweet child. She could already say a few words, and she was always in a good mood, always smiling. She didn't look Jewish. With her blonde hair and heart-shaped face, she looked more Norwegian than Jewish. But his sister would not change her mind.

Monsieur Renard took Michelle home with him. He kept her hidden in the back of the bakery. Several times a day he would step out of the shop to see if he could see any sign of Loti coming back. After four months Monsieur Renard knew that he had to make a decision about Michelle. Although she was an obedient child, and kept very quiet while the shop was open, it was becoming more and more difficult to hide her. Once, when he hadn't been able to pop into the back and see her for a few hours, she ran into the shop and hugged him.

She was his cousin's child, he explained to a curious customer, and he was looking after her while his poor cousin recovered from tuberculosis.

But he was nervous. There were many Nazi collaborators, and it was impossible to recognise them. Monsieur Renard's sister heard of a Catholic woman who would take Michelle in, for a small fee. "Just until her mother comes back. Just until after the war,"

Monsieur Renard said to Madame Guillaume. Michelle screamed and screamed when Monsieur and Madame Guillaume came to the bakery to collect her. She clung to Monsieur Renard. It took both men to disengage Michelle from Monsieur Renard. After Monsieur and Madame Guillaume left with Michelle, Monsieur Renard howled like a child.

Michelle stayed with the Guillaume family for eight years. Pierre and Marie Guillaume were good to Michelle. They took her to church every Sunday. She was a curious child, and a quick learner. By the time she was three she could recite the rosary. Several times a day she would say "Hail Mary full of grace the Lord is with thee. Blessed art thou amongst women and blessed is the fruit of thy womb, Jesus." She would, if she was asked, say that her mother was Jeanne Lafitte, cousin of Monsieur Renard. "My mother is very sick in a sanatorium," she would say.

Monsieur Renard sent a small weekly stipend to Madame Guillaume, but he never came to visit Michelle. A visit, he thought, would disturb her. It would do her more harm than good.

When Michelle was six, Madame Guillaume gave birth to twin boys, Alain and Auguste. Michelle doted on them. She fed them, she sang to them, and she walked them round and round the square in their big double pram.

"I don't know how I would have managed without Michelle. She is a gift to me from God," Madame Guillaume said to her husband. When the war ended, Madame Guillaume became very agitated. Every day she ran down to the letterbox to see if there was any news of Loti Luftman.

One day a letter arrived from Monsieur Renard. Loti Luftman had perished in Auschwitz, he said. Madame Guillaume could not contain herself. She wept with relief. She did not want to experience her happiness at the expense of somebody else, she told the priest at confession, but she was overjoyed that Michelle was now hers.

* *

On the other side of Paris, Monsieur Renard's sister was bothered by her conscience. Finally, she phoned the Jewish Welfare. "I have to do this," she said to her husband. "I have to make sure that that poor little girl knows who her real people are. I deserted her once, and I am not going to desert her again. It is not right that she is being brought up as a Catholic."

The day that the people from the Jewish Welfare came to collect Michelle, the whole Guillaume family was crying. Michelle clung to Madame Guillaume. "Maman, maman, don't let them take me," she screamed. "Maman, maman, don't let them take me!"

Mrs Polonsky from the Jewish Welfare escorted Michelle on the train to Marseilles. "This woman is taking me away from my mother," Michelle told everyone in the carriage. She repeated it whenever anyone walked through. Nobody took any notice. When Mrs Polonsky tried to put her arm around Michelle, Michelle bit her. When they reached Marseilles, Mrs Polonsky put Michelle on board the boat for Australia. The purser agreed that it would be best if they locked Michelle in her cabin until the boat was ready to leave. When the boat sailed Mrs Polonsky heaved a sigh of relief.

To celebrate Michelle's first birthday in Australia, the Borg family went out to dinner at Giuseppe Botticelli's Italian Cuisine Restaurant in the city.

"Have you got a French onion soup?" Esther Borg asked the waiter.

"We have a beautiful minestrone, but madame, if you wish, we will make you a French onion soup," said the waiter.

"Good," said Esther. "This girl is French, from France you understand, and she likes an onion soup."

"Excuse me, this is not onion soup," Esther announced when the soup arrived. "This is kapushniak."

"Madame, I assure you that this is French onion soup," said the waiter.

"This is kapushniak. Polish cabbage soup. And it is not such a good kapushniak," said Esther.

"You expect an Italian to make a good kapushniak? You are crazy," said Josl Bensky. The Borgs had invited the Benskys to join the celebration.

"You have to be very careful about what you eat in a restaurant," said Renia Bensky.

"Yes," said Josl. "I did eat some worms last week and oy Gott was I sick. Sick like a dog. I usually don't eat those worms, but they were in a special dish a girl did bring to the factory for her birthday."

"Josl, they are not called worms," said Renia. "They are called prawns."

"You are, like always, right, Renia, they are called prunes," said Josl.

"Prawns, Josl, not prunes," said Renia.

"Prunes and prawns. Sounds like the same thing to me," said Josl.

"Josl, you have to learn to say the right word," said Esther. "We are in Australia and in Australia we speak English. Oy, look who is at the table in the corner. It's Mr and Mrs Belgiorno from the fruit shop. Good evening, Mr and Mrs Belgiorno. Good evening." Esther lowered her voice: "She is eating crapes. Crapes is a fish with a shell. It is not trayfe, but maybe one day we will try a crape. After all, none of us is religious."

"It's not a crape, Mum," said Rivka. "It's a lobster."

"It's for sure not a lobster, it's a crape," said Esther.

"I think Esther means a crab, not a crape," said Max Borg.

"Oh. I know what Mum meant," said Rivka. "She meant a crayfish."

"That is what I said, a crapefish," said Esther.

"It's not for me, such a crapefish," said Josl.

The next day Max Borg came across Mario Belgiorno in Lygon Street, Carlton.

"How you like that meal last night at Giuseppe Botticelli's?" asked Mr Belgiorno.

"It was very nice," said Max. "The kapushniak was not so nice, but I can't complain if an Italian can't make a kapushniak."

"I had a polenta," said Mario Belgiorno, "and this morning I ring Botticelli and I say to him, 'Why you put on the menu something you can't cook? I come from Venezia and every Friday we have polenta and fish. You must have a German cook because he put bacon in the polenta.' I say to Botticelli, 'We don't put bacon in the polenta.' "

Max reported this conversation to Esther.

"I knew this restaurant didn't know what they were doing," she said. "The kapushniak was shocking."

When Michelle was twelve, Esther Borg went to see Mr Herbert again. "Herr Professor," she said, "I beg of you to put Michelle into at least grade six. She is a very intelligent girl. So she doesn't want to learn about the grazing lands of Gippsland or the discovery of the Darling or the story of wool, so is this so terrible? What is it about these things that she should be so interested in? Herr Professor, it is something shocking that a twelve-year-old girl should be in grade three. Herr Professor, she is an orphan. Don't you make special allowances for orphans?"

"Mrs Borg, I can see your point of view, but I have a school to run and I can't put a child up who refuses to do her projects," said Mr Herbert.

Michelle was happy in grade three. She was with the same children she had started school with in grade one. Michelle liked her classmates. She often told them stories about the Guillaume family. The children loved the stories of the twins and how no-one except Michelle could get them to eat beans.

Sometimes, on the way home from school, Michelle would stop at St Kevin's church around the corner from the South Street Primary School. She could still remember her prayers. She never

prayed for anything in particular. She was just soothed by the presence of God.

The few times that Michelle mentioned God or the Guillaume family to Esther Borg, Esther would try to stop her from speaking. "Shush, shush, Michelle," she would say. "You mustn't upset yourself. That is in the past, and the past has gone. You are our daughter now and we love you like our own daughter. You must forget the past and think of the future. And better still, you could think of your schoolwork. A girl like you in grade three, it is shocking. Also, you could stop, once and for all, dipping your bread in your milk."

"I don't know how Esther manages with that Michelle," said Josl Bensky to Renia. "This morning Max came to pick me up. He had Michelle in the car. She jumped into the front seat. I said to her: 'Excuse me, I am going to sit in the front seat.' She said to me: 'No, I am. It is my car, not your car.' Is that a nice way to behave?"

"You know, Josl, I feel sorry for Michelle," said Renia. "She was dragged away from a family who loved her. I hear Esther doesn't even let her write to them. So what, so they were Catholic? She was happy. Is it such an important thing to be Jewish? Look at all the people who died because they were Jewish. Why is it so wonderful to be Jewish? And what sort of a Jew is Esther Borg? Josl, what sort of a Jew is she? Does she go to synagogue? Does she observe even the holiest of holy days? Of course not. So this poor child got dragged from a good family to come and live a Jewish life. Is it such a good life, Josl, that it is better for her?"

Michelle left school at fifteen. She had completed grade five.

"I did my best," Esther Borg wailed. "The child wouldn't do her projects. What could I do?"

Max Borg got Michelle a job in the Baumes' grocery shop. Michelle worked there with Mrs Baume and her son, Shmul. Mr Baume worked in a factory. Baume's was the first kosher grocer shop in Melbourne. Michelle weighed and served pickles and herrings. She sliced sausages and packed breads and bottled oil. Sometimes women left their children with Michelle while they went next door to the butcher's.

"Michelle is a wonder with children," Mrs Baume told everybody, "and she is a wonder in the shop. I don't know how we managed without her."

Michelle talked to the customers and she talked to Shmul. She talked to Shmul every day. And Shmul listened. On the eve of Michelle's sixteenth birthday, Shmul asked Michelle to marry him.

"I need this like I need a hole in the head," Esther Borg said to Max when Shmul asked for Michelle's hand in marriage. "What for does she want to marry a religious boy? Is this what she came to a modern country to do? To be a religious fanatic? Thank you, no."

But Max Borg gave the couple his blessing. "He is a good boy, Esther, and he will be a good husband to Michelle," said Max.

On their wedding night, Michelle said to Shmul, "Shmul, maybe if we are very lucky we will have twins."

"Maybe we will have two sets of twins," said Shmul.

"You know, Renia, Michelle won't eat at my house any more," said Esther. "That's what I needed, a religious maniac. She goes to synagogue, she keeps a kosher house. My God, she even wears a shaytl, with such beautiful hair, she wears a wig. I said to her last week: 'Come on, just take one piece of klops home.' She wouldn't. What did I need this for? Soon she won't even have a glass of water in my house. And with that shaytl on she looks like she lives in a village in Poland. I should have been able to see what was happening between her and that Shmul."

"What you should be able to see, Esther my darling cousin," said Renia, "is that Michelle looks happy."

"Happy, happy, what does Renia Bensky know about happy?" Esther said to Max that night.

"Esther darling, if Michelle won't eat with us maybe you could cook at her house and then everything will be kosher and we can eat there with them?" said Max.

"I have got a shocking headache from being with Renia Bensky, so please leave me in peace," said Esther.

A year after the wedding, Esther saw Mr Herbert outside the school. "Hello, hello," she called to him. "I would just like to tell you, Herr Professor, that my Michelle has done very well. She has found herself a beautiful husband. He is good to her like gold. And any minute now we are going to be grandparents. And let me tell you, Herr Professor, that she has done all of this without your help. She has done all of this without the projects about the mighty merino or the death of the dinosaur. Yes, Herr Professor, my Michelle has done very well and she has done it all by herself."

An Illness

Lola Bensky looked at her mother fussing around her younger sister, Lina. Lina had been born with one leg shorter than the other. So what, thought Lola. All it meant was that she limped. But her mother seemed to think it meant Lina's life was in danger.

Mrs Bensky was sitting on Lina's bed. "Lina darling, it's time to get out of bed and get ready for school. Sit up and drink your orange juice, darling."

Lola grimaced. She didn't think Lina was a darling.

Lola didn't feel like going to school today. Bruce Matthews had been bothering her in class. Although he was in grade six, he was six feet tall. He had moved into the desk behind Lola. He stuck rude signs on her back, and he looked menacing.

Mrs Bensky was still fussing around Lina. "Watch her carefully on the way to school, Lola," she said. "She can't go without a cardigan."

"I don't feel well, Mum," said Lola.

Mrs Bensky looked startled. Lola never got sick. "You'll feel better after you have something to eat. Your breakfast is on the table," she said.

Lola knew she would have to try harder if she wanted to stay at home today. "I feel too sick to eat," she said.

Mrs Bensky stopped buttoning Lina's cardigan. "What is wrong with you?" she asked Lola.

"I've got a stomach ache," Lola said.

Mrs Bensky did look worried now, thought Lola. And no wonder. Lola was always eating. She ate everything that Mrs

Bensky fed her and more. She ate so much that Mrs Bensky had to keep all her biscuits, cakes and chocolates locked in the kitchen cupboard.

But Lola knew where the key was. She was an expert at biting off both ends of the walnut horseshoes until they formed smaller horseshoes. She licked the middle of plump, chocolate-filled macaroons, and left them marginally slimmer. She could pick the sultanas and poppyseed out of the strudel and leave it looking untouched.

"Have a nice piece of cantaloup, darling. A piece of fresh cantaloup will make you feel better," said Mrs Bensky.

This is not working, thought Lola. Maybe Mrs Bensky knew she was lying? Mrs Bensky always said that mothers and policemen could read the truth in children's eyes. Lola kept her eyes averted.

"I think I'm going to vomit," she said. Nothing happened. Mrs Bensky didn't move. Lola opened her mouth, clutched her stomach, and screamed. Lina started crying. Mrs Bensky rushed to comfort Lina. "Get into bed, Lola," she said.

When Lina had calmed down, Mrs Bensky came and sat on Lola's bed. She took Lola's temperature. "You haven't got a temperature, darling," she said. "Maybe it was something that you ate that is giving you the upset stomach? I will take Lina to school and if you are still not feeling well when I come back I will ring Dr Stone."

Lola was happy. She would spend the day in bed, reading. Mrs Bensky got ready to leave with Lina. Every now and then Lola let out a small groan or a loud whine. Lola felt pleased with herself. Mrs Bensky was starting to look really worried. Lola remembered that there were some fresh almond slices in the cake cupboard. This was going to be a good day.

Mrs Bensky and Lina finally left. Lola leapt out of bed and ran into the kitchen. She had a good fifteen minutes before Mrs Bensky returned. She grabbed three slices of honey cake, which she had neatly sheared off the sides of larger slices. She took half

of a wedge of cheesecake, and boy, was she in luck, there were loose scorched almonds. Her mother would never miss a few handfuls, thought Lola.

Lola hopped back into bed. She ate quickly. That breakfast would have to do her until three o'clock when Mrs Bensky went to pick up Lina.

Lola was swallowing the last scorched almond when Mrs Bensky arrived back.

"Darling, you look a bit red and hot. Where is the pain?" she asked. Lola pointed to the lower part of her stomach.

"Is it still as bad as it was this morning?" said Mrs Bensky.

"It's worse," said Lola.

"I think I will call Dr Stone," said Mrs Bensky.

Lola liked Dr Stone. She often chatted to him while he pressed tongue depressants down Lina's throat.

"Dr Stone will be here as soon as he has finished in the surgery," said Mrs Bensky. She tucked Lola into her bed.

"Are you sure you don't want some cantaloup?" she said. "No thanks," said Lola.

"What about an orange juice, freshly squeezed?"

"No thanks, Mum," said Lola.

Mrs Bensky started to clean the house. Lola settled down with a book under the sheets. From time to time she remembered to moan.

Dr Stone arrived just after lunchtime. Lola had refused to eat any lunch. She was starving. It hadn't been easy to say no to lunch. Mrs Bensky had offered her some apple compote, and some chicken soup with rice. Lola loved chicken soup with rice.

Mrs Bensky had looked very distressed when Lola said no to the chicken soup. Lola started to feel guilty about her mother. Had she taken things too far by refusing the chicken soup?

Dr Stone poked and prodded Lola. He told her to lift her right leg and then to bend it as close to her chest as she could. He asked her to pinpoint the pain in each of these positions. Lola was smart. She was consistent about which part of her stomach hurt most.

When Dr Stone finished, Lola smiled at him, but he wasn't smiling. Dr Stone and Mrs Bensky went into the kitchen. Lola could hear them talking. She was a bit hungry, but on the whole things were working out quite well, she thought. Maybe she would even get to spend another day in bed.

Dr Stone and Mrs Bensky came back into Lola's bedroom. "Well, my girl," said Dr Stone, "I think you have got appendicitis." Lola felt proud. She looked up at Dr Stone as he continued, "It seems to be in quite an advanced state. I think we might take you to hospital now."

Now? Hospital? Lola felt faint. Then she felt sick. Dr Stone helped her to the toilet. She had violent diarrhoea. Dr Stone helped her back to bed. He rang for an ambulance.

Mrs Bensky was weeping. "Oy, my Lolala, my poor Lolala."

"I'm going to vomit," said Lola. Mrs Bensky rushed for a bowl. Lola vomited and vomited.

Lola was still shaking in the ambulance. The ambulance men were very nice. One of them held her hand all the way to St Andrew's Hospital. "Get a move on," he shouted to the driver. "She's in bad shape."

The nurses were also sympathetic. "Poor kid, have you eaten anything today?" said a nurse.

"No," cried Lola.

"Good," said the nurse. "Give her a wash," she said to another nurse, "and we'll prep her."

Prep her? What was that? Lola felt sicker and sicker. Her heart raced and she couldn't stop crying. What had happened?

Mr Bensky came rushing in to see his daughter before they wheeled her away. "Don't worry, darling, you will feel so much better after the operation. My poor darling, you look so terrible. Mum is worried out of her mind. Just remember you will feel much better afterwards," he said. "I love you, darling," he added. Tears ran down Mr Bensky's face as he waved goodbye to Lola.

* *

Afterwards, Lola felt awful. Her throat hurt. She had a horrible ache in her stomach, and her mouth tasted terrible. She wove in and out of a nightmare in which a young nurse kept telling her it was all over and she was fine.

Later, Dr Stone came to see her. "You have been a very brave girl, Lola," he said. "The appendix didn't look too bad. It looked fine actually, but you can never be too safe in these cases. You have got a cut right down the middle of your tummy. We thought we should have a good look around, but all is well in there."

Lola looked up at him. She knew that he hadn't told her parents and never would.

"Don't worry, you'll be out of hospital in two weeks and we'll get you some ice-cream for that sore throat," said Dr Stone.

Mr and Mrs Bensky and Lina came to visit Lola. They looked at her solemnly.

"I heard you have got twenty-two stitches," Mr Bensky said to Lola.

"We are so proud of you, darling," said Mrs Bensky. "Acute appendicitis and she didn't even complain!" Mrs Bensky added to a passing nurse.

Lola tried to listen to *Take It From Here* on the radio, but it hurt her too much when she laughed. The kids in Lola's class sent her a big box of chocolates, but she wasn't hungry.

Dr Stone smiled reassuringly as he took Lola's stitches out. "Well, you're right as rain now. Don't carry anything too heavy for at least two weeks, and be careful going up and down stairs. You can go home tomorrow," he said.

Lola went back to school on the first day that Dr Stone thought she was well enough.

In later years, Lola envied people who got bronchitis or chickenpox or ingrown toenails. Anything that wasn't really serious. Lola had trouble even catching a cold.

A Drive

She always called him "Ma Motl". They only had each other. He called her "Ma Nusia". They were the same size. Both short and round.

Nusia and Motl lived two doors from the Benskys. Every summer, on the Australia Day weekend, the Benskys took Nusia and Motl to Lorne for four days.

On the drives to Lorne, Nusia used to wear a pair of underpants on her head. To protect her hair. Lola and Lina had to stuff hankies in their mouths to stop their giggling.

Josl Bensky drove like a maniac. He had a need to overtake everyone else on the road. Lola's job was to look out for the police. She had to take this seriously, as it was her fault each time he was booked for speeding.

Lola and Lina would glimpse the expressions on people's faces as they caught the sight of Nusia with her pink silk underpants flapping in the wind. The pain of the sisters' suppressed laughter was agony.

Every now and then Renia Bensky would turn around and glare at the girls. Before the trip she would tell the girls, yet again, what good people Nusia and Motl were. "Look, so they don't have money. They've got big hearts, bigger hearts than all the ones with big money. And they're poor people, they haven't got children."

This last poignant note never really rang true to the girls, as having children hadn't seemed to make their mother's life much happier.

All the Benskys' friends had come to this country fresh from

Auschwitz or Dachau, or if they had been lucky, a couple of years buried in a bunker. But once here they had made it. They had nice houses, nice cars, big factories that were big business. They built flats that destroyed half of St Kilda and defaced the bayside beauty of Beaconsfield Parade.

Their kids weren't much good. Even Renia Bensky, although she tried to deny it, could see that. So what were Nusia and Motl missing?

Motl sat with his arm around Nusia, next to the girls in the back. They kept smiling. They were enjoying the trip, too. Nusia repeated the same stories of Lola's childhood. "Remember, Motl, when she was a little girl? She would answer the phone: 'Hello, this is little Lola. I'll talk to you.' "

Josl, momentarily distracted from his goal of being first in line on the road, would launch into a diatribe about how nothing had changed, how much business he lost because no-one could get through to him on the phone at night. He would rant about the hours that Lola spent talking to girlfriends who, God help him, she'd only just left, after probably having talked to them at school all day. Renia, who didn't like most of Lola's friends, nodded in approval.

This distraction usually occurred on the Great Ocean Road, which curves and bends sharply alongside a drop of 500 feet to the sea. Every Christmas a car goes over the cliff.

Nusia and Motl smiled warmly. "It's nice to be a good talker." Nusia linked arms with Lola. The love flowed from her.

Nusia had the longest, most beautiful nails. They shone like dark red porcelain. Just as they arrived at the Lorne Hotel, Nusia would adjust the underpants with an elegant movement of the hands, smooth Motl's collar and sit back with an air of expectant excitement.

Every year the girls thought that she would take the underpants off before walking into the foyer. They prayed that she would take them off.

The front driveway of the hotel was full of people unpacking. They walked back and forth carrying fishing equipment, surfboards, rubber dinghies, beach mats, table-tennis bats, fly-spray and suntan lotions.

Lola and Lina looked at each other. It was one of their rare shared moments. Would she take them off? God, what if there were any boys watching? Could they stay in the car and find their rooms later? Would Renia miraculously understand and save them? How could they not hurt Motl's and Nusia's feelings?

Lina developed delayed car-sickness. Being sick worked miracles in the Bensky family; Lina was allowed to lie wanly on the back seat. Nusia looked at Lola. Through the ribboned pink lace frills, Lola could see the perfectly set blonde waves. "Oy, Motl, such a sweet face she has. I baked such a lovely apple cake, no sugar, plenty of apples. Darling, carry it carefully."

Lola carried the cake. Nusia and Motl walked either side of her.

"You know, darling," Nusia said loudly, "I've got a little piece of beautiful cheesecake in the bottom of the box. Mummy won't mind. It doesn't hurt to have one piece. Too thin doesn't look nice. Look at that one in her shorts. Looks like her mother doesn't feed her."

Lola and Nusia and Motl stood in the queue checking in. Lola smoothed down her new gingham dress, held her stomach in and tried for her most sophisticated expression. Motl put his arm around Lola. "Such a sweet girl."

Nusia sighed in reply: "Oy, Ma Motl, what a lovely holiday we're going to have."

A Family Portrait

Renia Bensky's hair was slightly bouffant and stylishly cut short. Blonde, with coppery highlights glinting through — a colour that was very popular in Caulfield that year.

Laid out on the bed were a grey herringbone light wool tailored suit and a black and white spotted silk blouse with a once-again-fashionable Peter Pan collar. The sheer, fifteen-denier Smoky Nights pantihose screamed: "High Leg. Sheer to the Waist."

The herringbone suit sat smoothly on Renia. She patted her tummy with pleasure. It was always flat. Even when she sat down there was no bulge. All her friends admired her figure.

At the dinner parties she hosted every fifth Sunday night, Renia never sat down. All night she rushed between the dining room and the kitchen. Every fifth Sunday she served gefilte fish that everyone agreed was just right, not too sweet. Then came hot fried flounder in a sauce of onion, tomato and dill, followed by an entrée of chopped liver. The secret of Mrs Bensky's smoother, lighter chopped liver was simply an extra egg. One kilo of chicken livers, two large onions and five boiled eggs was the recipe she guarded with her life. The main course was a roast shoulder of veal with large, hot, boiled potatoes. If she could find a duck lean enough when she went shopping in Acland Street, she served roast duck.

The meal ended with Mrs Bensky's sponge cake. Mrs Bensky was famous all over Melbourne for her sponge cake. She told anyone who wanted to hear that her sponge cake was not fattening: it had only a tiny bit of sugar and hardly any flour. No-one was quite sure what held it together, but they ate it in large slices with relish, secure in the knowledge that it wasn't fattening.

Later in the evening, when the men settled down to play cards, usually gin rummy, and the women nestled in groups whispering, usually about their husbands and children, Mrs Bensky cleared the table, put out the chocolates and washed the dishes.

On the other Sunday nights, when it was Mrs Ganz's or Mrs Small's or Mrs Zelman's or Mrs Pekelman's turn to have dinner, Mrs Bensky helped. They could rely on her to serve the latkes straight from the frying pan, before the grated potato mixture became cold. Mrs Bensky would swiftly spoon out generous portions of cholent and kishke. Before anyone could say they were on a diet, their plates would be full of oxtail, baked for twenty-four hours in a glue of chicken fat, onions, garlic, lima beans, barley and potatoes.

Very few of the group had ever seen Mrs Bensky have a meal. For that matter, neither had her family. They had watched her chew a crust of toast while she prepared dinner, or have a bowl of semolina to soothe her nerves.

Six nights a week Mrs Bensky served grilled baby lamb chops with salad, grilled calf's liver with salad, grilled whiting with salad or a lean roast chicken with salad. The helpings always came in under five hundred calories. Mrs Bensky washed the dishes loudly while her family ate.

She often told her fat Lola how she herself had no tolerance for sweets. "Do you ever see me with a chocolate? I can't eat them. They taste something terrible to me." While she said this she glowed and looked even more beautiful.

Mr Bensky and the girls were quite self-sufficient. They didn't really need her meals. Mr Bensky kept a large supply of Toblerone bars in the glovebox of his new Fairlane. He did messages for Mrs Bensky willingly: some minced chicken from Rushinek's, some challah from Monarch's. Whenever she said "Josl, can you pick up ...?" he rose from his armchair. "No trouble, Renia." On the way he stopped at Leo's for a triple chocolate gelato.

Lola fed herself at Pellegrini's in Bourke Street on her way home from school, and Lina had a fast and accurate aim in and out of the fridge. She could remove a cheese blintz and digest it in ten seconds.

Mrs Bensky stepped into her shoes. Light grey suede, pointy-toed and soaring on six-inch stiletto heels, they were made by Maud Frizon of Paris and bought from Miss Louise of Collins Street, Melbourne. At Miss Louise's winter sale, Mrs Bensky paid £20 for these £79 shoes.

Mrs Bensky had a real eye for a bargain. She saved hundreds of pounds a week. Mrs Bensky personally knew every manufacturer of swimwear, evening wear, hosiery, overcoats, underwear, knitwear, furs, suits and sportswear within a ten-mile radius of Flinders Lane.

She walked briskly into the bathroom, relishing the feeling of power that came with the extra height. Searching in the lipstick drawer, she decided that Unspiced Rose by Estée Lauder was the right shade for today. First she outlined her lips with brown eyeliner pencil. Then she applied a thick, glossy coat of Unspiced Rose. Pleased with the result, she smiled at herself in the mirror.

The bathroom had sixty feet of mirror attached to sliding doors around three of its walls. These doors concealed endless shelves: shelves crammed with cleansers, toners, exfoliating creams, neck, chin and eye creams, thigh creams, day creams and night creams, clay and mud and apricot masks, ampoules for firming your skin and lifting your breasts, cell extract treatments to remove wrinkles and dimples, and chimiozymolsat of yeast, which favourably affects the oxygen balance of epidermal tissue.

When Mr Bensky had built this oversized bathroom, he'd had high hopes of being able to shave in peace. Eventually, in despair, he'd removed his Remington electric razor with four different cutting blade selections and automatic overseas conversions to the small cupboard in the toilet next to the bathroom, and there he found his peace.

* *

Mr Bensky spent two hours a day in the toilet, between 7 a.m. and 8 a.m., and again from 9 p.m. to 10 p.m. The seemingly endless stream of volcanic farts erupting from him in there was a source of excruciating embarrassment for Lola, whose bedroom was across the hallway. If she had a girlfriend staying overnight, Lola set the alarm clock for six-thirty. At five to seven she nonchalantly turned her transistor on to full volume. Johnny O'Keefe screaming "Shout" at the top of his lungs on 3UZ was barely a match for Mr Bensky's early-morning evacuation.

Touching up her eyelashes, already lengthened and strengthened by Fabulash, Mrs Bensky reminded herself that it was their turn to pay for the pictures this Saturday. She looked up the phone number of the Rivoli and rang straight away, because it wasn't always easy to get seventeen seats on a Saturday night.

The gang, as Lola called them — the Benskys, the Smalls, the Ganzes, the Zelmans and the Pekelmans — were joined by the Feiglins, the Glicks, the Blatmans and poor divorced Mr Berman for their regular Saturday-night excursion to the pictures.

They'd seen almost every film shown in Melbourne since 1952. Mrs Bensky thought of herself as the intellectual of the group. She liked *Wild Strawberries* and *Last Year at Marienbad*, while others enjoyed *The Pink Panther* and *My Fair Lady*.

At interval, Mr Bensky liked to be the one to buy the snacks. He could get as much as he needed, and it was dizzyingly satisfying for him to buy scorched almonds for seventeen people. Seventeen people could eat a lot of scorched almonds. Mr Bensky liked to make sure that nobody missed out.

Sometimes after the film they went to a supper dance at the Top Hat cabaret. Mr Ganz, with his lean figure and cornflower-blue eyes, was unanimously recognised as the most handsome man in the group. He danced with Mrs Bensky. The knowledge that they made a stunning couple swept them through the quickstep with even greater grace.

Mrs Zelman danced with Mr Bensky, who could be relied upon to have a few leftover scorched almonds in his jacket pocket. They ate them with a furtive happiness while they foxtrotted in the far corner of the dance floor. Mrs Ganz and Mr Zelman often danced the cha-cha and the rumba together. They both liked the livelier dances.

Mrs Glick and Mrs Small and Mrs Blatman and Mrs Feiglin and Mrs Bensky took it in turns to dance with Mr Berman. In the last few years Mr Berman had become even more nervous and distant. He hadn't gone out with a woman since his disastrous affair with Mrs McKenzie ended in 1962.

Their affair had thrown the entire group into turmoil. The group had all made sure their children had grown up understanding that it was essential to have a Jewish partner. Now, here was one of their close friends infatuated with a shikse, holding her hand in Carlisle Street and grinning like a fifteen-year-old. Mrs Glick and Mrs Feiglin decided that she was after his money. They visited Mrs McKenzie privately. They offered her five hundred pounds to stop seeing Mr Berman. Mrs McKenzie offered the women tea and biscuits. Ten days later she was gone. She had moved to Moe to be closer to her mother, a broken Mr Berman told the group.

The phone rang. Mrs Bensky, who was just about to put the final coat of Imbi's Mellow Mauve on her nails, shook her head in annoyance. It was probably Mr Bensky calling from Myers to say that there was no white Tissus Michel material left. She should have bought it when she saw it there last week, she admonished herself. She knew she looked good in white, and could wear it without any worry about its fattening effect.

She answered the phone. It was Mrs Ganz. Mrs Bensky cradled the phone on her shoulder with her upper arm. She swung her nails to and fro to catch the dry breeze of the air-conditioning. "Renia darling, I don't think we will go to the pictures tomorrow, darling. Moishe has a terrible cold. I asked him to go to the doctor because I'm sure he has got a virus, but you know Moishe, stubborn like an ox. Me, myself, I've got a sore throat already. So, Renia darling, make it fifteen tickets."

Mrs Bensky nurtured a not-so-secret dislike of Mrs Ganz. Mrs Bensky knew that Mrs Ganz thought of herself as highly intelligent and very beautiful. Mrs Bensky reassured herself that anyone could see that Mrs Ganz was no beauty. The fact that the Ganzes' Champs Elysees Blouses had one hundred and seventy-eight retail outlets around Australia did not mean that Mrs Ganz was intelligent. Mrs Bensky bit her lip, thinking about the many very stupid people she knew who were good at business.

Mrs Bensky toasted herself a slice of black rye bread. It was so black it could have passed for pumpernickel. Mrs Bensky liked peace and quiet when she ate. She was comforted by the warm density of the thick toast.

When Mr and Mrs Bensky arrived in Australia, Mr Bensky had wanted to abbreviate their name to Benn, but Mrs Bensky liked the name Bensky. She didn't want to change it. Many people had changed their names when they came to Australia. The Silberbergs, the Rotkleins, the Mokruschkis, the Pirkoskis and the Minofskis had become the Silvers, the Rotes, the Moors, the Pikes and the Mints. They now sounded like a gathering of good Presbyterians.

As Renia Kindler of Lodz, and then Renia Bensky, Mrs Bensky had been the most beautiful girl in the town, some said in the whole of Poland. Her red-brown hair was waist-length and flowed behind her like a dark curtain, framing her high pink cheekbones and intense eyes. Even though she was from one of the poorer families in Lodz, with no dowry to speak of, she was constantly pursued by admirers.

She was also very clever. In later years Mrs Bensky never tired of telling her two daughters: "I gave maths tuitions", which she always pronounced "choosons", "to pay for my schooling, from when I was eight. I was always very good at mathematics. I was the only Jewish girl to finish high school in Lodz and be offered a place at university."

As Mrs Bensky was about to begin her first year of medicine at the University of Vienna, the war broke out. Six years later Mrs Bensky graduated from Auschwitz.

Mr Bensky was a good husband. He had always been grateful to Mrs Bensky for marrying him. His family were displeased by the marriage, for they were property owners and timber merchants, and one of the wealthiest Jewish families in Lodz. Mr Bensky still felt upset when he remembered the hysteria he'd caused in his family when he had married Mrs Bensky. All that fuss and all that heartache, and all for nothing, because soon they were all in concentration camp and equally poor.

To give Mrs Bensky a break, Mr Bensky took Lina and Lola out on Saturday afternoons. When the girls were smaller they would go to the zoo. Mr Bensky enjoyed those afternoons. He would sit in the small park next to the bandstand and read the latest Perry Mason thriller. Lina and Lola would wave to him from the top of the elephant, which walked round and round the track circling the park. Lina and Lola liked to buy ten tickets each. That way they stayed on the elephant for exactly an hour. This suited Mr Bensky. When the hour was up, the three of them walked to the kiosk and bought six Eskimo Pies. Then they strolled around, looking at the animals. When she was older, Lola looked back on those afternoons as the nicest part of her childhood.

If there was a new show on at the Tivoli, Mr Bensky took the girls there on Saturday afternoons. They saw acts from all over the world. Sexy dancers and all sorts of singers, acrobats and jugglers, exotic striptease artists, a blonde underwater stripper, comedians and performing dogs, magicians and evil-looking hypnotists.

Hundreds of semi-nude, beautiful showgirls decorated the stage. The showgirls wore high heels and high-cut fishnet tights. On their heads they balanced spectacular soaring head-dresses made from hundreds of brightly coloured feathers and sequins. By law the showgirls had to stand perfectly still. They were not allowed to move at all. From their front-row seats, Mr Bensky and the girls had a very good view.

The comedians were Mr Bensky's favourites. He laughed at their jokes so heartily that other people in the theatre stood up to see who was laughing like that. Sometimes he laughed so hard that his shirt buttons popped and tears ran down his face. Sometimes Lola worried that he would burst with happiness. At interval they always shared a packet of Jaffas, a packet of Fantales and a packet of Columbines.

Mr Bensky applauded each act vigorously and was the first to leap onto the stage if a juggler, hypnotist, comedian or magician asked for volunteers from the audience.

Now, Mrs Bensky was starting to feel edgy. A faint headache hovered at the back of her head. Mr Bensky should have been home by now. She'd told him that the photographer was due at two o'clock.

She parted the plush gold velvet curtains in the family room. Outside it was sunny. Mrs Bensky was pleased. Later on she could lie out on the grass for half an hour or so.

Mrs Bensky had a deep golden tan all year round. She saw her suntan as public evidence of her energy, vitality and youthful spirit.

When Mrs Bensky lay in the sun, she could think about her daughters without anxiety. In the sun she could forget about Lola's weight and not worry about whether Lina would ever find a boyfriend. Sometimes a ray of pleasure crept through Mrs Bensky's thoughts about her daughters; at least neither of her children had ever had an abortion or experimented with drugs.

Mrs Bensky liked to sunbathe in solitude. At home this was easy, for Mr Bensky loathed the sun. Even on his summer holidays he spent his time indoors reading Raymond Chandler. Lina had very pale skin, which blistered if she crossed Collins Street in the sun, and Lola was too embarrassed to put her flesh, olive though it was, into a bathing suit.

There was a loud knock at the front door. "Renia, Renia darling, it's Josl." Mrs Bensky switched off the indoor and outdoor burglar alarms and Mr Bensky unlocked the mortice lock and Lockwood deadlock. He was beaming. "Darling, I went to Buckleys and I went to Georges and I had no luck. And then I had a very good idea, I went to Yanek at the top of Bourke Street and Yanek had two and a half yards of white Tissus Michel."

Mrs Bensky looked at him. "Josl, you know I need three yards for a dress." Mr Bensky lost his beam.

Mrs Bensky had prepared Mr Bensky's lunch: four slices of Pariser sausage, a tomato quartered, two radishes, a spring onion, some lettuce and three Vita-Wheat biscuits. On their bed she had laid out Mr Bensky's new white shirt, a finely striped maroon and gold tie, and Mr Bensky's best suit, which was grey with cream flecks. Mr Bensky ate and got dressed.

At exactly two o'clock Michael Beets, the most successful and talented Jewish photographer in Melbourne, arrived with his assistant.

Every year Michael Beets photographed the Bensky family. Mrs Bensky chose the photograph she liked best and ordered a twenty-by-thirty-inch copy, which she put into an ornate gilt-edged frame and displayed with great pride in the lounge room.

"Good afternoon, Mrs Bensky. You look wonderful. You're getting younger every day. It's true, you look more beautiful every year. It's a pleasure to see you."

"Oh, Mr Beets, I look terrible. I've got a headache and I've had sinus trouble for three weeks. I've taken Amoxil and Abbocillin and Moxacin and nothing helps. Look at how my nose is swollen."

Lina and Lola arrived separately, at the same time. Mr Bensky kissed Lina hello. Lina had a habit of averting her head when she was kissed, so that the kisser came in contact with a mouthful of hair and the back of her head.

Lola picked up the book that Lina had bought her parents as a gift. It was inscribed: "To the best Mum and Dad in the world." Lola felt nauseous with disgust.

"Lola darling," her mother was saying. Lola looked up, still feeling sick. "Maybe you'd like to put on a little bit of mascara?" Mrs Bensky trilled.

"No thanks, Mum." Lola walked away, smoothing down her dress, which had bat-wing sleeves, was gathered at the yoke and was made out of satiny, black crushed velvet. The dress flowed past Lola's hips, the part of Lola that Lola tried to hide, against all odds.

"OK, OK, OK, everybody," Mr Beets called as he shepherded them into the dining room. The dining room was low-ceilinged and rectangular. The bottom panels of the windows, which overlooked the garden, were made of opaque blue glass, a style that was fashionable in Caulfield and East St Kilda in the 1960s. Lola called it Jewish-Chinese architecture.

The Bensky family stood in a row. Mr Bensky patted a block of Small's Energy chocolate in his pocket. Lina blinked rapidly, her face twisted with tension. Lola arranged herself so that she stood between but slightly behind Mr and Mrs Bensky, a position that she hoped would cut her hips down a bit. Mrs Bensky glowed. Her eyes were luminous. A soft expression of serenity lit her face. Everything was ready. One, two, three, click. They smiled for the camera.

What Do You Know About Friends?

In Renia Bensky's world, people were pigs. "Don't be a greedy pig," she would say when Lola reached for another potato. Renia's neighbour, Mrs Spratt, was "a dirty pig". Her favourite grandchild was "a little piggy", her cousin Adek "a big pig".

Josl chauffeured his two daughters around every Saturday morning. To the city, to the dressmaker, to the hairdresser. On the way home he liked to stop and buy himself a double chocolate gelato. "What a pig!" Renia said when they arrived home.

When Renia talked about Josl's father, who had died in the ghetto, she said, "such a pig". Sometimes she would say a bit more, although the past, their lives before they came to Australia, was definitely out of bounds, their own private territory. Sometimes a small sliver of detail would slip out. "Such a pig he was. In the ghetto he cried because he was so hungry. Children were dead in the streets and he was crying because he was hungry."

Until she was twenty Lola had never seen a pig. When she saw her first pigs, she was fascinated by how unself-conscious they were. They snorted their way through their food, big and pink and bulky. They weren't holding their stomachs flat or sucking in their cheeks. They weren't expecting judgements. They seemed quite happy to be pigs. If people weren't pigs, then they were idiots. Even when she was quite small Lola knew that Mrs Bensky was an authority on pigs and idiots. "Such an idiot!" Mrs Bensky would shout. "Such an idiot is that Mrs Berman. An idiot, an i-d-i-o-t. She thinks she speaks a perfect English. In the butcher I heard her say 'Cut me in half please.' Such a perfect English!"

Mrs Berman had been Mrs Bensky's friend. Until Mrs Berman left Mr Berman and Mrs Bensky could no longer be friends with her, the two women had baked cakes in Mrs Bensky's kitchen on Saturday afternoons. Mrs Berman made her honeycake and rugelachs and Mrs Bensky baked her lakech. Working in the kitchen together, they looked like good friends.

"Friends," Mrs Bensky said to Lola. "What do you know about friends? Friends, pheh! You can trust only your family."

And what did Lola know? She had watched the Benskys and their friends, their "company", as they called themselves. The company went to the pictures together every Saturday night and then to supper afterwards. On Sunday evenings they played cards. If there was a good show on, sometimes they went out during the week. They celebrated each other's birthdays, anniversaries, barmitzvahs, engagements and weddings, and were present at the operations, illnesses and funerals.

Lola thought that the company were family. She called them Uncle and Aunty and believed that they would always care about her. What did Lola know?

Mrs Bensky hated Mrs Ganz. She was irritated by the way that Mrs Ganz kept inviting her to fashion parades, card afternoons and charity luncheons. Couldn't Mrs Ganz see that she was very busy? Every day Mrs Bensky had to wash six sheets, four pillow cases, three eiderdown covers and seven towels. She had to scrub and polish the floors, and vacuum the carpets. And on top of this she had to cook and to wash up. She was not the kind of woman who had time to go to a fashion parade. Why couldn't Mrs Ganz understand this?

Mrs Bensky thought that Mrs Ganz had always been spoilt. In the ghetto Mrs Ganz's father had been a Jewish "policeman". Their family had rarely been hungry. In 1943 they were smuggled out of the ghetto and spent the rest of the war hiding in a cellar. Mrs Bensky often chatted to Mrs Pekelman on the phone. She felt that Genia Pekelman had her problems, but above all she had a good heart. Mrs Bensky advised Mrs Pekelman about which clothes suited her best, how to cook a good gulah, where to buy the freshest Murray Perch. Shc also shared some beauty tips with her, including the fact that if you rinsed your hair with a bit of beer after washing it the waves stayed in much longer. Renia Bensky and Genia Pekelman, both non-drinkers, often trailed an alcoholic air around with them.

Lola learnt about friendship from listening to the two women on the phone. Last week Mrs Bensky had said in an affectionate tone, "Genia darling, I bumped into Yetta Kauffman in the city. Such an ugly face that woman has got. You think you are ugly, Genia darling? Next to Yetta Kauffman you are a big beauty."

This may have seemed harsh to an outsider, but Lola knew that it was affectionate and well-intentioned. In this company one of the friendliest and most enthusiastic responses to anything was: "What, what, you are crazy or something?"

Things cooled off between Renia Bensky and Genia Pekelman when Genia took up dancing lessons. She was forty-seven. At thirteen, Genia had been a promising young dancer. She had won a ballet scholarship to study in Paris. She was counting the days to her fourteenth birthday, waiting to leave for Paris, when the Germans arrived in Warsaw.

Now, Mrs Pekelman was learning Indian dance. She went to dancing classes twice a week. She was taught by Madame Sanrit. Mrs Pekelman wore leotards under her sari and practised at home every afternoon. She loved to dance and danced at every opportunity.

If a group of women were having a charity luncheon, Mrs Pekelman asked if she could dance at the lunch. When Mrs Pekelman learnt that Mrs Small was taking a group of voluntary Jewish Welfare kitchen helpers on a tour of the Victorian National Gallery, she begged her to bring the group to her home, where she would dance for them.

Some of the company were embarrassed by Genia Pekelman and her dancing. Mrs Small was furious. She said to Mrs Bensky,

"Look at her! She is so big and fat and ugly, and she wants to dance for everybody. When she moves her big tuches around the room it is shocking."

"She can't help it," Mrs Bensky replied. "She doesn't know how she looks. She is not so intelligent."

As well as pigs and idiots, Mrs Bensky knew about intelligence. She dismissed most people as "not intelligent". One year Mrs Small, who spoke Russian, Polish, Yiddish, French and English, interpreted for the members of the Moscow Circus when they came to Melbourne. Mrs Bensky was clenched with anger for the entire season.

"She thinks she is such a big intelligence," Mrs Bensky railed. "What does she read, this big intelligence, this Mrs Intelligentsia? Maybe a *Women's Weekly* under the hair dryer once a week? I remember her mother delivered our milk in Lodz. Two big cans across her shoulders, she walked from house to house in bare feet. And both daughters finished school at twelve. Now, suddenly, Ada Small is a genius. She tells everybody that she matriculated in Poland. Soon she will say she was almost a doctor. Everybody who came here after the war was almost a doctor. Mrs Ada Intelligentsia thinks she is important because she is translating for an acrobat."

Mrs Bensky did know about intelligence. She was the only one of the group who had been at university. She still kept her student card in her handbag. In 1972, Mrs Bensky enrolled at Melbourne University. She did one semester of "Physics In The Firing Line". Lola had suggested that Mrs Bensky study Russian or German, languages she was fluent in. Lola thought that this would have been a gentler introduction to university life, but Mrs Bensky insisted on "Physics In The Firing Line". Science had been Mrs Bensky's great love in Lodz. When she spoke about Copernicus and the planets, Mrs Bensky was at her most tender. It was science that Mrs Bensky wanted to go back to.

In Lodz, Mrs Bensky came top of her class every year. She was every teacher's favourite student. Her curiosity was as immense as her ambition. Other people in the neighbourhood laughed at her father for wasting his money on a daughter. "You'll make her too clever for a husband," one neighbour repeated regularly.

At the University of Melbourne, Renia Bensky was so tense she could hardly hear the lecturer. His words flew around the auditorium. Mrs Bensky had to grab each word and put it in its correct place. Sometimes she lost a few words and the sentences didn't make sense. She sat in a sweat through most of the professor's speeches. Later she learnt that this heat was menopausal.

Renia worked feverishly on her first assignment, "Molecules and The Future". At last it was finished. Fifteen pages on bright yellow notepaper. Lina corrected the English, and they hired a professional typist to type the essay.

Mrs Bensky got a "C" for "Molecules and The Future". She wept and wept.

Mr Bensky tried to comfort her. "This assignment, Renia darling, is out of this world. Something special. There is no question about it. It is perfect, believe me." But Mrs Bensky went on weeping.

Mrs Small gave Mrs Bensky her sympathy and support. "I think it is anti-Semitism," she said. "For what other reason would he give such a beautiful piece of work only a 'C'? He is an anti-Semite, for sure."

Most of the company called around to offer their condolences. They knew it wasn't Mrs Bensky's fault. A "C" for Renia Bensky, whoever heard of such a thing? Everybody knew she was too intelligent. But Mrs Bensky was inconsolable.

She rang her tutor, a young, pale-faced boy of twenty-five, to ask if maybe it was her English that wasn't perfect. Maybe that was why she had got a "C".

"Excuse me, tutor," she began, "I want to know if you have made a mistake with my essay. I think the English was very good. My younger daughter who is a lawyer with an honours degree did correct my writing, so it couldn't be my bad English. And my English is very good. She didn't find many mistakes at all. I understand you did give young John Matheson an 'A'. Well, he told me himself that I did understand the molecules much better than him. In fact, I explained some of the facts to him. So, he got an 'A' and I got a 'C'? Maybe I shouldn't have hired a typist? Maybe you think I have got money to burn or to throw away that I hired a typist? My husband worked very hard for fifteen years in factories so I could afford a typist. Maybe you were prejudiced against my typing? Did Mr Matheson type his essay? I'm sure not. As a matter of fact I know his mother, Mrs Matheson. She told me he was talking about how much I know about molecules. You know, I, myself, don't think you are an anti-Semite. My friend Mrs Small does, but she is not intelligent. She doesn't see we are in a modern world and this is not Poland.

"So, do you have an answer, Mr Tutor? Do you know how many years I dreamed of going to university? Do you know this? I dreamed of studying at university when I was a small girl. And I kept dreaming. Even in Auschwitz, when I didn't dream any more, sometimes when I was standing in roll-call for six hours, barefoot in the snow, I would try to think about what subjects I could study one day."

Now Mrs Bensky was crying. "Do you have an answer, Mr Tutor? When I came to Australia my sister-in-law said to me that all women work in Australia. She said to me I should have considered if I could afford to have a baby before I got pregnant. So I took my baby every day to Mrs Polonsky, a woman in Carlton. I had never been apart from my baby. Sometimes I vomited on the tram on the way to the factory. I felt so frightened. Josl told me that Mrs Polonsky was a good woman and nothing would happen to little Lola, but I couldn't stop being frightened. When I finished work I picked Lolala up. Mrs Polonsky lived just next to the university, and when I stopped vomiting, I made myself a promise that one day I would go there. Did you hear me, Mr Tutor?"

Mrs Bensky left "Physics In The Firing Line" six weeks after she had begun. She left the University of Melbourne a wiser person. The rest of the company acknowledged this and accorded her new respect. "She studied at Melbourne University," they now said when they spoke of her.

I Wonder Why She Looks So Happy

Genia Pekelman looked at herself in the mirror. Her thighs looked strong. They were muscular, not fat. Her breasts had fallen, but they were looking better than they used to. Less limp.

She positioned herself in front of the full-length mirror, adjusted the legs of her leotards and began to dance.

Genia felt alive. She could feel her muscles. She could feel her heart. She could feel her strength.

She moved gracefully and rhythmically. She moved in time to the chorus of her veins and arteries. In tune with the movement of her blood.

Her head and arms and legs were in harmony with the stars and the moon and the sun. That was how Genia Pekelman felt. Connected. Anchored. Part of the world.

When Genia Pekelman was dancing, she could forget everything else. Genia had a lot to forget. She often thought that she had so much to forget that she could dance her way through ten lifetimes and still not have danced enough to forget everything.

The memories that Genia Pekelman was trying to forget would leap out unexpectedly and leave her breathless.

Last week, in Pruzansky's butcher shop, a customer had asked for a kilo of calf's liver. Mr Pruzansky was carefully slicing the liver. His blade was sharp and slid easily through the soft liver. Genia was watching, but she saw another blade slicing another liver.

She saw Shimek Greenbaum cutting a liver with a blunt piece of tin. The liver belonged to Abe Korner. This was in Bergen-

Belsen, in the last few weeks before the camp was liberated. Genia had just turned nineteen. Germany was losing the war. The front lines were disintegrating. The Germans were evacuating their forced-labour camps and concentration camps. Thousands of prisoners were brought to Bergen-Belsen on foot and by rail. In the week of Genia's nineteenth birthday, in April 1945, twenty-eight thousand new inmates were dumped into Bergen-Belsen.

Typhoid raged. Corpses rotted in the barracks. Rats ate prisoners' fingers and toes while they slept. And starving prisoners ate the inmates who had died.

There were things that Genia kept forgetting, memories that she fought to remember. Genia struggled to retain a clear picture of her parents.

Shmul and Mania Buchbinder, Genia's parents, were both dentists. Genia was their only child. They doted on her. Genia had piano lessons and ballet classes. A tutor came to the house twice a week to teach Genia French. At ten, Genia had read *Madame Bovary* in French.

Mania and Shmul had such hopes for their beautiful and clever Genia. Mania would tell Genia about the writers and the musicians they had had in the family. For hundreds of years the Buchbinders had produced extraordinarily gifted people.

Shmul's mother, Yetta, was one of the best-loved Yiddish actresses in Poland. Genia adored her grandmother, and often travelled with her parents from their home in Lowicz to watch Yetta Buchbinder perform in Warsaw. "What fine silk you are spun from, my child," Genia's mother used to say to her.

Genia was pampered by all of her relatives in Lowicz. Her uncles brought her presents from Europe, and her aunties combed and plaited her long auburn hair. Genia never minded being an only child. She felt as though she had many mothers and fathers and many brothers and sisters.

Mania and Shmul Buchbinder died in Auschwitz. Yetta Buchbinder died in the Warsaw ghetto. All the aunties and uncles died.

There had been eighty-seven Buchbinders in Lowicz. After the war, Genia was the only one left.

At home this morning, Genia was practising her arabesques. For a few years she had studied Indian dance. She had enjoyed that, but it was ballet that made Genia Pekelman truly happy.

Genia was in the Advanced Senior class at the Dancing Academy in Brighton. She was the oldest member of the class. She was twice as old as her teacher.

Genia knew that people laughed at her. Sometimes she laughed at herself too. Sometimes she could see that she looked absurd. A crazy woman. There she was, fifty years old, the owner of eight pairs of leotards, endless legwarmers, and two white tutus!

Genia didn't mind people laughing. They were not her real audience. When Genia danced she was in another world. She wasn't in Melbourne. She wasn't in Bergen-Belsen. She was in a dream. This dream was in a place where everything was as it would have been if it were not for the war.

Her parents were there. Her grandmother was there. Her uncles and aunties were there. They had all known that Genia would be a ballerina, and they were such an appreciative audience. This morning Yetta had clapped and clapped when Genia had balanced an arabesque perfectly. Her ballet teacher from Lowicz, Madame Kasner, was there. Last week Madame Kasner had said to Genia, "Genia darling, we have to be grateful to Olga Ramanova, who told us when you were six that you would be a great dancer. Do you remember when she performed in Lowicz?"

Of course Genia remembered Olga Ramanova. The Russian ballerina had patted Genia on the head, and told her that if she practised hard she could possibly one day dance with the greatest of the Russian ballet companies. And little Genia had practised and practised.

Last Thursday Genia had danced for a small group. It was the Eastern Division Bridge Players' luncheon. Genia knew that some of the women were mocking her, and that the rest of them felt sorry

for her. After her performance, Genia was getting dressed in the bathroom when she heard Mina Blatt say to Marilla Rose: "It looks something shocking to see a woman of her age jumping around as if she is a young girl. I wonder why she looks so happy."

"You are right, Mina," said Marilla. "Who knows why she looks so happy?"

Genia had been dancing for forty-five minutes when the telephone rang. It was Renia Bensky. Renia had rung to see if Genia needed any towels. Josl was going in to Shavinsky's warehouse. Both women had linen cupboards large enough to service a small hospital.

"All right, Renia, ask Josl to buy me six of those nice cream bath-size towels."

Genia could never have too many sheets or towels. The feeling of clean, pure cotton sheets on her bed gave her such a sense of well-being. It was the same with good towels. Genia felt pampered and indulged every morning when she dried herself with the thick, king-sized bath towels.

"I'll bring you the towels on Saturday," said Renia. "I can't speak to you for too long today, because I have to cook something for Lola. I am cooking her a cabbage and rice dish. It is her new diet. I make a big pot for the whole week. But, Genia, I looked at Lola last week, and to tell you the truth, I think she is eating the whole pot in one night. Then she goes on another diet for the other days. I don't know what to do. It's killing me."

Genia felt depressed about Lola. Lola had been a beautiful little girl. With her dark, sausage curls and her lively eyes, she had looked like a doll. Now she was very fat, and her eyes were flat.

"Renia," Genia said, "shall we go together to the German Embassy? I have to go this week. Why don't we go together again?"

Renia and Genia received "reparation" money from the German government. Genia got slightly more than Renia because she had been a teenager during the war. The German government,

Genia's lawyer had told her, considered it had more to make up for to those people who had also lost their youth.

Renia had been eligible for this extra payment, as she had only been twenty-one when she arrived in Auschwitz, but by the time Renia found out about the extra "reparation" money the German government's deadline for applications had passed.

The amount of money that they received was such a pittance that to label it "reparation" and "restitution" was offensive. Some Jews refused to accept this money, but to most Jews it was an important symbolic gesture.

The "reparation" money, Josl was fond of saying, was not enough to cover the monthly ice-cream bills he used to run up in Lodz.

Once a year, all the Jews receiving these payments had to present themselves to the German Embassy, to prove that they were still alive.

Last year Renia and Genia had gone to the German Embassy together. Genia had picked Renia up and the two women, who talked on the telephone for an hour every day, had driven to South Yarra in silence.

"Well, can you see that I am alive?" Renia had asked the man at the German Embassy.

"Yes, Madam, I can see that," he had said.

"Well, you are blind, sir," Renia had said. "Because you killed all of us. Those of us who are still walking and talking are not alive, sir."

Afterwards the two women had walked along Punt Road to the car. A sudden feeling of lightness had come over Genia. She was alive, and she wanted to prove it. "Renia," she had said, "let's go shopping and spend this 'reparation' money all at once. Let's decide what we can do with it. Should we invest it in BHP, Renia, or should we buy a pair of shoes?"

Renia and Genia had driven into the city. They had gone to Miss Louise in Collins Street and bought a pair of Maud Frizon shoes each.

* *

"All right, Genia," Renia said. "We will go to the embassy together again. Is Tuesday morning all right for you?"

"I'll pick you up at ten o'clock, after my ballet class," said Genia.

"Genia darling," said Renia. "I have been thinking about Pola Ganz and Joseph Zelman. I think that there is something funny going on between them. It would be shocking. After all, Moishe is a wonderful husband to Pola. What is that crazy woman doing? At her age she needs to shtoop so much? And what about poor Mina Zelman? I know that she is very tall, and maybe Joseph needs to feel he is a big man, so he shtoops with little Pola Ganz. But there are other ways of being a big man. What's happening to the world today, Genia? I remember when I thought that we had had so much pain and suffering that we would never cause pain or suffering to each other. I was stupid."

It worried Genia that Renia was so suspicious. If Pola and Joseph were having an affair, then it had probably been going on for a long time and not hurting anybody. Who knows whether they are or they are not? thought Genia. She didn't care.

What had gone wrong with Renia Bensky? Genia wondered. When Genia had first met Renia in 1950, Renia had been so kind. Renia was still hopeful then. Later she had hardened. They had probably all hardened, thought Genia.

What had been taken away from them in the war, Genia thought, what they had lost, was their trust. Renia had never regained her trust. She was suspicious of everything. In 1950, thought Genia, Renia had still thought that she would be able to regain her trust.

"Anyway, I am not going to think about Joseph Zelman and dear Pola Ganz any more. I have got better things to worry about," said Renia. "Poor Lina, she has got this week such an allergy. It wasn't enough that she did become allergic to food, now she is allergic to her dog. And she loves her Pandy so much. Such a stupid dog, and she loves him."

Renia had talked for months about Lina's allergy to food. "Poor

Lina," she had said to anyone who would listen, and many who didn't want to hear. "She eats nothing at all. As soon as she puts anything into her mouth, she puts on half a stone. So, she eats nothing. The doctors said it was an allergy to food. My poor Lina is allergic to food."

Genia's husband, Izak, was sceptical. "She doesn't eat anything and she puts on weight? It doesn't sound like an allergy to me. Maybe Lina could market this allergy. If the doctors could find out how a person can eat nothing and not die, we can save the whole Third World."

After talking for fifteen minutes about Lina's blotches caused by her allergy to her dog, Renia was sounding a bit flat. "How is Esther?" she said.

Esther Pekelman, Genia's younger daughter, stammered. She couldn't finish her sentences. Esther's thoughts always trailed off in a nervous stutter. All the fears that Genia managed to contain, Esther displayed. In many ways Esther was a barometer for the whole Pekelman family. If things were difficult for the family, Esther wore the symptoms of that distress. When times were calmer, Esther looked better.

Genia felt closer to Esther than she did to Rachel, her first-born daughter. Genia felt that Esther understood her. Esther had been in the audience at the luncheon last week. As soon as the performance was over, Esther had rushed up to her. "You were fabulous, Mum," she had said. She had hugged Genia tightly. It had been a hug that had shut out all Genia's fears and nerves. Esther didn't have the beauty of her sister, Rachel, but Esther had the heart.

Genia thought that Rachel was one of the most beautiful young women she had ever seen. Many other people thought the same thing about Rachel. Rachel had large, green, almond-shaped eyes, flawless olive skin and an elegant aquiline nose. Her face was framed by a head of thick auburn ringlets. At the moment Rachel was between husbands. She had divorced number three, and had just met Boris Zayer, who fulfilled all the prerequisites for husband number four.

Each of Rachel's husbands had been richer than the husband before him. Rachel had started by marrying a struggling young lawyer. She had left that marriage with a small house in South Yarra. Rachel's last divorce had netted her a settlement of two and a half million dollars.

"She doesn't have an economics degree or a Diploma of Business Administration, but she could be president of the World Bank, the way that she has escalated her assets so rapidly," Izak used to say about his elder daughter.

Rachel was now beautiful and rich. She believed that every man in Melbourne was in love with her. She had told Genia that Rabbi Blatt had propositioned her at her son's barmitzvah. She had also said that the rabbi who had handled her last divorce had wanted to handle her. Genia couldn't believe that a rabbi would behave like that. "Rachel darling," she had said to her daughter, "I think you must have made a mistake. Rabbis are more concerned with the Torah than a nice-looking tuches."

With her striking curls and smooth skin and polished nails, Rachel looked full of life, but Genia knew that there was not a lot of joy in Rachel. Rachel was made happy by the transient things in life, and she had to keep getting more and more of them. Esther, Rachel thought, had more life-force in her, more spirituality, more balance. Yet to most people, Genia thought, Rachel appeared alive, and Esther appeared mad.

"Esther is fine," Genia said to Renia.

"It's lucky that she's got a good husband like Stan," said Renia. "Someone like Esther is not always appreciated. What do people appreciate?" continued Renia. "They appreciate the things that are not so important. Do you remember what Rabbi Bloom said when he married Stan and Esther? He said Esther had a good heart. Usually Rabbi Bloom says that the bride is beautiful. If he can't say that she is beautiful, he says she is clever. If he can't say clever or beautiful, he says how rich the parents are. He doesn't say rich, he says successful, but everyone understands what he is saying. And if he can't say one of those things, Rabbi Bloom says that the bride has got a good heart. When Rabbi Bloom said Esther had a good heart, I did nearly cry, Genia."

Genia thought that this was a good time to say goodbye to Renia. She could feel herself starting to feel gloomy.

"Genia darling, before you hang up," said Renia, "please let me make an appointment to the hairdressers for you. Ada Small rang me this morning to say that she heard Malka Spiel and Fela Brot in the chicken shop saying that it was shocking that a woman of your age has such long hair. Genia, I am telling you this for your own good. Do you want people to talk more about you?"

Genia had been growing her hair for four years. It had almost reached her waist. She wore it in a single plait.

"Don't listen to them," Izak had said when Genia had told him about Renia and Ada nagging her to have her hair cut. "If it makes you happy to have long hair, then have long hair," Izak had said.

"Renia darling," said Genia, "I know that you tell me these things for my own good, but it is me that people are talking about, and I don't mind. At least I am giving people something to talk about. I have to go now, Renia. I will speak to you tomorrow. Goodbye."

Genia felt unsettled now. She should take the phone off the hook when she wanted to practise her ballet. She had tried to take the phone off the hook many times, but she was always overcome with the worry that Izak or Rachel or Esther might want to get through to her and not be able to.

She really had to make sure that she could practise uninterrupted, Genia thought. She would never progress if her practice was constantly interrupted. She would take the phone off the hook. She would do it today, Genia decided. She took the phone off the hook, and walked back to Rachel's old bedroom, which was now Genia's rehearsal room.

Last night Josl Bensky had gently asked Genia why she drove herself so hard to dance. "I feel happy when I am dancing," she had replied. "When I'm dancing, Josl, I feel very happy, and it takes my mind off things."

Josl understood about taking your mind off things. Josl read three or four detective novels a week. They had titles like *Cold Blooded Revenge* and *From Death to Death* and *Who Killed The Boss?* and *The Crippled Snout.* When Josl read his detective novels, he was utterly immersed in them. Nothing else existed. He read after work, and he read in the evening before bed. He read all day when he was on holidays. He belonged to three libraries in different areas, and there were never fewer than half a dozen unread detective novels in the house.

When Lola was fourteen and beginning to read serious fiction, she had asked Josl why he read such rubbish.

"It keeps my mind off things," he had answered.

Lola had asked her mother the same question. "Why does Dad read such garbage?" she had asked.

"It keeps his mind off things," Renia had replied.

Lola had a very vague idea of what it was that Josl was keeping his mind off, and she was too frightened to enquire further. She was already frightened enough about her parents' past. She had grown up with all kinds of phrases spinning around in her head, like "you don't know what it means to suffer" and "you don't know the meaning of trouble" and "you think this is trouble?" and "you think this is a tragedy?" Lola didn't want to ask any more questions. She didn't want to know what real trouble was.

"If it takes your mind off things, then go and dance, and dance in good health," Josl had said to Genia.

With the phone off the hook, Genia practised and practised. She was learning the part of Odile in *Swan Lake.* She was rehearsing the ballroom scene in the third act.

She had mastered the mime and the movements when Odile tries to force the prince to marry her. Her arabesques were balancing nicely, but she was having trouble with her fouettés. Her teacher, Marilyn Warner, had told her that she was too old to attempt fouettés. Genia had felt depressed when Miss Warner said this. Genia told Esther, who always rang her after her classes.

"Look, Mum, maybe you could learn another role, or maybe Miss Warner could choreograph the part differently for you," Esther had suggested.

"I'm only having trouble with my spotting," Genia had said to her daughter. "When you do fouettés, you are spinning around and around on one leg, and you have to spot while you are spinning. Spotting stops you from being dizzy when you turn. Your eyes should be the last thing to leave the front of the stage, and the first part of your body to return. You have to turn your body first, then move your head quickly around so that it gets to the front again before the rest of your body," Genia had explained to Esther.

Now Genia wasn't spotting properly, and she was feeling dizzy. Her back hurt and her feet ached. She could hardly move her shoulders. She felt nauseous. She sat down.

She closed her eyes to stem the dizziness. She saw her mother's face. Mania Buchbinder's face was full of pride. "Remember, Genia darling, when Olga Ramanova said you would be a beautiful Giselle?"

"Yes, Mama," said Genia. "I remember."

Genia stood up and took a deep breath. She threw herself into a fouetté. She spun around and around and around. She had known that she could do it.

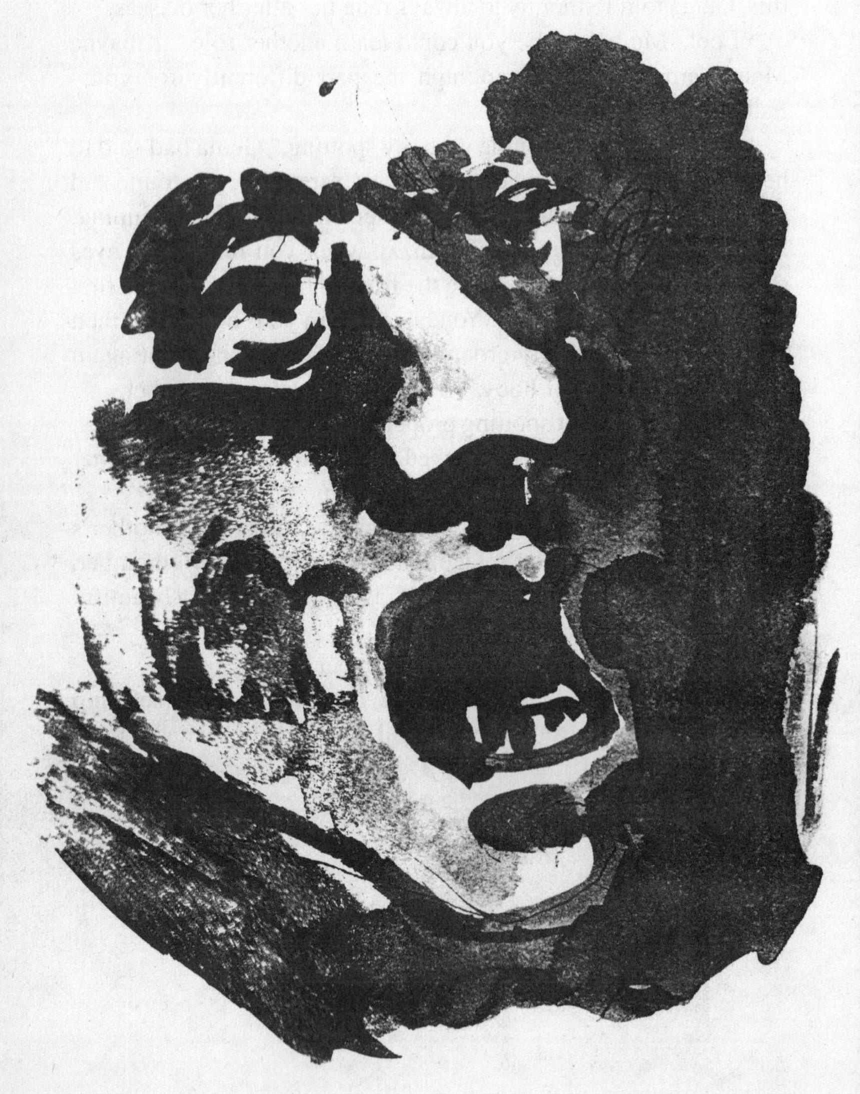

Every Death

Renia Bensky read the obituary columns of the *Age* and the *Herald* every day. The death notices were the first thing she turned to in the *Jewish News* when it arrived on Fridays.

She read every death. She knew who had died and who they had left behind. She could guess the age of the deceased. She knew if the dead were good or bad people, and whether they had many friends. She knew when they were dearly loved, or when their death notice was only a formal acknowledgement.

Renia could feel the levels of grief behind the announcements. She could detect the pain or anguish or anger behind these public notices.

Every day there were families left without a mother, and families who had lost a father. Every day there were small children left fatherless and motherless. Every day a child died. Many times Renia would see that a husband had given up and died a few months after his wife's death. There were also quite a few wives who didn't want to live without their husbands.

Fathers and mothers and sons and daughters, and even brothers and sisters, wrote poems for the dead. Such touching poems. They were bad verses, but Renia was always touched by the depth of pain and sadness, and the great effort it took to put this into a poetic form.

Renia was scathing about the death notices that came in large boxed advertisements. She scoffed at the ads that began "The Managing Director and the Staff of".

"Mr Bigshot, Mr Important!" she would say out loud.

Renia often wondered why it was so hard for these notices to say how very much someone was loved. People tried, but always came up with the same half a dozen sentiments. The same neatly packed phrases at the end of a notice. The announcements usually ended with "Forever In Our Hearts", or "Will Be Sadly Missed By All Who Knew Him", or "Forever In Our Thoughts". Why was it so hard to write out a scream, or an ache, or a cry of pain?

Renia had never buried anyone she had loved. She had never written a death notice. In the ghetto, Josl had carried their stillborn son to the cemetery, but there had been too many bodies waiting to be buried, and Josl had had to leave the baby. Renia had stayed in bed. She had been too sick to walk to the cemetery. Renia wasn't sure exactly how her mother and father and her four brothers and three sisters had died. She knew that her mother and two of her sisters had died in Auschwitz. Her last image of them was of the three of them walking towards the gas chambers. Her mother was holding Renia's niece Hanka by the hand.

Renia had often wondered who had knocked her on the head and pushed her out of the queue for the gas chambers. Was it a Kapo? Was it a fellow prisoner? Was it a member of the Gestapo? She never knew.

Renia had heard several conflicting reports about the deaths of her father and brothers. After the war, she heard that Jacob had died in Bergen-Belsen, and that Felek had been shipped to Mathausen and was shot when he tried to jump off the train. Someone said that Abramek and Shimek and Renia's father, Israel, died in Dachau. But there was no conflict about the fact that they were all dead.

In 1972, when the passengers on an American plane were taken hostage in Lebanon, Renia Bensky was beside herself. The news almost paralysed her. She couldn't read. She couldn't talk on the phone. She sat in her kitchen all day, and waited for the radio news bulletins. Nothing could distract her from the fate of the hostages. Genia Pekelman said to Ada Small, "I think Renia has lost her mind." When Renia knew that the hostages had been released, she rang Lola.

Lola was twenty-five. She was so overweight that even her face had doubled in size. She was wearing a long, blue, voluminous, flower-patterned dress. Lumps of mashed pumpkin had dried on her cuffs. Lola was sitting in her kitchen looking at a huge bucket of nappies soaking in Milton solution. It was ten o'clock at night.

"Lola, darling, I hope I didn't wake you," Renia said. "I want to tell you what you should do if you would be one day hijacked on an airplane. First of all you must never say you are Jewish. If anyone should ask you why you are born in Germany, just say it is because you are Polish. Say that your Polish parents went for a holiday to Germany after the war. You see, Lola, Jews who survived the camps were, a lot of them, in Germany after the war."

Lola was used to calls like this. "Wouldn't it be easier if I said I was German?" she asked.

"Yes, maybe you are right," Renia agreed. "Yes, maybe you are right. And see, Lola, how handy it will be that you did study German at school. You can say a few words in German to the hijackers. In Auschwitz, quite a few times I was saved because I had such good German."

"You know, Mum," Lola said, "I don't think anyone would even ask me if I was Jewish. I've got an Australian passport. Why would they ask me?"

"Oh, Lola," wailed Renia Bensky, "You know nothing. The Jews are the first ones they will kill. Look, it happened already, I think the American soldier the hijackers did kill was a Jew. Everybody wants to kill the Jews first, Lola. But what do you know? You grew up a free child in a free country. You know, Lola, maybe it is not so bad that you didn't marry somebody Jewish. Rodney is so blond, and the baby is blond, and they've both got blue eyes. The hijackers would never think the baby is Jewish. Anyway, Lola darling, I shouldn't hold you up. Give the baby a big kiss from me. You sound a bit tired, so try and get an early night."

Lola put the phone down. The bits of shit had come off the nappies and floated to the top of the bucket. She thought her mother was getting confused. Wasn't it another group of terrorists who had shot the Jew first? She would ask Rodney. She put the nappies in the washing machine.

The next day Renia rang the Immigration Department to ask if they could remove the entry on Lola's passport listing Germany as her place of birth. Renia was switched from one clerk to another. Nobody seemed to understand why this was so important, and nobody could give her an answer.

Renia wrote to the department. Her neighbour, Mr Spratt, checked her letter for her and told her that it was an excellent letter. The Immigration Department replied that if Renia came in to discuss the matter, it would be considered. Renia thought that she would go in with Lola. After all, Lola could talk anybody into anything.

"Mum," said Lola, "I'm having enough trouble staying alive in one place. I feel in such a mess. I can't even think about the danger of having Germany as my place of birth in my passport when I travel."

Renia felt angry. Lola had always disappointed her. It was as if Lola was going out of her way to make sure that she never gave her mother any pleasure. The only thing that Renia had ever asked of Lola was that she be slim. She had been putting Lola on diets for over twenty years. But somehow, despite all the diets, despite all the lettuce and tomatoes, despite the Ryvita biscuits, the thin-trim wafers, the Metracal drink, the sugarless chewing gum and the calorie-less lollies, Lola had always been fat.

Lola had completed slimming courses at Silhouette, the Elsternwick Weight Loss Clinic, the YWCA gymnasium and Weight Watchers. And she had remained fat.

Renia rang up her local Member of Parliament, Mr Charles. Mr

Charles lived around the corner from the Benskys. Renia made a point of always saying hello to him. She also let him know that she voted for him. Mr Charles would help her with the Immigration Department.

Renia was elated the day that Josl picked up Lola's new passport. Next to "place of birth" was a nice, cream-coloured space.

"Couldn't this make the hijackers suspicious?" asked Topcha Rosen. "After all," she continued, "everyone has a place of birth on a passport. Maybe they will wonder why this girl has nothing next to her place of birth? Anyway, don't worry, Renia. The main thing is not to worry about it. You'll worry Lola, and then she'll be worried, and the hijackers will see a worried person, and they will wonder why the person should be so worried."

Renia knew that Topcha knew what it was to be worried. And what it was to be in danger. Topcha had been hidden in a bunker in Poland for five years. Topcha's family had shared the bunker with another family. Fifteen people living in a bunker for five years. The bunker was twelve feet by eight feet. They couldn't all lie down at once. They had to roster sleeping hours.

After the war, Topcha's parents couldn't walk. Their muscles had atrophied. Topcha's father never learnt to walk again. Every day, Topcha's brother had gone out to the forests to buy and scavenge food. Topcha's father had built the bunker in 1933. All his friends had laughed at him. When Poland was invaded, he had taken the family's jewels and furs to the bunker. By the end of the war, the family had nothing left to sell. Another few weeks and they would have perished.

Renia also read reports of car accidents in the *Age.* If there was an extra large crash, she also bought the *Sun,* which always had more details. Renia wept for the car-accident victims. She scoured the articles for information. She learnt which streets and which intersections in Melbourne were the most dangerous. She learnt which times of day car accidents were likely to happen. Twilight was a bad time. She learnt that Volvos and Mercedes stood up well in accidents and that, on the whole, the bigger the car, the less damage was likely to be caused to its occupants.

"Drive carefully," Renia said to Josl every morning. "Drive carefully," Renia, Lola and Lina Bensky chorused when they farewelled friends. "Drive carefully," the two Bensky daughters said to their husbands whenever the husbands drove anywhere. "Drive carefully. Drive carefully," they repeated several times. "Drive carefully. Drive carefully." The Bensky women sang it like a mantra.

When Lola was sixteen, she had a boyfriend who was a tow-truck driver. For the Benskys, this young man's other defects paled into insignificance next to the fact that he was a tow-truck driver. The Benskys didn't complain about his long hair, they ignored his tattoos, and they overlooked the fact that he wasn't Jewish.

The tow-truck driver and Lola went out in his tow-truck. They went to the pictures, they went for walks, and they went for drives in the country. When the tow-truck driver brought Lola home after these outings, the tow-truck would come screaming to a halt, late at night, outside the Benskys' bedroom window. Josl and Renia would have to get up and have a cup of hot milk and honey to soothe themselves after Lola's return. "Jesus, why do you always have to wait up for me?" Lola would ask.

On Lola's eighteenth birthday, the Benskys bought her a large pink Valiant.

"Lola darling," Renia said, "We are giving you this car, not because you have been such a wonderful daughter that you deserve a new car, but because we want you to drive in something safe. I want to sleep at night, and so does Daddy. And now you won't have to drive in somebody's old bomb." Renia loudly emphasised the last "b" in bomb.

Lola had corrected her mother many times. "Mum, you don't sound the 'b' at the end of bomb. It's like bum. It's pronounced bom."

Renia always had the same reply. "So, you are so clever, my Lola, that you are now teaching me English? When you are clever enough to not go out in the old bombs, then I will listen to your English lessons."

By the time she had her pink Valiant, Lola was no longer with the tow-truck driver. She was going out with an African. He was the blackest man she had ever seen. His name was Abu.

The Benskys and their "company" prided themselves on their lack of prejudice. Josl often said to his daughter and to his friends, "After the discrimination that we Jews did suffer, we should have only tolerance and understanding towards anybody in a minority, and towards all races and all religions." The whole group agreed with Josl.

All of the Benskys' friends had different suggestions for splitting up Lola and Abu.

"Just be firm," said Izak Pekelman. "Tell her that you won't put up with it and that's final."

Genia Pekelman had the best solution. "Send her to Israel straight away."

From the moment she arrived, Lola hated Israel. She was contemptuous of the young American Jews who had migrated there. When they asked her if she didn't feel that this was her grass, her earth, her sky, here in Israel, she said she had never been fond of the outdoors. Lola thought that they were all running away from something.

The Jews in Israel didn't look like real Jews to Lola. She had thought that Israel would be full of Aunty Genias and Uncle Izaks. She had thought that she would be greeted by everybody as a long-lost relative. Instead, people had a brusque manner and didn't feel any more affectionately towards her because she was Jewish. Here, everyone was Jewish.

In Israel, perfect strangers asked Lola why she didn't lose weight. A man in the bus one day looked at her and said: "Young girl, it is lucky that you have such a nice face. Why are you so fat?" A woman in the supermarket offered her the Israeli Army Diet.

After three months in Israel, Lola was very happy to be back home in Melbourne. She was a bit upset when she found out that Abu had gone back to Nigeria. He hadn't written to say that he was going. The Benskys' friends congratulated Renia and Josl on a mission successfully completed.

Renia Bensky always expected the unexpected. She tried to predict the unpredictable. She liked to be prepared for all possibilities, and to be one step ahead of whatever lay in the future.

The perfectly normal, the absolutely routine, always took Renia by surprise. She gasped with horror or disbelief if anyone caught a cold. She then rushed into overdrive. This was an emergency. She bought high-dosage vitamin C tablets before they were fashionable. She made inhalation clinics in the bathroom. She would fill the basin with eucalyptus oil and turn on the two hot-water taps in the shower. The patient had to sit in this steam three times a day.

As well as this, Renia squeezed dozens of oranges and ran around dispensing the juice. She took the victim's temperature every hour. She made extra chicken soup. Josl and the girls joked, when Renia was out of the room, that if the cold didn't kill them, they might just drown in chicken soup.

Some of Lola's most pleasant childhood memories were of being nursed through a cold by Renia. All Renia's anger seemed to dissipate. The harsh looks she often gave Lola were gone. She was soft and sympathetic. She no longer focused on Lola's diet. "Eat up," she urged.

All the Benskys' friends could rely on Renia to look after them when they were sick. She visited them. She shopped for them. She rang twice a day to enquire after their progress. She was full of love for them.

In the Lodz ghetto, Renia had found her school friend, Raisl, lying in Palacowa Street. Raisl's face was covered in blood. Renia knew it was tuberculosis. She carried Raisl the four blocks to her apartment. Josl's parents and brother, who shared a room with Renia and Josl, were horrified. They told Renia that Raisl had to be put back in the street.

"Let her at least have a few hours' sleep," Renia pleaded. Renia cleaned Raisl up and tucked her into her own bed. Raisl kept coughing blood.

Suddenly there was a great commotion outside. It was another raid, another round-up of Jews to be transported out of the ghetto for "a better life". Renia, Josl and his parents were trapped. They had no time to run anywhere. Up until then they had been lucky. Josl had a cousin in the Judenrat who had managed to tip them off when a raid was due on Palacowa Street.

Josl's father, Shimek, looked defeated. Josl pushed the four of them into a small cupboard. They all knew it was no use. The SS had dogs. They were done for.

A few minutes later, the door was bashed in by an SS officer. He took one look at Raisl and fled. The SS, Josl's father later laughed, were such cowards. They were terrified of contagious diseases.

The next morning Raisl was dead. Renia walked beside Raisl's body, in the cart that picked up the unclaimed dead, and said Kaddish for Raisl.

Renia bought four loaves of bread a day for the birds in her garden. She bought rye, white sliced, wholemeal and vienna. She walked to Acland Street to get the best bread.

She always had plenty of bread in the house. The few stories about Renia's past that she shared with Lola were about bread. She used to say, "Lola darling, you don't know what it is to be without bread." Renia was often eating the toasted rye with caraway seed that she loved when she told this to Lola. "You know, Lola, there were some people in the ghetto who killed people so that they could have their bread. Mrs Berg, my high-school teacher, didn't report the death of her daughter. She kept the body with her for two weeks so she could claim her daughter's rations. Finally, the neighbours couldn't bear the smell and told the authorities.

"I, myself, one day was carrying my bread ration home. I was stupid and was holding the bread in my hand. A young boy did snatch the bread from me. I ran and ran after him. I did catch him, but he had already gobbled my bread while he was running. He was only about eight years old. His stomach was swollen from starvation. I couldn't even cry for my bread."

Sometimes, at night, Lola was woken by her mother's nightmares.

"Mama," Mrs Bensky would call out. "Mama. Mama. Mama."

Even when she was little, Lola knew that her mother was not just in the world of sleep. She knew that Renia Bensky was in another world, in another time, with another family.

Lola suspected that this family that her mother was joined to in her nightmares was her mother's real family.

When Lola was seventeen she had crept into the Benskys' bedroom, late one night, to get her alarm clock from their sideboard. Renia and Josl were fast asleep.

As Lola picked up the clock, it slipped from her hand and fell to the ground. Mrs Bensky jumped from her bed. Her eyes were wild. "Go on, kill me!" she shouted. "Go on, I don't care what you do to me. Kill me. Kill me."

Josl woke Renia up gently. He calmed her down. "It's all right, my darling. It was just a bad dream. Everything is all right. Go back to sleep."

When Renia was asleep again, Josl went to find his daughter. Lola was in the bathroom washing herself. She had locked the door.

Josl called out to her: "I am sorry, darling, but when your Mum goes to sleep she can't get away from the past. As soon as she shuts her eyes, she is back again. Are you all right?"

"Yes, I'm fine," Lola answered. She finished washing her legs and her feet. Her bowels had given in to the shock. She had shat herself.

* *

Renia sat in her kitchen drinking a cup of black tea with cloves. Today the *Herald* was very good. There were two very good death notices today. They both had wonderful quotations. "Death surprises us in the middle of our hopes," Mr Jack Lane's wife had put at the end of the notice of her husband's death. And at the end of another notice was: "Death borders upon our birth, and our cradle stands in the grave."

The *Jewish Times,* which came from Sydney, also had a very nice death notice this week:

His life was gentle and the elements
So mixed in him that Nature might stand up
And say for all the world, "This was a Man."

Renia had heard that the editor of the *Jewish Times* was a very poetic woman.

Renia added these quotes to her notebook of obituary quotations. Her two favourites were: "A man's dying is more the survivor's affair than his own." Thomas Mann had written this. And John Donne's beautiful passage, "Any man's death diminishes me, because I am involved in mankind; and therefore never send to know for whom the bell tolls; it tolls for thee."

Renia folded the *Herald* and put it away. She had to prepare dinner. Josl liked to eat at 5 p.m. She thought that she would just ring Lola quickly before she began the dinner. Genia had told Renia yesterday that Malka Frenkel had lost three stone at the Jenny Craig Weight Loss Centre. This was not the first good report that Renia had received about the Jenny Craig Centre. She'd heard that Nusia's friend Fela had lost two stone, and that Topcha's daughter, who had always been a big fatty, was now thin. Renia walked to the telephone and dialled Lola's number.

The Holiday

It was the holiday in Olinda, they all agreed, that marked the beginning of the end. Mr and Mrs Bensky, Mr and Mrs Small, Mr and Mrs Pekelman, Mr and Mrs Ganz and Mr Berman had been a group for thirty-two years. "Our company", they called themselves. Every Easter and every Christmas they went somewhere together.

At first the holidays were modest. They were all migrants, newly arrived refugees, when they met in Australia. They met in the summer of 1950, at Solly Nadel's Guest House in Hepburn Springs. Mr and Mrs Bensky had arrived at Nadel's on a truck. Mrs Bensky and Lola had travelled in the cabin with the driver, and Mr Bensky was strapped to a chair on the back of the truck.

Josl Bensky had paid Jack, the driver, to drive them to Hepburn Springs. In two weeks, Jack would come and pick them up and take them home. The return trip cost Josl five shillings. Mrs Bensky had wept all the way there. She was sure her Josl was going to fall off the truck. And Lola, unnerved by Mrs Bensky's cries, had screamed all the way to Hepburn Springs.

When they arrived, Mr Bensky had had to wait for Jack to unstrap him. He felt a bit humiliated when a group of guests gathered to watch.

It was the Benskys' first holiday in Australia. Mrs Bensky entered Lola in the fancy-dress competition. From some cardboard and newspaper and glue, and a bottle of black ink, Mrs Bensky made Lola a witch's outfit. A black pointed hat, a black fringed cloak and a big false nose. Little Lola, the witch, won second prize.

By the end of the fortnight the "company" had been formed. Mr and Mrs Bensky, Mr and Mrs Small, Mr and Mrs Pekelman, Mr and Mrs Ganz and Mr and Mrs Berman had gone for walks together after dinner at night. They had bottled the mineral water from the springs together. They had eaten together. They were firm friends.

Mr and Mrs Pekelman had arrived in Melbourne only four weeks earlier. Mrs Bensky took Mrs Pekelman under her wing. She introduced her to Mrs Papov and to Mrs Berg. It was essential, Renia Bensky explained to Genia Pekelman, to be on the good side of these gossip-mongers.

Later, in Melbourne, Renia took Genia shopping. The two women bought a length of black knitted fabric from the Victoria Market. From this material, Renia made two tops with scooped necklines and three-quarter sleeves, and two straight skirts.

Renia made a whole wardrobe for herself and Mrs Pekelman. The total cost of this wardrobe was less than the price of one dress at Myers. Mrs Bensky felt very proud of herself. Mrs Pekelman was grateful, and she remained in eternal admiration of Mrs Bensky.

The two women looked so stylish, so elegant, so beautiful in their new clothes. Mrs Bensky's hair was cut in the new, chic, short, gamin style. She had taught Mrs Pekelman how to roll her thick auburn hair into a chignon. Both women were olive-skinned and strong-limbed. Looking at them, it was impossible to believe that five years ago Renia Bensky was in Auschwitz and Genia Pekelman was in Bergen-Belsen.

At Solly Nadel's Guest House, the men (and an occasional woman) sat inside and played cards. One hundred and two degrees Fahrenheit, and they sat with the windows closed, the air thick with cigarette smoke. And they played cards. They played Red Aces, poker and gin rummy.

The women sat in small groups outside. They chatted to each other and fussed around their own children and other people's children. Shouldn't little Johnny be wearing a sun hat? How could

Harry's mother let him out without some sunburn cream on his nose? And look at that Layla, didn't Mrs Hersh know that a young girl shouldn't be allowed to get so fat? And the Horowitz boy, he was already out of control. What would it be like when he was a teenager? For the women on holiday, here at Solly Nadel's in Hepburn Springs, these were the questions of the day.

At night there was dancing. The guests at Solly Nadel's could be divided into six categories. The good dancers, the bad dancers and the non-dancers, and the good card-players, the bad card-players and the non-card-players.

The good dancers enjoyed the highest status at Solly Nadel's. Their importance could only be surpassed by a professor or a doctor. There were not too many professors or doctors at Solly Nadel's, so the good dancers were the élite.

"Look at that Mr Gruner, what a dancer," Genia Pekelman said almost every morning at the breakfast table. "He dances the tango and the foxtrot like he was in a world championship of dancing." Genia Pekelman, who was awkward in the kitchen and around the dinner table, turned into a light-footed, delicate slip of a girl on the dance floor. All her self-consciousness left her. She side-stepped and back-stepped. She whirled in neat, graceful circles. She swivelled her hips and held her head at a coquettish angle.

During the day, the ballroom at Solly Nadel's was used as a dining room. Breakfast, lunch and dinner were served there. At meal times the noise was deafening. One hundred and twenty people ate and talked simultaneously. They ate while they talked. They talked over the top of one another. If they felt they weren't being heard, they shouted. Some of the guests shouted everything they said. The same conversations were repeated every day. The sentiments that were voiced were interchangeable among the guests. Mrs Bloom would probably be saying the same thing as Mrs Fink, and Mrs Freedman's thoughts often echoed Mrs Rose's.

Slivers of sentences shot through the room like crossfire. "How old is little Esther? Oh, she's not talking yet? My Johnny says many words. And Esther is still in nappies? What a shame. Johnny says for quite a few weeks already, 'I need pishy. I need cucky.' "

Most of the men were looking for ways to better themselves. The same conversations travelled from table to table. "Did you hear that Mr Brown was looking for a good tailor? You can get a job at the Renee of Rome Factory. He doesn't pay so good, but he always gives the Jews work. Watch out for Mr Sal. Never do piecework for him. He complains about every garment."

Every summer Solly Nadel employed Mr Muller, an elderly Austrian baker, to bake bread. Mr Muller worked seven days a week in December and January. He baked from 5 a.m. to 5 p.m. He baked rye bread, pumpernickel and vienna, and he baked special challah rolls for dinner.

There was never any bread left on the tables after the meals. Mr Grossman saved the leftover bread from his table. After two weeks, he took home three cardboard boxes of bread. Other people did the same.

"He is a peasant, that Mr Grossman," said Mrs Lipshutz. Frieda Factor interrupted her. "We should understand, Mrs Lipshutz, that this is not his normal behaviour. I don't know if you know this, Mrs Lipshutz, but Mr Grossman was in Mathausen concentration camp." "Well, he is now in Melbourne, Australia, where there is plenty of bread," Mrs Lipshutz replied. "That sort of behaviour causes anti-Semitism," she added.

Mrs Lipshutz, who had been in Australia for ten years, was not happy with the postwar influx of Jews. "They are a different brand of Jew altogether," she told her Australian neighbour, Mrs Cunningham. "They are peasants. We, Adam and I, came from cultured families. We read books, we went to the theatre, we went to the opera, we always had the best seats. We travelled in Europe. My father spoke fluent French. We were not peasants. You will see, these Jewish refugees will make the Australian people into anti-Semites."

"Oh, no, Mrs Lipshutz," said Mrs Cunningham. "I feel so sorry for some of them. They're still young girls. With those numbers on their arms they remind me of branded cattle. And Mrs Lipshutz, I met a young woman who was a dentist in Warsaw before the war, and now she is a cleaner. And her sister, who was a doctor, is working as a machinist."

"Pheh!" said Mrs Lipshutz. "They all say that they were doctors in Poland."

Later that night, Mrs Lipshutz told Mr Lipshutz that her greatest fears had been confirmed. Mrs Cunningham, their hard-working, church-going neighbour, had told her that these new Jewish migrants looked like cattle.

If it was so easy for a good, kind person like Mrs Cunningham to be an anti-Semite, said Morry Lipshutz, what hope was there for the world?

The company went to Solly Nadel's for their Christmas holidays every year until 1959. By then they had a bit more money. Things were looking up for most of the group. The Smalls and the Pekelmans were partners in a knitting factory. Mr Bensky owned Joren Fashions, a small factory that manufactured ladies' suits. Costumes, Josl called them. Pola and Moishe Ganz already had six machinists working for them at Champs Elysees Blouses, and Mr Berman wholesaled plastic bags. Joseph Zelman was the wealthiest of the group. He was already building his sixth block of flats. He bought the land, built the flats, and sold them as they were being built. He worked day and night. He undercut his competition by settling for a smaller profit. In 1959 he was on his way to banking his first million.

In 1959 the company went to Surfers Paradise. They rented four units in the same block in Cavill Avenue. Mrs Bensky brought her own frozen chicken stock. Mrs Zelman brought six pounds of lean beef, which she made into three big klops on the first day. One klops for lunch, and two for later in the week. Mrs Ganz stewed a big pot of apples and baked a sponge cake, and everyone felt at home.

They ate their meals outside, around the swimming pool. At night they walked along the beach. For Mr Bensky, the highlight of this holiday was the matzoh brei that Mrs Zelman made for everyone most mornings. Josl was the first at the breakfast table each morning. He looked so happy eating the matzoh brei that Mrs Zelman thought she could have happily made it for him forever. Some men, she thought, are so easy to please.

Surfers Paradise, the company decided, was a very successful holiday place. They went there often after that.

The company had other memorable holidays. They went to Rotorua in New Zealand. They had mud baths and mineral spas. Mrs Bensky loved this. She sat happily for hours covered in hot mud. Josl had to be ordered into the mud. He hated it. On the second day Josl sprained his ankle, and had to spend the rest of his New Zealand holiday doing what he liked best. He lay on the bed in the motel room and read detective novels. He finished a book and a box of chocolates a day.

Mrs Ganz and Mr Zelman went to the mineral baths together. Mrs Bensky was worried. She feared that the attachment between them was more than it should be. No-one else appeared worried.

In New Zealand the company discovered duty-free shopping. All the families came home with new cameras.

In 1982 the company went to Israel. They had planned this trip for months. Mr Bensky was in charge of the itinerary. They stopped in Las Vegas on their way to Israel.

Mr Bensky was one of the keenest card-players of the group. He loved to gamble. Mr Zelman and Mr Pekelman thought that Las Vegas wasn't really on the way from Melbourne to Tel Aviv, but they kept their thoughts to themselves.

Josl Bensky was deliriously happy in Las Vegas. He lost at blackjack, he lost at roulette. He lost playing chemin de fer and five card stud poker. He played the poker machines in the main gambling hall, and he played the mini poker machines in the toilets. In two days Josl Bensky lost $700. "Las Vegas", he told everyone in Melbourne when he got back, "was the best part of the trip."

"There's too many Jews here for me," said Izak Pekelman in Israel. "I don't feel so good among so many Jews." The rest of the group thought that what Izak said may have sounded a little strange but, in different ways, they all knew what he meant.

Renia Bensky stayed in the hotel room with the 'flu for most of their three weeks in Israel. Genia Pekelman wouldn't go to the pictures, or to the theatre, or to any concerts. "If it's all the same to you," she said, "I would prefer to stay in the hotel. It makes me too nervous to be with a crowd." To her husband Genia said what the others had understood she was trying to say: "Izak, I can't stand being in the middle of so many Jews. It makes me too nervous. What if someone starts to shoot at us? It reminds me too much of too many things."

George Small couldn't eat anything in Israel. "This is not what we ate at home in Poland," he said. "This is the food of Arabs, not the food of Jews."

In Mea Shearim, the Orthodox area of Jerusalem, Josl Bensky bellowed: "Who do they think they are, these Orthodox? What are they doing? Why do they have to draw such attention to themselves? Where in the Talmud does it say you have to wear such a long black coat, and the short black trousers, and the black hats? This is the modern world, not the old world. Stupid bastards. They cause trouble for everyone. Haven't the Jews had enough trouble?" By now Josl was almost in tears.

That night the company were having dinner in Jerusalem. A group of Orthodox young men came and sat at the next table. Josl looked at them and said loudly, "Oy, I'm going to vomit."

Mr Berman liked Israel. But Chaim Berman was a quiet man. He always agreed with the majority. He kept to himself the elation that he felt at being in the homeland of the Jewish people. He loved the robustness of the people, the honesty, the lack of artifice. He loved the commitment and the loyalty. Chaim thought that it was a privilege to live for an ideal, and in Israel people were living for an ideal. They had, Chaim Berman thought, something more valuable than central heating and new television sets.

Pola Ganz had hoped that she would be able to find Chaim Berman a new wife in Israel, but after a few days Pola decided that a Jewish woman from Melbourne might be more suitable.

"You have to be careful with these Israelis," she said to Ada Small. "We wouldn't want to find Chaim a wife who married him because he owns a nice house and a good business in Australia."

Ada Small agreed that they had to be careful.

The group visited a kibbutz in the Negev. They all loved the kibbutz. They were very impressed by the size of the kitchen, and the laundry facilities. "Did you ever see such a stove in your life?" said Joseph Zelman. With all his blocks of flats, Joseph knew about kitchens.

"Australia is paradise," Josl Bensky said on their last night in Israel. He raised his glass and proposed a toast to Australia. "To Australia," they all chorused.

In Israel, Renia Bensky had become increasingly agitated about Pola Ganz and Joseph Zelman. Several times, she thought, she had caught them looking at each other tenderly.

By the time she was back in Australia, Renia Bensky was sure there was a heat between Pola Ganz and Joseph Zelman. And Renia Bensky felt hot watching them.

"Poor Mina Zelman," Renia said to Josl. "She hasn't suffered enough? It wasn't enough what she did go through in Bergen-Belsen? Now she has to have a Romeo for a husband? And what about poor Moishe Ganz? Maybe he is not so intelligent as our dear Joseph Zelman, but he has always been a first-class husband to Pola. The trouble with Pola is that she doesn't know when she's got something good. She is always looking for something new. She says to me, 'Oh Renia, I've found a new hairdresser. Oh Renia, I've found a new dressmaker. Oh Renia, this manicurist is better and cheaper.' Now, whatever Joseph Zelman has got in his trousers is something Pola Ganz thinks is better than what she's got at home."

Renia knew that after the war there were strange and hasty alliances formed. Women married for security. Men married mothers. Strangers married strangers. People were starved of comfort, companionship and affection. Odd matches were made. There was not always time to wait for love.

Young girls married older men. Students married their teachers. Neighbours and cousins got married. Everyone was in a hurry to begin a normal life.

Dead wives, dead husbands and dead children were present at many of these marriage ceremonies.

Renia decided that something had to be done about Pola and Joseph. She hired a private detective. Two weeks later, the private detective gave Renia a photograph of Joseph Zelman sitting in his car outside Pola Ganz's house. Renia felt very pleased with herself.

It was Easter, and the company went to Olinda. Renia packed the photograph carefully at the bottom of her suitcase. She hadn't told Josl about the detective.

In Olinda, it seemed as though it was going to be another nice Easter break. The group settled into their holiday routine. They ate nice big breakfasts, they went for walks, they sat in the autumn sun. They had good lunches, a nap after lunch, another small walk and it was time for dinner. After dinner they played cards. After three days they were all in good spirits, and felt invigorated by the country air.

On Sunday night, Renia showed Ada Small the photograph. Ada didn't say much. "Why have you got a photograph of Joseph in his car?" she asked. Renia explained the location of the photograph, and its implication.

Ada Small went straight to Pola Ganz. Pola laughed and showed the photograph to Moishe. Moishe looked carefully at the photograph. He didn't say anything. Later, he said to Josl: "So what, what does that photograph prove? Nothing." Josl had to agree.

Nobody mentioned the photograph to Mina Zelman.

"She's got enough trouble," said Ada Small. "She's so tall. At her height she would never find another husband."

Pola refused to speak to Renia Bensky. Renia tried to explain that she had done this for Pola's own good, but Pola wouldn't even come near her.

"If she is going to be so unintelligent about this," Renia said to Josl, "she can go to hell. I am finished with Pola Ganz."

The atmosphere became so unpleasant that the company left Olinda a day early.

What was really shocking about all of this, Ada Small said to her manicurist, was that Renia Bensky and Pola Ganz had almost been machatunim. There was no word in English for machatunim, Ada explained. Machatunim was the word for the relationship between a couple's parents-in-law. Renia and Pola were almost the mothers-in-law of each other's children. Renia's daughter Lina had almost married Pola's son, Sam.

There was an unspoken, unanimous decision among the company not to tell the children why they were no longer friends. The children had to be protected.

One of Lina's colleagues at the law firm where she worked told her that she'd heard a rumour that the rift between Renia and Pola was caused by Renia's accusations that Pola had committed adultery with Joseph Zelman.

Sam Ganz laughed when Lina told him. "My mother, having an affair? You're joking. She goes to bed in flannel nightgowns and wears face cream, throat cream, neck cream, arm and leg cream. As a kid, I used to watch her hop into bed and wonder why she didn't slip straight out again. There must be another reason Renia and Pola aren't speaking."

Mrs Zelman also wondered why Renia and Pola weren't speaking. Maybe Mrs Ganz had done something she shouldn't have been doing with Mrs Bensky's Josl. She wouldn't put it past that Pola Ganz to meddle with someone else's husband.

Mr Zelman and Mrs Ganz also stopped speaking to each other.

"He was a rotten lover," Mrs Ganz said to her sister. "He wore his socks to bed."

The company collapsed. Mr Small and Mr Pekelman and Mr Berman met Mr Zelman and Mr Ganz to try and patch things up. They agreed that it was important to forgive and to forget. To make a fresh start. But the women wouldn't budge.

Moishe Ganz believed his wife, and wouldn't hear a word against her. Josl, although he thought that Renia shouldn't have interfered, knew that she didn't do it out of malice.

People took sides. Mr and Mrs Small sided with the Ganzes, and Mr and Mrs Pekelman stayed loyal to the Benskys. Chaim Berman remained friendly with everyone.

For thirty-two years the company hadn't missed a Saturday night at the pictures. Now they stopped going to the pictures. They stopped playing cards. They stopped going out for supper. They stayed at home.

Mr and Mrs Small and Mr Berman took short walks around Caulfield, but their hearts weren't in it. The Zelmans tried to learn bridge, but everyone else at the Herzl Club could play well, and they gave up. Izak Pekelman took up golf. He dropped it a week later.

At weddings, barmitzvahs, engagements and anniversaries and birthdays, people knew to put the Benskys and the Ganzes at different tables.

Genia Pekelman talked separately to Renia and Pola. She begged them to make up. She said to each of them, "Couldn't you just put this behind you and make a new start?" That approach hadn't worked with Genia's daughter Rachel, and it didn't work with Renia and Pola.

Genia tried again. "If you can't be friends, at least don't be enemies. Let us all go out together again, and maybe things will get slowly better. And we will be a group again. And people will stop talking about us. And if things are not as good as they look, at least it will look as though they are good." Genia's mother used to quote this old saying to her. It had a melodic lilt in Yiddish that got lost in the translation. Nothing that Genia Pekelman said moved Renia or Pola.

This was the price of success, thought Genia. This is what happens when you can afford to hire a private detective. Life used to be so straightforward in the old days in Melbourne, thought Genia.

When they first came to Australia, some of them had lived two families to one room. Even the most comfortably off of the group, the Smalls, lived in a room at the back of their factory.

On weekends all their children played together. Now, when Genia reminded Rachel that Jack Zelman was unattached, Rachel replied, "I hate Jack Zelman." Rachel and Jack had played together so nicely when they were small.

Genia had thought that she had created cousins for her Rachel and her Esther in Australia. A new family. She thought that the company and their children would regard each other as family. As cousins, aunties, uncles, nephews, nieces. As it turned out, none of their children were friends, except for Lina and Sam. And now the company themselves were no longer friends.

They had all ended up, Genia thought, in the same position that they had been in in Germany after the war. No family. No close friends. At least they had their children. But the children were another story. Even the children had brought them troubles.

Soon, Genia thought, they would all start dying. And they would die alone. One of Genia's most comforting thoughts had been that she would never have to die alone. Not like the hundreds and hundreds of dead in the streets in the ghetto.

So this is how things had turned out, thought Genia Pekelman. This is how things had turned out in the goldeneh medina, the new world.

The Children

Sam Ganz was the Managing Director of Champs Elysees Blouses. Sam was on the phone negotiating the purchase of a turn-of-the-century musical sideboard. When you opened its glass doors, this sideboard played *Für Elise.* Sam was on the verge of agreeing to pay the asking price when his father walked into the office. "I'll call you back, and we'll discuss it this afternoon," Sam said to the antique dealer. "Just talking to the mechanic about the Volvo. It needs its front brake pads replaced," he explained to his father.

Moishe Ganz was the Chairman of Eiffel Tower Fashions, which owned Champs Elysees Blouses. Pola and Moishe had set up the business in 1950.

Pola and Moishe had met in Paris, in the Hotel Lutetia, in 1946. They had both just survived the war in Poland — she in hiding, and he in a labour camp. Now they were being looked after at the Hotel Lutetia.

During the war the Hotel Lutetia had been the Gestapo headquarters in Paris. Now it was a welcoming centre for the few Jews who had survived Nazi Europe.

Pola and Moishe had rooms on the same floor at the Lutetia. They began talking to each other. Soon they began to meet in the foyer of the hotel in the mornings. Then they spent their days together.

After two weeks, Moishe proposed to Pola. Pola said: "No, never! I don't want to get married. I want to live a bit, to grow up. I am twenty-one, and I haven't had any boyfriends. I haven't done

many things a normal girl does. I don't know who I am, where I am. I only know I don't want to get married. Not now, never."

"Never say never," said Moishe. Three weeks later, Pola and Moishe were married.

They moved out of the Lutetia and into a small bed-sitting room in the Rue de Rennes. Pola and Moishe shared their sixth-floor flat in the Rue de Rennes with a family of dark-brown rats. Pola and Moishe kept their bread, coffee, tea, sugar and even butter wrapped in newspaper, and hung these parcels in pillowcases from a hook on the wall.

One day Pola reached for one of her shoes from the bottom of the cupboard. She surprised a sleeping rat. The rat ran up Pola's arm. Pola wept. The rat had shat on her skirt. "I knew I shouldn't have got married," she said to Moishe.

Pola and Moishe did have good times in Paris. They went for long walks along the river. They went to the zoo. Even then, straight after the war, Paris was a city of lovers. Pola and Moishe got to know each other slowly. It was a time of rest and recuperation. A honeymoon of sorts.

They were waiting for their immigration papers to be finalised. Moishe taught Pola to ice-skate. They fed pigeons in the Luxembourg Gardens. They walked arm-in-arm alongside other lovers in the Tuileries and on the Boulevard St Germain.

Years later, when people talked about the beauty of Paris, Pola could only remember the rats.

Baby Sam was born three months before Pola and Moishe were due to leave for Australia. Pola wept with happiness at the birth of her son. The night after Pola had been freed from the cellar in which she had spent the last year of the war, she had had a dream. Her father, who had died in the cellar, had come to her in her dream. "Pola, my daughter," he had said, "you will one day give birth to a son. And this son will have in him all the fathers and all the sons from our family. I will be there in him. Your grandfather will be there. And your grandfather's grandfather. We will all be there. As soon as you see your son, you will see us."

Sam was a beautiful baby. He had a wise face and a quiet disposition. Pola saw that her father had been right. Sam looked just like him.

Moishe was also in love with Sam. He kissed him hundreds of times a day. When Sam was two months old, Moishe took him to the Punch and Judy show at the Bois de Boulogne. He pointed out dogs and cats and birds in the street. He repeated the Yiddish, French and English words for these animals to Sam. As soon as he had set eyes on Sam, Moishe had seen that Sam was the image of Moishe's mother. Moishe also recognised Sam's eyes: they belonged to his youngest sister, Chana. Chana and her mother had died of tuberculosis in the ghetto.

Moishe had hoped that Sam would be born in Australia. He had gone to the Australian Embassy every day to ask if the visa had been approved. "I want my child to be born in Australia. I want that he should be very Australian," Moishe had pleaded. But the process couldn't be hurried.

The Ganzes arrived in Australia in May 1949. They spent the first month at the migrant hostel at Bonegilla. Pola and Sam slept in the women's quarters. Moishe was in the men's dormitory. Pola's bed was in the middle of rows and rows of beds. The toilets were outside. There were no lights at night. Sam wasn't well. He had diarrhoea. At night, Pola changed his nappies in the dark. As soon as she had a clean nappy on him, he had another bout of diarrhoea. Pola had been nervous about coming to Australia. Australia was proving to be worse than her worst fears.

Moishe found a nice room in Brunswick. The Jewish Welfare Agency furnished the room, and the Ganzes moved in. Moishe was happy. Things were looking up.

Pola put on her best dress and went to Georges, the most exclusive department store in Melbourne. She took a pencil and a notepad. In the dressing room of the Ladies Daywear department, Pola sketched half a dozen of the blouses that they had in the store.

Moishe bought some fabric. Together, in their room in Brunswick, Pola and Moishe made copies of the blouses. Moishe got orders for these blouses from several small retailers around Melbourne. Champs Elysees Blouses was in business.

"Mum," said Sam, "I've put a deposit on a sideboard. It's antique and it's very beautiful. It will be a good investment. In another few years it will be worth twice what I am paying for it." "Good, darling," said Pola. She liked Sam to be happy.

"It was very expensive," said Sam. "But this sideboard is one of a kind. You'd never find another one like it, and it's going to look fabulous in my den. I took Ruth to see it, and she adores it."

Mrs Ganz, unfortunately, didn't adore Ruth. She thought that Ruth had married Sam to better herself. Ruth came from a poor family. She had adapted herself very well to a moneyed lifestyle. Too well, thought Pola.

"Well, darling, enjoy this sideboard," said Pola. "How much did you pay for it?"

"Fifty thousand," said Sam.

"What, are you crazy? Fifty thousand? Does it have eighteen-carat gold cutlery in the drawers? Are you a meshugana? You are, you are mad."

Eventually Pola calmed down. It was only money, she thought. Sam was their only son. What did it matter? Nobody was hurt by the purchase. Pola did feel, though, that it would be unwise for Moishe to know that Sam had paid fifty thousand for a sideboard.

When Moishe was angry with Sam, he would call him a "little prince". "He doesn't know what it is to work hard, to earn your own money," Moishe would say.

Moishe was disappointed in Sam. Not that he voiced this disappointment. Moishe believed that to air a problem only made the problem seem worse. Sam had been a mediocre student at school, and had failed his matriculation year. The Ganzes had no alternative. They had taken Sam into the business.

Pola and Sam worked out a scheme whereby Sam would pay for the sideboard with three separate cheques. He would tell his father that he was buying three pieces of furniture, not one. Fifty thousand for three pieces would seem reasonable.

Moishe didn't notice Sam's purchases. He had other things on his mind. His two daughters both wanted to leave their husbands. Moishe didn't know what to do.

Last week Debbi, the elder daughter, had told him that she was leaving her husband, Oscar. She was in love, she said, with Adrian Gartener. Moishe didn't see that there was much difference between Oscar and Adrian Gartener. Why Debbi was transferring her love from one to another bewildered Moishe.

"Love, love," he raged to Pola, "They all talk about this big word love. It is not 'love', but 'LOVE'. Tell me Pola, can you see that that Adrian Gartener is any more of a mensch than Oscar Kreutzer? They are both pishers."

Helen, the Ganzes' other daughter, was also looking for fulfilment. She had said to her father, "Issy is a nice enough person. He's good-hearted and kind to the children, but I can't bear him to touch me. It's not that he wants to touch me so often. Luckily, he is not all that interested. But when he moves towards me in bed I feel sick."

Pola Ganz knew that Helen had been having an affair with one of her colleagues at the University of Melbourne. She had told Helen to be sure to be absolutely discreet. "Darling, for a few hot minutes in someone else's bed, you don't throw away a good husband," she had said to her daughter.

The Ganzes had supported their sons-in-law through university. Afterwards, they had set them up in business. They had bought Issy a law practice, and Oscar a dental surgery.

Moishe felt tired thinking about his daughters. Moishe had thought that the days of having trouble with his children were over.

What was wrong with young people today? They had no stamina. They had to be gratified immediately. Their love life had to be perfect. Their sex had to be the latest up-to-date manoeuvres. If they were not having simultaneous orgasms they looked for another partner.

What about love? And tenderness? And patience? And loyalty? Life, for his children, was too transient to allow for love, thought Moishe.

Pola and Moishe had given their children everything. The children had been spoilt and coddled. Moishe had set up Champs Elysees Blouses one block from Elwood Primary School so that Pola could take hot soup to school at lunchtime for Sam and the girls.

Still, his girls were better than other people's girls, thought Moishe. Look at poor Renia Bensky. Her Lola, who was so clever at school, had refused to go to university. And then she had married a goy. At least, through marriage, thought Moishe, Lola had become a wife and a mother. Before that she had been a hippie. She had walked everywhere, even in Collins Street, barefooted, with bells around her neck and long dirty dresses. Moishe had felt so sorry for Renia Bensky.

And, Moishe thought, his Debbi and Helen were better than Genia Pekelman's Esther. Esther was always preoccupied and distracted. She couldn't finish her sentences. Her anxiety blinded her. Last year she had driven through an amber light and killed an elderly man. She hadn't seen him. Izak and Genia Pekelman had visited the man's family to see if there was anything they could do to help. The family had said that there was nothing that the Pekelmans could do for them. There were no witnesses, and the death was recorded as an accident. Izak made a large donation to the Royal Children's Hospital in the dead man's name.

Sam Ganz had a problem. The price he had agreed to pay for the sideboard was seventy thousand, not fifty thousand. He knew his parents would never understand. They really weren't very educated, thought Sam. They knew nothing about antiques. He had to find twenty thousand dollars.

All Sam's and Ruth's expenditures went through the company's books. That was how Pola knew exactly how much Ruth spent at Figgins and Georges and David Jones every week.

Sam frowned. He would have to find a way to pay the extra twenty thousand dollars. Maybe he could give his friend Solly Rosenberg a cheque for twenty thousand. Sam could tell Moishe that he was buying Solly's computer for a very good price, to use at home. Solly could then write out a cheque for twenty thousand, which Sam could give directly to the antique dealer.

At Champs Elysées Blouses, Sam earned a hundred thousand dollars a year. He also received one-fifth of the company's profits. Sam was a wealthy man, but he felt like a small boy who was not allowed to be in charge of his own pocket money. Sam tolerated this discomfort. Now and then he thought of doing something that interested him more, but he couldn't think of anything.

Every winter Pola and Moishe went to Surfers Paradise for three weeks. Pola went at the beginning of June, and when she came back, three weeks later, Moishe went. They both felt that they couldn't be away from Champs Elysees Blouses at the same time.

"If Sam is the Managing Director, he should be able to manage the factory," Ada Small often said to the Ganzes. "Moishe, Sam is thirty-two. He is not a baby. He can look after the business." But Pola and Moishe both agreed that it would be unwise for them to be away from the factory together.

Every Sunday the Ganz family had lunch together. Sam, Debbi and Helen, their spouses and their children came to Pola and Moishe's house. Pola's housekeeper, Mrs Staub, prepared the food. Pola was one of the few women in their group who had a full-time housekeeper. "I work all day. Why should I work more when I come home?" Pola would say. She always felt a need to defend her use of a housekeeper. The food that Mrs Staub made was delicious. Pola's friends and Pola's children regarded Mrs Staub's meals as inferior because they were not cooked by Pola.

Today Mrs Staub had prepared gefilte fish, chopped liver, a grated egg and onion salad, a potato salad, roast chicken, and chicken schnitzels for the children, and a salmon patty for Issy.

Issy Segal was a fussy eater. Every day for breakfast Issy had a bowl of Kelloggs cornflakes. He had been having this breakfast for twenty years, since he was ten. For lunch, he had one cheese sandwich. White bread with Havarti cheese. For seventeen years, Issy had had a slice of Kraft cheddar in his sandwich. One day Debbi had said to her brother-in-law, "Couldn't you try another cheese? A real cheese. That stuff you're eating is plastic. Try Havarti." Issy did. And now he ate Havarti cheese in his sandwich. Last year, Debbi had suggested Issy try some Jarlsberg cheese in his sandwich. Issy said that he was perfectly happy with Havarti.

Every Sunday Issy picked at his salmon patty. The rest of the family ate heartily. "This is a very good gefilte fish today," said Pola. "Last week you couldn't get Murray Perch in Melbourne. The places that had a Murray Perch were selling them for a fortune. It happens every Pesach. The fish shops save their stocks of Murray Perch for just before Pesach, and then they put up the price. They know that at Pesach they can get double the price."

"Mum, we can afford to pay a bit more for a Murray Perch," said Debbi. "It is easy for you to say that," said Pola. "Listen to her," continued Pola. "She says 'we can afford'. Who is this 'we' that can afford this? Who is this 'we' that has earned the money to pay this price for a Murray Perch? Is it you, my darling daughter?"

Luckily, just at that moment, one of the grandchildren dropped a piece of beetroot onto his white shirt, and everyone was diverted from the issue of who earned the money in this family.

The matter of food took over from the matter of money. Pola, Debbi and Helen all tried to push food into the children.

"Harry, have some chicken."

"Melanie, please eat the schnitzel before the potato."

"Jonathan, you have to eat the fish before you can have any salad."

"Jason, you know that salmon patty belongs to Daddy. Have a chicken wing."

"Have you had a drink yet?"

"Don't drink the lemonade before you finish your meal."

"Don't eat so much egg, you'll be sick. Have some potato instead."

"Eat more egg salad, it's good for you."

This was the main conversation at the lunch table.

After the meal, Pola and Moishe played with the grandchildren, and Debbi and Helen washed the dishes. The sisters had never got on well. They had never confided in each other. Each thought that the other was the favoured daughter. But they had a few things in common. They both wanted to leave their husbands. They both despaired of their brother Sam. And they both hated Ruth.

"Did you see that outfit that Ruth was wearing?" said Helen. "I saw it in Gucci. It cost three thousand bucks."

"Three thousand bucks!" said Debbi. "Jesus, by the time our kids grow up there'll be no money left in the business, the rate that Ruth's going through it. I noticed, too, that she had another new ring. Sam keeps buying her jewellery. First of all Sam bought himself a wife. He did, he bought Ruth with that car and that big engagement diamond. And now he just keeps paying. He's an imbecile."

"I wonder what she's got that makes her worth all that expenditure?" said Helen.

Helen contemplated telling her sister about her affair with Malcolm Bourke. Sometimes she longed to be close to her sister, but something prevented her. Helen decided against telling Debbi. Debbi might use the information against her in some way.

Helen knew that her affair with Malcolm Bourke had no future. Malcolm wasn't Jewish, and Helen couldn't imagine being married to a non-Jew. There was a comfort and a familiarity and a trust that she felt when she was with Jews.

Helen had rarely found Jewish men sexy. Standing at her mother's kitchen sink, Helen closed her eyes for a moment. She thought of Malcolm licking her, manipulating her. She thought of Malcolm caressing her buttocks, his head between her legs. Helen had to steady herself. She felt limp.

On the few occasions that she and Issy made love, he left his pyjamas on. Helen would lift her nightie to just above her waist. For three minutes they would be joined in a wordless union.

Helen wondered if she would ever find a Jewish man she couldn't wait to fuck. Would there ever be a Jew that she would lust after? Be hungry for? Feel hot about?

There was Charles Roth. He was their solicitor. He was small, articulate and fiery. He had a spark and a swiftness that Helen found attractive. He wasn't overly concerned with himself. He seemed indefatigable. His enthusiasm was infectious. Charles Roth had put himself through law school by playing the piano in jazz bars at night. Now his law practice was very successful and he was a wealthy man. Charles Roth was, however, married. And happily married, Helen had heard.

Never mind, Helen thought. She would make an effort to meet as many Jewish men as she could. It was better to try and find another husband now than in ten years' time when she would be middle-aged. Anything would have to be better than the brief intertwining of the pyjamas and the nightie.

"It's better that I leave now," Helen had said when her mother suggested that she wait until the children were older. "Mum, the kids will be happier if I'm happier. Issy is at the surgery until eight every night. They'll see just as much of him. If I wait until I'm forty, I'll probably have forgotten what it feels like to feel like a real woman."

"Helen, darling, there is more to a good marriage than a good shtoop. Believe me, I know what I'm talking about," said Pola Ganz.

Helen and Debbi had finished the dishes.

"Debbi, I'm not happy with Issy," said Helen. "Can we have a cup of coffee somewhere tomorrow, and talk?"

"Sure," said Debbi. "I'll meet you at The Place at nine."

Debbi and Helen left Oscar and Issy in the same week.

"Look, Pola," said Moishe, "if people are going to talk, let them get all the talking about us over with at the same time. It's better that the girls did it together. Otherwise we would have everybody talking about us this week, and then again everyone talking about us next week, or next month, or next year. Now, they will get double the pleasure in their talking, and we will get it over with at once."

Pola could see the good sense in that. Everyone in the community would get twice as much joy in the Ganzes' failure as parents, and the Ganzes would only have to endure the humiliation for half the time. Moishe could always see the good side of a bad situation, thought Pola.

"You think, Moishe, that I should speak to Sam about that Ruth?" said Pola. "I mean, Moishe, if we have to have people talking, and marriages finishing, and grandchildren who are going to suffer, then maybe I should suggest to Sam that he leaves that bitch Ruth. Three divorces wouldn't be any harder than two divorces. We could get a special bulk price from a divorce lawyer. Things couldn't be worse. Sam could be comforted and looked after by his sisters, who would understand exactly what he is going through. What do you think, Moishe?"

Moishe started laughing. He had known Pola for thirty-four years, but her efficiency still surprised him. "Pola, I think that maybe we should leave the matter of his marriage or his divorce to Sam himself."

Pola was disappointed, but she knew Moishe was right. Still, Pola couldn't resist making a few enquiries.

"Sammy, my darling, does Ruth cook you the schnitzel the way that you like it?" she said to her son.

Sam looked bewildered. "No, Mum. Ruth doesn't cook schnitzel. She doesn't fry any foods. She can't bear the frying smell. She says it stays in her hair for hours."

Pola put her hands over her mouth to keep her response inside her.

Sam was puzzled by his mother's concern about Ruth's cooking. He was glad that Pola was distracted. He needed some peace and quiet. Yesterday Sam had bought a hat stand for ten thousand dollars. It was a beautiful hat stand. This hat stand had cerulean blue ceramic balls at the end of every hook, and a ceramic sculpture of an owl at the base.

Now Sam had to figure out how to pay for the hat stand without the transaction going through Champs Elysees Blouses' books. Sam thought that Pola and Moishe might just be preoccupied enough with the divorces not to question the purchase of another home computer. He could repeat the cheque-swapping routine with Solly Rosenberg.

Moishe was with his solicitor and his accountant. They were trying to organise the family finances so that their assets would be protected in case of financial disputes in the property settlements of their daughters' divorces.

Moishe had a headache. Everything was in joint names, in trust funds for the children, in trust funds for the grandchildren. They had already had two lawyers and two accountants working on it for a week.

Moishe noticed that Sam had bought himself another computer. Some people are easily pleased, he thought. If only his daughters would settle for another computer.

A Mixed Marriage

From the day that Lola fell in love with another man, her husband smelt bad. The smell was like stale, sweet cheese. It came from his body and hovered in a thick net around the bed. It made Lola feel bilious.

She began sleeping with the window open. For thirty-five years she had lived with deadlocks, combination locks and iron bolts; her home security system was updated annually. Now, her fear of rapists, burglars and murderers paled next to the horror of the smell.

It came from his ears, his feet, his hands and his neck. She could smell it in the bathroom when he showered. In the kitchen, it crept across the breakfast table. It soaked into her coffee and filtered itself through her grapefruit juice.

Was Rodney suspicious? Was this his body's reaction? Like a skunk putting out a stink when it feels in danger?

But Rodney didn't know that she was in love with anyone but him. She had been devotedly faithful to him for thirteen years. More than that, they were the ideal couple. Lola loved the image of herself, a dark, wild-haired, large-eyed Jewess, standing next to the tall, pale son of the city's establishment.

The smell lodged itself in Lola's throat. She was unable to eat. She got up and called to her children through the intercom system. "Kids, we have to leave in five minutes or you'll be late for school." Lola had never been late for anything. In all her years of psychotherapy, she had not missed one minute of one session. Lola liked to deliver her children to their schools an hour early. This allowed time for possible delays due to heavy traffic, a flat tyre, a mechanical failure or other emergencies. Lola felt that she would be able to tackle any emergency clear-headedly, secure in the knowledge that she would still be on time.

The night before Lola's first day at school, her mother had sat her down for a talk. The family had been in Australia for three years. Mr and Mrs Bensky worked behind sewing machines in a factory during the day, and behind sewing machines at home at night. "Lolala, my Lolala," Mrs Bensky said, "You will be in a school now with Australian children. I want you always to remember that a Jewish boy will make you the best husband. Australian boys, they learn from their fathers to drink beer and to smack their wives. My Lolala, what do you know what it is to be smacked? To be treated worse than a dog?"

Lola couldn't imagine anyone smacking the beautiful Mrs Bensky. She knew that the Nazis had. They had tattooed a number on Mrs Bensky's slender strong arm. Lola told anyone who asked that this number was their new phone number.

"Lolala, look at Mrs Stein's daughter. She married someone who is not Jewish. A nice man he seemed. An accountant. Look at her, Lolala. Three children, no money, dirty everything. He is in the pub every day straight after work, then he comes home and gives her a nice klup on the head. That's what will happen to you, Lolala, if you marry an Australian."

Lola wasn't surprised at this prospect of violence. Lola knew that she didn't yet know half of how frightening the world was. She did know that there was danger everywhere, and that life was a series of narrow escapes. By the time she was thirteen she had a highly evolved, complex system of warding off evil. She had to touch all the doorknobs and cupboard handles in her bedroom ten times each in the correct order, from left to right, before going to bed. Then she could sleep.

On Sunday nights the world looked better to Lola. In the afternoon Mrs Bensky would bake a sponge cake. It always came

out with a soft brown covering, like lightly spun velvet. Next she laid out the bowls. A bowl of dark, shiny chocolates, a bowl of delicately sprigged branches of muscatel raisins scattered with almonds, a bowl of black, fat prunes, and a bowl of fruit-flavoured boiled lollies.

Then she prepared supper. It was always the same. Grated egg and spring onion salad, schmalz herring, smoked mackerel, chopped liver, dill pickles, radish flowers, sliced tomatoes, some rye bread and some matzoh. After that, she unfolded four card tables and chairs and arranged them in the small lounge room. At four o'clock Mr and Mrs Bensky had a nap for an hour. By eight o'clock the air was scented with heady perfume and cigarettes. Mrs Ganz's long, polished nails sparkled as she dealt the cards. Lola loved Mrs Ganz's husky voice and the way that her breasts moved with her breath.

Mr Ganz argued with Mr Berman: "Chaim, you are an idiot! You walk with your eyes shut. You will be finished if you go into partnership with such an idiot like Felek Ganzgarten. You mustn't do it."

"Gentlemen, gentlemen," Mr Bensky admonished them in his most formal English.

Mrs Small sang in a low voice as she played. "Motl, Motl vos vat sein mit dir, der Rabbi sogt du kanst nisht lernen," she sang — "Morris, Morris what is going to become of you, the Rabbi says you are not learning."

And Mr Small, as usual, slipped Lola a couple of very expensive, large, chocolate-covered liqueur prunes. Mr Zelman whistled an old Polish lullaby as he smoothly swept his winnings over to his corner.

Sometimes the hum of the room was low and calm, and other times the atmosphere was feverish. Moves were disputed, news was dispensed, rumours were scotched or debated, advice was given and taken, and money was won and lost.

Mrs Bensky never played cards. She made cups of black lemon

tea, refilled the glasses of soda water, emptied the ashtrays and served the supper.

Driving the children to school, Lola remembered Rodney, twenty-three years old, his speech almost a stutter that was expelled in short bursts. He had looked much happier when he was not speaking. And Lola was then free to imagine his thoughts.

One day, Rodney told her that he was never going to marry. He said that he would be too worried that his wife would leave him. This revelation was at odds with Lola's understanding of Rodney. She saw him as independent, self-contained and peaceful. The thought of not being the one who had to worry about being left appealed to Lola. Six weeks later they were married.

Lola and Rodney became good friends. They laughed together. They blossomed as parents and were bound together by a fierce pride in their two beautiful and clever children.

For the first few years of the marriage, Lola was captivated and wholly satisfied by Rodney's blondness. She would lie awake next to him for hours, looking at the golden hairs glinting on his arms.

Lola dropped the children off and parked the car in the supermarket car park. She walked to a taxi rank and caught a taxi to Garth's apartment.

In the taxi, the lies, the deception and the tension of the last month visited Lola briefly, but her happiness crept up and covered her.

Garth was waiting for her. His smile looked as though it might lift him off the ground. He trembled as he held her. He had prepared coffee. She watched him pour the coffee.

The first time they made love, Lola had felt like a virgin. She and Rodney had shuffled in and out of sex comfortably, companionably. Now she ached. She had forgotten what it was like to ache for a man. It felt like a violin screaming between her legs.

That evening at dinner, Rodney said "I think Garth Walker is in love with you."

"What?" she said.

"I've seen the way he looks at you," Rodney answered. "He doesn't take his eyes off you. He talks to the kids and he looks at you. He talks to me and he looks at you."

"Don't be silly," said Lola. She felt bilious.

"It's infatuation," said Lola's closest friend, Margaret-Anne. "It wears off. After a few years you and Garth will be like you and Rodney. It's not worth the bother."

Lola fantasised about finding another wife for Rodney. She would find someone intelligent, well-read and with a good sense of humour, and they could all be friends. They could buy a small block of flats and create two large apartments. They could eat together. They could share holidays. And the children wouldn't miss out. The prospect of this happy communal life made Lola feel exhausted.

Lola knew it wasn't going to be easy to tell Mrs Bensky that she was going to leave Rodney.

"So, Hitler didn't kill me, now you are going to do it for him!" screamed Mrs Bensky.

Mr Bensky said: "I lived through the labour camp to hear this news? I wish I would have died."

Mrs Bensky rang Rodney to tell him that she would do his laundry. She said she didn't want Rodney to suffer the humiliation of having his clothes washed by a wife who was in love with someone else.

Lola had not had such an effect on her parents since the day she told them that she was going to marry Rodney.

"Lolala, Lolala, how can you do this to us?" Mrs Bensky had wailed. "What will our friends say? They will say that we didn't bring you up properly. They will say that we should have sent you to Mount Scopus, not to an Australian school. Lola, get me some Stemetil. I feel sick."

Now, Mr and Mrs Bensky were hysterical. "Lola, you and Rodney were our big hope, our example of how a mixed marriage can work. Everyone says what a wonderful man Rodney is and what a wonderful couple you are. Lolala, wake up!" Mrs Bensky screamed.

For most of her adult life Lola had had trouble waking up. She used to daydream while she was cleaning, while she was driving, while she was reading or watching television, and while people spoke to her. She would nod from time to time, and on the whole no-one noticed.

She had a whole set of fantasies she could slip into. When Mrs Bensky delivered her regular lectures about losing weight, Lola would plug herself into the dream in which she had just completed her fifth best-selling novel. A novel that had made millions of readers weep. A novel that had earned Lola hundreds of thousands of dollars. A novel that had caused passionate debate in dining rooms in Paris, London and New York. Last week, when Mrs Bensky finished her speech, Lola was being interviewed by Johnny Carson on the *Tonight* show.

When she was with Garth, Lola was wide awake. So awake she could feel every part of her body. She could feel her nervous heart. She could feel her knees. She felt as though she could inhale the earth and touch the stars.

Garth taught her about art. He played her music. Mahler, Satie, Berg, Poulenc, Glass, Stravinsky. He read her poetry. Poems by Akhmatova, Tsvetayeva, Brodsky, William Carlos Williams. Poems by Anne Sexton. And he never stopped looking at her. He looked at her as they walked. He looked at her when they talked. He looked at her while they ate. He looked at her as they made love. And he painted her. He painted her happy and he painted her sad. He painted her pained and he painted her exuberant. He painted her as a madonna and he painted her as a warrior queen, a Boadicea streaking across the canvas. Hundreds of portraits of her were stacked around the walls of his studio.

* *

Mr and Mrs Bensky had observed every detail of Lola's life. What she ate, how often she changed her underwear, who she spoke to in the school ground. Mrs Bensky would watch Lola every lunchtime, after she had delivered her daily hot lunch. Later on, Mrs Bensky kept a record of Lola's menstrual cycle on a chart inside the pantry cupboard. And the intercom system that connected all the rooms in the house was always switched on.

Everything was a potential catastrophe. A sneeze indicated pneumonia, a cough was a sign of asthma, a stomach ache pointed towards kidney and liver trouble. An unexpected knock at the door would leave Mrs Bensky breathless, and if Lola was ever late home from school, Mrs Bensky prepared herself for the worst.

Lola, who still complained that nothing she did escaped her parents' scrutiny, became an observant parent herself. Lola adored her son Julian. For the first year and a half of his life she recorded his every bowel movement. She drew up a chart and headed the columns "Time", "Size", "Consistency" and "Colour". Another chart recorded every mouthful of food baby Julian swallowed. This was headed "Food", "Description", "Amount", "Time" and "Attitude".

By the time her daughter, Paradise, was born, Lola was not so intense about being a parent. She allowed Paradise to pat stray dogs and to eat her food from the kitchen floor. Paradise spent hours smudging her meals into the brown quarry tiles under the table before scraping the food into her mouth.

Lola worried about the consequences of allowing Paradise to eat off the floor, but she consoled herself with the thought that at least Paradise was a good eater. Julian was such a fussy eater that Lola had had to pretend that everything she fed him was chicken. Most of Julian's chicken chocolate custard or chicken fruit salad or chicken chops went into Lola.

Mr and Mrs Bensky spent the Saturday afternoons of most summers at St Kilda Beach. The whole gang would go. Mrs Bensky always brought cold boiled eggs and rye bread, and Mrs Ganz made her special carrot and pineapple salad. The Zelmans brought ham and Mr Pekelman brought long cucumbers from his garden.

They sat under the tea-trees on the foreshore, on thick, soft rugs, and ate and drank and talked. The Italian man who sold peanuts was always happy to see them. They bought twelve large bags. Enough peanuts to last until dinner.

Every now and then, someone would go for a dip in the water. Most of the gang couldn't swim. Mrs Bensky was the only good swimmer. She would stride into the water in her gold lamé bikini, or her silver and purple polka dotted pair, or the green pair covered in latex leaves.

As a child, Lola used to wear lumpy, frilly bathers. They had a gathered yoke and a full skirt, which Mrs Bensky said disguised Lola's hips and thighs.

Now, Lola would soon be able to wear her first pair of bikinis. The weight was dropping off her. Every day she was thinner. Garth satisfied all her appetites and she no longer felt hungry.

At five o'clock, Lola started getting ready to go home. Garth phoned for a taxi and then came and sat down next to her. "Lola, I love you. I'll always love you. There'll never be anything in my life more important than loving you. I feel as though I was born to be with you."

The next day, Lola told Rodney that she was moving out with the children. All he said was "Have you slept with him?"

"No," she lied.

Garth, with his dark hair and large, heavy-lidded eyes, looked Jewish. Lola hoped that the Benskys would see this as progress.

You Will Be Going Back To Your Roots

Garth's new trousers had three pleats on either side of the zip. Until now he had worn skin-tight, peg-legged Levis. Lola looked at Garth. She found the loose space between his legs alluring. She started to think about what lay behind those parallel pleats.

Not since Lola was seventeen had she felt lustful just looking at a man's crotch.

Out of bed, Lola rarely felt sexually aroused. She had enough trouble feeling that way in bed. Where were the children? Could they hear? Was she ovulating? Should she use Ultrasure With Spermicidal Creme or Nuda Natural Feeling condoms? What was the time? Did she have to get up early in the morning? These were the questions that occupied Lola when sex seemed imminent.

A distant memory flickered in Lola's head. She quickly tried to calculate how old she would have been in the 1950s, when all men wore pleats in their pants. She had been just young enough still to sit on her father's lap and crush him with hugs when he came home from work.

Lola had always adored her father. She still did. She couldn't resist his generosity and his sense of humour. She loved the way that he turned beetroot red and cried when he laughed. If he laughed at the dinner table, pieces of fish or chicken would fly from his mouth and land on the other side of the kitchen.

Lola's girlfriends also adored her father. "Mr Bensky, Mr Bensky, can you drive us to Luna Park?" they would beseech him. On Saturdays and Sundays Mr Bensky could be seen driving through the streets of Melbourne, his pink Pontiac Parisienne full of chattering, gum-chewing fourteen-year-olds.

If they passed Leo's Spaghetti Bar in Fitzroy Street, the girls knew that they could rely on Mr Bensky to shout them a round of chocolate gelatis.

Mr Bensky loved gelati. Before the war, in Lodz, Mr Bensky used to spend more money on ice-cream than most people earned in a week.

Mr Bensky came from one of the wealthiest Jewish families in Lodz. They owned apartment blocks and a timber yard. At sixteen, Mr Bensky was in charge of the timber yard. He doubled the turnover, fiddled the books and pocketed the profit. Nobody noticed.

Even as a schoolboy, Mr Bensky never used public transport. He went everywhere by droshky. He single-handedly supported two droshkies and their drivers. At eighteen he bought himself a dark red Skoda sports car.

Mr Bensky met Mrs Bensky when she was the very quiet, studious, extraordinarily beautiful Renia Kindler.

Mr and Mrs Kindler lived in two small rooms with their seven children. Mrs Kindler paid the caretaker of their block a couple of zlotys extra a week to keep one of the external toilets solely for the use of the Kindler family.

Renia's ambition was to study medicine. She was not easily deterred from her studies.

Mr Bensky wooed this slim-hipped, serious sixteen-year-old fervently. He bought her an eighteen-carat solid gold Rolex watch. He bought her French perfumes and Swiss chocolates. He bought her peaches and strawberries, and the first pineapple that she had ever seen.

Just as Renia was preparing to leave for the University of Vienna, Germany invaded Poland. All the Jews living in Lodz were ordered to move to a slum area of the city, where they were completely cut off from the rest of the world.

Mr and Mrs Kindler urged Renia to marry Mr Bensky. They thought that she would be better off with his family.

In their haste and confusion, the Benskys had only been able to pack a few valuables. At the end of that first year in the ghetto, they were as poor and as hungry as everyone else. They had sold their last diamond, a blue-white, 2.4-carat stone in a heavy eighteen-carat gold setting, for a sack of potato peels.

Potato peels were a luxury in the ghetto. You had to have good connections in the public kitchens to buy this delicacy. You also had to know whether the kitchens used knives to peel their potatoes. Peels from the kitchens that used potato peelers were mostly just films of dirt.

Lola hated hearing about the potato peels. It seemed too pathetic. Worse than the stories about children dying in the streets and relatives killing each other for a piece of bread and trainload after trainload of people being shipped out of the ghetto never to be heard of again.

When Lola was twelve, she had boiled herself a pot of potato peels. She had often wondered what they tasted like. She was halfway through her first mouthful when Mrs Bensky came home unexpectedly. Mrs Bensky, who had never laid a hand on either of her daughters, took the bowl of potato peels. Then, screaming and crying, she shook Lola by the hair until Lola fainted.

The thought of her father's penis made Lola feel nauseous. If she thought about her father in sexual terms, she would have to think about him fucking her mother. She tried to blink that thought out of her head.

At seventeen, Lola was having furtive sex regularly, if erratically, with her first serious boyfriend. One evening, with her puce-faced boyfriend hovering above her, Lola was suddenly seized with the thought that maybe her parents were doing the same thing in their bedroom across the hallway. Her stomach heaved, and she vomited and vomited.

Fortunately, Lola's boyfriend considered himself an existential eccentric. He felt that this messy, smelly, potentially humiliating episode merely added to the interesting experiences of his life.

Melbourne is a small city. Years later, people still asked Lola if it was true that she had chucked all over Johnny Rosenberg while he was fucking her.

Mrs Bensky rarely touched Lola or her sister. When she kissed them hello and goodbye, she planted the peck firmly in mid-air.

Every evening when Mr Bensky came home from work, he would grab Mrs Bensky by the bum, and kiss her loudly. Mrs Bensky would try to shrug him off. "Look at your beautiful mummy," he would say to the girls. "My little Renia. What a beauty!" By this time, Mrs Bensky would have wriggled out of his grip and busied herself serving dinner.

"You'll be going back to your roots if you marry me" was one of the lines that Garth used to persuade Lola to leave her husband. He pursued her relentlessly. He phoned her several times a day, wrote poems for her, painted her portrait, bought her an eighteen-carat gold Parker pen and a leather-bound notebook. Then came the jewellery. Lola loved rings. Garth bought her garnet rings, emerald rings, ruby rings, sapphire rings and a magnificent art-deco diamond ring.

In the end, Lola couldn't resist the adoration. Even before her analysis, Lola knew that she loved being adored. And Garth adored her. He was always looking at her. In seven years he had painted over five hundred portraits of her. Last year he had had an exhibition of his paintings in Sydney. The exhibition was called *Pictures of Lola.* One hundred and eight portraits of Lola hung from the walls of the Creighton Galleries.

Lola got up from the breakfast table. "I think I'll have a shower," she said to Garth.

Lola found it difficult to wash. She found it an ordeal. Lola only showered when she had to wash her hair.

Mrs Bensky showered every morning and every evening. And at night, if Mr and Mrs Bensky had made love, Lola used to hear the bathroom taps gushing at full throttle while Mrs Bensky furiously washed herself out.

Mrs Bensky kept her house as clean as she kept her body. She washed the floors every day. Twice a week she stripped the stove and the fridge. Once a week, balancing a large bucket of water on top of a ladder, she cleaned the windows. Mrs Bensky vacuumed the carpet when Mr Bensky and the girls left in the mornings, and again after dinner.

Sometimes Lola didn't change her pantihose for a fortnight. The feet would become rigid. Lola wondered if the dirt held the pantihose together and made them last longer.

Mr and Mrs Bensky visited Lola every Tuesday and Friday night. They usually stayed for about three-quarters of an hour.

For years Lola felt that they only came to see the children. They were besotted by their grandchildren. Mr Bensky would look at Lola's son, Julian, who at sixteen was already six feet tall, and say "Whoever would have thought I would live to have grandchildren?"

Mrs Bensky would go straight to Lola's kitchen sink, in her Yves St Laurent silk blouse, her Kenzo trousers and her Maud Frizon shoes, and wash and scour and dry until everything gleamed.

Even at home, Mrs Bensky never wore an apron or work clothes. She cleaned in her ordinary clothes, although Mrs Bensky's clothes could hardly be described as ordinary. She had satin dresses beaded with pearls, taffeta coats dripping diamantés, lamé and lurex cocktail dresses, linen and leather trousers, all from the best fashion houses in Europe.

Margaret-Anne and Ivana, Lola's best friends, kept spotless houses. Ivana felt compelled to clean up whenever she visited Lola. Margaret-Anne said that she found Lola's mess relaxing.

Margaret-Anne and Ivana were both tall and thin. Mrs Bensky was very slim too. Lola wondered whether ectomorphs had a mania for cleanliness.

Lola never used to wash the dishes. She owned enough crockery to keep going between the cleaning woman's twice-weekly visits. After her first year in analysis, Lola began to wash her own dishes. Late in life, Lola discovered the joy of well-scrubbed saucepans and shiny surfaces.

Lola had always had trouble with the concept of moderation. For a while she became a bit obsessive. She washed every teaspoon or fork or coffee mug as soon as it was used. She cleaned out the pantry and bathroom cupboards and put everything in labelled jars. She rearranged the cutlery drawers and the crockery cabinets. She vacuumed the front veranda and polished the letterbox. She drove everyone crazy, and the kids begged her to go back to being a slob.

Garth stood next to Lola. He wound his leg around her leg and stroked her face. The children were at school. They lay down and had a noisy fuck.

After she came, Lola wept and wept. She often cried after a strong orgasm. She knew that it usually meant that she had been shutting herself off from any intense emotions, been out of touch with her sadness.

Lola used to say that she felt that she was born with a backlog of sadness. She didn't really know what she meant. Was it all those dead relatives — uncles, aunts, cousins, grandmothers and grandfathers — all fed to the sky? The ashes of the victims of Auschwitz almost choked the Vistula river.

Mr and Mrs Bensky shared a past that Lola could never belong to. Lola longed to drive a wedge into their togetherness. She had one such moment of triumph when she was ten. She had been begging and pleading to have her ears pierced. Mrs Bensky said that ear-piercing was a barbaric custom and they were a civilised family. Not while Lola lived in her house could she have pierced ears.

Lola stopped practising the piano. She no longer took the dog for a walk. She sat in her room for hours looking miserable. Mr Bensky relented. Behind Mrs Bensky's back, he took Lola into the city and held her hand while a nursing sister pierced Lola's ears.

For the next week, Mrs Bensky made twice as much noise as she washed up while the rest of the family ate their dinner.

Lola still wore the gold sleeper earrings that Mr Bensky had bought. Now a gold, heart-shaped Victorian locket carrying a lock of Garth's hair hung from the sleeper in Lola's right ear.

"Lola, my love, my beautiful wife, my delicious chicken, shall we go out for coffee?" Garth called from the bedroom.

"OK, I'll be out of the shower in a second," she answered.

Lola loved going out for coffee. Going out for a coffee meant going out for a walk, going out for a cake, going out for a talk. She had seen some new earrings up the street. They were small ruby studs. Maybe she would have another look at them.

Chopin's Piano

Lola Bensky was about to arrive in Warsaw. She tried to decide whether she was nervous or anxious. Nervous was all right. Being anxious made her dizzy. She wondered if she should take a Valium. She didn't want to take a Valium if what she was feeling was a normal kind of tension. If it was anxiety, she needed the Valium.

The plane landed. An indecipherable blast of blurred Polish came from the loudspeaker system. Lola began to feel breathless. She hated not being able to understand or to make herself understood. In the bleak immigration and customs hall, long queues of people stood waiting. Lola was dismayed. She always tried to avoid standing in queues. It was one of the things that made her very anxious. Her analyst had explained to her that she felt this anxiety because she could not bear to have to wait for the breast. That she was angry about the fact that she was dependent on her mother. That she was outraged that her mother had something that she didn't. That she was jealous and envious of her mother, but couldn't face the pain of these bad feelings, and so denied her need for her mother. This insight hadn't helped Lola with her queue problem.

The yellow-haired, sallow-faced young man behind the immigration desk tapped his blue biro violently as he asked Lola questions.

"Your nationality?" he snapped.

Lola tried not to panic. He was holding her passport. Why would he ask her her nationality?

"Australian," she said meekly.

"Purpose of visit?" he barked.

"To see Poland," Lola whispered. She could see that he thought that this was a reasonable answer. With a brusque gesture, he motioned her to move on.

Outside it was dark and bitterly cold. Lola was flushed and hot. She could feel drops of sweat trickling down between her breasts. She was wearing a woollen spencer and long woollen underpants, a three-piece woollen suit, angora socks, boots, an astrakhan hat, elbow-length gloves and a voluminous, thick coat. A cashmere scarf was wound around her neck. She caught a taxi to the Victoria Hotel. Driving in, she was astonished to see that Warsaw looked like an ordinary city. The streets were lined with graceful neoclassical four and five-storey apartment buildings. A soft, yellow light that suggested happy family life seeped out from the sides of the curtained windows. There was no sign of menace in the air.

The Victoria Hotel was a 1960s late-modern building. Lola recognised the style. Caulfield was full of fine examples of this sort of building.

Lola was unnerved when she walked inside the hotel. The interior was a large replica of the loungerooms of Caulfield and Bellevue Hill. The same granite and marble surfaces, the same rich, rounded woodwork, the same heavy raw silk drapes, the same large leather lounge suites, and the same 1950s expressionist ashtrays and vases. Chandeliers hung from the ceiling.

The short, stocky woman who was to be her guide was waiting in the foyer. Lola explained to Mrs Potoki-Okolska that she had come to Poland to see her parents' past, the small piece of their past that was left.

She wanted to go to Lodz, she told Mrs Potoki-Okolska, to see where her parents had lived before the war. Where they had studied, where they had played, where they had walked. She would also like to see what was left of the Lodz ghetto. She explained that her parents had spent four and a half years in the Lodz ghetto before they were shipped to Auschwitz.

"My mother was the sole survivor of her family. Her brothers

Shimek, Abramek, Jacob and Felek, and her sisters Fela, Bluma and Marilla, and her mother and father were gassed and then burnt. My father lost his parents, three brothers and a sister."

"It was a terrible, terrible tragedy, yes," said Mrs Potoki-Okolska. "But Polish people lost people too. It was not just the Jews who were killed by the Nazis. We suffered. Oh, how we suffered! My mother's cousin lost her mother, an innocent woman who never hurt anybody." Here, Mrs Potoki-Okolska had to pause. Tears were streaming down her face.

Mrs Potoki-Okolska showed Lola to her hotel room. A sign on the back of the door asked that no guests remain in the room after 10 p.m. Lola assumed that that meant guests other than those who were paying.

The fridge in the room was full of bottles of blackcurrant juice, blackcurrant juice with vodka, and Coca-Cola. Mrs Potoki-Okolska drank four bottles of Coca-Cola. She thanked Lola profusely for the Coca-Cola, said goodnight and left.

Lola looked out of the window. Warsaw was asleep. The city was covered in a fine layer of snow. Everything looked peaceful.

"It will be the end of you. They will put you in jail," Mrs Bensky had warned Lola. "They won't let you leave Poland. The Poles were worse than the Germans. They used to laugh at us in our concentration-camp rags. Small children would kick us when we were walking to work in the towns near the camp. Oh, those nice Poles, those good people, they couldn't wait to point Jews out to the Germans. They couldn't wait to take over our apartments when we had to move to the ghetto. They took our clothes, our china, our furniture. They took over the Jewish businesses. They just helped themselves. The caretaker of my parents' building, who my mother had looked after like she was one of the family, went running to the Gestapo to report on us.

"And after the war, there was a miracle. Not one single Polish person did know anything about what happened to us. You could smell the flesh burning for kilometres from Auschwitz. Those chimneys were blowing smoke twenty-four hours a day. The sky was red day and night, but the Poles didn't notice.

"And when my cousin Adek went back after the war, what did he see? He saw that they were surprised that he was still alive. Mrs Boleswaf, the caretaker, said to him: 'Oh, I thought all of you were dead.' Her son was wearing my father's suit, Adek said. My brother's grand piano was in the middle of their living room. And Mrs Boleswaf offered him a cup of tea from the beautiful white-and-silver china that was part of my mother's dowry. What do you want to go to Poland for? Something terrible will happen to you."

In the morning light, the city looked less vibrant. Lola was shocked at how depressed and oppressed the people looked. They walked with their heads down. Even the children were quiet and expressionless. Men and women wore grey clothes and grey faces. Their hair was lank and dull. No shampoo, Lola remembered.

Long queues of people waited outside the sparsely stocked shops. There was no movement in the queues. No-one spoke. Lola found this collective depression frightening. She had always thought of depression as an individual and isolating experience.

At the bus stop, people stood in silence. The bus arrived. The crowd clambered aboard, elbowing each other and Lola out of the way. Lola was left behind. From the bus, Mrs Potoki-Okolska screamed at Lola that she would get off at the next stop and walk back.

By midday Lola had seen the Radziwill palace, the Potoki palace, the Tyszkiewicz palace, the Uruski palace, the Czapski palace, the Staszic palace, a dozen churches and several cathedrals. Mrs Potoki-Okolska left money in each church, and wept as she dedicated the gift to her mother. In the Church of St Cross there was an urn that contained Chopin's heart. The Old Town Market Square, like most of the city of Warsaw, had been destroyed by the Nazis. Mrs Potoki-Okolska pointed to one quaint seventeenth-century building after another and announced:

"Built in 1953," or "Built in 1956," or "This building is still being finished."

Lola was exhausted. Her feet hurt. She was suffering from the anxiety that she experienced when she was ignored. Mrs Potoki-Okolska had refused to listen to her when she had expressed her lack of interest in churches, palaces or monuments to famous generals.

Lola had arranged to have lunch with Mr Konrad Serbin, the father of a friend of a friend. She felt that it could do her no harm to have a connection with Mr Serbin, who was one of Poland's leading barristers, and his wife, a highly acclaimed surgeon.

Lola wanted to buy some flowers for Mrs Serbin. Mrs Potoki-Okolska took Lola to a small, dimly lit, shabby shop. The back wall of the shop was lined with shelves. Each shelf held three vases, and each vase contained two flowers. A carnation and a freesia. A round, red-faced man was meticulously wrapping a pink carnation in a small square of butcher's paper.

Lola asked Mrs Potoki-Okolska to ask for a dozen carnations. Mrs Potoki-Okolska looked horrified.

"It is very rude to buy so many flowers," she said. "Your friend's father will think that you want to show him how much money you have. It is not good manners, no, not good manners."

Mrs Potoki-Okolska was very concerned with good manners. This morning at breakfast she had wrenched a toothpick from Lola's hands. "This is not good manners in Poland," she had shouted.

The carnations were thin and stringy. Lola thought that twelve of them would at least produce some volume.

"What to do? What to do? What to do?" sighed Mrs Potoki-Okolska.

Mrs Potoki-Okolska ordered a dozen carnations. A rumble of hostility went through the waiting queue. The florist glared at Lola and wrapped the carnations carelessly. Twelve carnations cost as much as most people earned in a week. Flower-growers were the new rich in Poland.

Mrs Potoki-Okolska was right. Mrs Serbin looked furious when Lola gave her the flowers.

Mr and Mrs Serbin were wealthy Poles. Their two-room apartment was filled with nineteenth-century romantic and historical paintings, oriental rugs, leather-bound books, silver and crystal.

The Serbins were very pleased with the parcel of pencils, biros, soaps, toothpaste, pantihose, silver foil and kitchen cloths that Lola had brought from their daughter. Mr Serbin's brother and sister-in-law joined them for lunch. Mrs Serbin served an entree of smoked trout with horseradish sauce. In the middle of a mouthful of trout, it occurred to Lola that all five Poles at the table were in their mid-sixties. The same age as Mr and Mrs Bensky. Where were they when the Jews were being rounded up for the ghetto? Where were they when the Warsaw ghetto was burning? Were they part of the heated, cheering crowd on the Aryan side? Were they watching Jews explode into the night?

Lola felt nauseous. She excused herself, and ran to the toilet. The toilet was in a tiny room, ten feet away from the dining table. The door wouldn't close properly. Lola tried to hold the door shut with her foot while she sat on the toilet. She felt bilious and giddy. Sweat ran down her face. She could hear every word of the lunch-table conversation. She coughed loudly to disguise her own violent eruptions. Half an hour later, she emerged. Mrs Potoki-Okolska rushed to greet her. "You look terrible. Was it your liver or your kidneys?" she asked.

Mrs Serbin brought in a large jar of Nescafé on an enormous Georgian silver platter. She put six spoonfuls of the coffee powder into each person's cup. Lola asked if she could have tea. The other guests drank their coffee with relish.

* *

The next morning Lola met Mrs Potoki-Okolska at the railway station at eight-thirty. At eleven o'clock there was an announcement that the nine o'clock train to Lodz had been cancelled. Mrs Potoki-Okolska rushed Lola to the taxi stand.

Lola looked at the miserable faces in the taxi queue. She felt buoyed by their hardship.

"You've got what you deserve," she whispered to the man standing on her left.

Lola sat in the back of the taxi. Mrs Potoki-Okolska sat in the front seat. She ordered the taxi driver to turn the heater on high, and settled down with a bag of boiled sweets.

Lola had packed her own provisions. She had packets of Life Savers, Minties and Steam Rollers. Steam Rollers, Lola felt, were particularly good for combating nausea.

After an hour in the car Lola felt sick. Her skin burned and itched. She unbuttoned her coat and jacket. Her chest was covered with angry red blotches. She thought that she was probably the only person in Poland suffering from a heat rash.

She opened the car window a little.

"What is that?" bellowed Mrs Potoki-Okolska. "Shut it, shut it, shut it. You will catch a disease of the lungs. It is very dangerous. Very, very dangerous." Lola closed the window.

They arrived at Zelazowa-Wola, Chopin's birthplace. Lola was glad to be able to get out of the car. An hour and a half later, Lola had seen Chopin's piano, Chopin's mother's piano, Chopin's bedroom, Chopin's mother's bedroom, Chopin's garden and Chopin's bathroom.

Lola thought that maybe she would never get to Lodz. She thought, once again, that maybe Lodz didn't exist. Maybe Mr and Mrs Bensky's past would always be inaccessible to her. Mrs Potoki-Okolska left Zelazowa-Wola reluctantly, humming *La Polonaise.*

They passed kilometre after kilometre of flat, snow-covered countryside. This soft, white stillness was punctuated occasionally by small forests of spindly, black fir trees.

They were now ten kilometres from Lodz. Lola was already weeping.

Friday Is A Good Day For Fish

Lola lay facing away from Garth. She was almost asleep. Garth had been rubbing her shoulders. He had patted her and rubbed her and stroked her. She felt suspended in a state of bliss.

Garth lowered his head and kissed her in a line across her back. He pressed himself against her. His rubbing became more intense. He was no longer soothing her into sleep. He was waking her.

Lola, at forty, could still sometimes feel nervous and shy about sex. She turned towards Garth. She buried her head in his chest. She loved his smell. They hadn't made love for over a week. She stroked him and smoothed him. She stroked his penis. She rocked it from side to side between her thumb and her forefinger. She felt good.

"My mother really loved the dress we bought her," she said. "I'm glad I didn't buy a book or that kettle. I felt so happy seeing my mother's pleasure."

Garth started laughing. "You're playing with me in the same absent-minded way you twist your hair. My dick is flying backwards and forwards and you're talking about your mother's birthday present."

Garth pulled her on top of him.

"Can we change positions before we come? Can you lie on top of me then?" she said.

He laughed. "Do you have to orchestrate everything? Do you have any more instructions?"

They made love. Lola gripped the sheet. She used it to lever herself. "It's OK," she said. "We don't have to change positions."

Lola had a long orgasm. She felt as though she'd been away. In another dimension. In another time. She fell asleep.

Lola was in Lodz. She was in the loungeroom of the apartment. Everything was exactly as her father had described it. The rounded couch and chairs, the white-tiled heater. All that was missing was the family. Her father's parents, his three brothers and sister.

They had known the end was coming. Jengelef Boleswaf, the family's Polish caretaker, who was eighty-three when Lola visited him in Poland, had told Lola this.

"Your grandfather came to me before he left for the ghetto. He said to me, 'I may not be here in a few years time, but my building will still be here in one hundred years,' " Jengelef had said.

Nobody had ever said "your grandfather" to Lola. Jengelef still lived on the ground floor of the apartments that Lola's grandfather had built. Jengelef lived in one small room. Everything in the room was spotless. A small table next to the window was covered with a starched white linen tablecloth. The corners of the tablecloth were embroidered with red roses. In the middle of the room was a plain brass bed.

Jengelef's wife was lying in the bed. She was dying. She was lying perfectly still. She seemed to be barely breathing. Her skin was pale and clear, and her hair was brushed and fluffed. She was wearing a white pin-tucked nightie. Jengelef's devotion to his wife had made Lola cry. But then, Lola had cried all the time that she was in Lodz.

When Lola had arrived in Lodz, she had gone straight to 23 Zakatna Street. The taxi driver had pulled up across the road from the apartments. From the car window she could see the first-floor balcony her father had told her about so many times. His father used to sit on the balcony and watch his children come home from school. Lola's father always made sure that he had his school cap on before he came into his father's line of vision.

Lola got out of the taxi and stood on the footpath. She was too frightened to cross the empty street. Her heart was pounding and she was trembling. She crossed the street. The main entrance of the building was open. Lola stepped inside.

She stood in the deserted hallway. Her chest tightened and her throat constricted. She found it hard to breathe. She stood in the deserted hallway. The air felt thick with people. She could feel their presence. She could hear their voices. The voices of people going about their daily business. Going to work, to school, to market. She could feel the movement. She could feel the life. She stood in the hallway and wept and wept.

Lola cried every time she went to the building. She went there every day. Often she stood in the hallway for hours. She would touch the tiled wall with her cheek. She would stroke the balustrade. She wanted to sink into the marble staircase. To mesh herself with the air. To be part of the past.

Jengelef had told the tenants in the building who Lola was. Some of them had looked at Lola as though she was a ghost. "I thought they had killed all the Jews from Lodz," Mr Krupnik from the second floor had said to Lola.

Lola was washing her hair when the phone rang. She had never been able to ignore a ringing telephone. She answered the phone. Shampoo dripped down her.

"It's me, Morris," said Lola's friend, Morris Lubofsky.

"Hi, Morris," said Lola. Morris sounded a bit flat.

"What's wrong?" she asked.

"I've just found out my brother is coming to Melbourne for two months," said Morris. "My folks are putting pressure on me to invite him to stay at my place. I'm not happy about having him back in the country, let alone in my house."

Morris and his brother Boris were twins. Fraternal, not identical twins. Boris, a banker, had lived in New York since he was twenty. Lola thought that Boris was OK. She couldn't see that Morris had all that much to complain about in Boris. He hardly saw him.

"Maybe you and Boris will patch things up this visit? We're a bit old to be quibbling with our siblings," said Lola. Quibbling with our siblings. Lola liked the sound of that line. Quibbling with our siblings. She repeated it to herself a few times while Morris complained about Boris.

Morris was calling from Sydney. He'd been there for a week. "Sydney's depressing me," he said. "Everybody looks slightly seedy. On the make. I must be getting old. And the drug scene here is depressing. Everyone's on cocaine or Ecstasy. Really, fifty per cent of my friends are on cocaine."

Lola thought that she and Morris were both getting old. This was the same Morris Lubofsky who used to slip her joints and speed and phials of LSD when they were twenty. These drugs, Morris used to tell her, would expand her mind and her horizons. Lola was having enough trouble with her mind at the time. Her grip on things already seemed marginal and skewwhiff, and Lola didn't want it tilted any further. The contortions that LSD produced were too chaotic for Lola. As a fellow seeker of purity, enlightenment and truth, Lola had been a great disappointment to Morris.

Lola had pulled on a dressing gown while Morris was talking. Her hair was still dripping. She felt uncomfortable. She felt fat this morning. She'd eaten too much poppy-seed cake last night. Lola allowed herself a slice of poppy-seed cake every Thursday. Last night's slice had been just short of half the cake.

"Yeah, fifty per cent of my friends have got a coke problem," said Morris.

"Fifty per cent of my friends have got a cake problem, Morris," said Lola. "I better go," she said. "I was in the shower when you rang and I've probably already caught pneumonia."

"See you in Melbourne next week," said Morris.

Lola hopped back into the shower. She rinsed out the shampoo, towel-dried and moussed her hair, and got dressed. She looked around. Her two desks were clear. Her poems were filed. Her pencils were sharpened. Everything was ready for her to begin work.

Lola looked at the poem that she was currently struggling with.

What was she trying to say? She was trying to say that she was getting better. That she was changing. That she could see that she could no longer occupy the role of the victim.

Spotting the fault had been her speciality. Lola always knew whose fault it was. It was always someone else's. She was also an expert on what was wrong. Lola could find the flaw in anything. You could tell Lola the most elevating news, and in less than ten seconds she could tell you what was worrying about it.

Just before lunchtime, Lola's mother rang. "Lola darling, Genia Pekelman is giving me a lift to the Georges sale. They have got a sale of all their imported underwear. Darling, would you like to come with us?" said Renia.

"I don't think so, Mum," said Lola. "I've got such a lot to do."

"They have got silk petticoats and beautiful strapless bras and backless bras and Swiss cotton underpants. Lola darling, they have got Lily of France bras," said Renia.

Renia always wore beautiful underwear. She had drawers and drawers of bras and girdles and suspender belts and petticoats.

For years, Lola had refused to wear any underwear. Then she went through a phase of wearing ragged and discoloured underwear. She would wear torn and stained underwear underneath beautifully beaded and embroidered dresses.

"We won't be long in the city, darling," said Renia. "Genia doesn't feel so good today, so we will just go straight in and straight home. I just want to buy some bras and Genia just wants to buy some underpants."

Lola was beginning to get a headache. She didn't want to go shopping for underpants with Genia Pekelman.

When Lola was thirteen, Genia Pekelman had told her a story that had horrified her. "When I was your age," Genia had said to Lola, "the Germans invaded Poland. I was walking down the street, and a whole car of German soldiers stopped me. They made me take off my underpants and clean the windscreen of their car with my underpants. All five of them stood outside the car while

I was cleaning. One of them kept lifting my skirt so everyone in the street could see."

"Mum, I really don't think I can come with you," said Lola. "Maybe you could buy me a white Lily of France bra in size 14C, and a black half-slip in a 16?"

"You don't need a 16," said Renia. "You've lost so much weight."

"Yes I do," said Lola. "My hips are enormous."

"No, you have lost enough weight. You don't need to lose any more. You look very nice. You shouldn't be too thin," said Renia.

Lola was still not used to this turn of events. After being harangued all her life to lose weight, she now had to worry about being too thin. Too thin. If only she was too thin. If she was too thin she could have some more poppy-seed cake.

"Lola darling, give Lina a ring," said Renia. "She is your sister. Sisters should be sisters. And after all, you are the older one." Lola wondered how old she would have to be before she was no longer considered the older one.

Last week Renia and Josl had had a large dinner party to celebrate their forty-seventh wedding anniversary. Everyone was eating and talking except for Lina. Lina was picking at a plate of lettuce and cucumber.

Lina asked Renia if there were any chicken bones.

"Yes, of course, darling," said Renia. She brought out a platter of chicken bones. Lina picked up a thigh bone and chewed it. Lola leaned across the table.

"If you're on a diet you shouldn't be chewing chicken bones," she said.

"Chicken bones can't have any calories," said Lina.

"Well, they do," said Lola. "The marrow is very fatty, and there's fat wedged in behind the gristle." Lina put the bone down and returned to her lettuce.

"Are chicken bones really calorific?" Garth asked later.

"I don't know," said Lola.

* *

"Oy, darling, I have to go," said Renia. "Genia and Izak are here to pick me up. Bye bye, darling."

So, Izak Pekelman was taking the women shopping. Jewish men were amazing, thought Lola. They did everything for their wives. They shopped, chauffeured, accompanied. Even on underwear excursions.

Lola liked Izak Pekelman. He always seemed to be in good spirits. Izak was respected and admired by all of his friends for his gardening skills. Not too many Jews were good in the garden. In his garden in Caulfield, Izak had almond trees, walnut trees, chestnut trees, apricot, pear, peach and plum trees, and orange, lemon and lime trees. Izak grew his own vegetables, too. He grew zucchinis, cauliflowers, cabbage, carrots, beans, peas, potatoes and spring onions.

When he was a child in Lowicz, Izak was in charge of the family's vegetable plot. He grew carrots, beetroots, onions, potatoes and radishes. Before and after school, every day, Izak had looked after his vegetables.

In the ghetto, where people were dying of starvation every day, Izak kept his mother and father alive with his vegetables. Izak grew onions and radishes and potatoes in an old pram. He had bought the pram from his cousin for a loaf of bread and his mother's wedding ring. Izak had kept the pram by his side all the time. He slept with the pram next to his mattress, and during the day, while he worked, he parked the pram outside the window where he sat sewing uniforms for the Germans.

"People did laugh at me," he had told Lola. "If there was some sunshine I would rush outside to move the pram. I had a chain to lock the wheels of the pram, and some wires over the vegetables so no-one could steal them quickly. One day I was at the pictures in Melbourne when a man came up to me and said: 'You are the boy who grew vegetables in that old pram. My mother used to say to me that you looked after those vegetables like they were the most precious children in the world.' To tell you the truth, Lola, I started to cry in the middle of the picture theatre when he was talking about my pram."

Izak Pekelman always wore sandals. Sandals and socks. He wore sandals and socks in summer and in winter. To the beach and to barmitzvahs. When he was poor he was laughed at, in his socks and sandals. Now that he was wealthy, business associates admired his eccentricity.

Izak couldn't wear shoes. His toes were twisted and bent. His toenails were black, layered and chalky. They sat, raised and rounded, on top of his toes.

Lola had once asked Izak Pekelman why he always wore sandals. "My feet don't look so nice," he had said.

"What's wrong with them?" Lola had asked. For a moment Izak had looked as though he wasn't going to answer Lola's question, and then he spoke.

"In the concentration camp, Sachsenhausen, where I was in," he said, "they had an area for testing shoes. One of the local manufacturers wanted to test their merchandise on a variety of surfaces. So they did some research, and they built tracks with nine different surfaces. Every day some of us prisoners had to put on new shoes and walk for about forty kilometres over tracks of different sorts of cement, cinders, broken stones, sand, gravel. To make life more interesting for themselves, the SS guards made us wear shoes that were one or two sizes too small, and we had to carry sacks filled with twenty kilos of sand. So you can see, Lola, that I am lucky that I have still got toes."

Lola couldn't speak. She felt terrible for asking Izak about his sandals. Izak didn't look upset. He looked calm.

"I always knew I was a lucky man," he said. "I was lucky even when I arrived in Sachsenhausen. When we got off the train there was a big crowd of people to greet us at the station. The spectacle of watching the prisoners arrive was an exciting pastime for the townspeople of Oranienburg. There were men and women and mothers with their children all watching us. When we got off the train they sang and shouted and screamed terrible things about the

Jews, and they threw stones at us, and pieces of wood, and dirt from the street. We had to walk two miles from the station to the concentration camp, and the SS guards kicked us and beat us all the way. If somebody fell, they shot him. We had a whole trail of dead and injured. A few patrol cars drove along the road behind us to pick up the victims. It didn't matter whether they were dead or alive, they were all picked up because the SS had to deliver the correct total number of prisoners that had been consigned to the camp. This was German efficiency.

"One of the first things I saw when I arrived in Sachsenhausen was a sign which said: 'There is a road to freedom. Its milestones are obedience, industry, honesty, order, cleanliness, sobriety, truthfulness, spirit of sacrifice and love for the Fatherland.'

"I was lucky to see this sign. My friend Felix had died in the train that brought us to Sachsenhausen, and my cousin Moishe was beaten when he got off the train, and was shot when he fell down."

At four o'clock, Lola decided to pack her work away for the day. The poem was working well, and she felt happy. She decided to prepare dinner early; she liked the feeling of being ahead of schedule. Maybe tonight she would make a nice potato and onion soup, and a light pasta.

Lola was chopping up her fourth large onion when the front door bell rang. It was Renia and Genia and Izak.

"Hello, hello, hello," they chorused. Genia and Renia looked flushed and elated. The shopping had obviously been a success.

Renia looked beautiful. Her skin was golden and smooth. She was wearing a double-breasted, black Chanel suit. She looked stunning. Renia had looked much happier lately, thought Lola. It had happened slowly, over the last few years. Her happiness suited her, thought Lola.

"It was a very good sale, darling," said Renia. "I bought you six Lily of France bras, and three petticoats. Genia bought herself the most beautiful Swiss cotton underpants with a matching camisole singlet, and I did buy myself Christian Dior silk stockings for a quarter of their normal price."

"We also went to Myers," said Renia. "I bought you a challah, some brisket and some gefilte fish. Everything from Myers. You can buy a very good challah in Myers. The fish is very good too. Friday is a very good day for fish. It is always fresh on Friday."

Izak took Lola aside. He had a new joke. He knew Renia didn't approve of his jokes.

"Did you hear about Mrs Rosenberg?" Izak asked Lola. "The phone rang in Mrs Rosenberg's flat. She answered the phone. 'Hello,' she said. It was a man on the phone. 'I know what you want,' he says. 'You want me to come over and tear your clothes off. You want me to shtoop you stupid. You want me to tie you to the bed and shtoop you silly,' he says. 'From one hello you can tell all this?' said Mrs Rosenberg."

Lola laughed.

"We should leave now, otherwise we will catch all the traffic," said Renia. "Goodbye, darling, enjoy the fish."

Lola kissed Renia, Genia and Izak goodbye. "Goodbye, goodbye, goodbye," they called.

Five minutes later the trio were back.

"I forgot to give you the horseradish to eat with the fish. Garth loves this horseradish," said Renia.

"Thanks, Mum. Goodbye," said Lola.

"Goodbye, goodbye," called Genia and Izak. Lola didn't know whether to laugh or cry. She could see the goodness, the kindness and the love in this frenzy, this intensity. So why did it still give her a headache? Maybe after another couple of years of analysis she would know the answer.

Lola and Garth ate alone that night. The children were in Sydney visiting Garth's parents.

"This is fabulous gefilte fish," said Garth.

"It's from Myers," said Lola. "My mother has always said that

the gefilte fish in Myers is very good. She's said so many things that I haven't listened to. I wonder what else I've missed out on."

After dinner, Lola and Garth went to the opening of Stephen Newsome's exhibition of paintings at the Smithson Galleries. Newsome was an old friend of Garth's.

Lola disliked openings. The harsh lighting in galleries often heightened her anxiety. Standing up and talking to people also made her anxious. Tonight she would made an effort not to focus on herself. She wouldn't examine herself minutely for symptoms of anxiety. She wouldn't concentrate all her energy on the question of whether she was feeling anxious. She wondered if other people had to make such a conscious effort not to think about themselves all the time.

Lola and Garth told Stephen Newsome how much they liked his paintings, but Newsome was so drunk he could hardly recognise them. He was so drunk he could hardly stand.

"Newsome and I have both, over the years, had a lot of trouble standing up," Lola said to Garth. "He's been pissed, and I've been dizzy." Lola and Garth said hello and goodbye to half a dozen people, and left the gallery.

At home, Lola prepared herself for bed. She cleansed and scrubbed and creamed her face. She looked at herself in the mirror. She looked so Jewish. Jewish eyes, Jewish curls, Jewish expression. She had a Jewish face. A face that looked semi-anxious when she was happy, and distressed when she was sad.

Lola turned her face away from the mirror. If she was going to work at making this analysis successful she would have to place less emphasis on what she looked like. She used to think that if her curls were at the right angle, everything else would be all right.

Lola walked out of the bathroom, through the loungeroom and into Garth's studio. Garth was painting. Luciano Pavarotti was singing "Nessun dorma". Garth's hips and legs moved in time to the music. He was immersed in his canvas, and didn't hear her come in.

She stood and watched him. She thought about how lucky she

was. She was lucky to have Garth. Lucky to have the children. She was lucky. The thought took her by surprise. She felt temporarily disconcerted. It wasn't an aberrant thought, just a new one.

She kissed Garth goodnight. Still feeling lucky, Lola walked back to the bedroom. She knew that Garth was going to paint until late, so she had made herself a hot-water bottle. She got into bed. The new sheets she had bought felt nice. She hugged the hot-water bottle. Still feeling lucky, she fell asleep.

I Heard You Got Another Husband

For ten years Lola had not been able to mix with Jews. For ten years, even to walk along Acland Street, past the Scheherezade Restaurant, past the Benedykt Brothers Delicatessen, caused Lola anxiety.

She knew most of the people who stood in small clusters on the footpath, talking. "Lolala, hello, what's happened to you? Last time I saw you, you were thin, now look." Lola didn't have to say much in these encounters. "Good morning, Lola, I heard you got divorced and now I heard you got another husband."

Garth loved Acland Street. He always greeted Tivele, who had Parkinson's disease and shook dangerously as he drank his lemon tea, with a pat on the back and a handshake. He asked Abe how the hosiery business was going. He smiled like a benign parent while Adek, Edek and Isaac talked. They talked and talked. Over the top of each other. At the same time. What energy they had, this gang of elderly men! thought Lola. Everything mattered. Everything was important.

Lola went into the Scheherezade. She sat at a table near the counter. She ordered a glass of borscht and a plate of boiled potatoes. She watched Mr Krongold, who was at the back of the restaurant, eating his latkes in his parka and his peaked cap. He had already had schnitzel and boiled potatoes. Mr Krongold was a slightly built, fine-boned man. He ate vigorously.

Lola often ate bent over the rubbish bin. She tore clumps of bread from a loaf. One piece of bread into her mouth, one piece into the bin, some more for her, and a few crusty pieces for the rubbish bin. Lola had to finish the loaf. It would have been damaging evidence. Another couple of bites, and the last piece could go into the bin.

Lola could evacuate any thoughts that disturbed her. She blinked them out of her head. Three blinks and all bothering thoughts vanished. The only problem was that most of anything else that was in Lola's head was also blinked out.

Lola had difficulty feeling the life in her. She often breathed herself dead. Her breathing would become slow and shallow. She could sit in one spot for hours. She could be with her children, she could be in the middle of a group of people and appear enchanted by the conversation, but she was somewhere else, and she was dead. If she was not as dead as all the dead, then she was almost as dead.

Mr Lipnowski, who often ate at the Scheherezade, came up to Lola. "I did see the wonderful drawing Garth did do in the newspaper. Such a beautiful drawing. You can see the suffering of the whole world in the eyes. The way he drawed those eyes. Beautiful."

"What about my article?" said Lola.

"Too short," said Mr Lipnowski. "Too short, and I didn't learn anything from it."

Lola was in a good mood. Her analyst had told her that unless she worked at this analysis she would have to leave. The news had shocked her. She felt more alive than she had for weeks. She smiled at Mr Lipnowski.

She remembered a conversation she had had with Mr Lipnowski last summer. Her book of poetry about life in a concentration camp had just come out. Mrs Frydman from the bookshop around the corner didn't want to order any copies until she saw whether there was a demand for the book.

"I was in Auschwitz," she said, "so, do I write poems?"

Mr Lipnowski had said to Lola, "I told Mrs Frydman she should be selling gutkes, not books."

Gutkes, Lola had explained to Garth, were underpants.

* *

Halfway through her analysis, Lola saw that this apparent harshness, this callousness, this bluntness, was an endearing directness, a brisk and efficient communication. They all spoke like that. Mr Lipnowski, Mrs Frydman, Mr and Mrs Bensky. "This is right. This is wrong. This is bad. This is terrible. This is no good. This is how I see things. This is this." They all knew.

Their children had trouble knowing whether this was this, or this was not this. Lola's friend Ben, whose father had fought with the partisans in Poland and now owned Sunsoaked Swimwear Industries, belonged to the Shiva Yoga Centre. Every morning, between 5 and 6, Ben danced to Indian chants. From 6 to 7 he meditated. For the rest of the day he worked on his idea for a contemporary theatre production of the Ramayana Ballet.

Ben smiled at everything. In recent years, as he had climbed the executive rungs of the ashram, he had become more interested in his Jewishness. He now interspersed his "oms" with "oys".

And then there was Morris Lubofsky. Lola found it hard to believe that Morris was the offspring of Rivka Lubofsky. Orphaned at thirteen by the Nazis, Rivka had spent the war hiding in the forests of Poland. Lola was mesmerised by Rivka's beauty. Rivka had fiery, dark-red hair and enormous, seductive and inviting eyes. She spoke six languages. And she laughed. She laughed with her whole body.

Rivka completed her Master of Laws degree in the same year that Morris dropped out of dentistry to edit the *Teenybopper.*

One hour after he had arrived at his parents' place, and twenty minutes after he had finished his regular Sunday lunch with them, Morris Lubofsky, forty years old and thrice divorced, lay on the couch in his parents' loungeroom. His stomach heaved gently and he slept.

Last Sunday at lunch Mr Lubofsky had given Morris the brochure for a new Jaguar Sovereign.

"Delivery will be in December. Happy Birthday."

"Oh. Great. Thank you," said Morris, and he went to the couch and slept.

Lola had observed this impossible-to-stay-awake-in-front-of-your-parents disease. She had discussed it with Morris's Catholic first wife, who was infuriated and bewildered by it. Lola had seen it in herself.

Lola never looked excited or enthusiastic in front of Mr or Mrs Bensky. She rarely expressed surprise, and never showed any joy, light-heartedness or happiness in their presence. She appeared to have no sense of humour. She never laughed when she was with them.

Occasionally they had caught her laughing with a friend. Lola once saw Mr Bensky look at her with great surprise when she exploded with laughter while telling her friend Margaret-Anne the story of how she had met Dean Robertson, who was a top political journalist and a former colleague of Lola's. Lola's son was five at the time, and going through a stage of adding "l" to every word. He said bookl, smokel, dogl, catl. Dean Robertson had asked Lola what she was doing now. "I'm just a housewifel," she had answered. Dean Robertson had fled with a nauseous grimace of farewell.

Lola looked at a photograph of Garth that she carried around in her wallet. He didn't look Jewish. He looked too happy.

Even the language tapes that Lola and Garth were learning Yiddish from were not too cheerful. Each phrase was stated slowly and then repeated. The conversation on the subject of "How Are You?" went like this:

How are you?
Fine, thank you.
Not bad.
So so.
I don't feel well.
What's wrong with him?
He has a headache.
She doesn't feel well.
What's the matter with her?
She has a toothache.
We are ill.
What's wrong with you?
We have stomach aches.
I don't feel well.
What's wrong with you?
My feet hurt.
My parents aren't well.
What's wrong with them?
They have heartaches from their children.
My head hurts.
Her back hurts.
His hands hurt.
Your bones hurt.
Our feet hurt.
Their feet hurt.

* *

By the time she was twenty, Lola knew no Jews. She worked as a rock journalist. Her three close girlfriends were pale, tall and angular, and, she realised on reflection, all prone to constipation.

She fell in love with blond, blue-eyed men whose fathers were president of the golf club and whose mothers had been the school hockey captain. Jewish boys looked awful to Lola. They looked spoilt and soft and unmanly. They looked frightened of their mothers, frightened of their fathers. "Jewish boys have still got their mother's breastmilk on their faces," said Margaret-Anne.

When Lola and Johnny Rosenberg were eighteen, he had driven his father's Vauxhall into the back of another car. Lola had had several stitches in her knees and Johnny Rosenberg had broken his nose. He sat in the Royal Melbourne Hospital and wept. "How can I ring up my parents? The shock will kill them."

Killing their parents was something that most Jewish children felt they had the power to do. Common fragments of conversation among the children were: "This is going to kill my mother." "I can't tell my mother, it would kill her." "I couldn't do that, my father might die." "I can't leave my wife, it would kill my parents."

Lola was no exception. Rather than kill her parents, Lola lied about everything. She lied about her non-Jewish boyfriend. The Benskys were perfectly happy to see Lola going steady with Angus Nankin, a "Scottish Jew". Mr and Mrs Nankin played along. Mr Nankin wore a yarmulka at dinner, and on Yom Kippur they all went to synagogue together. Mrs Bensky explained to her friends that these Anglo-Jews could never speak Yiddish. The Benskys thought it was a shame when Lola and Angus broke up.

Lola lied about being a virgin, she lied about what she ate, she lied about studying at the Sorbonne. After she finished high school, Lola had begged the Benskys to send her to Paris to do a Diploma of Languages at the Sorbonne. Lola spent two days at the Sorbonne. She felt lonely, lost, and unable to be understood. She flew to London, bought an old London taxi cab and drove around Europe for six months. She drove through Italy, Spain, France,

Germany, Austria, Switzerland. She put the car on a ferry in Naples and went to Israel, where she visited her cousin on a kibbutz in the Negev. A Parisian student rerouted Lola's mail, and everybody was happy. Mr and Mrs Bensky still boasted about Lola's gift for languages, and how she topped her class at the Sorbonne. Lola knew that people didn't die of lies.

She did fear her parents' deaths though, and did feel that whenever and however they died, it would be her fault.

She sympathised with Morris Lubofsky. When people talked about what a rich man he would be one day, Morris always said "I hope I die before my parents." Lola knew exactly what he meant.

"You will cry on my grave but it will be too late," Mrs Bensky said to Lola over and over again. What if she didn't even cry then? Lola used to wonder.

Now she wondered how she could have been so cruel. So indifferent. How could she have been so unsympathetic, so uninterested in what Mrs Bensky had been through?

When Lola began to think about Mrs Bensky's life, she couldn't understand why, after the war, Mrs Bensky had still wanted to live, or why she had wanted to have children. Lola felt that she herself would have given up. She had given up many times. She had felt that nothing was worthwhile. This feeling, Lola now recognised, was a sad luxury. That nothing-really-interests-me, everything-is-so-tedious syndrome. It was usually accompanied by the my-parents-have-ruined-my-life philosophy, and had as a postscript, and-they-can-pay-for-it.

Lola folded her copy of the *Jewish News.* She had had a slice of apple cake, even though this was the first day of her new diet. She paid for her coffee and cake. She waved goodbye to Tivele. She smiled at Mr Rosenberg and Mr Schwarz, who were sitting at the front table, and she went home.

If You Live Long Enough

"Mmm, Elizabeth is so beautiful." Morris Lubofsky was talking about his twenty-five-year-old girlfriend. "She's got such strong limbs. You should see her close up. I mean really close up. People look very different really close up."

Lola Bensky and Morris Lubofsky were walking along Lygon Street. Morris continued his conversation enthusiastically. "You know, she's a really fabulous singer. There's no-one in the country who can sing like her." Lola said nothing.

Sometimes Lola had to remind herself that she was very fond of Morris. She liked his sense of humour, and his dogged loyalty. When Morris held these conversations about his girlfriend, Lola didn't have to look interested. Morris was entertaining himself. He didn't notice Lola's lack of response.

Morris usually rang Lola several times a week. He rang to say how beautiful Elizabeth was, or how brilliantly her photography was progressing. Sometimes he wanted to relate what he had bought for his house, or what he intended to buy. Morris lived in a 20,000-square-foot converted dairy in Williamstown.

"She says I'm a fabulous lover," Morris said. Lola didn't know what to say. They went on walking. "We spent all yesterday in bed, and I'm meeting her for a production conference at home this afternoon."

Morris was emerging. He was re-entering the world. He had been a dilettante. An editor of unsaleable newspapers. Morris had founded the *Teenybopper* and the underground 1970s weekly *The Joint.* His last venture had been the *Vegetarian Monthly.*

Now, with an initial capital investment of $500,000 provided by his father, Morris had formed an advertising agency. He specialised in television jingles.

Even when he had worked on the *Teenybopper,* whose circulation had peaked at five hundred a week, Morris was always on the phone. Now that he was in advertising, he had installed a telephone with eight lines, a fax machine and four computers. Whenever you rang Morris Lubofsky, whether it was 6 a.m. or 11 p.m., he was always on another call. "Hello, hold on, I'm on another line," he would say.

When Lola rang him up, she made sure that she had a book to read or some work to do while she waited for Morris to finish his other calls.

Now, listening to Morris, Lola realised what it was that she couldn't bear about him. He was always absorbed in himself. This was too close to what Lola was fighting in herself. It was that self-centred part of her that she knew she had to get rid of.

Why was it, Lola wondered, that a generation of robust, earthy, vigorous parents had produced cool cats like Morris, or comatose hypochondriacs like Fay Farber or Susan Wiener, or repressed depressives like Ben Hertz, who meditated and ommed all day?

Their parents had been in concentration camps, labour camps, ghettos. They'd survived for years during the war in bunkers, in forests and in haystacks.

They came to Australia damaged and penniless. But they were also resilient. They came here with gratitude, and spirit, and optimism, and a readiness to begin again. They built new lives. And they had children.

They wanted only the best for their children, and they gave them everything. "I am doing everything for the children. I want nothing for myself," Renia Bensky used to say to Lola from the time Lola was a small child.

Lola never believed her. Renia would come home from the city with a new cocktail dress. "Look, Lola, Mr Gross did give me this dress for almost nothing. It was a sample, and I am lucky that I am, of course, a perfect SSW, and it fitted me perfectly."

There was always something for Lola in this shopping. "Lola darling," Mrs Bensky would say, "I did buy you some new singlets. Pure cotton. Imported from England. They were so expensive. It is something shocking how much they cost." Lola added them to her pile of pure cotton singlets and underpants.

Morris was still talking. They had walked to the Café Roma, where they were to meet Garth for lunch. Garth was late. After half an hour, Morris and Lola began lunch without him.

"My mother's chosen this fabulous lounge suite for me," said Morris. "It's grey leather, art deco. It's got three couches and two armchairs," he said. He took another mouthful of spinach lasagne and continued talking. "This new diet I'm on is really good. I went off it last week and gained half a stone, but as I'd lost one and a half stone, that's still a net loss of one stone. It's just a matter of what foods you eat with what. Like, you never mix carbohydrate and protein."

Lola yawned. Morris Lubofsky was the centre of his world. And his world was the best world. His chiropractor was the best chiropractor. The coffee at Café Nero, next to his house, was better than the coffee at the café next to your house. In fact, according to Morris Lubofsky, the coffee at Café Nero was the best coffee in Melbourne. His barrister was the best barrister in Australia, and his proctologist was the best proctologist in the world. When Morris Lubofsky was a vegetarian, meat was poison. Now that he was a carnivore, raw eye fillets of beef minced with seaweed and soy sauce could save your life.

Morris Lubofsky was now talking about his haemorrhoids. "You know," he said, "haemorrhoids are often a sign of bowel cancer. I'm getting rid of mine. Nowadays they can just tie an elastic band around them, and snap them off. Like crutching sheep." Lola felt worn out. Not talking about herself had exhausted her.

Garth finally arrived. Lola was overjoyed to see him. They had been married for ten years now, and Lola still felt a soaring happiness when she saw him. Garth kissed Lola for just a moment too long for Morris. Morris coughed uncomfortably. "OK, break it up, boys," he said.

Garth was luminous, Lola thought. His smile lifted him out of the ranks of mortal men. She was besotted by him. And he was devoted to her. He quietened her fears and her nervousnesses. He never panicked. He relished the present, and looked forward to the future.

Lola was mesmerised by people who made long-term plans. How could anybody be certain of what could happen in the future?

Often, in the morning, Lola woke before Garth. She would lie in bed and look at him. He always looked as peaceful as a baby. As contented as a cat. Comfortable with himself. This morning, he had had one leg stretched out on top of the doona, and half a buttock exposed.

Lola slept with the doona wound around her. She slept curled in a ball. She hugged herself in her sleep.

"Freedom was never something you allowed yourself," her first analyst had written, in a letter he had sent her years after she had left him. Lola didn't quite understand what he meant, but she had been pleased with the sympathetic tone.

Renia and Josl Bensky had been appalled when Lola left Rodney for Garth. Now, things were different. Josl proudly told anyone who would listen that he "wouldn't exchange Garth for twenty Jews". Garth could always gauge his rating with Josl. On a really good day, Josl wouldn't swap him for fifty Jews.

Garth had a good sense of humour. He made even Renia laugh. He introduced a levity to the meals that they shared together. Garth loved Renia and Josl Bensky. He wasn't in awe of them or afraid of them. He wasn't shackled by the notion that anything he said could kill them. He teased them. He confided in them. He was generous to them. The relationship between the Benskys and Lola

began to have a fluidity and a freedom and ease that they had not experienced before.

Morris, Lola and Garth shared a Zuppa Inglese and a crème caramel. Morris had said that he wouldn't have any dessert. He had then eaten most of the custard from the Zuppa Inglese, and now he was demolishing the crème caramel. "Garth, did I tell you about my diet?" he asked.

Jews are all diet experts, Lola thought. No Jews overlooked the importance of weight loss. Last week, Lola had been at Izzy Staub's funeral. It was a very moving service. Izzy had been a much-loved man, and many people among the mourners were weeping. After the funeral, Lola waited in line to offer her condolences to Izzy's daughters, Eva and Irena. Eva and Irena were both distraught. Irena's eyes were swollen and red. She looked up as Lola went to speak to her. "Look, Eva, look at how much weight Lola has lost. How did you do it?" Lola felt cheered by the thought that, even in the middle of death, weight loss was important. She made herself laugh, driving home from the cemetery, with the thought that at a Jewish funeral weight loss was a grave issue.

Morris was still talking about his diet. Lola could see that Garth was cross-eyed with boredom. Garth had never been on a diet. Morris was communicating with great intensity. He was giving Garth the details of how much weight he had gained and how much he had lost.

The obsession with food must be genetically built into Jews, Lola thought. Josl Bensky had been thirty-two when he came to Australia after the war. The few details of the first thirty-two years of her father's life that her father talked to her about were to do with food.

Once or twice a year, Josl would reminisce about the ham he used to eat. "Oy," he would say. "Oy, was that a special good ham they made in Poland! I used to go to the Grand Hotel in Lodz. They made the best ham. It was almost sweet tasting. My father would have killed me if he had known that I was eating ham."

Lola's earliest memories were of herself at Bialik kindergarten.

She remembered hoping that she would have time to fit in a second helping of chocolate custard before her mother came to pick her up.

Lola's most humiliating memories were also to do with food. While the rest of the ten-year-olds at the Marilyn Brown School of Dancing were performing the final dress rehearsal of "Fella With An Umbrella", Lola was in the dressing room, eating Shirley Berry's lamington.

When Mrs Brown confronted the class and said sternly, "OK, who has stolen Shirley Berry's lamington slice?" Lola kept quiet. She hoped that she didn't have any crumbs on her face.

Later, feeling uncomfortable, Lola comforted Shirley Berry. They both agreed that the thief was probably Cheryl Buchanan.

The other humiliating episode Lola almost couldn't bear to recall. It was when she'd stolen Dr Bender's bananas. The Bender family and the Bensky family had gone away together for a week to Rosebud. Lola had been seven. Dr Bender was their dentist. She was a quiet, thin and intense woman. Dr Bender and her husband and daughter had been in Bergen-Belsen for six months. When they were liberated, Mr Bender had to spend six months in hospital before he could eat without vomiting.

Dr Bender couldn't work legally as a dentist. The Australian government didn't recognise her Polish qualifications. She was halfway through a Bachelor of Dentistry at the University of Melbourne. She had, however, bought dental equipment and set up a practice at her home, working mostly at night. Most of her patients were newly arrived Jews. She was an excellent dentist, and she was cheap. Her practice thrived, and she could afford to keep studying.

This week in Rosebud was the Benders' first holiday in Australia. The two families kept their food in separate cupboards. This wasn't the way that Renia Bensky would have liked it. Renia would have preferred to pool the food, but she was gracious about Dr Bender's need for division and order.

On the first day, Lola took three bananas from the Benders'

cupboard. "Was there any particular reason why you ate our bananas?" Dr Bender asked Renia Bensky.

"What a stingy pig that Dr Bender is," Renia said to Josl after the debacle had been sorted out. "Here she is, an educated woman, and she acts like a pig. She has to count every piece of food, and she did accuse us like we were big criminals." To Lola, Renia Bensky said "Lola, you are a greedy pig."

Lola couldn't look Dr Bender in the eye for years. She still felt uncomfortable when she thought about the bananas. When Lola was twenty-two, she had come across Dr Bender in Regent Street in London. They had had a cup of coffee together.

"You know, Lola, your house, when you were a child, was the tensest household I was ever in." Lola didn't know what to do with this information. It shocked her. She wanted to ask a thousand questions. Why was it tense? In what way? What had Dr Bender observed about their lives? Dr Bender was the only adult who had ever suggested that the Benskys' home life was anything less than perfect.

Lola opened her mouth. But nothing came out. The questions stayed stuck in her.

Was Dr Bender talking about the noise in the house? There was always a lot of noise. There were doors opening and shutting, cupboards and drawers banging. There were kitchen noises and bathroom noises, and instructions and orders being shouted. Was that what Dr Bender had meant?

As a child, Lola had longed for silence. She envied those girlfriends whose parents took no notice of them. Lola felt that her parents were omnipresent. At the same time she felt that they were not there. She felt as though she couldn't get a grip on them. When she spoke, she felt that they didn't listen. They were distracted by something. Something larger. Something Lola couldn't share.

Morris Lubofsky ordered another crème caramel and three more coffees. "Today is a write-off diet-wise, so I may as well pig myself," he said. "I'll go back on my diet tomorrow."

Lola had a scientific theory about why all Jews were on a diet. She had told Garth about this theory last week, and he seemed to think that there could be some truth in it. She explained the theory to Morris.

"Morris, I think that you and I are genetically predisposed to putting on weight. See, I think that the Jews who survived concentration camps must have had very efficient metabolisms, and that's why they could survive on very little food. It stands to reason that the offspring of people with such slow metabolisms would have extremely slow metabolisms. That would explain why Garth can eat anything he likes and not put on weight, whereas you and I can eat hardly anything and get fat."

"I think you've got something there," said Morris Lubofsky.

Just then, Aviva Jacobsen walked into the Café Roma. Aviva was the child of concentration camp survivors. She was two or three stone overweight. Morris and Lola nodded at each other. Aviva was evidence of the validity of Lola's theory.

"Hi, guys, how are you?" Aviva said. "I'm just between cases. I've got a sentencing at four o'clock, and I've got to get to the children's court before then, so I won't stop." Aviva, a barrister, lived her life on the run. She was busy defending this murderer, that thief, this distraught father, that battered child. Lola often thought that Aviva was driven. When Aviva wasn't working, she went to the theatre, to the opera, to the cinema, to concerts, to art openings, to museums. She was always doing something. And always in a hurry. Lola found Aviva's ceaseless activity exhausting.

Aviva's sister, Fay, moved very slowly. Fay looked permanently tranquillised. She lived in Israel. Very few Israeli men were limp or insipid, but Fay Jacobsen had found one such Israeli and married him. They had four boisterous, unmanageable children, and their fifth child was due any day now. Fay and her husband were supported by her parents.

Lola had met Aviva and Fay's father last week. He told her he had just spoken to Fay. "I did ask her," he said to Lola, "how the economic situation in the country is. She said to me 'I don't know, Dad. I don't have to work, Igal doesn't have to work. How do we know how the economy is?' " Mr Jacobsen looked both proud and troubled by his daughter's reply.

"You know, Lola," Mr Jacobsen said, "I had a dream when I came to Australia. My dream was to earn enough money so that my children would never have to worry about money. And I did it." Mr Jacobsen looked bothered.

Morris Lubofsky was talking to Garth about his girlfriend Elizabeth's legs.

"She's got amazingly long legs," he was saying.

"Morris," said Lola, "this relationship with Elizabeth will never last. Even if she marries you, she'll leave you in a few years. And then what will you do, look for wife number five when you're fifty? I saw the way Elizabeth looked at you when you had that hayfever attack. Her concern was efficient, not affectionate. Anyway, she's not Jewish, and she's too young for you."

One of the nice things about Morris Lubofsky, Lola thought later, was that he was very good-natured. "At the moment I'm not really worried about how long the relationship will last," Morris replied. "I feel happy with Elizabeth. She's given me a confidence that I didn't have. She tells me I'm a fabulous lover, and that's been very good for me."

Lola had someone in mind for Morris Lubofsky. It was her friend Roslyn. But Roslyn had a penchant for non-Jewish men. Her two husbands hadn't been Jewish. Lola was trying to show Roslyn the error of her ways. She was trying to persuade Roslyn that her next husband should be Jewish.

Roslyn and Morris would be a perfect match, thought Lola. Roslyn's mother had been in hiding, in Poland, during the war, and so had Morris's mother. Roslyn was very bright. She wouldn't take any crap from Morris if she was his wife. She'd put Morris on the right track, thought Lola.

A friend of Lola's had once said to her, "Lola, you should marry someone who will make you more than you are, not someone who will make you less than you are." Roslyn would make Morris Lubofsky more than he was. And Roslyn would no longer have to struggle. She had struggled all her life. She had worked full-time while getting her degrees. She had always had to support herself. Things would be easier for her as a member of the Lubofsky family. And Roslyn wouldn't exploit their wealth. Roslyn was a modest and independent girl.

Yes, Roslyn would make a perfect wife for Morris Lubofsky. Lola talked to Roslyn about the importance of marrying a Jewish husband. "What about Garth?" said Roslyn. "Garth is more Jewish than I am," answered Lola. "He knows more about Judaism than I do. Anyway, there are no other goys like Garth."

Josl Bensky had been at Lola's house one day when Lola was talking to Roslyn. "You have to stop running away from your Jewishness," Lola had lectured Roslyn. "You think that having a ham sandwich on Yom Kippur is the action of a mature person who has come to terms with themselves?" Lola asked Roslyn. "You are Jewish," Lola continued emphatically, "and it is a very attractive part of you."

Josl Bensky had been sitting between the two women. He looked amused. Was this the same girl, the same Lola, his daughter, who'd gone out with tow-truck drivers, who had dated a black African from Nigeria, who had been in love with drug-addicted rock-and-roll singers? Was this the same daughter who had rejected all her mother's matchmaking efforts? The same daughter who hadn't gone out with a Jewish boy since she was eighteen? Was this Lolala Bensky speaking?

"Lolala, my darling," Josl Bensky said. "There is an old Yiddish saying. It says, 'If you live long enough, you see everything.' "

Lola and Garth said goodbye to Morris on Lygon Street.

"Will you be here for coffee on Saturday morning?" asked Morris. Lola nodded. "Good," Morris said. "See you then."

Things Could Be Worse

Lola Bensky saw herself on the screen. There she was. She was the second guest on the right at Tsaytl and Motl's wedding in *Fiddler On The Roof.* It was her. The same hair, the same eyes, the same mouth, the same expression.

Now, the Lola on the screen was dancing. Look at her. Her skirts were whirling. She was turning this way and that way. Stepping to the right. Stepping to the left. Now she was clapping and dancing. She was dancing the hora. She was dancing the mitzvah-tensl. Now Lola Bensky could see that it wasn't her up on the screen in *Fiddler On The Roof.* Lola Bensky couldn't dance.

Lola had tried to dance. At sixteen, when her friends were jiving to Chubby Checker, Bobby Darren and Crash Craddock, Lola had tried to look like a carefree rock-and-roller. She had had the right rope petticoats, the right T-bar shoes, the right lipstick and the right hairstyle. But she had had the wrong expression. She looked anguished, embarrassed and uncomfortable. She had tried to keep smiling through "Only The Lonely" and "Boom Boom Baby", but her discomfort had dislodged her smile.

Lola had tried again in her early twenties, when dancing had become more creative. You could make up the movements or follow the go-go dancers. At Ziggy's discothèque, Lola had kept her eyes glued to the go-go dancers. Six go-go dancers danced in cages suspended from the ceiling. Lola often felt dizzy looking up at the dancers while she copied their arm and leg movements, but Lola had no talent for choreography. Her imagination didn't extend to dance steps. If she couldn't see the go-go dancers, she couldn't dance.

At twenty-three, Lola gave up dancing. She didn't dance again until she met Garth. Garth was a fabulous dancer. Lola clung to Garth as he turned and stepped and twisted around the dance floor. Garth held Lola close to him, and clutched her tightly. From this secure position, Lola Bensky could smile while she danced.

Lola had seen herself on the screen before. She had seen herself in old footage of the prisoners of Dachau being liberated by the American army. She knew that the young girl behind the barbed-wire fence in Dachau, in front of the ditch filled with dead bodies, was her.

Lola saw herself in photographs, too. She saw herself in photographs of street urchins in the Lodz ghetto. She saw herself in a photograph of a small girl sitting next to her dead mother in the ghetto. She saw herself in photographs of Jewish women smiling for the camera in displaced persons camps.

Lola also looked for relatives in these photographs. She searched through photographs, books and films for members of her family. She looked for the son that her parents had had before the war. She looked for her grandparents. She looked for her aunties and uncles and cousins.

In her handbag she kept a notebook with the names of her parents' parents and brothers and sisters. In this notebook, she also kept an index of the titles of the books on the Holocaust that she owned.

Lola hated the word Holocaust. It was too neatly wrapped into a parcel. There were no loose ends and no frayed edges. The Holocaust. It was a nice, compact abstraction. But what else could she say? The alternatives were so wordy. She could say the Nazi extermination of European Jewry. She could say the destruction of the Jews by the Nazis. She could say Hitler's murder of six million Jews.

Lola had a library of over one thousand books on the Holocaust.

She had read most of them. Lola had a good memory. She had always had a good memory. She could remember hundreds, if not thousands, of phone numbers. Conversations she had ten years ago, she could recall verbatim. Yet the facts and statistics of the Holocaust flew out of her head. She had to check and recheck the information. Was it in Bergen-Belsen that British troops had found over ten thousand unburied bodies? Was it there, in BergenBelsen, that five hundred inmates a day had died from typhoid and starvation in the week after liberation? Was it in Mathausen that the Nazis had murdered thirty thousand Jews in the last four months of the war? Lola had to check and recheck.

When she was thirty, Lola had begun to ask her parents about their experiences in the war. They had answered her questions, hesitantly at first, but they had answered. Lola had listened. She had listened quietly. She had taken notes. She had tape-recorded some of the conversations. She had videotaped a long interview with each of her parents. And still their stories blurred and wandered in her head.

Lola had been shocked to find that other Jews her age didn't know or couldn't remember what had happened to their parents during the war. Solomon Seitz, with his Oxford D.Phil, didn't know. Susan Shuster, a researcher for the Prime Minister, couldn't remember. Boris Kronhill, the physicist, had a vague idea. He told Lola that his mother had been in hiding in a convent and his father had been in a labour camp in Russia. Lola knew that Boris had it all wrong. Renia knew the Kronhills and had told Lola that Mrs Kronhill had been in Auschwitz and Mr Kronhill had been hidden in a haystack on a farm in Poland for two years.

Renia and Josl's friends thought that Lola, with all her questions and all her books, was crazy. "What does she want to read books about concentration camps for?" said Genia Pekelman. "Does she want to go crazy?"

* *

Lola came out of the Adelphi theatre in Mordialloc. Mordialloc was a long way from Russia and the world of Tevya and Tsaytl and Motl.

Lola's mother had died nine months ago. Last night, Lola had been feeling out of kilter. She had seen in the *Herald* that *Fiddler On The Roof* was playing at the Adelphi, and she had decided that she needed to see it. This morning Lola had bought a packet of Fantales and a packet of Minties, and driven for an hour to Mordialloc to catch the early matinée session at the Adelphi.

There had been only five other people in the cavernous theatre. Lola thought that she and the four elderly women and one very old man must have been the only people in Melbourne who hadn't yet seen *Fiddler On The Roof.*

Now, outside the theatre, Lola felt a bit disconcerted. It was a bright, blue, hot day. Mordialloc looked prosperous. People were eating Chiko rolls and pies in the pizza shop next door to the Adelphi. Poor Tevya had been so poor that he had to carry his milk deliveries himself when his horse had become too old. Here everyone had a car and could afford a milkshake.

Lola bought a custard tart and drove back to Melbourne. On her way home she stopped at Texoform, the factory in which her father worked. Josl had been with Texoform for nine years. Josl's clothing company, Joren Fashions, like many small businesses, had closed down in the seventies. At first Josl had felt devastated. Now, he enjoyed his job at Texoform. He had his own office, and he was in charge of ordering the fabrics. Josl felt as though Texoform was his own company. He was overjoyed when he saved the firm money, and he worked hard to create a high morale and a sense of loyalty among the workers.

Josl was surprised to see his daughter, but then nothing that Lola did really surprised Josl. For many years, Lola had been at odds with herself. At odds with him. At odds with his beloved Renia, who had died just when everything was looking promising. Renia had died when both of her daughters were happily married and her

grandchildren were turning out to be everything she had hoped for in her own children.

Josl wiped away the tears that came when he thought about Renia. He still got up early every morning and tiptoed around the bedroom so that he wouldn't disturb her. And every morning he was jolted out of his quiet by the realisation that Renia was no longer there. His darling Renia, the woman he had loved since he was twenty-two and she was sixteen, was dead.

Josl kissed Lola hello. He looked at her. Lola had changed. In her thirties Lola had changed, and all the things that Josl had loved in her as a small child had returned. He had loved her curiosity and her enthusiasm. And he had loved her laugh. When Lola was little she used to laugh and laugh. If something struck her as funny she would laugh with her whole body, with her whole being. She would be completely immersed in her laughter. It used to give Josl so much joy.

"Hi, Dad," said Lola. "The photo of Mum looks good on the wall. I like this new office. How are you, Dad?"

"I'm all right, Lola. I'm all right," Josl answered.

"You know what I did today?" said Lola. "I drove out to Mordialloc and went to the pictures. I haven't been able to work well lately, and I noticed that *Fiddler On The Roof* was playing, so I went and saw it."

"You haven't seen *Fiddler On The Roof* before?" said Josl.

"No, I'd never seen it," said Lola.

"You never saw *Fiddler On The Roof*? But everybody did see *Fiddler On The Roof.* What a picture! I loved *Fiddler On The Roof.* Topol was very good in the film, but that Hayes Gordon, who did play Tevya on the stage in Melbourne, he was terrific. He is not a Jew, yet he was one hundred per cent a Jew on the stage. Your Mum and I, we loved him. We saw him twice. I can't believe that until now you didn't see *Fiddler On The Roof.*"

"I'm glad that I went to see it," said Lola. "I loved it. Dad, I know it's not Wednesday, but will you have dinner with us tonight? I'm making a beautiful veal and beef klops with sauerkraut."

"I don't want you to start again with the 'can I eat with you' business," said Josl. "I told you, I'll come once a week and that's it. Klops with sauerkraut? Is it the same way that Mum made it?" Josl asked.

"It's exactly the way that Mum made klops and sauerkraut," said Lola.

"It is a little bit hard to say no to klops with sauerkraut. All right, all right, I will come, but don't put me in this position again. I'm not going to be a burden on you or anybody," said Josl.

"Dad, you know that it makes us happy to see you," said Lola.

"OK, Lola, OK. I will come but I won't stay long. I want to have an early night. I didn't sleep so well last night. I started thinking, and I couldn't fall asleep. It's no good to think too much. It can get you so mixed up. I started to feel crazy. First I was thinking about Mum. She did everything right. She was slim, she didn't smoke, she did do exercise, and still she died. She was young. Sixty-three is not old today. Then I started to think about the past, and that maybe what happened to Mum in Auschwitz was what did give her the cancer. After a few hours thinking like this you can think you are crazy. It's better not to think too much," said Josl.

"It's better not to think too much" was something Josl had said repeatedly since Lola was small. Lola had stopped thinking altogether when she was sixteen. Until then she had topped all her classes, played the piano well and won prizes for her French and German poetry recitations. At sixteen she failed two of her five final year high school subjects. The following year she had passed the two subjects that she had failed and failed the three that she had passed. The third time, to everyone's relief, she passed all five subjects.

Lola had drifted through the next ten years. She became a journalist. She became a wife. She became a mother. She seemed like a good journalist, a good wife and a good mother. But Lola was crooked. She was skewwhiff. She was at an odd angle. And no-one noticed.

Arrows of anger and shafts of self-pity pitted her thoughts. Fear ruptured her nights. Fantasies and dreams were intertwined with her daily life. She thought she was Renia and Josl. She thought she had been in the ghetto. She thought she had been in Auschwitz too.

Lola had always been plump. But from the age of sixteen, she grew, slowly and steadily, until she was huge. She grew a cocoon around herself. And in this unoccupied territory, this haven, this no man's land, Lola, a bit breathless and tired, spent her youth.

Lola didn't start thinking again until she was twenty-six and went to see a psychoanalyst about her weight problem.

"What sort of answer is that to a weight problem?" Renia had said when Lola asked her to look after Julian while she went to the analyst. "Is this a solution to being fat? To go to a psychiatrist? What sort of a solution is that?" said Renia.

"Lola is going to see an analyst about losing weight?" said Ada Small. "Why doesn't she go to Weight Watchers? Whoever heard of somebody going to see a doctor for mad people, for meshuganas, when she just wants to lose some weight? It's crazy."

"What about a hypnotist?" suggested Genia.

"What about Limmits biscuits, or the egg-and-grapefruit diet?" said Renia to Lola. "I have heard some very good reports about that egg-and-grapefruit diet. You can have as many boiled eggs as you like, as long as you eat half a grapefruit first. Lola, what did we do to deserve the shame of a daughter who goes to see a psychiatrist?"

"You think too much and you don't do enough dieting," Josl had said. "Anyway," he had continued, "I have heard some not very good things about this Herr Professor, this expensive doctor psychiatrist. I heard he got divorced from a very nice woman. I heard that he is the meshugana, not the patients that he treats. The worry about this is making your mother sick. Her daughter is going to see a lunatic doctor. She needs this like a hole in the head."

Lola had decided that it hadn't been a good idea to ask Renia to babysit Julian. She came to an arrangement with her friend Margaret-Anne. Margaret-Anne would look after Julian twice a week while Lola went to her analyst, and Lola would babysit Margaret-Anne's Jonathan while Margaret-Anne was at meditation classes.

Lola had always had close women friends. She spoke to them every day. She had cooked food for their husbands when her friends were in hospital having children. She had scoured the real-estate pages of the newspapers and visited properties with them when they were buying houses. Her friends were her substitutes for sisters.

Although she had tried to see little Jonathan as family, his shit stank and she couldn't understand him. After six months Lola had hired a babysitter for Julian.

Lola had tried other ways of creating a large family. She had arranged book clubs, film clubs and card nights. She had tried to organise a communal housing project. Lola had wanted her friends to sell their houses and build new houses on a large block of land that had come up for sale in Melbourne. This land was fifteen minutes from the city, and had a thousand feet of river frontage. Lola had envisaged a beautiful environment where they could all still have their privacy, but they would be able to develop deeper friendships with each other. They would be able to share some of the domestic drudgeries of having young children, and they would also be able to afford luxuries such as a swimming pool and a tennis court.

Lola had cajoled, arranged, organised, pressed and begged her friends. The proposed project had divided the group. The book and film clubs and the card nights came to an end.

Charlie Goldstein, Lola's old school friend, had asked Lola why this large group of friends no longer spoke to each other.

Lola had replied, "We were split up by my proposal that we become closer."

This was a liberated era. Charlie Goldstein, still wide-eyed, had told his partner Hyram that, although Lola Bensky didn't look the type, she had told him, and he had heard it with his own ears, that she had tried to organise a wife-swapping commune.

The news had spread through Melbourne. Mrs Goldstein, Charlie's mother, had rung Renia Bensky.

"Renia darling," she had said, "I hear you are having a bit of trouble with Lola. Just be strong, Renia. Like my dear departed mother used to say, 'Small children small worries, big children big worries.' "

"That idiot Mrs Goldstein rang me today," Renia had said to Josl that evening. "She rang to let me know that she knows how fat Lola is. 'Be strong, Renia,' she said. With friends like Mrs Goldstein, who needs enemies?"

"Renia darling," said Josl, after he had agreed that Mrs Goldstein was a philistine, a peasant and an idiot, "Renia darling, I think that Lola is losing a bit of weight. Do you think there is a chance that that lunatic doctor is doing her some good?"

"Who knows what would do Lola good?" said Renia. "I think I will make her a dish of zucchinis and tomatoes. I got the recipe from Nusia who got it from Mrs Braunstein who is going to Weight Watchers."

Lola was just leaving Josl's office when he called her back. "Lola, I nearly forgot. I bought some dog food for you. Pal dog food. The brand Mum always bought. It was on special, so I bought two boxes. I'll put them in the boot for you."

Lola had inherited her mother's dogs. Lola, who had no interest in dogs or cats, was now the owner of Cleo, Benny and Blacky.

Lola was sure that Renia had been the only Jew in Melbourne to own three dogs. Cleo, Benny and Blacky had all been strays. They had attached themselves to Renia, who couldn't bear to see homeless or hungry animals.

Josl put the boxes of dog food in the car. "Thanks, Dad," said Lola. "I'll see you tonight."

Lola drove towards St Kilda. She felt better. Seeing *Fiddler On*

The Roof had cheered her up, and she was happy that Josl was coming for dinner. She wished that her mother wasn't dead. Why did her mother have to die? In the last few years she and her mother had been getting on so well. Lola's throat constricted with choked tears. She hadn't been able to cry for her mother since the funeral.

On St Kilda Road, Lola started to think about how good her life was. She loved Garth, and he loved her. The kids had turned out well. Julian was a medical student.

"My son is two-thirds of a doctor," Lola boasted. When Renia was in hospital dying, Renia had told every nurse, every intern, every orderly and every specialist that her grandson was a medical student. It had made Lola weep. It had also consoled her. At least she had given Renia a grandson who had given her a lot of pleasure.

Even when he had been a small boy, Julian had been able to make Renia happy. When Renia was with Julian all her anger evaporated and all her anguish vanished. Renia had played with Julian, fed him, walked with him, talked with him. Lola had felt that little Julian had healed and soothed Renia in a way that her own children had never been able to.

When Julian was older, Renia collected his prizes and certificates. The two of them went for long walks along the beach together. Sometimes, on these walks, people had complimented Renia on her handsome son, and she had glowed. "Julian is as good at maths as I was," Renia used to say to Lola. Lola had always been hopeless at maths.

Lola arrived at Polonsky's kosher butcher shop. Though her parents had never been Orthodox, Lola bought kosher meat. Josl used to laugh at her. "The kosher meat is twice the price and it doesn't taste any different," he would say. Lola knew it was irrational, but she felt that the veal and beef were better for having been blessed.

Mrs Kopper was inside Polonsky's.

"Hello, Lola," she said, "and how's things? How are you keeping? Are you and your sister still broygis with each other? It's a shocking thing that two sisters should not speak to each other.

Thank God your poor dear mother, God rest her soul, didn't see this. It is shocking. I saw your father the other day and he told me how upset he was about you two girls. I tell you, Lola, there was a tear in his eyes. I told him, I said to him, 'Josl, things could be worse.' And it is true. To make your father feel better I reminded him about the old Sholem Aleichem story. You know, the story about the bags of worries. You don't know this story? You didn't hear about it? Well, I will tell you, Lola.

"There was a village where many people had troubles. They came to the rabbi and said 'Rabbi, why do I have to have so much trouble? My neighbour doesn't have such troubles. Why was I chosen to have this trouble?' The rabbi heard these complaints many times. One day the rabbi said that everyone who had troubles should put their troubles in a bag, and bring the bag to the market place. The people of the village did this. Then the rabbi said that everyone should choose someone else's bag to take home. When the people got home and saw what was in the bag of troubles that they had chosen, they said, 'Oh God, please give me my own troubles back. My own troubles were not so bad.' The next day everyone returned to the market place to get back his own bag of troubles."

"Excuse me," said Mrs Singer. "I know that you are telling this story, Mrs Kopper, but it is important to tell it right. I don't think that Sholem Aleichem said that many people in the village had troubles, just a few people."

"All right, all right, Mrs Singer," said Mrs Kopper. "What does it matter? That is not so important. What is important is what I was trying to tell Lola. And that is that things can always be worse."

"I can tell you straight away about two sisters who are worse," said Mrs Singer. "My neighbour has got three nieces. The two younger girls hate the oldest girl. I hear that she is not such a nice person but that is another story. My neighbour's brother, the girls' father, died last month. The younger girls told their older sister, who lives in Canberra, that the funeral was at eleven o'clock. When the older girl arrived at the cemetery, the funeral was finished, because the funeral was really at ten o'clock. And of course, everybody was talking about how shocking it was that the older daughter didn't come to her father's funeral."

Lola knew that things could always be worse. It was something that she had always been sure of. Mr Polonsky gave Lola her minced veal and beef.

"Well, Lola," he said, "you are a big star now. A famous person. I see your photograph in the *Jewish News* every week. When you left here last time, Mrs Leber asked me if that was Lola Bensky the writer. 'Yes, Mrs Leber,' I said. 'Lola Bensky always buys her meat and chickens here.' "

Lola drove home. At home she prepared the klops mixture. This was her mother's recipe. Two eggs, two chopped onions, two grated cloves of garlic, two tablespoons of breadcrumbs, two teaspoons of salt and half a teaspoon of pepper for every kilo of meat. It made a delicious meatloaf.

Lola kneaded and kneaded, listening to the soft sound of the meat on her fingers. The meat and onions and eggs and garlic and breadcrumbs blended into a smooth universe.

Maybe one day she would be able to patch things up with her sister, Lola thought. Although it wasn't really a patching job, more like a total overhaul. She put the klops into the oven.

Technical Trouble

The Prime Minister had finished his speech. Everybody was clapping. There were five hundred people here, in the forecourt of Parliament House. The Prime Minister had planted a tree in honour of Raoul Wallenberg, the Swedish diplomat who had saved tens of thousands of Jews from the Nazis.

Lola Bensky stepped up onto the podium to read her poem about Raoul Wallenberg. Lola was nervous. She was so nervous that her hands and legs shook almost as though they had been choreographed.

Lola cleared her throat away from the microphone. She began to read. The words came out of her mouth and dissolved in the hovering humidity. The microphone was not working.

There were mutterings and stirrings from the crowd.

"The microphone has broken," said Mr Rosen.

"Oy, it's broken," said Mr Berg.

"The microphone has broken down," said Mrs Roth.

"It's not working," said Mrs Fink.

"That microphone is not working," said Mr Mendelson.

No-one moved.

The Prime Minister got back up onto the podium. He tried to fix the microphone. He turned and twisted the knob at the base of the microphone.

"It's broken," said Abe Rothberg.

"Yes, it's broken," said Sadie Levin.

The Prime Minister tried again. He found a switch at the side of the microphone and switched it on and off. But nothing happened.

"It's definitely broken," said Mrs Dunov.

"It's broken," said Mr Fishman.

"You'll have to shout," the Prime Minister said to Lola.

How could Jews be so clever, and so inept? thought Lola. Jews could feed three thousand people without a hitch, but it was beyond them to find one microphone in working order for a special occasion.

Lola looked at the crowd. There was Sol Apelbaum, managing director of Consolidated Metal Industries. Consolidated Metal Industries had offices in Hong Kong and Singapore. Next to him were Wolf Nathanson of Proctor Properties and Sam Baume, head of the Sweet Evelyn chain of retail stores. How, wondered Lola, had they managed to build such successful businesses without knowing how to fix a microphone?

In the past year Lola had read her poetry at many Jewish functions. The microphone had not worked once. Josl had explained to her that microphones were not what Jews knew about.

"It's not their field," he had said.

The crowd was becoming more agitated. People shook their heads and said "It's not working." Lola looked feebly at the Prime Minister. "I think you'd better shout," he said again.

Lola shouted the sad poem about Raoul Wallenberg.

Four hours later, the dinner after the tree-planting ceremony was progressing well. The guests had already had hors d'oeuvres, soup and an entrée. The waiters were serving the main course. The dessert, the cakes and the coffee were yet to come.

Lola was enjoying herself. There she was, sitting among five hundred Jews, and she was enjoying herself.

Lola looked around the room. The atmosphere was buoyant and celebratory. Most of the guests had come from Melbourne and

Sydney. Lola could see the energy of the people, the vitality, the good humour, the warmth.

She could see what she had prevented herself from seeing for years: she could see that she was at home here. This was a familiar world. She understood the language, the mannerisms, the meanings and the intentions.

A woman in her sixties came up to Lola. "Lola, you don't remember me, but I am Mrs Klineman. I used to know your parents when you were a young girl. I remember you well. What trouble you gave your parents, Lola! I remember when you were arrested for shoplifting. Your poor mother, it nearly killed her."

Lola said that she would pass on Mrs Klineman's regards. Mrs Klineman was sitting at a table with Mr and Mrs Beir, Mr and Mrs Pilsen and Mr and Mrs Dorovitch. Mrs Klineman and Mrs Beir had been in Auschwitz together. Mrs Pilsen had hidden in the forests in Poland for four years during the war. Mr Beir had been in Dachau, and Mr Dorovitch had fought with the partisans.

When Lola thought about their pasts, and the pasts of many of the Jewish people in the room, she felt full of admiration for them. Mr and Mrs Klineman had canvassed for the release of Russian Jews for years. Mrs Beir was at every commemoration, every seminar and every book launching in the community. Mrs Dorovitch was on the Jewish Heritage Committee. They were tireless. They made speeches, delivered lectures, collected petitions, baked cakes, raised money and raised children. They were exemplary grandparents and were devoted to their grandchildren.

Somebody tapped Lola on the shoulder. It was Jack Zelman.

"I came up to Canberra for some business and heard you were in town, so I thought I'd drop by and say hello," said Jack Zelman.

Lola hadn't seen Jack for at least ten years. She'd heard bits and pieces about him from her mother. Lola had also heard news of Jack from Morris Lubofsky. Morris knew what everybody was doing.

Lola knew that Jack was forty-four and unmarried. She knew that he had had plenty of short-term relationships.

"Jack can only feel excited by women who are not his," Morris Lubofsky had told her. "It's true," Morris had said. "Jack always falls in love with someone else's wife. He stays in love with them until they look as if they might leave their husband for him, and then he falls out of love. He once told me that as soon as he imagines the woman as his wife, he becomes impotent." Morris had felt that he should elaborate this point: "Jack can't get an erection if he thinks that the woman might want to marry him. And this is a guy who is supposed to be one of the greatest shtoopers in town. Phew, what a problem."

Lola hadn't been sure whether Morris Lubofsky had been ironic or envious. She hadn't had time to ask him, because Morris's real area of interest was himself, and he had already been derailed for too long on the subject of Jack Zelman.

Morris had wanted to tell Lola about his new shoes. "I had to get these new sports shoes," he had said earnestly. "I was falling over, walking in ordinary shoes. I can't wear ordinary shoes anyway. After three hours of wearing ordinary shoes, I'm so exhausted I have to go to bed. These new ones that I'm wearing have got three soles. The first sole hits the pavement, the second sole slides in along and absorbs the shock, and the third sole throws you into the next step."

Lola thought that it must be a great help in life to have shoes that gave you a lift into the next step.

What a trio they made, Lola had thought. There she was, a former bad girl, a reformed anti-Semite. And there was Morris Lubofsky, divorced from his third wife, and still buying himself toys. Cars, furniture, shoes. And Jack Zelman, a property developer who could only fuck other people's wives.

"You look very good. You look fabulous, actually, Lola," said Jack Zelman.

Lola started to laugh. One of her strongest memories of her adolescence was of Jack Zelman.

"Lola," he had said to her, "if you went on a diet and lost weight I'd take you out." He had then gone on to explain to Lola just how much weight he would like her to lose. He wanted her to get down to the same size as Louise Samuels.

Louise Samuels was five foot nine and weighed eight stone. Lola was told this by Jack's sister Mary. Lola was the same height as Louise Samuels. Lola had often thought that they must be the two tallest Jewish girls in Melbourne. Unfortunately, Lola had calculated she was fifty per cent heavier than Louise. She would have had to lose the equivalent of half of Louise's body. Lola decided to give up on Jack Zelman after that.

Jack looked embarrassed when she laughed. She wondered whether he was remembering too. They had a few memories in common, she and Jack Zelman. She thought of one of the many holidays they had had in Surfers Paradise. The Benskys had been there with the whole company of friends. Lola and Jack were sitting on the lawns of the Chevron Hilton. It was early evening. They had known each other since they were small children. They were talking. Jack had stopped talking, and Lola was listening to the quiet of the night. Lola loved silence. A cicada sent out a long shriek, and suddenly Jack Zelman was kissing her. He lay on top of her and pushed himself against her. She could feel his hardness. It felt wonderful. Lola had an orgasm.

"Oh God, what a mess," was what Jack had said when he spoke again. Lola had thought that the mess that he was talking about must have been the intimacy they had shared. She thought that he had regretted the closeness. That he felt sullied.

Lola felt flushed, remembering that summer in Surfers Paradise. Jack was smiling at her. Lola introduced Jack to Garth. "Garth, I'm so pleased to meet you. I hear from my mother all the time that you are the perfect son-in-law. Renia Bensky always said to my Mum that she wouldn't swap you for one hundred Jewish sons-in-law." Garth laughed.

"Sit down and join us, Jack," said Lola. She suddenly felt sorry for Jack Zelman. He didn't have a wife. He didn't have any children. Lola wondered why. Other people also wondered why. Jack Zelman was the bane of every Jewish matchmaker in Melbourne. He was their dream match. He was good-looking, educated and rich. He wasn't a faigele — on the contrary, he had a reputation for being a lion in bed. So why didn't he get married?

Lola knew that Jack had had a hard time at home as a kid. His parents, Mina and Joseph, had each been married to other people before the war. Mina's first husband, Tadek, Lola's mother had told her, had been the great love of Mina Zelman's life. Mina and Tadek had lived in the same street in Warsaw. Tadek was several years older than Mina. He used to take her on outings from the time that she was two and he was seven. At ten, Tadek had announced to his mother that he was going to marry Mina. When Mina was sixteen they were married. Their son, Henryk, was born the following year. Tadek and three-year-old Henryk died in Bergen-Belsen. When the British troops liberated Bergen-Belsen, they found Mina half-dead, on top of a pile of corpses.

Renia Bensky had once told Lola that she thought that Mina Zelman worked so tirelessly for charities in order to store up credit with the Almighty, so that when she died she would be reunited with Tadek and Henryk. This thought had given Lola the creeps.

Once her mother had said to her, "Lola, Mina Zelman is giving away all of Joseph's money. She gives to this charity. She gives to that charity. The more Joseph earns, the more Mina gives. Joseph doesn't understand why Mina does so much giving, but he doesn't say anything. It keeps Mina happy, he thinks, and she doesn't ask him any questions about Pola Ganz. And, for the moment, he has still got plenty of money left."

Lola didn't like Joseph Zelman. She thought that he was crude. She could understand Mina Zelman not being upset at the thought of Joseph having an affair with Pola Ganz. Lola thought that there was not a lot of tenderness or sensitivity in Joseph Zelman, so what difference would it make whether he was faithful or not? Pola Ganz probably wasn't getting anything that Mina Zelman needed, thought Lola.

Lola sometimes saw Joseph Zelman at her parents' place. He always wanted to tell her about his daughters, Mary and Susan. Lola hadn't seen the Zelman girls since they left Melbourne to live in Israel sixteen years ago. She had, however, seen endless photographs of them, their husbands and their children. Joseph always carried a walletful of photographs on him.

Joseph Zelman boasted about the sacrifices that his two daughters had made by choosing to live in Israel.

"It's not so easy to live in Israel," he used to say. "Susan and Mary could have a much more comfortable life in Melbourne, but they are committed to Israel, and Mina and I are very proud of their commitment."

Lola thought that Susan and Mary were probably most committed to living away from their father. That way they all got on well together.

"It's a blessing to have such a close family," Joseph would tell Lola.

The Zelmans always seemed to have just returned from another wonderful holiday with their daughters. "We just had a marvellous holiday in Monte Carlo with the girls and their husbands and the children. We all get on so well together. We share the same interests. We went out every night. We had the most wonderful holiday. Yes, it's a blessing to have such a close family," Joseph would say.

During the years when Lola was having trouble just being civil to her parents, let alone entertaining the thought of romping in Monte Carlo with them, Joseph Zelman's speeches used to make her hair stand on end.

Before the war, Joseph had been married to Mina's eldest sister, Malka. Malka and Mina were distantly related to Renia Bensky.

"Malka was a different sort of woman," Renia used to say, mysteriously. "She was a perfect match for Joseph. She was as hungry as him in every department. My aunty used to tell me that Malka could never keep her hands off Joseph."

Mina was Malka's quiet, younger, taller, more awkward sister.

Mina had met Joseph in Germany, hours after he had heard that Malka had perished in Dachau. Mina already knew that Tadek and Henryk were dead. She had watched them die.

Two months after they were married, Mina and Joseph arrived in Australia. They spent their first month in Australia at Bonegilla.

The air at Bonegilla was thick with the smell of boiling mutton. The smell lingered in people's clothes and in their hair. Mina felt as though her skin had absorbed the stench of the mutton. Mina avoided going to the huge pit that was used as a toilet as much as she could. She would wait until her bladder ached or she felt ill before she went to the toilet at Bonegilla.

Jack had been conceived at Bonegilla. The barracks at Bonegilla were segregated. Mina slept in the middle of a large, crowded women's dormitory. One afternoon, Joseph had wound two sheets around four chairs to create an area of privacy around the camp stretcher that was Mina's bed. He had then made love to Mina. Mina had wept with humiliation. When they had both emerged, Mrs Lovic and Mrs Platt and Mrs Antman, who slept in adjoining beds, were grinning.

One morning in Bonegilla, Mina thought that she could hardly remember what it was like to live in a normal home. For almost ten years she had gone from one set of barracks to another. From labour camp to concentration camp to displaced persons camp, and now to this "Reception and Training Centre".

Mina tried to remember the small apartment in Warsaw where she and Tadek had lived. Just as the memory was beginning to warm her, Mrs Lovic called her to come to what was called an English class. Very few people in Bonegilla spoke English. It was unnecessary. Living in the camp you could have picked up German, Polish, Italian, Latvian, Russian or Yiddish, but not English. The English class, that day in Bonegilla, was learning to sing "Roaming in the Gloaming". Mina still knew the words.

Joseph Zelman had had a good head for business. He had

worked very hard, and now the Zelmans were very wealthy. Joseph had built large blocks of apartments all over Melbourne.

Joseph liked to live well. He went to the theatre, to the opera, to the cinema. Twice a year he flew to Switzerland to the Brechen-Bilt Clinic for a rest. He went to Germany for Alpine Air Inhalations at the Baden Rejuvenation Centre, and he went to Austria to have mud baths for his arthritis.

Joseph ate at the best restaurants and drank the best wines. Joseph dined at these restaurants with business colleagues, with friends, or with his son Jack.

Mina wouldn't eat in restaurants. She was suspicious of them. The few times she had eaten out, she had been ill afterwards.

When Joseph and Mina travelled, Mina ate raw vegetables, which she bought herself. Restaurant food was never clean enough for her. She had tried several times to explain this to Joseph. "I don't want to eat food that has been touched by other people," she used to say. "I don't know who has touched the food, and if the cook has washed his hands, or if he has got a running nose or a bad cough." Joseph was aggravated by Mina's attitude, but he never said anything.

Joseph felt that his own experiences during the war were so mild compared to Mina's that he could never criticise her. Joseph had been lucky. In 1939 he had been sent to a Russian labour camp. It may not have been a picnic, Joseph often thought, but when he compared it to Mina's wartime experiences he knew he had nothing to complain about.

In the centre of the sideboard in the Zelmans' dining room, in a large silver frame, was a small, yellowing, sepia photograph of a small boy. He had large, hooded eyes, chubby cheeks, and a sweet, bow-shaped mouth. The small boy looked just like Jack Zelman. He was Henryk Fischer, Mina's first son. The photograph was all Mina had from her life before the war.

When Jack was sixteen, he had told Lola that he didn't think he was Mina's real son. He thought that the boy in the photograph was Mina's real son. The boy in the photograph was never mentioned in the Zelman house. Jack didn't even know his name.

Jack had asked her if her parents had had any children before her. She had said no, even though she knew that her parents had had a stillborn son in the Lodz ghetto.

Lola didn't know why she had lied to Jack Zelman. Lola had woven so many of her own fantasies into the fabric of her parents' past that she could no longer remember what was true and what wasn't.

She had concocted a whole story about how her parents had been separated in Auschwitz, and had searched for each other after the war for six months. The story up to this point was true. From here, Lola added a scenario worthy of Cecil B. de Mille. Lola's story was that her mother and father had separately criss-crossed Europe by train looking for each other. They had often missed each other by seconds, and often passed each other on parallel train tracks going in opposite directions. After six months, neither had yet found out whether the other was alive. Finally, in Lola's story, her mother was asking a British soldier at a railway station in Germany if he had seen her husband.

"Yes I have, madam, and he's on that train," the soldier had replied, pointing to a train that was just pulling out of the station. But all was not lost. The British soldier drove Lola's mother to the next station and she boarded the train. She walked through the carriages looking for her husband. Then she saw him, and fainted.

The Master of Ceremonies, Nathan Spatt, tapped the side of the lectern with a teacup.

"Ladies and gentlemen! Ladies and gentlemen! Quiet, please. I am going to call on Mr Sol Spigal, our president, who shall say a vote of thanks to the many people who have helped to make today a memorable day."

"Jesus, look at all that saccharin," said Jack Zelman. Lola looked around at the tables. There were two bottles of saccharin for every four place settings. An avalanche of saccharin was about to be dropped into five hundred cups of coffee.

"It's always puzzled me why Jews are so fixated by saccharin," said Jack. "They've just eaten apple strudel and ice-cream, and chocolates, and now they're making up for that by not putting sugar into their coffee. It's madness."

"Yes, it's madness," agreed Lola.

Mr Sol Spigal had twenty-five minutes of thank-yous. Everybody from Melbourne had to be thanked. Everybody from Sydney had to be thanked. And, of course, the local committee from Canberra had to be thanked. Each individual was thanked, and the audience applauded each thank-you.

The Master of Ceremonies returned.

"And now we have something very special to end our very special day. We have the honour to have with us tonight the wonderful poet Lola Bensky, and she is going to read her wonderful poem again for us."

Lola stepped onto the platform. She was not so nervous now. She quietened herself for a minute. She took a deep breath, and began to read. There was an uproar in the hall.

"We can't hear. We can't hear," echoed around the room.

"I think the microphone is not working," said Nathan Spatt.

"I'll shout," said Lola.

What God Wants

Moishe Zimmerman's Wife

Ruthie Brot had a problem. She was trying to find a wife for her father. She finished applying her mascara and tousled her hair with her fingers. Her hair had a contemporary, messy look. To achieve that effect she had to mousse and scrunch her hair with her fingers, then blow-dry it upside down. After this, she sprayed her hair with hairspray, and shook her head.

The whole procedure took an hour. Now each strand of hair was suitably skewiff. Ruthie put on her leotards and waited for the girls. Every Tuesday at 9 a.m. Zoe and Golda and Ella came to Ruthie's for an aerobics class with Peter Jones. Peter Jones was everybody's fitness instructor. By 9 a.m. he had already conducted four aerobics sessions in Toorak.

Ruthie sat at her kitchen table and wondered how she could persuade her father to buy some new clothes. He seemed to think that not spending money on clothes made him superior. It had been five years since Ruthie's mother had died, and her father had refused to buy a single new item of clothing in that time.

"Is my daughter ashamed of me?" he would say every time Ruthie suggested they go shopping together. "I'm not a snob. I don't need to live in Toorak and I don't need to buy new clothes. I am happy with what I have got."

Ruthie took a deep breath. Not even her new leotards with their tummy-firming, elasticised insert made her feel better. She should be feeling good, she thought. She was thirty-eight. She was in quite good shape. She had had her breasts lifted and her tummy tucked. She was finally free of her children. They had finished school and

were both in Israel for a year. This was the year that she had fantasised about. She had had fantasies of going out dancing with Eddie and fucking all night. But Eddie was as preoccupied with his work as ever, and here she was, sitting at the kitchen table wondering how she could find a wife for her father.

"It doesn't have to be the love-match of the century," she had said to her father. "Just some company for you. Someone to go to the pictures with, someone to go for walks with."

"I don't like to walk," he had answered.

Ruthie had already had several match-making arrangements fall through or misfire. She had persuaded her father to accompany her to a lunch at Sofia Ritman's place.

"I have to go to lunch because she has asked so many times that it would be too rude if I refused," she said to her father. "She wants to say thank you to me for hosting that Wizo luncheon. Dad, I hear that Sofia Ritman's chulent is out of this world."

Sofia Ritman knew that a possible match was in the making. She had cooked chicken soup, chulent and kishke, and roast chicken and tsimmes.

Ruthie hadn't met Sofia before. Sofia had been in Surfers Paradise when Ruthie had hosted the luncheon. As soon as Ruthie set eyes on Sofia Ritman she knew that the whole thing had been a mistake. Sofia was short and fat. Moishe himself was short and fat, but he looked down on fat people. Bluma Zimmerman, Ruthie's mother, had been petite. Bluma had been very proud of her figure. She had never weighed more than seven and a half stone. Ruthie, who had never carried an excess pound, felt like an elephant next to her mother.

Ruthie had been so nervous at Sofia Ritman's lunch that she hadn't stopped eating. Sofia had been so nervous she hadn't stopped talking. And Moishe Zimmerman had sat there, wordlessly eating. For four days after the lunch Moishe complained to Ruthie that he felt sick.

"I did eat so much that I didn't sleep again last night. I had to get up in the middle of the night to take tablets. What are you trying to do to me, Ruthie? Are you trying to kill me?"

"Dad, I didn't force you to eat."

"You know, I am a pig," he said. "If the food is there in front of me I will eat it. I still feel shocking."

Ruthie hadn't felt too well herself. It had taken her a week to recover from that lunch.

Lots of people had made helpful suggestions to Ruthie about finding a wife for Moishe. Ruthie's mother-in-law, Minnie Brot, had said to her over and over again that Melbourne was full of Jewish widows. Yesterday Minnie had said, "Moishe Zimmerman isn't the biggest catch in the world, but it's a buyer's market out there. Moishe could choose whoever he likes. He should choose a rich woman. Why not have a rich wife? There's nothing wrong with money."

"I don't think Dad's interested in money," said Ruthie.

"Interested, shminterested. Everybody's interested in money. I heard that Mr Slonim is going to marry Janek Kovic's widow. Such a shame for two such rich people to marry each other. And in the meantime poor Mrs Shinkel doesn't have enough money to help her son buy a house," said Minnie.

"Maybe Moishe would like to meet Dunca Lipman," she went on. "She is slim. She is not too clever, but dear Moishe isn't Einstein."

Ruthie laughed. She liked Minnie. Minnie was so much more straightforward than anyone in her own family. Minnie said what she thought. In the Zimmerman family everything had to be interpreted and decoded.

"What about Moishe for yourself?" Ruthie asked Minnie. She had asked Minnie this before and Minnie had brushed the question aside.

"Ruthie darling, when my husband was alive I was happy to live with him," said Minnie. "It wasn't the biggest love match in the world, but I liked him and I was used to him. Now, to tell you the truth, I am happy by myself. I can smoke if I want to. If I clean the house, it stays clean. I have my girlfriends to play cards with. I prefer their company, you know. Maybe if I were a modern person I would be a lesbian. Who knows?"

Eddie Brot also had some suggestions for Moishe. "I think your father should go to Theodore Herzl Social Club," Eddie said to his wife.

"Eddie, you know my father has never belonged to a club in his life. I could never get him to go to a club," said Ruthie.

"Maybe you could go there one night with him," said Eddie. "Ronnie Blatt's neighbour met her husband there. Ronnie's neighbour was eighty-two and she had an artificial leg."

Ruthie felt that there was something offensive about Eddie using Ronnie Blatt's limbless neighbour as an example of the success that could be possible for her father, but she wasn't sure what it was. Ruthie wasn't sure about a lot of things about Eddie. He was developing a property in Surfers Paradise at the moment. Sufferers Paradise, he called it. He seemed to get more excited about his property development than he did about her. The development in their sex life was zilch. They had been fucking the same way for years. When Eddie wanted to fuck, he came to bed without his pyjamas on. She then masturbated him for a few minutes, and then they fucked for another minute or two.

Ruthie wasn't sure why she shaved and waxed and tanned and tinted herself. She wasn't even sure why she'd bothered to have her tummy tucked. Nobody touched it. Although when they all changed after their aerobics classes Zoe and Ella and Golda always admired Ruthie's figure.

Today, after aerobics, Zoe stayed for a cup of coffee. "What's wrong, Ruthie love? You look so downcast," she said.

"It's not any one particular thing, I don't think," said Ruthie. "My father is driving me mad. He looks more and more scruffy. He's hardly seeing anybody. I wish he'd find a nice woman, but I think that even the thought of going to the pictures with another woman feels to him like a gross disloyalty to my mother."

"The thing about you Jews," said Zoe, "is that you all complain endlessly about your families. You fight and argue and discuss with your mothers and fathers and brothers and sisters. But there you are, all together. You think you've got problems with your father? My father wouldn't give a shit if I dropped dead. I haven't spoken to him for ten years. I don't even know where he's living. Oh, Jesus, I'd better be off, I've got a dentist's appointment."

Zoe kissed Ruthie goodbye. "You want to have lunch with me tomorrow?" said Ruthie. "The forecast is for good weather. We could sunbake for an hour."

"OK," said Zoe.

Ruthie's phone rang. It was Moishe. "Ruthie, did you drop a yellow plate off on my porch?" he asked her.

"No, Dad, I haven't been out of the house today."

"Somebody dropped it off yesterday. I thought that maybe you thought that it was my plate and you brought it back to me. No? Never mind, Ruthie. Darling, what do you put in the washing machine to wash the clothes with?"

"Washing powder or liquid," said Ruthie, "Why, Dad? I thought that the cleaning lady was doing your washing."

"Yes, yes, the cleaning lady does the washing. But there is a woman from the flats next door, a Chinese woman I think she is, who asked me if she could use my washing machine because the laundromat is closed for renovations. So I said yes, but I don't know what to put in it."

"Dad, if she's been going to the laundromat she'll know what to put in it."

"Do you think I am stupid or something? Of course she will know what to put in it. I just want to make sure that I have got whatever it is that you use in the house."

"Well, I don't know. I usually buy Omo."

"I will buy Omo." Moishe hung up.

* *

Zoe and Ruthie lay on large towels on Ruthie's back lawn. It was perfect sunbaking weather — twenty-four degrees and a clear blue sky.

"I was thinking to myself yesterday," Ruthie said, "that I don't know why I diet and exercise. I don't know why I had my tummy tucked. It was so painful. It took me weeks to recover from the operation. No-one takes any notice of my beautiful new stomach. Eddie's more interested in screaming at his builder than creating any heat with me."

"Have the scars completely faded?" Zoe asked.

"Almost. Look, you can only see this thin line here."

"Can I touch your stomach?" said Zoe. "It looks so smooth."

"Of course you can," said Ruthie.

"It's so soft it feels like a child's skin," said Zoe. "I guess I'm used to men's stomachs. You know, Ruthie, I've been fucking with three different men this year. All married. Last week I thought it would almost be better to be celibate than to be always fucking with married men. Don't tell Golda. One of the men is her sister's husband."

"You're fucking with Abe Lipshitz?" said Ruthie. "I don't believe it. How could you?"

"What do you mean how could I? How could I fuck with Golda's sister's husband?" said Zoe.

"No, I don't mean how could you fuck with Golda's sister's husband, I mean how could you fuck with Abe Lipshitz? He's so revolting."

"He's not revolting," said Zoe. "He's actually very tender. He kisses me so delicately. It almost makes me cry. And he'll lick me into an orgasm. I've never had a man who would do that. My husband would have died rather than put his head between my legs."

"Abe Lipshitz does that to you?" said Ruthie. "God, Eddie would think it was perverted. I wonder what it feels like?"

"It feels fabulous," said Zoe.

* *

Ruthie, Eddie and Moishe were eating at Scheherezade. They ate at Scheherezade every Sunday night.

"Ruthie, do you have any old clothes?" Moishe asked.

"Of course I've got old clothes. What do you want old clothes for?"

"For Esmeralda, the Chinese girl from the flats," said Moishe.

"A Chinese girl called Esmeralda? That's an unusual name for a Chinese," said Eddie.

"Yes," said Moishe. "She's very poor. She's got only two skirts and two tops. She was brought to Australia by a terrible man. She was a post office bride."

"Do you mean a mail-order bride?" said Ruthie.

"I think she's probably Filipino, not Chinese. Esmeralda is definitely not a Chinese name," said Eddie.

"Chinese, Filipino, what difference does it make? She is very poor," said Moishe.

"OK, Dad," said Ruthie. "I'll put together a bag of clothes for her."

"Thank you, Ruthie," said Moishe. "Ruthie, there was another yellow plate on my porch yesterday. Somebody is returning plates to the wrong address. I don't know what to do."

"Don't worry about it, Moishe," said Eddie. "You're making a profit on the deal. You're two plates up."

"That's a good way of looking at it," said Moishe.

Zoe and Ruthie sat in Ruthie's kitchen after aerobics. Ella and Golda hadn't made it to the class this morning.

"Do you think Peter Jones is gay?" Ruthie asked Zoe.

"Why do you think he is gay? Just because he takes aerobics classes?"

"No," said Ruthie. "I thought he might be gay because he felt so comfortable to be with."

"I don't think he's gay," said Zoe.

"How are things with you and Abe Lipshitz?" Ruthie asked.

"Abe is a real sweetheart," said Zoe. "Would you like to meet him?"

"Me meet Abe Lipshitz? What for?"

"Well, we may as well pool our resources. I come here for aerobics classes. I sunbake in your garden. So would you like to share Abe Lipshitz with me? I share him with his wife anyway. At least you're my friend and I'll be doing you a favour."

"Share Abe Lipshitz?" said Ruthie. "What do you mean?"

"I'll introduce you to him," said Zoe, "and if you two hit it off, he can be your lover as well as mine."

Ruthie, Zoe and Abe Lipshitz met for coffee at the Hyatt Hotel. Abe Lipshitz was tall and small-boned. His thick lips looked at odds with his thin body. They were too lush and too red. Abe's lips looked as though they belonged to somebody else's face. Maybe somewhere, Ruthie thought, there was a strongfeatured, sturdy man wearing a pair of pale thin lips. Maybe God had slipped up. Slipped up. The pun had been unintentional. She was far too nervous to make puns. Abe did have a quiet sort of authority, Ruthie thought, despite his stringbean shape.

The three of them had been talking for about twenty minutes when Zoe announced that she had to go. Ruthie was terrified. "Zoe, don't go, please," she said.

"You'll be fine," said Zoe. "Goodbye."

Oh God, thought Ruthie. She felt a bit sick. What was she doing? She tried to pull herself together. She was a normal person. She was a mother. She was a wife. She felt like a devious pervert. A sexually depraved monster. She thought that she probably smelt promiscuous.

"You're a barrister, aren't you?" she said to Abe.

"Yes," he said. "And what do you do?"

"Nothing much, really. I wanted to do law. In fact I did do first year law at Monash, but I got pregnant and Eddie thought that I should leave uni." There, she had done it. She had been determined not to mention Eddie or the children, and it had taken her less than a minute to mention Eddie and a foetus. Eddie didn't feel all that present in her marriage, so why did he feel so omnipresent at even the prospect of an affair?

"I feel a bit tawdry," she said. "I'm here because Zoe said that you were a fabulous lover, and I thought that maybe I shouldn't die without knowing, just once, what it was like to have a fabulous lover."

"Are you sick?" Abe asked.

"No, I'm not dying, I'm just getting old."

"Would you like me to book a room here? I think we'd both feel more comfortable if we were somewhere private."

"OK."

Abe was gone for ten minutes. He came back and handed her a room key. "Meet me in 505 in five minutes. That sounds very clandestine, doesn't it?"

Five minutes later, Ruthie and Abe were sitting opposite each other in room 505.

"We'll just talk," said Ruthie.

"That's fine," said Abe.

"Tell me about your wife," said Ruthie.

"I like my wife," said Abe. "I've been married to her for twenty-two years. Since I was twenty. We met when I was sixteen and she was thirteen. I can't remember my life when she wasn't a part of it."

"Do you still fuck with her?"

"Sometimes. Not very often. We're very affectionate, though."

"And what about Zoe?"

"I don't really know why I said to Zoe that I would meet you," Abe said. "I think I was flattered. I've been very straight all my life. I hadn't ever slept with another woman until I met Zoe. I had been monogamous and faithful. I didn't even know I was a good lover until Zoe told me. I was forty-one, and I didn't know I was a good lover. Shall we take our clothes off and just touch each other? I feel very comfortable with you."

Three and a half hours later, Abe Lipshitz kissed Ruthie goodbye. He kissed her goodbye for five minutes. He gave her a last quick kiss before the lift doors opened. They left the lift in separate directions.

Ruthie drove home. She rang Zoe. "Zoe, I am fucked. I am so fucked. I have been fucked and fucked. Zoe, I am so happy. Abe said that maybe you would like to join us next time?"

"Really?" said Zoe. "I'll think about it. I can't speak now; my ex-husband has turned up. I'll speak to you tomorrow. I'm glad that it all went well."

"Went well?" said Ruthie. "I can still feel his cock in me. And if I close my eyes I can still feel his mouth, and Zoe, I can smell him. I've got his cum all over me. He rubbed it on my breasts. He said it was very good for breast tissue. Is that true? Does he do that to you?"

"I don't like having my breasts touched," said Zoe.

"Oh, I'm sorry," said Ruthie.

Moishe dropped in to see Ruthie on his way home from work. At seventy-five, he still worked a full day at Harry's Fabrics. Moishe had been working for Harry King for forty-five years. Harry himself was now seventy-eight. Harry worked with the customers, and Moishe did the paperwork in the office.

"You look well, Ruthie," said Moishe.

"So do you, Dad." Moishe really did look young for his age, she thought. "Would you like to stay and eat with us tonight?"

"That is nice of you, Ruthie, but to tell you the truth I have got so much food at home. Esmeralda cooked me a dish of noodles in soup. She wanted to repay me for using the washing machine and the vacuum cleaner. She borrows the vacuum cleaner on Fridays. I didn't need any thanks but I couldn't be rude. I tell you the soup was not bad. The noodles were nearly the same as the lokshen Mum used to make."

Something about Moishe's sentence jarred Ruthie. It took her a few minutes to work out what had disturbed her. It had been the mention of her mother and Esmeralda in the same sentence. No, she decided, she was being ridiculous. She felt so happy. Nothing could dent her happiness. As she waved goodbye to her father she put her hand inside her shirt. Her breasts were covered in a light, crusty coating of Abe Lipshitz's sperm.

On Tuesday, after their aerobics class, Golda looked at Ruthie. "Ruthie, you look wonderful. What's up? Are you having an affair?"

"Don't be stupid, Golda," said Ruthie. The question had depressed her. Why did everyone assume that you only blossomed if you were fucking someone other than your husband?

"You're right, though, I do feel good. I feel terrific, actually. I'm thinking of studying something next year. I might try to do two law subjects."

"Weren't you going to do law when you were at school?"

"Yes, I was," said Ruthie.

That night, Ruthie got a phone call from Sofia Ritman. Sofia sounded hysterical.

"Your father is a very rude man," she said. "Somebody should teach him some manners. If somebody does something nice for you, you should say a thank you," she shouted.

"What happened, Mrs Ritman?" Ruthie asked.

"I baked your father some biscuits. Beautiful almond biscuits. I didn't want to make a big fuss about them. I left them near his front door. So, so he doesn't want me for a wife, but why should he be so rude to me? Not one thank you did I hear from him for these biscuits." Mrs Ritman was almost crying now.

"Mrs Ritman," said Ruthie, "did you leave them on yellow plates?"

"Yes."

"Someone must have eaten them," said Ruthie, "because the plates were empty when my father saw them. And I don't want to upset you, but how was my father supposed to know that they were from you?"

"Ruthie, he complimented me very much on my almond biscuits. Don't you remember? He said they were the best he had eaten. I thought for sure he would know who had sent them."

The next day, Ruthie told Moishe about Mrs Ritman. "She is an idiot," said Moishe. "Who leaves a plate of biscuits on a porch? Who leaves a plate of biscuits in a house where there is a dog? It is a shame, because they were really very good, her almond biscuits. I don't think the dog did appreciate what good almond biscuits he was eating.

"Ruthie, darling," said Moishe, "I have something very important to tell you. I wanted you to be the first to hear the good news. Esmeralda and I are getting married."

Ruthie had to sit down. What was Moishe saying? "You and Esmeralda are getting married? But she's so young. She's probably my age. And she's not Jewish."

"Jewish, not Jewish," said Moishe. "What does it matter? I lived all my life as a Jew. Now, I'll see what it is like not to be so Jewish. Ruthie, Esmeralda is not taking the place of your mother. If I had married Renia or Sofia or Rivka your mother, wherever she is, God rest her soul, would have been uncomfortable. But Bluma will be happy to see me married to Esmeralda. Bluma always liked me to look nice. You didn't even notice, my dear daughter, that I have got new clothes."

Ruthie looked at her father. He was right; she hadn't noticed. She had been aware that he had been in a good mood most of the time, but she hadn't noticed how well he had been looking. Now she looked at him. He looked terrific. His hair was combed. His wild silver waves no longer wandered off in different directions. He was wearing a new navy knitted shirt. He even had new shoes on.

"Mum will always be my real wife," he said, "but Esmeralda and I will look after each other."

Suddenly, it seemed all right to Ruthie. Esmeralda and Moishe were going to look after each other. Wasn't that what life was about? They were all trying to look after each other in the best way they could. Things mightn't be perfect. They mightn't be the way they should be, but they were all trying.

"It's a very good idea to look after each other, Dad," she said. "Now, let's talk about the wedding. Eddie and I will make such a beautiful wedding for you and Esmeralda. Bring Esmeralda around tomorrow night and we will all talk about it."

Something Shocking

Susan Silver was in the front garden of her house at 24 Walnut Avenue, Caulfield. She was standing on the third top rung of a large ladder. Hanging from a hook at the side of the ladder was a pot of Hot Ochre gloss paint.

She was concentrating intensely as she applied the final touches of paint. She hadn't looked down once in the two hours that she had been painting. Heights made her dizzy. She couldn't sit in the dress circle at the theatre. She didn't even like the stalls to have too steep a slope.

Susan smoothed the brushmarks out of the last stroke of paint. She was amazed that she had done it. She had never even stood on a ladder before. She put the brush into the pot. She would get one of the boys to carry it down later. She trembled slightly as she climbed down the ladder, but she was happy. She felt proud of herself.

Her father would have been proud of her if he were still alive, she thought. He had often called her a mouse. "You are frightened of the dark, you are frightened of strangers, you are frightened of heights, you are frightened of me. What's there to be frightened of? We are living in a free country. Every day the sun shines and the sky is blue. I think your mother gave birth to a mouse, not a daughter," he would say.

She had loved her father. She knew that he was a coarse man. He looked coarse, too. He refused to buy new clothes. He wore the last pair of trousers that he owned for twenty years. There were brown stains on the seat of the trousers. It amused him enormously that they looked like shit stains.

He refused to cut the hairs from his nose. They protruded from his nostrils like wiry silver brushes. He had a sharp word for everyone. But Susan loved him. She knew that underneath the gruffness and the indifference he was soft-hearted and easily moved.

The day he'd died she'd thought that she was going to die too. Her mother had said to her after the minyan. "You know, he was very harsh to you. Always. From the time you were a small child. And you loved him. From the time you were a small child you loved him. You could see that he had another side to him. Your brother couldn't see it, and your dear sister couldn't see it, and I, dear God forgive me, I couldn't always see it. But you always knew it, so you can be at peace with yourself, Susan."

Susan examined her paintwork. It looked good. Hot Ochre had been the right choice. It looked just right against the matt brown brick work. Susan took a deep breath. The air was thick with the sweet smell of jasmine. It was mid-spring and Walnut Avenue was perfumed with the scent of jasmine.

Wendy Fairweather came out of her house across the road, saw Susan and walked towards her. Wendy and Susan had been nodding to each other for nine years.

"Hello, Susan," said Wendy. "I noticed you were doing some painting. That sign you've painted on your house, is it religious?"

"It says 'My husband is shtooping a shikse'. In English that means my husband is fucking a non-Jewish woman." Wendy Fairweather flushed and rushed off.

"What is that Susan Silver doing?" Malka Berger asked her sister Bronka.

"I think she is painting the outside of her house," said Bronka.

"What? Is she crazy or something? Her husband doesn't earn enough money to pay for a painter? I heard he is a millionaire. He should be ashamed of himself."

The Berger sisters continued walking up Walnut Avenue until they were in front of the Silvers' house. They read the sign at the same time. For two minutes the sisters stood, open-mouthed.

"She should be ashamed of herself," said Bronka.

"It is something shocking," said Malka.

"Do you mean that it is something shocking that she painted such a thing on her house?" Bronka asked her sister.

"Of course," said Malka.

"I thought that maybe you thought that it was something shocking that Mr Silver is shtooping a shikse."

"Everybody is shtooping somebody, dear Bronka, so what is the big occasion?"

"They looked like such a happy couple," said Chaim Berman to his son Michael, who was visiting from Israel. "I always saw them walking in Acland Street together on Sunday afternoon. They used to go to the Cosmos bookshop and they used to stop in front of the Monarch cake shop and look at the cakes in the window for quite a long time."

"Dad," Michael replied, "you think that the family who eats cakes together stays together. You're so naive. Harry Silver is having a mid-life crisis. His little dickie got weighed down with chulent and kishke and children and mothers-in-law. He took a look at it one day and thought that he better use it while he can."

Chaim Berman wondered, again, how he had fathered such a coarse son. After the war Chaim had decided that the only thing worth teaching a child was tolerance. Tolerance for his fellow man. And what sort of a child did that teaching produce? A bigot. A bighead. Michael was living in Israel, Chaim thought, not out of any noble motives but because his American wife's parents needed a family member to keep an eye on the Israeli branch of their family business. So Michael sat in Tel Aviv and ran the head office of an American car-rental company.

Chaim felt sad. He had enjoyed talking to Harry and Susan Silver on Sundays. And despite the fact that he himself had been divorced for more years than he had been married, he still had high hopes for the state of marriage.

"I knew something was up," said Susan's mother, Minnie Brot. "That Harry has been looking ten years younger. He walks with a different step. I said to myself, 'Minnie, something has happened.' It's not a good sign when a middle-aged man starts to look younger. You can make a bet for sure something is up. He is shtooping somebody, but not his wife. Everybody is shtooping their wife. Does it make them look younger? I don't know what you can do, but I don't think this notice that you have painted on the house is going to help things at all. Where is Harry?"

"He's in Sydney on business, but I know that she is there with him," said Susan. "I rang the hotel and they said that he was out. I asked if Mrs Silver was in, and they said that she was out too."

"Oy, my Susan, we needed this like a hole in the head," said Minnie. "Trouble with one's children never stops. Small children, small problems. Big children, big problems. And now I've got a son-in-law who's shtooping a shikse. To tell you the truth, Susan, Harry didn't look to me like he was someone who was too excited about shtooping anyway."

Harry Silver lay in bed next to Diane Burnett. She looked so peaceful. Jews rarely looked peaceful, thought Harry. Her breasts were so pink. There was a pinkish tinge to her hair. He wondered if that was what was called strawberry blonde. He didn't know whether Diane was awake or not. He was in a daze. He could still taste her in his mouth and on his hands. He felt enveloped by the smell of her breasts and her thighs. He could smell her body whether they were together or apart.

She opened her eyes and smiled at him. He had rarely felt so at peace with himself. He could feel the peace. It was a large, still space in his chest. Diane moved her left leg on top of him. She started rubbing his stomach and his thighs. She slid herself on top of him and lay there. They were connected from head to toe. Then she sat up, astride him, and eased him into her.

"Don't do anything," she said. "Just lie there." She made love to him until they both came.

Afterwards, she kissed him on his fingertips, behind his ears, on his feet. She put her fingers inside his mouth, inside his bum. He felt as though she had entered his bloodstream and was travelling through him.

"I feel insatiable," she said. "I feel as though I'm making up for lost time."

"Tell me about your husband and his special spiritual line," he said.

"It's called kundilini," she said. "He was preserving his kundilini. By not fucking me he was saving his sperm and strengthening his soul. He joined a yoga group twelve years ago. Before that he was so randy he'd fuck anything that moved. When he joined this yoga centre I thought that it was a good move. He didn't know what he wanted to do, and I couldn't see any harm in him meditating. It seemed to give his life a focus. He became completely involved in the centre. He went to India to study at an ashram for six months. When he came back he told me that he needed to be celibate in order to become a higher being. For ten years I cooked and cleaned and brought up the children while he ran yoga courses. Sometimes I used to die for him to touch me, but mostly I felt so fucked by the children and the nappies and the school lunches that I was glad not to have anything more to do at night.

"The day I found out he'd been fucking this Indian yoga teacher he'd met in India, I drove into the centre and walked into the evening meditation group. It was their biggest session of the day, the 6 p.m. meditation session. I was hysterical. I stood in the middle of the rostrum and shouted. I can still remember word for word. I shouted: 'John Burnett is an arsehole. He hasn't fucked his wife for ten years. He's been celibate. He's been preserving his kundilini. But some of his fucking kundilini has been leaking into Shanti Shankhar for ten years. For ten years he's been fucking Shanti Shankhar, ladies and gentlemen.'

"That was three years ago. When you touched me on the shoulder that night at Florentino's, it was the first time in years that I wanted a man to continue touching me."

Harry didn't understand why he had put his hand on Diane's shoulder that night at Florentino's. Diane had been there with her father. Harry was having a business dinner with a client, Abe Grossberg. Abe was an old friend of Diane's father, and he had invited Diane and her father to join them for a drink.

Harry had thought of nothing else but Diane since that night. He was addicted. He missed meetings. He didn't return calls. He stood up clients. For thirty years he had had a reputation as one of the best lawyers in Melbourne. Now, nothing mattered. His business, his reputation, his wife, his family. It was as if his desire for Diane took up all of his feelings. There were no other feelings left. He just wanted to be with her, to be part of her.

"I'm hungry," said Harry. "You must be hungry too. Let's go to Doyles at Circular Quay. I really feel like seafood. Let's get dressed."

As he was getting dressed, he felt a flicker of his old self return to him. The old Harry Silver. The one who until three months ago had worn white boxer shorts, not these black Calvin Klein stretch underpants. The old Harry Silver wasn't interested in underpants. He was a modest, well-spoken, responsible lawyer. He was a fifty-six-year-old family man. He was on the boards of the Victorian State Opera, the National Gallery and the City General Hospital. He was married to Susan Silver. Susan, who was so quiet that her own mother referred to her as having a gentile nature. Harry had been proud of Susan's reserve. He was proud of her English. She had a very upper-crust English accent. "Mrs Posh", her father used to call her.

It was Susan who had suggested that Harry go to elocution classes. Harry had been nineteen when he had met Susan. He had been in Australia for three years. He had taught himself to speak English in the DP camp in Germany. In 1949, he topped his

English class at Melbourne Boys High in his final year of high school.

When he met Susan he was already studying law. He also worked at night as a car-park attendant at the Southern Star Hotel. For five years he had studied for his law exams in the cold, neon-lit attendant's booth. The booth was still there. Harry sometimes visited it. Twice a week in his final year of law, Susan manned the booth while he went to elocution classes. Now Harry spoke beautifully. He spoke as beautifully as any of the men he sat on committees with. He spoke so beautifully he could pass for a gentile. When he first went into practice he considered changing his name to Harold. He didn't really know why he hadn't. Harry was already far enough removed from Chaim. Chaim Silberberg, he had been. He became Harry Silver when he arrived in Australia on 3 September 1946.

He watched Diane put on her bra. She was so pale and pink. Peach coloured. She had peach coloured nipples. He walked over to her and took her breasts out of her bra. He put her right breast in his mouth. She sat there quietly and cradled his head while he sucked.

At Doyles, they sat at a table right on the water's edge, overlooking the Opera House. Harry ordered oysters and crayfish. Forbidden fruit.

"Isn't the Opera House the most beautiful building?" said Diane. But Harry couldn't think about the beauty of the Opera House. He moved his chair closer to Diane. He put his hand under her skirt. He drove himself wild. He felt demented. He wanted to push his hand deeper and deeper insider her.

"Let's go back to the hotel," he said. The oysters arrived at the table just as they cancelled their order.

He put his fingers inside her again in the taxi. She looked utterly happy, utterly at ease. In the hotel he licked her and fucked her. He felt delirious. He licked her eyes, her feet. He wanted to put his whole head inside her.

At midnight she said she was hungry.

"Should I order some oysters and crayfish from room service?" she asked.

"That's a terrific idea," he said. He groaned. "I've got to have a piss, but I'm not sure if I can get up." They were lying on a black and maroon rug on the floor.

"Don't," she said. "Just piss here. On top of me. I'll clean it up later. Go on, just piss. Everything else has flowed out of you."

"I can't," he said. "I'll go to the toilet."

"Just piss here," she said. "I want to see the piss coming out of you. I want to feel it on my body. Come on, piss, piss, piss."

For the first time in the three months that they had been together, Harry felt uneasy. "I'll just go to the toilet," he said. In the toilet he felt sick. He began to sweat. He sat there trying to stem the nausea. What was wrong with him? Probably guilt, he thought. This feeling of infinite freedom was too good to be true. There had to be a price. And this was the price. He had no chest pains; otherwise he would have been sure he was having a heart attack. Didn't middle-aged men have heart attacks if they fucked too vigorously?

Diane came into the bathroom. "God, you look awful. Let me get you a drink. I'm sorry if I pressured you. It was only a whim. Would you like an Alka Seltzer?" Harry drank the Alka Seltzer.

He still felt sick. He started to cry. Tears ran down his face. He hadn't cried since he was a child. Diane stroked his back. Her touch made him feel worse. "I think it would be better if I sat here alone for a few minutes," he said. He sat in the bathroom by himself. He kept crying. Diane came in and sat on the floor. She looked tearful.

"It's not you, Diane," he said. "It's nothing to do with you. It's something that happened in my past. Something that I've never talked about."

"Please tell me," said Diane.

"You know, not even my wife knows about this," he said. Not even my wife, he repeated to himself. He had given Susan an importance in that statement that he hadn't accorded her in real life for months. For three months he had been so careless. He had booked hotel rooms on his credit cards. He had sent Diane flowers and books. He had hired cars. He had disappeared. All with no explanation. No subterfuge. He had separated himself from Susan. Now, when he was crying, he was talking about "my wife". He bent over the toilet bowl. He thought he was going to throw up.

Diane was crying. She looked lost and bewildered. "Don't cry, Diane. It's not you, it's me. It is such a messy story, such a heap of shit, that I wouldn't know what to tell you about it. And maybe you're too young," he said.

"Too young. I feel ancient, Harry. I'm thirty-eight. Please tell me," she said.

"In the forty years that I've been in Australia I haven't told anyone," he said. "When I was ten, my father was shot by the Nazis and my eight-year-old brother and I were taken to Buchenwald. Have you ever heard of Buchenwald? It was a concentration camp in Germany. In Weimar. The house that Goethe used to live in was near Buchenwald. There was a tree that Goethe used to rest under when he went for his walks. They built Buchenwald around that tree. It was a large old oak tree. I often used to wonder what Goethe would have said if he could have seen what was going on around this tree.

"On our first night in Buchenwald, a guard took my brother and me and another boy to his cubicle. He made us undress and lie on the floor. Then he pissed on us. I bit him on the leg and he clubbed me so hard with his rifle that I was unconscious for two days. My brother carried me back to our bunk. The SS and the kapos had their choice of the prettiest boys. They were called 'doll boys'.

"Buchenwald was a very good posting for the SS. The Commandant, Koch, was fleecing his party. Instead of documenting everything that was being taken from the prisoners, he was pocketing a lot of the loot. He was a multi-millionaire. He had the prisoners build anything that he fancied. Buchenwald had a mirrored riding hall for Frau Koch, who liked to ride horses. The prisoners also built a wild game preserve. They had deer, wild boar, bears, tigers, foxes. Commandant Koch liked to amuse himself by throwing prisoners into the bear cages. The prisoners built a zoo, too. The zoo had monkeys, pheasants, and even a rhinoceros. The SS opened the game preserve to the public. They advertised it locally and made quite a profit from sightseers.

"Frau Koch, Ilse Koch was her name, used to go riding in the riding hall nearly every morning. She was always fucking some guard or other. I heard that she liked to fuck close to her horses, in the riding hall. She liked the band of prisoners to play music for her while she rode. She was so evil that her evil stood out in the middle of all the evil. She loved tattoos. If she saw an interesting tattoo on a prisoner she would ask to have it. The prisoner would be killed and the tattoo delivered. Every prisoner who had a tattoo in Buchenwald was catalogued. The pathology department was very skilled at skin removal. They treated the skin in two ways. They either made it transparent or they tanned it so that it became tough like leather.

"One of Frau Koch's favourite lampshades came from the skin of a man from our village. It was a tattoo that said 'Hansel and Gretel'. The base of the lampshade was made from his bones, or maybe they were someone else's bones, I'm not sure. Bones were something else they were very good with in Buchenwald. The scientists in Buchenwald were taught by somebody who had been to Africa how to shrink heads. These shrunken heads were given by the SS as special presents."

"What happened to your brother?" asked Diane.

"He was transported to Auschwitz in 1944, and I have been on my own ever since," he said. He felt exhausted. His throat hurt. His eyes ached. How could he say he was alone? He had Susan and he had the two boys. He even had Minnie Brot. As a mother-in-law she wasn't too bad. How could he say he was alone?

Susan had often said that part of him was missing, was not available to her. She only ever said it, he thought, when they were making love. One of the things he had found very attractive about Susan was the quiet crisp way she fucked. She was hungry enough to want him, but she was distant. She didn't drag him inside her. Making love with Susan, he could feel comfortably separate. Intact. In no danger of disappearing.

He felt so alone. His legs shook. His breath smelt. He felt sorry for Diane. He looked at her. She was sitting very still.

"Diane, love, I'm very tired," he said. "I've got to go home."

Not a Simple Matter

Ruthie Brot and Abe Lipshitz were in the Dame Nellie Melba Suite of the Southern Star Hotel. Abe was talking to Ruthie. Ruthie was trying not to listen. She was playing with his balls. She loved them. She loved their weightiness and their warmth. She loved their smell.

"Ruthie," said Abe, "I want to tell you something. Ruthie, I want to marry you."

Ruthie slid further down the bed. She burrowed her face in between Abe's legs. She and Abe had just made love. She was feeling calm. She didn't want anything to intrude on this stillness.

"Come and kiss me," said Ruthie. "Kiss me and rub my feet."

"Did you hear what I said, Ruthie?" Abe asked.

"I heard," said Ruthie, "but couldn't we just kiss each other?"

"Is that what you want? That we kiss each other twice a week and make love twice a week, and never work out what we're doing?"

"We know what we're doing. We're feeling fabulous together. We're fucking each other and loving each other. I never want to stop being fucked by you. Sometimes at home I think of you and I almost come just thinking of you. That's not bad for a thirty-eight-year-old mother of two. That's not bad for a good Jewish girl who's never fucked with anyone more than once a week, and that was with her husband. Abe, I adore you. I've been so happy since we've been together. Why can't we just stay together like this? I don't know that there are too many married couples who are as happy together as we are. Abe, you've got such a beautiful mouth, come and lick me. Lick me and then we can fuck again."

"Oh, Ruthie," said Abe as he lowered himself onto her.

"Why don't you leave Eddie?" said Zoe. "The boys are old enough to get over it. Christ, they'll probably both leave home in the next year or so anyway, so you can't fall back on that old excuse of staying together for the children. My parents stayed together for the children. It was a fabulous sacrifice, a real gift. We had the privilege of watching their hatred for each other every day."

"I don't hate Eddie," said Ruthie. "I love him. I've loved him for a long time. And Eddie and I are not at all like your parents. We're never nasty to each other."

"Yes, but you and Eddie are like two old friends," said Zoe. "You don't fuck much with each other. You don't even talk all that excitedly to each other. I don't think that's a good role model for children. They end up settling for the same thing in their relationships. They think it's the only way to live."

"Zoe, you know something funny?" said Ruthie. "About a month ago, Eddie and I had our first good fuck in about fifteen years. We were chatting in bed. I had my arm around him. I've felt much more affectionate towards Eddie since I've been with Abe. Anyway, out of the blue, Eddie took off my nightie, turned me over and fucked me from behind. It stunned me. I was so surprised that I was almost too embarrassed to look at him afterwards. It was a very strange thing to share that heat and urgency. Eddie and I have never seen it in each other. I felt guilty and confused afterwards. I felt as though I had been unfaithful to Abe. When I'm with Abe I don't feel unfaithful to Eddie."

"Did you tell Abe that you fucked with Eddie?" said Zoe.

"No," said Ruthie, "because I knew it would upset him, and I didn't really think it would happen again. And it hasn't. To listen to me you would think that my whole existence revolves around fucking. Well, it doesn't."

"What does it revolve around? Love?"

"I think when you stopped fucking with Abe, Abe and I started falling in love with each other. While you and I were both seeing Abe, the fucking between Abe and me was fabulous, but there was no extra involvement. It all felt a bit radical and sophisticated. Two girlfriends sharing a lover. I know we didn't fuck him at the same time, but it all still felt a bit wild and a bit unreal."

"You've really blossomed since you and Abe have been together," said Zoe. "You're almost a different person. Look at you, you're doing two law subjects. You're already a tenth of a lawyer. You look fabulous. You've always looked fabulous, but now you look so alive. You even speak more speedily. Isn't that a far cry from the Ruthie Brot of a year ago?"

"Yes, you're right. I can't believe how much things have changed. Everybody I meet tells me how I look terrific. And I feel as high as a kite when I'm at uni."

"So, if you love Abe, why don't you leave Eddie?"

"I don't know. How do you know what love is?" said Ruthie.

Ruthie had asked Abe that question last week.

"I love you," he had said, "and to me that is what love is. It's what I feel for you. I love you and I want to be with you."

"But what about Dora?" she asked.

"I still love Dora, and I'll always look after her. I'll make sure she has everything she needs," he said.

"What if she needs you?" Ruthie asked.

"Then she'll have me as a friend."

"What if she needs you for sex?"

"She's never needed me for sex," said Abe. "We didn't need each other for sex. Now I've been lucky enough to meet someone who fills me with passion. Dora might even meet someone else. I feel sorry for her settling for such a sexless life at her age. She's not even forty."

"I know," said Ruthie. "She's the same age as me."

"You love me, Ruthie, don't you?" said Abe. "I know that you do. I can feel it in the way you hold me and pull me inside you. I can see that you love me every time you say goodbye to me. I can see that it's not easy for you to say goodbye. I can see that it's not easy for you to disengage yourself from me and go home. You love me."

"I do love you, Abe," she said. "I feel overwhelmingly happy when I'm with you. I feel a real sense of myself for the first time in my life. Before, I used to think I was here to look good, to be a mother, to be a wife, but not to be a person. And because I wasn't really a person, I wasn't really a wife, or probably not even a mother. The only thing I did properly was look good. But why can't we just leave things as they are? I'm happy, you're happy, Dora's happy and Eddie's happy."

"We can't, because I'm not happy. I love you. I want to hold you every night. I want to go to the pictures with you. I want to go out to dinner with you. I want to walk with you. I want to go to Paris and New York with you. I want to fuck you in the morning and fuck you again at night. I want to kiss you goodnight every night. I want to live with you. Don't you love me this much too?"

"I do," Ruthie said. She was crying now. "I do love you, but I don't know that I know too much about love. I love you. I love Eddie, I love my father, I love my kids, I love my mother-in-law. How do you know who you love more? And should your love for one person hurt the other people that you love? How do you know what love is?" After this, Abe had cried too.

"I'm not an expert on love," said Zoe. "You only have to take one look at my ex-husband to see that I haven't made fabulous decisions about love. Even now, with Mike, I'm a bit worried that he's too like my ex-husband. But I still feel head-over-heels in love with him. For the whole six months that I was with Abe, before you were involved, I never felt that I was in love with him. Yet he's got all the qualities I'd want in a human being. But, bingo, as soon as I'd gone out with Mike once, I was a goner. So, I don't know. All I know is that you and Abe seem to have everything going for you. I could feel it between you."

"You're the only person who's seen us together," said Ruthie.

"Well, trust me," said Zoe. "There was a heat and an energy between you and Abe that I don't think too many people have. And it's not just the heat of fucking, Ruthie, otherwise I'd never say you should leave Eddie. I don't think you should throw that heat away, Ruthie, because the rest of life can get pretty tepid."

Zoe laughed at her own clever sentence. Ruthie could see that she felt certain about the advice she was giving.

Ruthie wished she could talk to someone else about her dilemma. Who did people go to when they needed to talk? To a friend? It was too dangerous to talk to anyone except Zoe. Melbourne was so small that it was a minor miracle that she and Abe hadn't already been discovered. Who did people talk to? To a psychiatrist? She didn't have a psychiatrist. To a rabbi? It wasn't the sort of thing you could talk to a rabbi about. She had never been to a rabbi in her life. She wondered what had made her think of it now.

Ruthie talked to her hairdresser. Valerie had been cutting Ruthie's hair for ten years. Ruthie invented a fictitious friend, Vicky. For an hour she talked to Valerie about Vicky's problems.

"If I were Vicky," said Valerie, "I'd get a good lawyer right now and make sure that she gets what she deserves from that marriage. Is Vicky's husband as successful as Eddie?"

"I think so," said Ruthie. "You don't think maybe Vicky should stay with her husband?"

"No," said Valerie. "She's had twenty years to sort things out with her husband. Things don't get better after twenty years, they get worse. If they're not having all that much to do with each other in the bed department now, it's not going to be better in ten years. You can't teach an old horse new tricks."

"But Vicky's husband isn't an old horse," said Ruthie.

"Well, he is when he's with Vicky," said Valerie. "Maybe if he was with someone else he'd smarten up. Maybe he'd even smarten up enough to win the Melbourne Cup, but in Vicky's bed all he's interested in is grazing."

Ruthie felt confused. Valerie had lost her with all the talk about horses and horse-racing. Valerie's turn of phrase and her adept shuffle of metaphors and proverbs had often mystified Ruthie. Valerie had got it wrong anyway; the saying was "teach an old dog new tricks", not a horse. At least she had worked that out. She felt silly for wanting to talk about Abe and Eddie. It wasn't a subject you could canvass opinions on.

Yesterday her mother-in-law had said to her, "You've changed, Ruthie. In the last six months I've noticed a big change in you. You've grown up. I've always liked you, Ruthie, you know that, but lately you've become much more of a mensch. Dunca Lipman's grandson is in one of your tutorials at university, and he told Dunca that you ask the most interesting questions in the whole tutorial group. I'm very proud of you, Ruthie."

"Thank you, Minnie," Ruthie said. "You know I've always loved you. I said to my father that I would have married Eddie even if he hadn't been such a nice person just to get you as a mother-in-law."

"Ruthie darling," said Minnie, "you will always have me as a mother-in-law. Keep on looking after yourself. In life you have to look after yourself. Nobody else, no matter how much they love you, nobody else can really look after you."

Ruthie had spent the rest of that day wondering whether Minnie suspected anything, and, if so, whether there was a message in Minnie's conversation that Ruthie hadn't decoded.

Abe was making a cup of coffee in the kitchen of the Executive Suite of the Kismet Car-O-Tel. Sometimes choosing a place where they could be together was fun, and sometimes it was depressing. Abe had seen an ad for the Kismet in the Yellow Pages. The feature that had caught his eye was advertised in bold type across the top of the page. "Large Aquarium In Every Room," it read.

And it was true. Built into each bedhead was a big fish tank. Ruthie hadn't been able to stop laughing when she had first walked into the room. "Abe, these fish must be addled," she said. "All they ever see are people fucking. Do you think they've been corrupted by their environment?"

"I think they probably see more people sleeping than fucking," said Abe.

Ruthie counted the fish. "There are twenty-four fish in this tank. And they're so close to us. There's one that's watching me. I think I might feel inhibited with an audience of fish."

"I think we might manage to forget the fish," said Abe. "Anyway, we can be generous and share our good fortune with these fish. It will do the fish good to see people in love. It will elevate their spirits."

"Abe, look," said Ruthie, "we've got a vibrating bed."

"I know. When I booked I had to choose between the vibrating bed in the Executive Suite or the mirrored ceiling in the Honeymoon Suite. I felt a bit sleazy just making the choice."

"How do you think they decided which features to put in which room?" said Ruthie. "Do you think they thought that executives may just draw the line at a mirrored ceiling, but could cope with a vibrating bed? Maybe the vibrating mattress could be seen as an aid in relieving stress?"

Abe tried to turn the bed on. Nothing happened. "You wouldn't believe it!" he said. "You have to feed this bed twenty cents before it will vibrate. The mirrored ceiling is clearly for the more economical guests." Abe put twenty cents into the bed. The bed shook in a series of fits and starts. The aquarium also shook. The fish looked rattled. Ruthie started laughing again.

"I don't think we'd better put any more money in," she said. "The fish have probably got a permanent migraine. Poor bloody fish!"

Abe laughed too. "Ruthie, you look like a schoolgirl when you laugh," he said. "I love you. Do you get bored hearing me say that I love you?"

"No, never," said Ruthie.

"I've been thinking about you and Eddie," said Abe. "What you and Eddie have between you is what old friends have. With a bit of work, I think you should be able to keep everything that you've got with each other except the marriage. You could see him almost as often. You can still be parents together. He doesn't need you in the way that I need you. He doesn't need to talk to you four times a day. He doesn't need to touch you and to fuck you. And I do. I want to touch you and look at you and fuck you all the time. And you don't need him in the way that you need me."

Ruthie looked miserable. The room felt leaden and grey. The bed had stopped vibrating. The fish swam in slow motion, stunned by their bout with the bed.

"Abe, if it could be done without distressing anybody, I'd leave Eddie," she said. "It's true, I'm happier with you than I've ever been. I feel a different person. And I do love you. I think you're the most gorgeous person I've known in my whole life. I feel pampered with you. And I feel clever. For the first time in my life I feel clever. I feel so excited when I understand something difficult in a tutorial. Most of the kids in my tutorials are half my age. They look blase most of the time. But I feel almost hysterical with excitement."

"I remember feeling like that when I was at uni," said Abe.

"Yes, but you were eighteen, and maybe at eighteen it doesn't feel quite so miraculous," said Ruthie.

"No, it felt like a miracle to me," said Abe. "Here I was, Abe Lipshitz, son of Shlomo and Rooshka Lipshitz, who'd come to Australia with nothing, who'd come to Australia after six years in camps and ghettos. Here I was, their son, studying law at the best university in Melbourne. I felt as though I was the representative of hundreds of dead Lipshitzes, and I had to work hard to do well for them. When I got tired I used to think of my father working as a cleaner. He worked as a cleaner in his first four years in Australia. He and my mother cleaned offices during the day, and at night my father cleaned factories."

"Maybe that was why you did so well," said Ruthie. "You topped every year, didn't you?"

"They were the best years of my life, until now. Now that I've got you, I feel that same sense of purpose, that same sense of elation. My colleagues have noticed the difference. I've always worked hard, but now I feel driven. Driven to do the best I can in every aspect of my life. I'm not going to let you go, Ruthie. We're going to be together."

"I don't know how we're going to manage it. I never saw myself as being married to anyone other than Eddie. We've been together for nearly twenty years, remember. Sometimes it seemed that everyone around me was running off with somebody else. People were getting divorced two and three times. I didn't admire them, Abe. It depressed me. It upset me that they couldn't look at what was good about what they already had; all they could do was focus on what they were missing out on. And I often thought that they missed out on even more by splitting families and running off with somebody else's husband or wife. I was happy with Eddie. If life with Eddie meant less sex, then it meant less sex. Life with Eddie also meant nice children, a nice family life, a nice home where people felt at home. And Eddie and I have quite a good time together. He's been very good to my father since my mother died. I don't think my father has ever really been thrilled with Eddie, but Eddie is very good to him.

"It's not simple, Abe, is it? You told me the first time we met how much you like Dora. You don't like her any less because you love me, do you?"

"No," said Abe. "I don't like her any less, but I like myself more. And I want to feel everything as fully as I can. I've been blunted for too long. Ruthie, we're not children any more. Dora will be all right and Eddie will be all right. They'll both continue to get all that they got from us anyway."

"What about your parents?" said Ruthie. "Did they survive everything that they went through, all that suffering, just to watch their family break up? Don't you think that we have a responsibility not to dissipate families? Aren't we trying to rebuild, to regenerate?"

"Ruthie, Ruthie," Abe pleaded. He was almost crying. "Ruthie, we've rebuilt. We've got four kids between us. They're almost old enough to get married and regenerate themselves. Ruthie, we've done that."

Abe was quiet for a few minutes. He wiped his eyes and put his arms around Ruthie. "I've been thinking about children and families too, Ruthie. We could have a child of our own." Tears started to run down his face again. "I can't even think about having a child with you without crying," he said. "You could have your tubes untied. I asked a surgeon friend of mine if a tubal ligation reversal was very difficult, and he said it was now not as complicated as it used to be."

Ruthie felt winded.

"Jewish life is centred around the family," Ruthie said to Zoe. "It's not so easy to break up a family. Judaism is based on family life."

"But you've never been religious," said Zoe.

"I'd never been unfaithful before this," said Ruthie. "I can't leave Eddie. I don't know why I can't. I don't understand it. But every time I think of not living with Eddie any more I feel terrible. I picture Eddie alone and lonely in the house, and I feel like crying."

"Ruthie, you are mad," said Zoe. "Eddie is hardly at home anyway, and when he's at home he's on the phone. Eddie is in love with his business. He's not going to be lonely without you."

"He's able to be happy in his business because he's got me," said Ruthie. "There's something fundamental that I provide for Eddie. It's not sex, and it's not even companionship. I don't know exactly what it is. It's a sort of a form or structure from which he can go out and operate happily in the world. I've never really understood it, I've just known that I provided something really essential for him."

"Well, you've done it for too long," said Zoe.

Ruthie and Abe were at the Kismet Car-O-Tel again. Ruthie had wanted to see the fish. She had been feeling miserable. She thought that seeing the fish might cheer her up.

"Ruthie, I'll come with you when you tell Eddie about us," said Abe. "I'll explain to him that the two of you will still be very close. I think if I'm there Eddie will feel more included than if I'm just a threatening presence."

"Why does anything have to change?" said Ruthie. "Couldn't we just rent this room at the Kismet for the rest of the year? We can come here twice a week and you and me and the fish can all be very happy."

"Ruthie, living at the Kismet isn't a solution to anything. Even if I'm not with you I think of you all the time. When I'm with Dora, I'm not really with her. It would be kinder to Dora to let her know that. And the same goes for Eddie."

"I don't think Eddie has noticed the difference, so it wouldn't be kinder to him."

"What else can we do? This is a hell of a way to keep going. I have to lie all the time. I have to lie to my secretary, I have to lie to my clerk, I have to lie to Dora. Ultimately all this lying will harm us, Ruthie. It will damage us and it will damage those around us. I was at the dry-cleaners this morning, and I thought of being free to go to the dry-cleaners with you, and it almost made me weep."

"I'd like to go to the dry-cleaners with you, too," said Ruthie.

"Well, let's tell Eddie and Dora," said Abe.

"I can't tell Eddie," said Ruthie. "I can't do it to him. Eddie had such an unhappy childhood. His father was a real jerk, and he was awful to Eddie. Eddie feels OK now, and I feel I can't take that away from him."

"Ruthie, Eddie is a forty-year-old, highly successful, very wealthy property developer. I don't think his happiness rests solely on your presence as his wife. And I don't want to hear about poor Eddie and what a tough time he had from his father. Fuck Eddie, and fuck his father."

"Don't say that," said Ruthie.

Abe sighed. "I'm sorry, Ruthie. Really I am. Things seem easier when I feel angry, much more straightforward. I think: I can divorce Dora and you can divorce Eddie. Everybody gets divorced at least once. It isn't such a big deal. But when I stop feeling angry I can see that it's not a simple matter.

"Last night I was going to talk to Dora. I wanted to explain that I would always be fond of her and look after her, but I was leaving. I watched Dora making the dinner. She is so methodical and determined when she works in the kitchen. She puts massive energy into the chopping and mixing and stirring. She always does, but last night she seemed distressed and I asked her what was wrong. She told me that Golda has decided to be interviewed by Rosa Cohen about being the child of concentration camp survivors. Dora was very angry. She said, 'My darling sister wasn't in the camp, so why is she being interviewed? My father was in Auschwitz, not Golda. He was affected, not Golda. What is Golda doing? She's got a good husband and two nice kids. What is she trying to do? Look for trouble? There's enough trouble in the world without looking for it.' I didn't have an answer. And I couldn't bring myself to tell her about us."

He put his head in his hands.

"Do you think we should stop seeing each other?" said Ruthie.

"No," said Abe.

They sat side by side at the end of the bed.

"Look at us," said Ruthie. "We look so forlorn." Abe looked up. Today they were in the Honeymoon Suite with the mirrored ceiling. Abe laughed. They did look pitiful huddled together at the end of the bed.

"I've only ever read about mirrored ceilings," he said. "I've never seen one. Let's see what we look like, Ruthie. Let's forget about Eddie and Dora and Eddie's father and Dora's father. Let's forget about everything just for a little while. Ruthie, you've got the most beautiful breasts. Jason and Jonathan were very privileged boys to be suckled by these breasts."

Abe licked Ruthie's nipples. He put his fingers inside her.

"Abe, stop," said Ruthie. "Please stop or I'll come, and I want to come with you in me." He stopped and slid himself into her.

"What did I look like?" Abe asked afterwards.

"I was too engrossed to notice much," said Ruthie, "but your bum looked very cute on the ceiling."

"Ruthie, I think I've got a solution," said Abe. "It's not a fabulous solution, but it's a start. I'm going to buy us an apartment. I'll buy one in Richmond or Fitzroy, somewhere where we won't bump into anyone that we know. We can go out and choose furniture, books, a television. Even if we go out and buy them separately, we'll be buying them for us to have together. It will be our home. We can buy a fabulous bed. Did you like the mirrors on the ceiling? If you like them, we can have mirrors on the ceiling too. We can share some of the normal things of daily life together."

"Abe, you're mad."

"No, I'm serious. I can see that it's not going to be easy for you to leave Eddie, and maybe I'd find it harder than I know to leave Dora. I want you and me to have a life together. Our own apartment mightn't be a whole life, but it's a step up from this place. We'll be able to drop into our apartment and leave messages for each other. We can have our own things around us. I can buy you presents. We can be more like normal people."

"I don't know that it sounds all that normal," said Ruthie.

"Where would you like to live, Ruthie?" said Abe. "Richmond? What about East Melbourne? Maybe we can even buy a car together?"

"Abe, you're a lunatic," said Ruthie. "What would we do with a car? Sit in it in the garage together?"

"I'd be happy to sit in a garage with you," said Abe. "I'm serious, Ruthie. I'm going to buy an apartment."

Abe put on his clothes. "Stay here, Ruthie. I won't be long. I'm just going to go to the shop next door. I want to get the real-estate section of the paper. I think there's a block of new apartments in East Melbourne that have just been put on the market. The apartments on the top floor should have spectacular views. You should be able to see right across to the Dandenongs on a clear day. I'll be back in a minute. Don't get dressed yet. I love you."

Ruthie sat on the bed and looked at the fish. The fish looked as unmoved as they had been when Ruthie and Abe had arrived. They were swimming relentlessly up and down the aquarium. A large black fish paused for a moment to look at her. Ruthie wondered if the fish knew that a momentous decision had been made today. She felt a bit light-headed. She wasn't sure what she felt about the new developments. There seemed to be something not quite right about Abe's plans. But then maybe nothing in life was quite right. Ruthie smiled at the black fish.

Not One Drop of Juice

Eddie Brot was waiting for his architect. He felt irritated. He hated waiting. This project was behind schedule. The apartments that he was creating out of a former tomato sauce factory in Spring Street were supposed to have been completed three months ago.

Several people had advised him not to build in the city. One of the benefits of being Jewish was that you received plenty of advice. Everybody in the community was willing and able to dispense advice. Person after person had told him that people in Australia were not yet ready to live in cities, and that he was crazy. Eddie thought that they were wrong.

Eddie was standing in the penthouse of the Zesty Tomato Development. Down below, Melbourne looked orderly and peaceful. Eddie saw Christopher Thompson, the architect he had worked with for years, pull up in his new car. Christopher was a large man. He stepped out of the black Peugeot and adjusted his hair and his jumper. He gave his testicles a quick scratch and tugged at the back of his trousers. Christopher was always touching his balls, thought Eddie. Touching his balls or scratching his bum. He was unselfconscious about it. He scratched and pulled and adjusted, whether he was in the middle of a business conference or walking in the street. For Christopher his crotch was a constant source of reassurance.

Eddie rarely touched himself. He rarely looked at his body. He hadn't thought about his body much either, until lately. Lately he had been thinking about bodies and ageing. He had felt bewildered when Ruthie had had her breasts lifted and then her tummy tucked

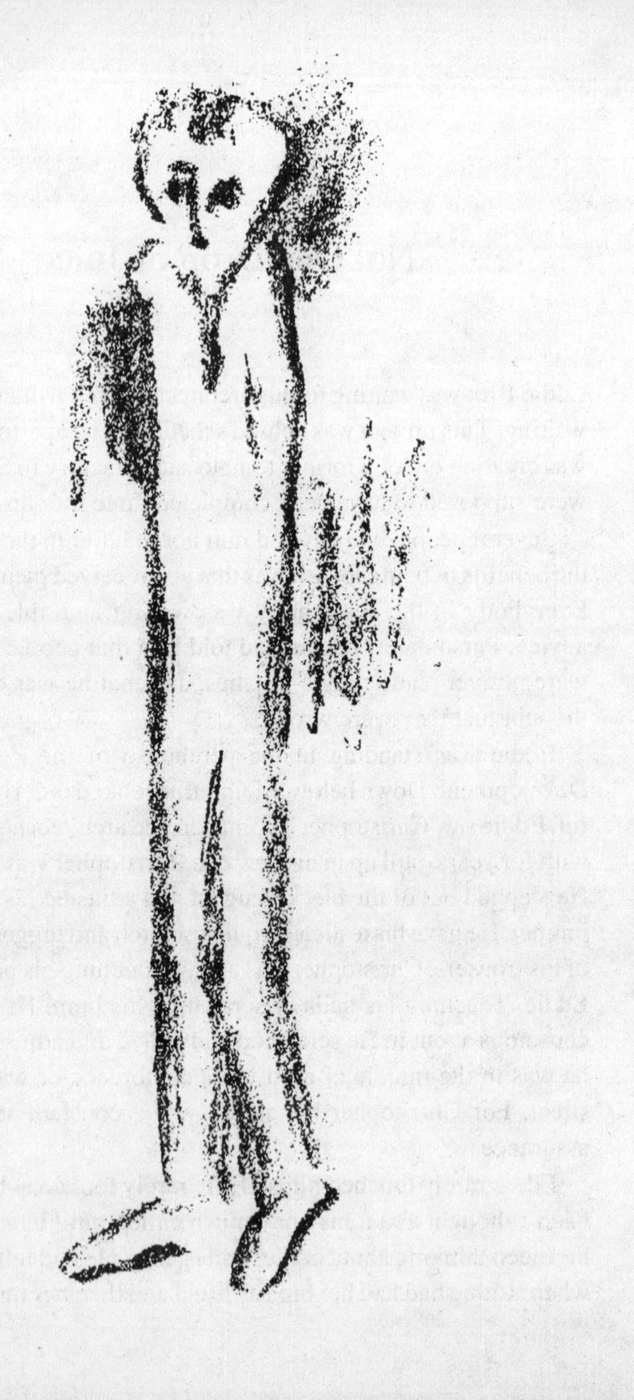

and tightened. He had had nothing against the operations, but it disturbed him to think about why she wanted to put herself through the pain and the possibility of something going wrong. Now Ruthie's figure looked boyish and flat again. He could see that she was pleased.

Across the hallway a carpenter was shooting nails into the oak flooring. Eddie was getting a headache. He walked over to ask him to stop for a minute. The carpenter was wearing earmuffs. He was bent over. Sweat ran out of his cotton shorts and down the back of his legs. Eddie had noticed this carpenter before. He was so blond. He was as blond as Ruthie. When Eddie had met Ruthie she was already a blonde. She had turned herself into a blonde at fifteen. Jews were obsessed with blondness, thought Eddie. His father, Shimek, had loved blonde women. "She is a blonde," he used to say, as though it was an extraordinary accomplishment.

It had often amused Eddie that Jews and Germans were in such accord over blond hair and blue eyes.

"My daughter has got two children now, and they have both got blue eyes," Mrs Bloom from the delicatessen had said to Eddie last Saturday.

"All three of my son's daughters have got blue eyes," a customer had interjected.

"Really?" said Mrs Bloom. "All three? Mazeltov."

Eddie had said, "My two sons have both got brown eyes."

"Oh, well," said Mrs Bloom. "I hear they are clever boys and nice boys and I'm sure they will be all right."

Eddie wasn't at all sure that seventeen-year-old Jason and eighteen-year-old Jonathan would be all right. They were in Israel for the year. Eddie thought that his generation sent their children to Israel when they finished high school as a nice corrective to a cushioned and comfortable Australian upbringing.

Eddie loved Jason and Jonathan, but he had never felt close to them. The boys had been Ruthie's domain. They were slender, slightly built boys, and Eddie wished that they were more muscular. He had a small frame himself, but he felt that he had a strength that his sons lacked. Jonathan would weep when he felt injured by a friend, and Jason wanted to be a poet. He was already writing poems and sending them out to literary magazines. He had had quite a few published in good journals, and Ruthie was thrilled by his talent. But Eddie was less than pleased about Jason and his poetry.

Neither Jason nor Jonathan had shown a great interest in girls, which also worried Eddie. He had hoped that his sons would be tough, robust football followers, if not football players. Lots of Jews followed the football these days.

One day Eddie had talked to Christopher Thompson about his boys. It was the first time he had ever voiced his concern.

"It's so easy to want your children to act out a role that you didn't get quite right yourself, isn't it?" Christopher had said. Eddie had sensed that there was no malevolence in Christopher's response, but he had bristled over it.

He had almost talked to Ruthie about his worry, but he thought that if he did it would become something concrete between them and dislodge their shared pride in their family. He had almost talked to his mother, but he didn't want to tarnish the one aspect of his life that meant more to Minnie than anything else that he had done.

Eddie knew that Minnie was pleased that he had made a lot of money, but he knew that what really made her happy was that he was a good husband and a good father. Every second Saturday afternoon Eddie took Minnie out. They usually visited a few art galleries and then had a cup of coffee at Tamani's, in South Yarra. Minnie loved her coffee at Tamani's. She always asked for double froth on her cappuccino. It made Eddie absurdly happy that she could indulge herself.

Everything about Minnie was familiar to Eddie. When he picked her up on Saturdays she would always have her walking shoes on and her handbag packed. She had been carrying the same things in her handbag since Eddie was a small boy. She always had a packet of Butter Menthols, a wad of Kleenex, her lipstick, a biro, a small Spirex notebook and her purse. Except now she had discarded her purse and used Shimek's old wallet.

Eddie found it disconcerting to see Shimek's wallet. He had struggled not to dislike his father. Shimek had been a cruel man. Eddie thought that Shimek hadn't really liked any of his children, and had barely tolerated his wife.

Shimek had died five years ago. The last time Eddie had seen Shimek was when he had driven over to show Shimek his new car. Eddie had bought himself a dark green Jaguar Sovereign. As soon as Shimek looked at the car Eddie had known that it had been a mistake to come over.

"In Poland you wouldn't have been able to be such a prince," Shimek had said. "In Poland it was much harder to make money. Here you can be Mr Posh."

Shimek called Eddie and his sister Susan Mr and Mrs Posh. "Mrs Posh," he would call from the kitchen when a boy arrived to take Susan out, or if someone called to speak to Eddie on the phone, Shimek would shout, "Mr Posh, it's for you."

At the dinner table Shimek ate loudly. He ate everything with his fingers. Every now and then he would look at Eddie and Susan and say, "You think that you need a fork and spoon to eat a compote? It's a miracle to me that I, with my own plain seed, created such royalty, such good manners. Look at Mr Prince and Mrs Princess sitting here. How did I do it? If there was anybody in the family still alive, if they hadn't all been finished off by the Germans, I could ask them if there was once any royalty in the family."

When their elder sister Gloria was still living at home, she would sometimes say, "Shut up, Dad, they're only kids," and Shimek would shut up. Eddie never understood the power that Gloria had over Shimek, or her lack of fear of him.

Gloria was bigger than Shimek, taller and fatter than him. Gloria was very fat. She had married her husband, Manny, when she was sixteen. Manny was short and thin. When Eddie was a teenager he used to try and imagine Manny struggling to get on top of Gloria.

Eddie had had his own struggles getting on top of girls. When Eddie was seventeen Shimek had asked Manny to take Eddie to the nurses' home at the Stenton Memorial Hospital in Richmond.

"You know what a nurse can do for you?" Shimek had said to Eddie. "A nurse can make a mensch out of you. She can get some blood flowing into that little pisher of yours."

Eddie had gone to the nurses' home with Manny. There had been a party on that night in a flat adjoining the home. Manny had given him a big wink and left him at the party. Eddie started talking to a girl called Patricia. Patricia was seventeen and in her second year of nursing. Her mother had died when she was thirteen. Patricia had wanted to be a vet, but her stepmother had insisted that she leave school and go into nursing. Nursing, her stepmother said, was the best profession for a young girl because nurses could always be sure of having a home. After he had talked to Patricia for half an hour, Eddie's throat was constricted and he had tears in his eyes.

When Eddie got home Shimek was waiting for him.

"Well, how did it go? Is my son a mensch yet?" he said. Eddie squirmed. He tried to tell his father about Patricia and her stepmother, but Shimek cut him short.

"What's wrong with you?" Shimek shouted. "Haven't you got any juice in you? Did I produce a son with no juice? Is the only thing that comes out of your little pisher a bit of wee-wee? A man is a man because he puts juice into a woman."

For years, Eddie couldn't hear the word juice without thinking of his father.

Six months after the nurses' home incident, while Minnie was in Surfers Paradise for three weeks, Shimek asked Manny to arrange for a prostitute to come to the house. Eddie was in his bedroom reading Manning Clark's *History of Australia* when Shimek banged on his door and strode into the room.

"Eddie, Manny and I have organised something very special

for you," he said. "We have got a clean young woman for you. I told her that you didn't have too much experience in this department, and she said that that was no problem. She said not to worry at all. I think that this is going to be a good one, Eddie. Take your time. I have paid for an hour. Manny and I will be in the front room. We'll shut the door and put some music on, so don't worry, nobody will be watching you or listening to you. Don't worry too much about the whole thing. It is very easy. You pull out your pisher, she will help you to get it ready, and you stick it in. I think you might even find that you like it."

Shimek turned towards the kitchen and shouted, "Bring her in, Manny."

Manny came into Eddie's bedroom with a short, plump, red-headed girl.

"Eddie, this is Pamela. Shimek and I will leave you two now." Shimek and Manny left, smiling at each other. Eddie was left alone with Pamela. Manning Clark's *History of Australia* was still on his knee. He couldn't speak.

"Do you want me to take my clothes off?" said Pamela. Eddie shook his head.

"OK," said Pamela, "I'll just take my stockings off. I've only got one rule and that's no kissing. I can't stand to be kissed."

Eddie hadn't moved or spoken.

"Are you all right?" Pamela asked. "Your father told me that you'd never done it before. Don't worry, there's nothing to it. I've had lots of first-timers. Let's get those trousers off you and I'll soon get things going."

An hour later, Pamela hadn't managed to get anything going. Eddie's penis was numb from being pulled and stroked. He felt exhausted and a bit sick.

"When you leave, could you tell my dad that it all went really well?" he said to Pamela.

Shimek wasn't fooled. He took one look at Eddie and screamed, "Not one drop of juice left his body, Manny, not one drop."

Shimek seemed to give up on him after that. His barbs and taunts were much less frequent. Minnie noticed this, too.

"I think your father is not so angry with you any more," she said to Eddie one day.

"I think he's not so interested in me any more," Eddie replied.

"Maybe you are right, Eddie," said Minnie, "and maybe it is better that he is not so interested. I think that Shimek is a man who shouldn't have had children. But I was young, and how do you know these things before they happen? You know, Shimek left Poland to get away from his father. His father wanted him to study, and Shimek wanted to leave school. I met him just six months after he arrived in Australia. He was full of plans. He was going to make a lot of money. He was going to show his father that he was a mensch. He used to talk about sending money for his sisters to come to Australia. Not too many years after he left Poland, his mother and father and his four sisters were all dead. The Germans took everyone from the village into the forest and shot them all. I feel sorry for Shimek. He didn't feel happy in Poland, and he doesn't feel happy in Australia. I used to think that I could make him happy."

"I don't feel sorry for him," said Eddie.

Christopher Thompson came flying out of the elevator.

"Eddie, I'm so sorry I'm late," he puffed. "I don't know if you've noticed, but I haven't been late for quite a while. I've had a shithouse morning. Marilyn is in Sydney and Lara had two friends staying overnight. I wanted to wait until they'd left before I came out of the bedroom. Lara's friends are such cool cats. Seventeen-year-olds think that they're infinitely superior. They make me feel fat and bald and geriatric. They were all talking flat out when I got in last night, and as soon as I stepped into the room all the conversation stopped. Even bloody Lara doesn't bother saying hello. The last thing she said to me was had I ever considered getting a hair transplant. She said she thought that Elton John's transplant made him look years younger. Who the fuck would want to look like Elton John? And how come I seem to have produced a daughter who doesn't have an ounce of kindness in her? She's full of concern for the planet, and cries her eyes out over baby whales being bashed over the head, but nothing about her family moves her except the money that she needs to support this ecologically and ideologically correct lifestyle. God, Eddie, I'm feeling so old."

Eddie laughed, Christopher's daily battles always disarmed Eddie. Nothing was easy for Christopher. He turned everything into an ordeal. Poor Christopher, thought Eddie, he was written up in *Vogue,* in *Harper's Bazaar*, in *Architectural Digest*, he was fawned over by an endless array of followers, and he felt none of it. He was as uncomfortable now as he was when he was twenty.

Christopher had designed the first building that Eddie had built. It was a small block of four flats in Caulfield. By the time Eddie was twenty-five he owned a construction company that employed forty-two people. When Christopher graduated, Eddie lent him the money to set up his architect's practice.

Eddie and Christopher walked through the building.

"Isn't the light wonderful in here?" said Christopher. "It's just as I imagined it would be." He looked happy for the first time since his arrival.

"Christopher," said Eddie, "do you think we could talk about why the plumber has charged us forty thousand instead of thirty thousand, and maybe we could talk about why these air-conditioning ducts are exposed?"

"You can't get reliable tradesmen any more," said Christopher. "I'll sort out that account with the plumber. I think I might have a breakdown if I have to speak to him too many more times. I shouted at him so loudly last week that I had a sore throat all weekend."

"And the air-conditioning?" said Eddie.

"I thought that the ducts would look really good exposed," said Christopher, "and they do. I know that you'll like them once you get used to them. Come and I'll show you the four-bedroom apartment. The air-conditioning ducts look fabulous in there. Eddie, do you know what I heard? A client of mine told me that Susan was having trouble with her husband."

"Oh, Jesus," said Eddie, "why does everyone in Melbourne have to know everything that everyone else is doing?"

Eddie felt annoyed at the gossip about his sister, but he was more agitated about the air-conditioning ducts. He couldn't believe that Christopher hadn't talked to him about them first. Sometimes Christopher irritated him enormously. There was something unpredictable about Christopher, Eddie thought. Sometimes he was so subservient and apologetic, and then at other times he would make a very aggressive move which always took Eddie by surprise.

Sometimes Eddie thought that Christopher's stumbling and halting apologies were concealing something. But Eddie didn't know what. There was something unknown and out of reach about Christopher, and it had often disturbed Eddie.

"What happened with Susan and Harry?" Christopher asked. "Their family life looked so perfect. It used to intimidate me. Remember I did their new kitchen and bathrooms? Everything in the house was always just right. The kids were clever and good-looking. Harry was good-looking and successful. Harry was nice to Susan. Susan was smart. I would arrive there, having left Marilyn playing the drums in her pyjamas and Lara still asleep. Susan and Harry's place seemed like an oasis of normality and propriety."

"God, I forgot about Marilyn's drum-playing phase," said Eddie. "Everything is all right now with Harry and Susan. It happened quite a while ago. Harry is back with Susan. He never left her. He just had some sort of mid-life crisis. I don't know. I didn't ask. I know he had an affair, but hasn't everybody? I think I'm the only person in Melbourne who hasn't had one."

"Have you ever wanted to?"

"No," said Eddie.

Eddie liked Susan. They weren't very close, but he felt a bond with her. He liked the way that she dressed well. She wasn't sloppy like Gloria. Gloria repulsed him. He felt ashamed of feeling that way. He thought that Gloria's hot-pink tracksuits and her gold jewellery shouldn't really matter to him.

If Shimek had favoured one of his children, it was Gloria. It had bewildered Eddie that Shimek had been moved by such a garish, voluble, large daughter. Everything about Gloria was large. Her face, her fingers, her breasts. Maybe it was because Gloria had been Shimek's first-born child that he was fond of her, although Eddie had often thought that the sight of Gloria should have been enough to stop Shimek and Minnie from having any more children. They had had Susan four years after Gloria, and Eddie had been born ten years later.

Eddie had always known that he had been an accident. "At least I could have been an afterthought," he had often said to Ruthie. There was something humiliating about being alive because a condom had leaked. Shimek had gone out of his way to remind Eddie that he owed his life to the Ansell Rubber company.

At Eddie's eighth birthday party, when Shimek took the balloons out of their packet, he had said to Eddie: "See, I buy only Ansell balloons. It is important to have all the family at celebrations. We should have called you Eddie Ansell Brot. It sounds like a good Jewish name to me."

Eddie hadn't cried at Shimek's funeral. He wasn't pained that Shimek was dead, nor was he happy to have Shimek gone. Gloria hadn't cried either. Even Minnie, who Eddie thought really had been fond of Shimek, didn't cry. Susan cried. She had cried and cried. Eddie had found it very disturbing. He couldn't understand how Susan could be crying for such a grubby, harsh old peasant of a man. Shimek hadn't shown Susan much love. From the time that she had taken elocution classes, Shimek had called her "My gentile daughter". "Meet my gentile daughter," he would say to people.

It seemed to Eddie that Shimek had few dilemmas. He rarely reflected about anything. The one question which had seemed to bother him was whether he would have agreed to be a kapo if he had been in Auschwitz.

"You can never judge anyone who went through the camps," he used to say. "Whatever they did, even if they were kapos, you can't judge them. It is a question I have asked myself many times. Would I have been a kapo? The truth is, I don't know. Maybe I would have and maybe I wouldn't have." Eddie was sure that he would have.

Eddie had to agree with Christopher that the exposed air-conditioning ducts did look good. Looking at them in an apartment that wasn't cluttered with building rubbish, he could see that they had a robust beauty, a sculptural quality.

"Have you got time for a cup of coffee when we finish here?" he asked Christopher.

"I don't really think so," Christopher answered. "I'm doing this small house for my mother, and she's driving me mad. I said I'd come and see her this morning. My mother has got no idea of how much work I've put into that house, or how much money I've saved her. She complains about everything that I do."

What was wrong with this generation? Eddie wondered. Here was Christopher, six feet tall, the architect of the moment, and he was still dementing himself about his mother. And here he was, Eddie himself, still unable to buy anything made by the Ansell corporation. When he and Ruthie were first married he had refused to wear condoms. He had been unable to explain his refusal to Ruthie. Ruthie had had Jonathan and Jason in the first eighteen months of their marriage.

Eddie had been pleased to be a father. It had made him feel more solid, more of a man. He felt less of an outsider. He felt the boys were a real accomplishment. Ruthie, exhausted by this accomplishment, had had her tubes tied at twenty-three.

Eddie had agreed to the operation. He didn't particularly want more children. But after the operation the thought that no seed could implant itself in her disturbed him and dampened his erection. At first he was bothered by it, but after a while he and Ruthie seemed to settle down to a less physical but just as friendly marriage.

"You like your mother, don't you?" said Christopher.

"Yeah, I've always got on very well with her, but I had that arsehole of a father to contend with," said Eddie.

"I must say that your father didn't appeal to me. He always made me feel uncomfortable and unacceptable. I always thought it was because I wasn't Jewish," Christopher said.

"God, no it wouldn't have been that. He hated Jews. He was always running Jews down, saying that all they were interested in was money, and then when they got money they gave themselves airs and graces."

"Let's go back upstairs," said Christopher. "I want to show you the main bathroom in the penthouse. I found some beautiful grey-flecked Italian marble tiles for the walls."

Eddie and Christopher walked up the stairs.

"How is Marilyn?" Eddie asked.

"She's fine," said Christopher. "She's learning the trumpet."

"The trumpet? Why the trumpet?"

"I don't know, but nothing that Marilyn does surprises me any more. Sometimes I think that the main goal of Marilyn's life is to not be like her mother. You've met Marilyn's mother, haven't you?"

"Yes," said Eddie, "I met her at Lara's birthday dinner a couple of years ago. I was very impressed with her. Wasn't she one of the first women barristers in Melbourne?"

"Yes, she was," said Christopher. "She was one of the first real feminists. She didn't go around preaching dogma, she actually strove for equality. I like her, and I think that Marilyn's quite fond of her too, but Marilyn seems driven to prove that she is so different from her mother. She gets a real kick out of appalling her mother. Maybe we all do. I remember how distraught her mother was when Marilyn was still breastfeeding Lara after three years. Lara used to undo Marilyn's bra wherever they were, and say 'I want some titty'. Marilyn's mother nearly died when Lara wouldn't stop screaming for titty at Maxim's one night."

"Is Marilyn good at the trumpet?" asked Eddie.

"I don't know," said Christopher. "She makes the most awful noise when she practises. I've been so busy lately that I've been getting home really late, and I've been pleased to have missed her trumpet practice. When she was playing the drums it amused me, but now watching her practise the trumpet makes me feel a bit sad. I don't even know why. I guess it's just a nebulous feeling that I'm not watching her grow. I don't know. I don't want to think about it too much."

Eddie looked at the marble tiles in the bathroom. They were small grey squares, with odd thin slivers of black. The black markings had a calligraphic quality. They looked superb.

Christopher watched Eddie admiring the tiles. "I've always felt comfortable with you," he said. "I know I've driven you mad with my lateness, and I know you've thought I could be more efficient, more professional, less of a rambler."

"Look, Christopher, none of us is perfect. You and I have worked well together. I think I feel closer to you than anyone apart from my mother and Ruthie."

Christopher looked as though he was going to cry. He turned away from Eddie. When he turned back, his face was red. "You don't know how much that means to me, Eddie," he said. "I sometimes feel so old and so friendless. My life seems like a chaotic race for one meeting after another. I've got so many people working for me now that I feel addled. Half the time, I feel that they're younger and cleverer than I am, and the other half of the time I feel as though they're taking advantage of me. I worry that they're fiddling the books, that they're cultivating my clients. I'm not sure how a top architect should act. I'm not sure how an employer should act. I don't know whether I'm their boss or their friend. I don't know that I'm all that superior to them. Some of the young ones are so bright. Yesterday I arrived in the office at nine o'clock and found Harold, a new young student that I've got, wearing Doc Martens shoes and a 1950s suit. I felt so fat and old and bald that I had to go out and have a milkshake. Isn't that pathetic?"

"Most of the people that you feel intimidated by are probably intimidated by you. You're talented, you're successful," said Eddie.

Christopher was looking at the floor. When he looked up his eyes were full of tears. Eddie was startled.

"Don't be upset," he said to Christopher. He put his arm around Christopher's shoulder. Christopher felt so solid. Ruthie felt ephemeral, and his mother's shoulders seemed so frail.

Christopher was quiet. Eddie put both arms around him. Christopher's body had a vitality that surprised Eddie. Christopher felt present. From the time he was a small boy, the world had seemed slippery to Eddie. People slipped in and out of focus, in and out of intensity, in and out of favour.

Eddie felt an enormous freedom. A huge happiness. He held Christopher in his arms. For the first time in his life, Eddie felt he had a grip on another human being. He held him tightly.

A Lunatic Proposition

Dora Lipshitz was worried about her husband. They had never had sex frequently, but now their sex life had ground to a halt. It had been ten months since they had last made love.

She was only thirty-nine. Abe was forty-two. Dora had read that men's sexual prowess peaked at a much earlier age than women's. She wondered whether that applied to men's interest in sex as well. She had read that women were just beginning to heat up sexually at thirty, while men that age were already running out of steam.

Abe seemed to have come to a full stop. He still hugged her quite often, and he kissed her on both cheeks when he came home from work every night, but he no longer made even the smallest movement towards her side of the bed at night.

She thought that maybe he was unwell. But he looked well enough. He looked healthy. And he looked happy. He didn't look as though anything was bothering him.

She furrowed her brow and held her head away from the fumes of the onions and garlic that she was chopping. She was making a goulash. Even though Vivian and Anna were quite grown up, they still liked to come home to a hot meal cooked by their mother.

While the onions were frying Dora chopped the beef into small cubes. She liked cooking. It formed the rhythm of her day. She shopped for the food in the mornings and began to prepare the evening meal in the late afternoon.

Three mornings a week she shopped at the Victoria Market. The same stallholders had been selling her fish, meat and poultry for over twenty years. Last week one of them had said that it seemed like only yesterday that she had told him that she was pregnant with her first child.

Every day Dora looked forward to cooking the evening meal. It gave her the same deep sense of peacefulness and purposefulness that she had felt when she was breastfeeding her daughters. It was a sense of doing something solid and fundamental, something important. Dora felt sustained by the thought that, whatever else happened to Abe, Vivian and Anna during the day, when they came home at night a hot nourishing meal would be waiting for them.

From 12 p.m. to 3 p.m. three times a week Dora worked in a voluntary capacity in the kitchen of the Rosenthal Homes for the Aged. Three days a week she chopped chicken, gutted fish, grated eggs, fried livers and kneaded kneidlach. She also helped to serve the food.

In many ways looking after the residents of the Rosenthal Homes reminded Dora of having small children. The elderly had the same complaints as infants. This was too hot, this was too cold. That was too large, too small, too hard, too soft, too spicy, too tasteless.

When she spooned chicken soup into frail Mrs Berner or testy Mr Zelig, Dora would say: "Eat up, it's good for you." Or: "Come on, have one more spoon, just for me." She had to restrain herself from saying "Open your mouth, here goes the choo choo into the tunnel."

Sometimes the aged were worse than the most tiresome teenagers. This afternoon Mr Zelig, who looked as though he had hardly enough strength to swallow chicken soup, had delivered Dora a sermon on the shocking treatment of the Palestinians by Israel. "We Jews should be ashamed of ourselves. It is shocking," he had railed. Dora had meant to ignore him. He was an old man and he deserved his peace, but she heard herself answering him.

"What is so shocking, Mr Zelig?" she had said. "Under who did the Palestinians have better treatment? Did the Jordanians treat them any better? Did the Syrians treat them better? The Palestinians have lived under the best conditions they've had in years. They were never better educated or more prosperous. And who can Israel negotiate with? While they are talking to one set of Arabs, another set of Arabs are preparing to destroy them. What will be shocking, Mr Zelig, will be the annihilation of all the Jews. Who is going to care if the PLO wipes out Israel? Is it going to break America's heart? Is it going to break Australia's heart? Who is going to cry for the Jews?"

There had been an uncomfortable silence in the room when Dora had finished. After a few minutes Mr Zelig had said, "Well, Mrs Lipshitz, if you always do the right thing by the Jews, and you are so clever, why do you drive a German car? I have seen you in your big Mercedes. Don't you feel like you are driving on the graves of millions of Jews?"

It was a sensitive subject for Dora. Several times in the six months that she had owned the Mercedes, she had come close to selling it. She had gone through all the arguments about contributing to the German economy and contributing to the wealth of people who had built their wealth from the wealth of Jews they had murdered. She knew that there were still executives of large German corporations who had been part of Nazi Germany. She felt a sense of outrage when she drove past the Siemens company building in Richmond, yet she drove a Mercedes. "It's the safest car on the market, Mr Zelig, and that's why I drive it," she had answered.

"How safe do you have to be, Mrs Lipshitz? Is it so dangerous out there?" he had said.

The goulash was simmering. Dora soaked some rice in a marinade of beef broth, paprika and pepper. Abe loved this spiced rice. She started thinking about Abe. Although she was bothered by Abe's lack of interest in sex, she had to admit she was also relieved not to have to think about sex. Ten years ago she had had her last IUD removed, and they had used condoms whenever they had made love. Abe didn't like using condoms, but he was far too sensitive to be difficult about it. Dora herself preferred condoms.

They were so much less messy. All the mess remained in the condom. And she no longer smelt after having sex. Before, no matter how much she had showered and washed afterwards, she had still been able to smell herself. When Vivian had been about eight or nine, she had walked up to Dora one morning and said, "I smell prawns." Dora had been horrified. What did other people do, she had wondered? How did they get rid of the smell? With condoms, the problems of the prawn smell had gone.

In the old days, when she and Abe had made love more regularly, Dora used to fantasise while Abe was on top of her. It was the same fantasy each time. She would pretend that she was a prostitute and Abe was a paying customer, and she had to do a good job. This fantasy didn't inspire Dora or liberate her. She lay on her back as quietly as she had ever done. She often thought that if this was the best she could do for a customer, she may not have made such a great living as a prostitute.

Dora heard a key in the front door. She looked at her watch. It would be one of the girls, probably Vivian. It was Vivian. "Hi, Mum," she said. "I've just had my German orals and I think I've done really well."

"Good on you, darling. I knew you'd do very well; you've got an excellent accent." Dora felt very pleased. Vivian had a real talent for languages. She was doing an Arts honours degree and majoring in German. Anna was also studying German as part of an Arts/Law degree.

Sometimes Dora saw the absurdity and the irony of her two daughters studying German. "The fact that I spoke a very good German saved my life in Auschwitz," her father had said time and time again. Dora had done four years of German at high school. She and her daughters had learned the same Goethe poems. She could still recite "Der Erlkonig". She used to help the girls with their German homework when they were younger. And somehow, although she knew it was stupid, her father's belief in the value of being fluent in German had become her belief.

"Is everything OK, Mum?" said Vivian.

"Of course it is, darling," said Dora. She was puzzled by the question. "Why do you ask?"

"No particular reason," said Vivian. "Well, maybe there is something. It sounds silly, and it shouldn't have bothered me, but Debra Rose asked me if my parents' marriage was in trouble. When I said no, of course not, she just looked awkward. I didn't even want to ask her why she had asked."

"Debra Rose has always been a busybody. Remember how unpleasant she was as a school girl? Remember when she told everyone that her mother was dying, and the whole class put in for flowers to send to Mrs Rose? And Mrs Rose wasn't dying, she was sunbaking in Surfers Paradise? I guess there are some people who just love to cause trouble. You really shouldn't have been upset by her." Dora wondered why Debra Rose had chosen her and Abe as targets for her gossip. It perplexed her.

On Friday morning, Dora woke up with an unexpected, inexplicable and pressing need to have false nails. One of the physiotherapists at the Rosenthal Homes had silk-wrap false nails moulded on to her own nails. Dora had been mesmerised by them. They had transformed the girl's whole image, these shiny porcelain finishes to her fingers.

For the two hours that Dora had been up this morning, she had been unable to think about anything except having her nails done. Should she have square or rounded tips? What colour should she have them? Cherry red? Tawny brown? What about something really different? What about grey nails? She had seen some grey nail-polish at the hairdresser's when she had had her hair cut. What length should she have the nails? She didn't want to have nails that were too long, or she wouldn't be able to work properly in the kitchen. She would have them just long enough to be elegant.

She held her hands out in front of her and tried to visualise how her fingers would look with their new nails. She thought they would look pretty good. She had nice hands. Abe had always admired her hands.

She felt as excited as a child. She looked up nail salons in the Yellow Pages and found one in South Yarra. She made an appointment for Monday afternoon.

She vacuumed the new carpet. It still had that new carpet smell. She thought she might spray some perfume on the carpet. She loved perfume. It was her one big indulgence. She wore Femme, by Madame Rochas, which cost over $100 an ounce. When she sprayed herself with Femme, she felt enveloped in a cocoon of dizzying sensuality. Every now and again, when she passed a mirror, she held her hands up and imagined her new nails.

She had never paid undue attention to her appearance. She dressed sensibly, and always looked well-groomed. She wore modern rather than contemporary clothes. She wondered briefly why she was so fixated about the artificial nails. It was as though an aberrant thought, intended for someone else, had flown into her head by mistake. She wondered if some young model had lost one of the thoughts meant for her, and was now settling for short, stubby nails.

Sometimes she despaired at the stupidity of her thoughts. She spent a lot of her life lost in thought. Daydreaming, the girls called it.

One of her favourite daydreams was the one in which she rescued somebody from a car accident. The person and the details of the accident changed regularly, but Dora was always the hero of the story.

Her current accident fantasy involved Daniel Goodman. Daniel was the son of their accountant, David Goodman. David Goodman annoyed Dora. His vast network of social and political contacts intimidated and irritated her. Dora thought that David Goodman looked down on her. He was less condescending to Abe, who was his client. Dora could see that David Goodman thought that she was just another Jewish housewife.

In Dora's current fantasy, which she played out several times a day, she was driving her car along Balaclava Road when the car in front of her skidded sharply and smashed into a pole. Dora jumped out of her car and ran to the scene of the accident. Daniel Goodman was slumped across the steering wheel of his Datsun, blood pouring from his ears and nose.

Dora shouted to some people standing nearby to get the ambulance and the police. The road was covered with petrol and Dora knew that she had to get Daniel away from the car fast. With the help of a passer-by, she pulled Daniel from the wreckage and carried him to the side of the road. Her clothes were covered in Daniel's blood. She straightened out his limp body, taking care not to move his back too sharply, and she began to apply CPR — Cardio Pulmonary Resuscitation. She continued to work on Daniel until the ambulance arrived.

In real life, Dora had been meaning to take a first-aid course for years. It was one of the things on her list of important things to do. She used to worry about what would happen if Abe or her father had a heart attack. She knew that she would be useless. She would have no idea of what to do.

Dora had recently bumped into Daniel Goodman. She had felt intimately connected to him, and had been surprised to find that he had hardly recognised her.

Mr Zelig was in good form today. "If you are so concerned about Israel, Mrs Lipshitz, why don't you go and live there?" was his opening remark. "Ha, ha," he cackled. "I see I've got you with that one. You are what I call a Top Jew. TJ for short. Top Jews do everything for Israel. They donate money. Lots of money. Well, they've got lots of money, so that's not so hard. And Top Jews talk about Israel all the time. Nothing matters except Israel. When they vote for someone in an election they check his policy on Israel. It doesn't matter what else this person stands for, if he is for Israel they vote for him. Does an Irishman check his politician's policy on Ireland before voting for him? Of course not. A Top Jew does everything for Israel except live there. And why don't they live there? Because Israel is not comfortable enough for Top Jews. You are a Top Jew, Mrs Lipshitz. Do you live in Israel?"

"Mr Zelig, you're worse than an anti-Semite," said Dora.

Mr Zelig's speech had made her nervous. She hated arguing with anyone older than herself. She had been feeling a bit on edge lately, anyway. It was nothing that she could pinpoint. Abe seemed a bit distracted, but he was often distracted by his work. And he was being very affectionate towards her. Last night he told her that she was a very good human being. She had felt his love for her. It had been a very tender moment, and Dora had wished that they could have kept that tenderness and stretched it into something more palpable. But Abe had gone back to his study, and she had phoned her mother.

Her mother had had the usual list of complaints. Dora wondered whether all Jews complained, or whether it was just those Jews who had been battered by the war. She didn't know. Dora couldn't feel angry with her mother and father. How could you feel angry with people who had suffered so much? Even as a small child, she had known that it was her job to make her parents happy. To make up for what they had gone through. And she had tried. She had done everything that they had asked of her. It hadn't made them happy, but at least, she comforted herself, she hadn't added to their pain. Golda had caused them enough pain. Golda had agreed to be interviewed by Rosa Cohen about being the child of concentration camp survivors.

Dora didn't know what her sister or Rosa Cohen hoped to achieve with these interviews. She did know that it was making her mother and father very miserable. Dora felt a fury with Golda. Couldn't Golda see that they'd had enough pain, enough heartache, enough trouble?

Mr Zelig had followed her into the huge industrial kitchen. The Rosenthal Homes may have been a bit light on sporting facilities for their residents, but they had one of the best kitchens of all the Melbourne homes for the aged. It was probably one of the best industrial kitchens in the country. Mr Zelig stood there looking at her as she fed six pineapples and twenty kilograms of carrots into the mincer.

Mr Zelig's gaze disturbed her. She felt a bit sick. She often had diarrhoea if she was upset about something. She went to the toilet. Her bowels erupted violently. Wiping herself, she suddenly saw what the flaw in having false nails would be. How could you wipe yourself properly with long plastic nails? It could be dangerous. You could hurt yourself. Her desire for artificial nails disappeared as swiftly as it had arrived.

She decided that when she finished at the Rosenthal Homes today she would go and look for a birthday present for her mother. It was her mother's birthday in two weeks. She always found it difficult to choose presents for her parents. She thought that she had probably never given them a successful present.

She had bought her mother kettles, blouses, appliances, perfume, books. Nothing had been quite right. None of the presents had been used. The kettles and the kitchenware had been relegated to the shower recess in the laundry. The toaster and the waffle iron were in the garage. The jumpers and ties she had bought for her father had disappeared. She wondered if somewhere in the house there was a huge collection of unused gifts. She knew that her parents did the same with gifts from Golda.

Golda had once said to her that she wished that she could feel as though she had contributed something to her parents' lives. She said that she usually felt redundant around them, attached by some sort of fierce connection that didn't altogether feel like love.

"Golda, why do you have to be so complicated?" Dora had said to her sister. "Of course you've contributed to Mum and Dad's lives. You've produced two beautiful children."

"That's exactly what Mum and Dad would have said," Golda had replied.

Dora tried to think of something that she could buy for her mother. She wished that she could sew. If she could sew, she could make her mother a beautiful dress. She used to fantasise about making her mother dresses. In her fantasies she was an expert dressmaker. She could make the most complicated cocktail gowns, the most ornate evening dresses. She could make dresses that would make her mother look so beautiful. She was also, in these fantasies, a superb tailor. She made immaculate three-piece suits for her father. Her mother and father were both very proud of the clothes that Dora made for them.

Sometimes she also gave herself a gift for hairdressing. In her daydreams she became such a brilliant hairdresser that she was indispensable to her mother. Occasionally she allowed herself to style and cut Golda's hair for a special occasion. But mostly she felt too annoyed at Golda to include her in her fantasies.

Lately, the hairdressing fantasy had not been as satisfying. Her mother, in real life, had stopped going to Gina's Salon, and was doing her hair herself. She was proud of her hairdressing skills, and told everyone how much money she was saving. This reality disturbed Dora's daydream. Even in her fantasies, Dora couldn't compete with her mother.

Dora did, in fact, exercise some hairdressing skills. Every morning Dora combed Abe's hair before he left for work. For Dora it was one of the most touching moments of the day. She felt in charge of how Abe was going to be presented to the world. And she felt an enormous bond with Abe as she moved the comb in and out of his hair. She felt that she had all of Abe for those two or three minutes every morning.

It was a ritual that they never spoke about. Abe would just call out "I'm ready" when he had showered and dressed, and Dora would come into the bathroom with the special wide-toothed comb that she used for Abe.

Abe still had thick, vigorous hair. A slight bald patch was appearing at the back of his head. It was the only sign of time passing. Dora combed this spot with extra tenderness.

Men were lucky, she thought. On the whole their bodies remained more youthful than women's bodies. Abe still had a spring in his thighs, and a lightness in his step. Dora felt that all of her was sagging. Her breasts, her stomach, her thighs were all being pulled downwards. She felt as though her body was inexorably and inevitably moving towards the ground.

Dora was late leaving the Rosenthal Homes today. Somebody had overcooked the kneidlach and they had to make a second batch. She still had time to look for a present, though. She thought that she might buy her mother a vase. She had seen an elegant tall rectangular glass vase in Toorak Road. It was so tall that her mother would have trouble burying it away somewhere. Maybe her mother would like it.

She thought that she might buy Abe a new desk diary. That was something else she did for him. She always chose his desk diary. Abe had a drawer full of past desk diaries, all used and all chosen by Dora.

As Dora was walking out of the front door of the Homes Mrs Berner called out: "Mrs Lipshitz, Mrs Lipshitz." Dora stopped and waited for Mrs Berner to reach her. "Mrs Lipshitz, I wanted to say something before, but I didn't know whether it was the right thing to speak to you or not to speak to you. I thought and thought and decided that I should tell you."

"Tell me what, Mrs Berner?"

"Tell you that my niece told me something about your husband."

"What did she tell you?" Dora asked.

"I don't know if I should tell you."

"Mrs Berner, tell me if you want to, and don't tell me if you don't want to."

"All right, I'll tell you," said Mrs Berner. "Just remember that I'm telling you for your own good. My niece came to see me yesterday, and she told me that your husband is shtooping two other women. He's got a shikse and a Jew. I thought that this was something a wife should know."

"Mrs Berner, do you know what a lunatic proposition this is?" said Dora. "If you knew my husband, you would know that he is not the sort to shtoop two other women. He works very hard. He cares about people, not like some other barristers. He takes on a lot of cases where the client can't pay him. He is a wonderful father and a wonderful husband. He hasn't got time to do this shtooping that your niece has told you about. I think your niece must have him confused with someone else. Actually, maybe your niece was talking about Abe Lipman. Everybody knows that Abe Lipman is a ladies' man. See you on Monday, Mrs Berner."

Dora strode briskly to her car. She might cook a nice barley soup for dinner tonight. It was just the right weather for a thick soup. And Abe loved barley soup.

Poor Abe, she thought. With rumours like this going around, he might just need a good barley soup to keep his strength up.

Half-There

"I feel mixed up," Golda Goldenfein said to Bella Fleker. Golda and Bella talked on the phone every day. They had been talking to each other for thirty years. They were both forty-two. They often repeated themselves. Sometimes, Golda thought, they had probably repeated entire conversations verbatim. "I feel mixed up and exhausted," she said to Bella. "I spent the whole morning at Rosa Cohen's house. Remember I told you that Rosa Cohen was interviewing children of survivors of concentration camps?"

"I remember," said Bella, "only I forgot that it was this morning. How did it go?"

"How did it go?" said Golda. "How did it go? I don't know. She asked me endless questions and I talked for three hours. But I don't think I said anything. I wanted to do it well. I feel that the fact that my father was in Auschwitz has always been a very important part of my life, but I don't know why and I don't know how. I think I thought that by talking to Rosa Cohen I might find out something."

"You've never talked to me about it," said Bella. "Did your mother know you were doing it?"

"My mother didn't want me to do it. My mother said it was a plot by Mr Bloom. She said that Mr Bloom knows Rosa Cohen's father and planted the idea in his head that I would be a good person for Rosa to interview. My mother said Mr Bloom wants to show the world that our family has problems. I don't even know which problems she is thinking about, but Mr Bloom didn't give Rosa Cohen my name. I volunteered. I heard about this book of interviews from Arnold Klepner, who was really upset that he didn't qualify because his parents were hidden in a cellar."

"So you don't think Mr Bloom had anything to do with it?" said Bella.

"Of course he didn't," said Golda. "You're starting to sound just like my mother. I asked Rosa Cohen and she said that she didn't know Mr Bloom and she didn't think her father did either. She said that the Mr Bloom story sounded very far-fetched to her.

"I felt incredibly nervous before I went to her place. I almost cancelled the appointment. I didn't know what I was so nervous about. Anyway, Rosa Cohen asked me all these questions, and I didn't really have many answers.

"Rosa Cohen told me after the interview that even the most articulate people have had terrible trouble talking about this subject. I'm not sure whether I was in the category of most articulate but I certainly had trouble. I felt so dumb. There were so many things I didn't know. When I started talking to Rosa Cohen I could see that I didn't know much about what my mother or my father had gone through during the war. It was strange, because the feeling of them being in camps was so strong to me. I thought about my girls and how they know every important thing that has happened to me. I felt a failure for knowing so little about my parents.

"When I was talking to Rosa, I couldn't really feel anything. I looked at her at one stage and thought how weird it was that here we both were, Rosa Cohen and I, comfortably off, living in Australia and sitting and talking in a very nice house about my father drinking another man's piss in Auschwitz."

"I didn't know about that," said Bella.

"Well it's not something you talk about, is it? I don't even think I've told Charlie. My dad told me when I was about eight. It was a hot day and I didn't want to drink this orange juice he had bought for me. I thought it tasted funny. He said to me that when you are thirsty nothing tastes funny. He said 'In Auschwitz I had to drink pishy from another man.' That's all he said. I thought about it for years. How did he get the piss? Did he drink it from a container, or did he drink it directly from the man? I told Rosa Cohen about it, and she said that in the final days in Auschwitz, when the Nazis had fled, there was very little water and many of the prisoners, who were on the verge of death anyway, had to drink their own piss.

"I didn't cry when I told Rosa Cohen about my father, and she didn't cry when she was talking about Auschwitz. She seemed very sympathetic, but it was hard to know how she felt. She's got a very composed face. She's got such a composed face that sometimes I thought she might be thinking about other things while I was talking. Both her mother and her father were in Auschwitz."

"What did Dora think about you talking to Rosa Cohen?" asked Bella.

"Oh, Dora thought I was stupid," said Golda. "She knows everything better than I do. Dora said that what happened to our parents has had no effect on her life or on my life. She said that the Holocaust was over with, and what did I want to talk to a stranger about it for anyway? Dora said that she's got no problems and I've got no problems. I said to Dora that I didn't feel that I had more than a normal share of problems, and she said that she and I were more normal than normal, and that there was nothing to talk about from the past. Oh, I almost forgot, Dora said that she thought that there might be some truth in my mother's suggestion that my interview was a plot by Mr Bloom."

"What did Rosa Cohen ask you?" said Bella.

"She asked me lots of things," said Golda, "but I can't really remember any specific questions. She told me that she had often had trouble separating her experience from her mother's experience. She said that she sometimes had not been sure that she too hadn't been in Auschwitz. It sounds crazy but I knew what she meant."

"It sounds really crazy to me," said Bella.

"It's not so crazy, Bella. Why is that any more crazy than going and sitting by a river and catching fish when there are plenty of fish in the fish shops?"

"I don't go fishing," said Bella.

"Bella, I think you don't really want to talk about my interview," said Golda.

"Yes I do," said Bella. "Tell me what else you talked about."

"I told Rosa Cohen that I used to dream that Nazis were chasing me," said Golda. "She told me that she dreamt about Nazis too. I never knew that other people dreamt about Nazis."

"I've never dreamt about Nazis," said Bella.

"Yes, but your father was only in a labour camp in Russia, and your mother wasn't even in the war, she was already in Australia," said Golda.

There was a silence. Golda thought that Bella probably didn't like the way she said "only" in a labour camp. She thought that Bella was probably bristling and contemplating saying that there was somebody at the door and she had to go. Well, she didn't care. Bella was being as thick as a brick today. Couldn't Bella see that this was a very sensitive issue? And couldn't Bella see that being in a labour camp couldn't be compared to being in Auschwitz?

"Rosie Berg's mother was in a labour camp in Russia, and Rosie is always talking about the Nazis," said Bella. "Rosie says that she has nightmares about the Nazis."

"Rosie Berg is another matter altogether," said Golda. "If Rosie Berg had been born to a mother who'd spent her whole life on holiday in the Bahamas she'd say she had nightmares about the Nazis. Rosie Berg just loves to be the centre of attention."

"When I told my mother that you were doing the interview with Rosa Cohen," said Bella, "she said that it was disgusting that the children of survivors thought that the attention should be on them and not on their parents. She said that the survivors went through the suffering, not their children."

"Well your mother certainly didn't suffer," said Golda.

She felt flat. She wondered whether this message about who experienced the suffering was from Bella or her mother. She half agreed anyway. Why should anyone spend time thinking about how she had been affected? She wasn't the one who had suffered. And maybe Dora was right, maybe there was nothing wrong with her. If there was nothing wrong with her, she thought, then there was also nothing that was spectacularly right with her.

There was nothing that was spectacularly wrong. She had two nice kids. Charlie was a good husband. He was a good accountant. They were well off. Charlie's mother had been in Bergen-Belsen, but Charlie didn't think it had affected his life. Golda thought that Charlie was frightened of his mother, and far too scared to ask her anything about the past. Charlie worried a lot about upsetting his mother.

Golda thought that Charlie didn't want to upset anybody. Everything was always fine with Charlie. In an argument he would always give in. If she said that she didn't feel like sex, that was fine. If she cooked fish it was fine and if she cooked tripe it was fine. If she was on an egg diet, Charlie ate eggs. People said that he was very good-natured. Golda appreciated his good nature, but sometimes she worried about his eagerness to please.

She was grateful to Charlie for never criticising her, and for not making an issue out of the fact that she didn't work. When she said that she was tired at the end of the day, Charlie was sympathetic. He never asked her what it was that was tiring her. Danielle and Simone were seventeen and fifteen, and quite independent. Milka the cleaning lady came three times a week. Golda didn't have to do much around the house. Golda wasn't quite sure what it was that tired her. When people asked her what she did, she said, "I'm just Golda, I don't do anything in particular."

Most of the women that Golda knew worked. If they didn't have a job they worked at their figure, or their suntan, or they worked for charity. Golda had mostly been too plump to worry about her figure. She thought that if she'd only been a stone or so overweight, she might have felt more motivated to lose the extra weight. But Golda weighed eleven stone when she should have weighed eight.

Three months ago Ruthie Brot had asked her if she would like to come to the aerobics class at her house on Tuesday mornings. Golda had felt so grateful to be seen as a possible candidate for aerobics that she had said yes. She had bought purple lycra leotards and blue tights. She didn't look as awful in them as she thought she would.

Now the aerobics session was the highlight of Golda's week. She liked moving to music. She liked just moving. She liked being with Ruthie and Zoe and Ella. Last week she had begun a diet that Ruthie had given her. It was a black-eyed bean and rice diet.

Golda felt upset. Why did Bella have to say it was disgusting for children of survivors to look at how they had been affected? She'd asked Bella not to tell anyone about the interview. Bella's mother had the biggest mouth in Melbourne. If you wanted someone to know something, all you had to do was tell Bella's mother about it. Golda knew that Bella knew exactly what her mother was like, so why had she told her? There was so much that was right about Bella, Golda thought, but every now and then a mean thin sentence would streak out of her and skewer whoever was around her. She was glad that she hadn't asked Ruthie if Bella could come to the aerobics classes.

Golda was bewildered by why it was so hard to be good friends. Why did people feel the need to distress and disturb others? Golda remembered the day that she and Bella had worn their first straight skirts. They had been fourteen. Bella had looked at her and said, "That skirt looks fabulous on you. You can't see your knees at all. The fattest parts of your legs are covered up and nobody would even know you were fat."

Golda's mother had always said to her, "You can't trust anybody except your family." Golda wasn't sure that she could trust her family. She didn't feel all that close to her mother or Dora, and she felt winded and breathless from the punches that her father threw at her from time to time. Yesterday when she had dropped around to visit him he had looked at her affectionately and said, "It's a good thing, Golda my darling, that Danielle and Simone look like Charlie. I love you very much and you've got a good heart, but it is easier for a girl if she is pretty. You and I can speak plainly to each other, can't we, Golda? We don't have to have big politenesses between us?"

"No, we don't," said Golda.

Something that Rosa Cohen had said to her this morning had startled her. Rosa had been talking about her husband Allan. Allan was not Jewish. "Allan's father used to thump him," Rosa had said. "Sometimes he'd beat the shit out of Allan, but at least it was a very clear message and Allan knew exactly where he stood. The real problem for kids is when the message is ambiguous." What was her father's message? Golda wondered. Was it ambiguous or was it in another language?

"Did you ask Ruthie Brot if I could join the aerobics classes?" said Bella.

"Yes," said Golda, "I asked her and she said that she would have loved you to come, but Peter, the instructor, won't take more than four people in a class. So sorry, Bella, I did try."

Bella sounded disappointed. Golda felt pleased. "I'd better go now," she said to Bella. "I haven't prepared anything for dinner. Speak to you tomorrow."

"Speak to you tomorrow."

Golda reminded herself to mention the business of Bella not being able to come to the aerobics class to Ruthie. Just in case Bella ever met Ruthie and brought it up. Melbourne was so small that you could never be sure that two people would not meet each other.

Golda prepared dinner. She put a chicken and some potatoes in the oven. Maybe she would forget the beans and rice tonight. Maybe she'd have chicken with the others. She was feeling too rattled to diet.

Charlie arrived home a bit earlier than usual. Golda was happy to see him. He walked in carrying two briefcases and a large folder of papers. He always brought work home with him. "Hello, darling," he said. "How are you? I thought of you this morning. How did it go with Rosa Cohen?"

"I guess it was OK," said Golda. "I don't know that anything that I said enlightened either of us. I talked for so long, but I can hardly remember a word I said. I don't think I was very intelligent. I felt absolutely wrung out by the time I left. I felt terrible, and I had no idea what it was that was making me feel so bad.

"It's all such a muddle, this business of our parents' suffering. I feel scared to think about it too much. But I feel scared of so many things. My parents are scared, but at least they have got a reason for being scared. You know, Charlie, I feel angry with my dad for always having such a good reason for what's gone wrong with his life, when I haven't got a good excuse for what's gone wrong with mine."

"But nothing is particularly wrong with your father's life," said Charlie, "and what is wrong with your life?"

"Well, my dad didn't make as much money as most of his friends," said Golda. "He feels inferior about that, even though he always scoffs at people who are really rich. He says money isn't what is important, but I know that he feels that he hasn't been as successful a human being as those of his friends who've made lots of money. Look at how my mother has to buy everyone more expensive presents than they give her. She's very keen to show people that she can afford everything they can. And when she does buy a bargain my father gets really furious and says we've got enough money to pay full price, we don't need to buy bargains.

"Managing a knitwear factory wasn't what my father saw himself doing when he was a young boy. He said he dreamed of becoming a lawyer. His father and two uncles were lawyers. Haven't you noticed how often he manages to bring that up in a conversation? When I was little he used to say to me that it didn't matter if I wasn't too pretty because if I became a lawyer I would have the world at my feet."

"What a mean thing to say," said Charlie. "Your father says so many mean things to you. I don't know why. You're very pretty, and you look adorable in those photos of you when you were a little girl."

"Oh, Charlie, you're so biased," said Golda. "I'm sure my father would have been a much nicer person if he hadn't gone through the concentration camp. I don't think he would have been so angry. I think he was angry with me because I didn't have any hardships."

"Maybe that's why he gave you some hardships. Maybe that's why he convinced you you were awful looking, so that you would suffer too," said Charlie.

"I don't know," said Golda. "You know something creepy about Rosa Cohen? She's got all these books on the Holocaust. Hundreds of them. No, probably thousands of them. And you know where she keeps them? In her bedroom. Isn't that weird? I asked her, actually, why she has to have them in the bedroom. I mean, she could easily have them in bookshelves in another part of the house. She's got bookshelves everywhere."

"What did she say?"

"She said that she likes to see them. She said that they anchor her. They stop her from feeling sorry for herself, or getting things out of perspective. Isn't that strange? And she said something else that sounded a bit mad. She was talking about one of the reference books on the Holocaust which is out of print and very hard to get, and she said that when she went away for a couple of months last year, she put the book in a friend's safe. I asked her if she had put her own playscripts in the safe too. She said no."

"Is she a bit weird?"

"No, she's really very nice," said Golda. "I felt comfortable with her, but I felt a bit like we were two children who were doing something that we weren't supposed to be doing. I don't think she felt like that, I think it was just me. Although I noticed that every time she talked about her own family she reminded me that what she was saying was confidential.

"You know, by the end of the morning I could see that, even though she has read all those shelves of books, the whole business is as difficult and confusing for her as it is for me. She told me that she had been reading books on the Holocaust for over eight years.

She said that she can't stop. That every time she thinks she's had enough and can't bear to read one more word on the subject she finds another book and starts reading again. It sounds to me like she's got a problem."

"Even if she didn't have a problem to begin with," said Charlie, "she'd sure as hell get a problem from reading all that depressing stuff all the time."

"I said that to her, Charlie," said Golda, "and she said to me that it wasn't at all depressing to face things. She told me to read *Survival in Auschwitz* by Primo Levi and *Night* by Elie Wiesel. She said they may be distressing books, but they were brilliant and uplifting as well. I think I might go to Balberyszski's and buy them."

"Are you sure, Golda? I think it may be asking for trouble to go looking into the past."

"But I feel as though it's my past and your past, not just our parents' past," said Golda.

"It's not my past," Charlie said, and went into his study.

Charlie sat in his study. He was agitated by all this talk about the Holocaust. It was the 1990s, not the 1930s. What good could it do to think about it now? He could see that it was important for other people to know about what had happened, so that it couldn't happen again, but Jews already knew about it. Golda said that even Jews didn't know too much about it. But how much did they need to know? Maybe it would be harmful to know too much? It could be very distressing. Golda had been hysterical last week when Miriam Pincas had said that she couldn't possibly read anything about the Holocaust because it would upset her too much. "Look at her," Golda had raged, "in her expensive clothes and her Victorian mansion. She's air-conditioned and heated and demisted and totally coated with her wealth. But it's not enough for her to be protected from the weather or from burglars, she wants to be protected from feeling anything." Sometimes Charlie was so full of admiration for the way that Golda put things. She really did have a talent for words. It was a pity she had been determined not to do law. She would have been a good lawyer. Instead, she was a good mother. Who was to say that that wasn't more important? thought Charlie.

Still, he felt upset. Why had Golda become preoccupied with the past? It had only happened in the last year or two. Recently in the *Jewish News*, he had read an interview with Elie Wiesel. Elie Wiesel had said that it was important not to trivialise the Holocaust. Well, maybe to think that the Holocaust had affected the children of survivors was trivialising it. He didn't know.

Last night he and Golda had had dinner at Scheherezade with Bella and her husband David. They were talking about how the food in Australia had changed, how now you could buy so many different varieties of food. "My father," Bella had said, "said that when he came here after the war, the food was shocking. He said that the cheese tasted like wax. It must have been awful because my father was fresh out of labour camp and he can't have been too fussy about his food." Charlie wondered if that was what Elie Wiesel had meant by trivialising.

The phone rang. Charlie knew it would be his mother. "Hello, Charlie darling," she said. "How are you? I've got a shocking cold, darling. I didn't have it yesterday, and today I am sick like a dog. And, of course, do I get some sympathy from your father? Not one bit. You know your father, he doesn't like to see any problems. He likes to pretend that everything is all right all the time. He said to me, 'It's not such a bad cold. Take an aspirin and you'll feel better.' Probably when I drop dead he will look at me and say, 'Take an aspirin and you'll feel better'."

Charlie usually sympathised with his mother. He usually spent most of the phone call listening. His mother called at this time every night. She knew that he would be home but that he wouldn't have started his dinner yet. Sometimes Charlie worked on a client's accounts while his mother talked.

Charlie took a deep breath. His stomach knotted slightly. Before his mother could get on to the next subject, Charlie asked her a question. "Mum," he said, "do you think you are still affected from being in Bergen-Belsen?"

"Charlie, are you stupid?" she said. "Of course I am. Not one day goes by when I don't think about what happened to me. Not one day goes by when I don't think about what happened to my mother and father and my sister. Of course I know that they died, but how did they die? I didn't bury them. No-one buried them. Charlie, I thought you were clever enough to know that something like this never leaves you. Why do you think I have so much trouble with my stomach? Because of the camp, of course. I don't know why I'm explaining so much to you. Nobody who wasn't there could understand anything about it at all."

"Do you think I was affected by you having been there?" asked Charlie.

"Of course not," said his mother.

Charlie and his mother chatted for another ten minutes. As soon as he hung up from his mother, Golda's mother was on the line. "Charlie," she said, "get me Golda. I know she's busy in the kitchen but I won't keep her long." Charlie got Golda.

"Hello, my dear daughter," Golda's mother shouted. "I did hear already that you did go to Rosa Cohen's house this morning."

"Who told you?" said Golda.

"What does it matter who told me? Did you enjoy telling the family secrets to a stranger? Did it make you feel better?" she shouted.

"Couldn't you calm down, Mum? I don't want to upset you," said Golda.

"Golda, it's a little bit late for you to be so concerned with upsetting me," she answered. "If you didn't want to upset me or your father you should have thought about it before you went to talk to this Rosa Cohen. I think I am going to ring Mr Bloom and congratulate him. I'll tell him his plot worked. My loyal daughter couldn't wait to talk about her family."

"Mum," said Golda, "what is it that you thought I'd be talking about? What are the secrets that I'm supposed to have given away? How can I give them away when I don't know what they are?"

"In a family there are always things that you don't talk to other people about."

"But what are they in our family? What are you so worried about?"

"Golda," said her mother "you were not in Auschwitz, and that is why you can so easily decide that this is a subject to discuss with a stranger. If you had been there you would understand what is wrong with what you are doing. Your father wants to speak to you."

"Hello," said Golda's father, "is this the traitor in the family? I suppose that you feel better after your long talk to Rosa Cohen. I am glad that you talked to her. It is good that a poor child like you, who grew up with plenty of food and her family around her, should be able to talk about her suffering. Was Rosa Cohen interested in your suffering?" Golda tried to answer but her father wouldn't stop.

"Did she ask you if I was a kapo?" he said. "I suppose she thought that I must have been a kapo. Probably you think the same. Well, you can tell her that I wasn't a kapo. Most of the people who survived were for sure kapos. I don't trust anyone who was in Auschwitz who says they were not a kapo. How did they survive?"

"How can you say that, Dad?" said Golda. "If Jews can speak like that what hope is there for anybody else?"

"I can see that you have already become an expert about Auschwitz," said her father. "It didn't take you long. My dear daughter, you are not an expert. I am an expert. I was there. I am saying goodbye now. I am too upset to talk any more." He hung up.

Golda sat down at the kitchen table. Tears ran down her face. What had she done? What was so bad about talking to Rosa Cohen? It had felt harmless. Hadn't all the harm been done a long time ago? She wiped her eyes with her apron. Maybe she would ring Dora. Maybe her sister would be sympathetic.

"What the hell are you doing?" was Dora's first question. "Don't you know how much you've upset Mum and Dad? Haven't they suffered enough already? What's wrong with you? Were you feeling a bit bored? If you were that bored you should have joined a club, or come and worked with me once a week in the Rosenthal Homes kitchen. What is wrong with you, Golda? You've got a good husband and two nice girls. What do you want to stir up so much trouble for? You'll kill Mum and Dad with all this trouble." Golda didn't have an answer. She said goodbye and hung up.

Two days later Golda said to Charlie, "I think I might ring Rosa Cohen and tell her that I have to drop out of this project."

"Are you sure?" said Charlie.

"I'm not sure that I don't want to do it, but I am sure that I don't want to cause my parents any more pain. They've had enough pain," she said.

"Yes," said Charlie, "they are the victims, and why should they be victims again?"

"But I'm not victimising them," said Golda.

"But they feel as though you are," said Charlie.

"Charlie, I feel so fucked up," said Golda. "I've never done anything much. And I've never known why I haven't done anything much. I didn't do law because my father wanted me to do it. The feeling of not wanting to do law was much stronger than any feeling I had of wanting to do anything else. I feel like I'm a half-person. I'm half-there. I'm half a mother. I'm half a wife. I'm half-pretty. I'm half-clever."

"Maybe you should go ahead and do the interviews," said Charlie.

Golda decided that she would ring Rosa Cohen on Monday and tell her that she wouldn't be able to come on Wednesday, and in fact she wouldn't be able to continue with the interviews. She felt flat and depressed. She wasn't sure how she was going to explain it to Rosa Cohen.

On Monday Rosa Cohen rang Golda. "Golda," she said, "I'm sorry, but I've got some bad news. Don't worry, it's not a catastrophe, well at least not for you. I've decided to scrap my book of interviews with children of survivors. In over thirty-five interviews I had two really good ones and a couple of others that might have worked. Well, my two best interviews both rang this week to say that they couldn't continue with the project. So I thought about it a lot and I decided that this book is too difficult to do. Maybe someone else could do it, but I can't. I'm going to file away my four hundred kilos of transcripts and go back to my normal life."

"I'm really sorry about that," said Golda. "I enjoyed talking to you. It made me feel better."

"Would you like a copy of your interview?" said Rosa Cohen.

"Yes, I would," said Golda.

Golda put down the phone. She didn't know how she felt. She decided to go to Balberyszski's and buy Primo Levi and Elie Wiesel. She looked for her car keys. She thought she might stop at Krauss's, on the way, and buy herself a block of that new Swiss bitter-sweet chocolate.

Locker 1012

Esther Schenkler was sure that she was dying. She walked around her house slowly. She was in mourning for herself.

She felt fragile. She sat down each time she had a cup of tea. She had naps in the afternoon. She didn't carry anything too heavy. She didn't strain too hard on the lavatory. She tried not to precipitate the disaster that she was knew was on its way.

No-one had told her that she was dying, but she knew it. She could feel the death inside her. She could feel it in her bones, and she could feel it in the air around her.

Esther looked at the things around her. She looked at the lawn in the front of her house. It was buffalo grass. It was good grass, she thought. She had neglected it badly, and yet it had kept on growing. It had stuck in there. She had never re-seeded it. In high summer she had often forgotten to water it. Once every few months she dragged an antiquated hand-mower over it. The blunt blades pulled clumps of the grass out by its roots. She was grateful to the grass for persevering.

She looked at her shoes on the bedroom floor. It was weird to think that they would still be in Clifton Hill, Melbourne, Australia, when she was dead. They were scuffed and worn down. She could see the shape of her feet in their outline. Her shoes would still be there, but there would be no feet to put into them.

For months she had been having short, sharp, shooting pains in the right side of her head. They had subsided now, but she knew that it was a temporary reprieve.

When the pains first started she had thought that they were early symptoms of heart disease. She had sat and listened to her heart for hours. Occasionally her heartbeat was irregular, but she wasn't too worried. She knew that everyone's heart missed a beat now and then. It was perfectly normal. Still, she slept on her right side to avoid putting too much pressure on her heart.

She had a cardiogram done. It had showed no abnormalities. She liked the feeling of having no abnormalities, although she thought the doctor was referring to her heart rather than her whole being. The cardiogram reassured her for a while. Then she thought of a stroke. Of course, that was it. It would be a stroke. Esther knew that it was hard to detect and predict when strokes would strike. She dreaded being left with half of her face paralysed, so that whatever it was that she was trying to express would be distorted into foolishness by her facial muscles. It was hard enough to feel a sense of dignity and worth with symmetrical features.

One night she sat down and pored through the 2,674 pages of *Hawkins' Medical Dictionary*. By 5 a.m. she had finally diagnosed herself. She knew that she had a brain tumour. She had had her head X-rayed last year when she'd had bouts of dizziness. The X-rays had been clear, but Esther knew that X-rays often missed things.

She probably didn't even have much time left. Soon the cancer would start taking over. She would save up her Serepax tablets, she thought. Then she would have a way out when she could no longer speak clearly.

She thought about the fact that she wouldn't see her children grow up into adults. The thought didn't really distress her. Her children weren't all that nice to her. Beau had already left home, and Daisy only approached her when she needed money.

They were rough kids, she thought, but they'd had a rough life. Their father had left them fifteen years ago, when they were four and five. And Esther knew that she had been a wreck for the first five or six years after Bernard had left. So the kids had had a raw deal.

Bernard had left her for Jill Robinson. Esther had suspected nothing. When Bernard told her that he was leaving she didn't know what to ask him first. Her mouth was so crowded with questions that she said nothing.

Jill Robinson had also been in the A grade at Academy High. Now she was a lawyer. Esther hadn't thought that Jill Robinson was all that bright. Academy High was a school for gifted children, and the kids in the A grade were the *crème de la crème* of the State. Jill Robinson was always struggling at the bottom of the class. Esther had occasionally helped her with her German.

Bernard and Esther had started going out together when they were fifteen. Bernard was at Victoria High, a boys' school for academically superior students. He topped his school and won a scholarship to the University of Melbourne. He had completed an Arts/Law degree with honours six months before he left Esther.

Esther and the kids rarely heard from Bernard. He paid their rent with an automatic periodical payment from his bank. From time to time he sent the children $20 in an envelope.

For the first five years Esther couldn't believe that Bernard was gone. And so completely gone. He had left her the same day that he had told her he was leaving, and he hadn't spoken to her since. She had tried to call him, but as soon as he heard her voice he would hang up. Now she didn't even know where he lived. She knew that he had a silent phone number.

People said to her later that there had always been something detached about Bernard, but Esther hadn't seen it.

The phone rang. It was her mother. Her mother rang her every morning. The call was never to tell her anything specific, it was just to check in, to show Esther that she was still alive, and maybe to let herself know that she was still alive. Esther's mother had been saying that she wouldn't live long since Esther was a child. Her mother was now seventy-five. Esther thought that her mother hadn't noticed that she had made it into old age. Esther's father was still alive, too. Her parents lived in the same small dark cottage they'd lived in when Esther was a child. The house still smelt of sauerkraut and beef bones.

Her mother and father were frail now. They were more hunched and more nervous. To Esther they had always seemed old. She thought that they were worn out before they had had her.

Both of her parents had been in concentration camps. Both of them had lost everyone, but they had survived. They were survivors. Survivors. What did it mean to survive? Esther didn't think that her parents had survived.

Esther wished that she wasn't dying. She felt she had been on the verge of fixing herself up. She knew there were things she hadn't done, things she had missed out on. Sometimes she felt sick with panic at the way that the end had crept up on her.

She had been planning changes. She had been planning to go on a diet and smarten herself up. Then she had planned to look for a job, and give up the supporting mother's benefit that she received. She had never got used to being on a pension. Every second Thursday her mother asked her if her cheque had arrived. When Esther said yes, her mother wailed: "This is what I lived for? To have a pensioner for a daughter?"

Esther could see the shock in people's faces when they bumped into her. She could see that people had trouble recognising her. She wasn't sure just how unrecognisable she was, because she had removed all the mirrors from her house ten years ago. But she saw former friends looking at her lank hair, her bare legs and scuffed cream sandals, and she saw their pity.

Occasionally she saw herself reflected in a shop window or an unavoidable mirror, and she didn't recognise herself either. In her head she still looked the way she had looked when she was twenty. Bright-eyed and shiny-haired. Bernard had loved her hair. He'd thought it was her best feature.

Hair had always been important. Esther's mother still talked about her own hair all the time. "I had such beautiful hair," she would say. "My hair was thicker than yours. I had a plait down to my waist, so thick that all the girls envied it. After Auschwitz, my hair never grew the same. It was thin and all the curl was gone."

Esther didn't know very much about her parents' past. She had only scraps of information, odd ends of images, fragments of unfinished conversations.

Her mother's right leg had a jagged scar, which ran from her thigh to her calf. She had been mauled by one of the guard dogs in Auschwitz. Esther knew that her mother had kept on working with blood pouring from her leg. She had continued to clean the building rubble from a new enclosure that was being prepared for the prisoners. "I didn't stop," she'd said to Esther, "because the SS hated injured people. They always killed them straight away. My cousin Fela had a connection in Canada, the barracks where they sorted all the clothes they took from the Jews, and Fela got a man's shirt which we did tear into pieces to bandage my leg. I was very weak but I kept on working. Two weeks later they took blood from me for wounded German soldiers."

Esther had never talked to anyone about any of this. After all, what could she have said? Did you know that my father was forced to drink from the unflushed toilets at Auschwitz? It wasn't the sort of thing that people wanted to hear. She had never even talked to Bernard about it. Bernard knew that her parents had been in Auschwitz. He had seen their numbers tattooed on their forearms.

When Esther was seventeen, she had had her mother's Auschwitz number tattooed on her right forearm. She looked at it now. A4257. The letter A was given to those who were chosen for work.

Esther had had a strange sense of relief after she'd been tattooed. As though some missing link had been relocated. Looking at her tattoo always made her feel calm.

Her mother and father had been hysterical when they had seen Esther's tattoo.

"What are you doing, you idiot?" her mother had screamed.

"You are making a mockery of our tragedy," her father had said, and turned his back on her.

* *

Sometimes Esther forgot that she was dying. Some mornings she woke up and thought that she might try and get her life into order. She might go to a good hairdresser and have her hair cut. And maybe she would buy some lotion for her bad skin. She had read that to still have oily skin at her age was a good sign. It meant that her skin was less prone to wrinkling. Maybe she would even try to meet somebody. Her parents had stopped urging her to find another husband years ago, and her children took her spinsterish existence for granted. She thought that they thought of her as sexless. She hadn't had sex with anyone since Bernard. She hadn't had sex with anybody except Bernard. She could hardly remember what it was like to have sex. She couldn't remember whether she had found it enjoyable or not.

She had started thinking about men and sex last year when she had turned forty, but she thought that maybe she had left it too late. Now she knew she had left it too late.

She had seen a T-shirt in a shop in Brunswick Street which had horrified her. Across the front of the T-shirt was a drawing of a worried woman saying: "Oh my God, I forgot to have children." Esther had forgotten to do so many things. The T-shirt had chilled her. Lists of things that she had forgotten to do started to fill her head. They disturbed her thoughts and interrupted her routine. She began to feel agitated.

Her mother noticed her agitation. "Esther, what's wrong with you?" she said. "You don't sound like your normal self."

"Nothing's wrong in particular," said Esther.

"Well, maybe it is the change of life coming early to you. Women who don't live with a man can get the change of life very early," her mother said.

The change of life. What a funny phrase, thought Esther. Her life had had so few changes. First she'd been a child, then she'd had a husband. The big change came when she lost her husband. After that she'd had very few changes. She did the same thing most days. She cleaned the house, did the shopping, the washing, the ironing and the cooking.

On Friday mornings she went to the Victoria Market, and on Saturday afternoon she went to the Athenaeum Library. She took out four books each Saturday, and she read them by the following Saturday. She had read Doris Lessing, Saul Bellow, John Updike, Gail Godwin, Joyce Carol Oates, Maxine Hong Kingston, Philip Roth, Bernard Malamud. She knew what went on in the world.

One of her plans had been to write a book herself. She thought that she might write a novel about a woman whose husband leaves her, but inadvertently takes her life with him. She had made notes in several notebooks. She had had trouble deciding what form this symbol of his wife's life should take. She had thought that the wife could have been suffering from cancer. Cancer of the bone marrow. And the husband, because he was the wife's first cousin, could have had compatible bone marrow. But the wife could not have a bone marrow transplant because they couldn't locate the husband. She had thought that she might give the story a happy ending, but then she had abandoned the whole project.

Some Saturdays, after she had left the library, Esther walked to Drummond House. Drummond House had a particularly nice lift in it. The lift had Victorian plaster cornices, a marble floor and subdued lighting. On Saturdays the building was almost empty, and Esther could ride up and down in the lift for as long as she liked. She loved being in lifts. She found it soothing. She felt cushioned and protected by whatever it was that held lifts up. She imagined that this was how foetuses must feel floating in their amniotic fluid. Esther had a selection of good, infrequently used lifts that she travelled in.

This morning Esther woke to the sound of two currawongs singing. She had slept well. She lay in bed listening to the birds. She felt much better. Maybe there was nothing wrong with her? Maybe she was exaggerating the symptoms? Maybe she had misdiagnosed herself?

Maybe her tattoo had jinxed her? Number A4257. It was a number that had clearly been earmarked for death. Esther knew that it was now possible to have tattoos removed. She was feeling so good that she decided to see if she could have her tattoo taken off.

Esther went to the new medical centre at the end of her street. Dr Sainsbury seemed to be not much older than Beau, Esther thought. She calculated that he must have been at least twenty-seven to be practising medicine. He was very sympathetic. He said he would refer her to a plastic surgeon who would be able to remove her tattoo. "Were you in the concentration camp for very long?" he asked her.

"I just passed through," she said. "I didn't really suffer." She felt upset. To Dr Sainsbury she obviously looked fifty or sixty. She changed her mind about having the tattoo removed. It had been with her for a long time.

She was feeling more frail now. The shooting pains had almost stopped, but she had a dull headache day and night. She estimated that she had about a month to live.

She felt as frail as she had felt after her abortion. She hadn't thought about her abortion for years. She used to think that she would never stop thinking about it.

She had had the abortion when she was sixteen. She had tried to abort herself first. She had jumped off the kitchen table ten and twenty times in a row. She had once heard a friend of her mother's say that that was what women in Poland did when they didn't want any more children. So Esther had jumped and jumped. Her feet ached, but nothing else happened. She remained pregnant.

In order to get a legal abortion Esther had to have two psychiatrists say that it would be psychologically dangerous for her to have a child. Esther saw six psychiatrists and four general practitioners. She told them about her parents and how it would kill them, and she said that she would kill herself if she was forced to have a child.

The first nine doctors all told her that she was perfectly normal, and said they could not sign anything that suggested that she was not in a fit state of mental health. They told her that she was naughty, immature, irresponsible and promiscuous. She had made her bed, one of them said, and now she would just have to lie in it.

The tenth doctor arranged for two of his colleagues to sign the necessary papers. By this time Esther was sixteen weeks pregnant, and it was too late for a normal abortion. She needed a caesarian.

The doctor arranged for Esther to be admitted to the psychiatric ward of the Newton Hospital. Newton was a large public hospital. The psychiatric ward was a mixed ward. Men and women roamed the ward, or lay in bed and talked to themselves. Esther was the youngest person in there.

Luckily it was the school holidays. Esther told her parents that she was going to Rosebud for two weeks. Bernard came to visit her once, but he was so depressed by the other people in the ward that he didn't come again. He did call the nurses' station every night to send Esther his love.

After the operation she couldn't stop crying. The doctor came to see her once. He told her that he had aborted her of male twins. He said that he thought she should know this as it might encourage her to be more responsible. He left her with a prescription for the pill.

Before the war Esther's parents had each had two children in other marriages. Esther didn't know the sex or names of these children. Between herself and her parents, Esther thought, they had lost six children.

When she got home from hospital her hair started falling out and she developed red, itchy spots. These spots swelled up and began oozing a clear yellowish liquid. "Hives," said Dr Janowski, their family doctor.

Mrs Jones, Esther's English teacher, called Esther's mother.

"Esther seems troubled," Mrs Jones said.

"She is troubled? Esther?" said Esther's mother. "The only thing that troubles Esther is how to get the best for Esther. She has got hives. She probably got them from eating too many strawberries. Strawberries that cost five shillings a box. My husband and I know what trouble is, Mrs Jones, and it is not what Esther is suffering from."

Esther wore black fish-net stockings to cover the purple and red welts on her legs. She couldn't resist scratching the scabs. Sometimes ten welts on one leg would be bleeding at the same time. She tried not to scratch. She covered the welts with bandaids, but it was no good; she just pulled the bandaids off. Every time a welt began to heal Esther would scratch it. The scars never went away. Today her legs still looked polkadotted.

Esther wondered whether she should write any letters while she was still strong enough. She decided that she wouldn't. She couldn't think of anything that she could say that would make any difference to her parents or to Beau or Daisy. She wouldn't be able to alter their image of her. It was too late for that. They would remember her by what they already knew of her, not by anything she could say in a letter.

Lately her hair had begun feeling very heavy. It felt like a great weight on her head. She decided to have it cut. She walked down to the nearest hairdressers and had it cut fashionably short. She admired herself in the mirror. The hairdresser had done a good job. He showed her the back view of her head. It looked very chic, she thought.

At home her hair still felt too heavy. She took a pair of scissors and cut the rest of her hair off. Then she shaved her head with Daisy's electric razor. Her body might be flabby, but her head had a nice shape. When she ran her hands over it her head was smooth and firm, sculpted by the contours of her skull.

She was feeling very tired. Some fresh air might do her good. She thought she would go for a drive. She packed herself a thermos of hot tea and got into the car. She drove around. It was a mild, sunny autumn day. She drove to Academy High.

It was Saturday and the school was empty. The gate was locked. Esther climbed over the back fence, swinging her leg over as she used to do when she wanted to take the afternoon off. She was pleased that she could still climb over the fence.

She walked into the shelter sheds. They looked exactly the same. Her old locker was there. Locker 1012. It was unlocked. She opened the door and climbed into the locker. She could still fit inside. She poured herself a cup of tea and put the thermos on the shelf above her. She counted the sixty-five Serepax tablets that she had saved. They were all there. It took three mugs of tea to wash down the pills. She put the lid back on the thermos. The locker was cosy and comfortable. She snuggled into the corner and closed her eyes.

A Glimpse of Stocking

In this morning's mail Ella Tennenbaum had received letters from all three of her ex-husbands. Husband Number 1's letter said that he still loved her and he would like to see her when he came to Melbourne at the end of the month.

Ella knew that when she had been married to him he had had an all-consuming affair with his first wife. Ella felt sorry for his current wife, who at twenty-three had just given birth to her husband's fourth daughter.

What was wrong with men? she thought. They lurched through life as though there were no more sensitive antennae than their genitals. Even the best genitals didn't do much more than perfectly ordinary genitals.

She was tempted to accept her first husband's invitation. She wouldn't, she decided, but she was tempted. He had been a lovely lover. A very touchable man. You could stroke him for hours, and he would want more. He loved to hug and kiss and touch. That had been his trouble. He had loved it too much. With too many different women.

"There is no maliciousness in my adultery," he had said to Ella. "I think I'm just genetically overloaded with sensory receptors, and I can't resist a sexual experience. But I never mean to hurt anyone."

Ella had left him when she had found him in bed with her arch-rival, a colleague on the daily newspaper where she worked. Ella had come home early from work. She had had an abortion two days earlier and had still been feeling weepy and edgy. In that

one-minute glimpse of the two of them jammed together, she had become immune to him. No amount of apologies from him had made any difference. The boyish smile that had always won her over had looked crooked and foolish.

The other two ex-husbands had written via their lawyers. Husband Number 2 wanted to renegotiate the property settlement, and Husband Number 3 was letting her know that their divorce was now final.

It was a funny thing, she thought, that people could completely vanish from your life, yet you could be interminably tied to them. Their lawyers wrote to your lawyers and your lawyers wrote to their lawyers, and all the correspondence was passed on to you and to them. The intensity between all the lawyers was possibly greater than the intensity in the marriages, she thought.

She hopped into the car and drove to work. At every red light, she plucked her eyebrows. Looking in the mirror was demoralising. In this mid-morning summer light she could clearly see every line and every wrinkle. Ten years ago she had had no lines and no wrinkles. Her eyes looked puffy too. She tried to concentrate on her eyebrows. In the past her attention had wandered, and she had ended up with pencil-thin eyebrows that had taken months to grow back.

It seemed to her that the puffiness around her eyes was taking longer and longer to go down in the mornings. She wondered whether this could be a sign of kidney failure. She half-wished that she was going to see her first husband. He was a good hypochondriac, and they could have had a terrific conversation about symptoms. She no longer felt angry with her first husband. All her anger was used up on Numbers 2 and 3.

She turned right into the top of Bourke Street. Melbourne looked very beautiful. Very European. The plane trees that shaded both sides of the street billowed and fluttered like ample mothers. The cafe tables on the pavement were already set up for the day. Ella could almost smell the coffee.

She drove down Bourke Street singing to herself. "In olden days a glimpse of stocking was looked on as something shocking, now heaven knows, anything goes." She was just about to go on to the next chorus when she remembered that she had forgotten to call her mother. She grimaced.

Although her mother was almost seventy, Ella was still intimidated by her. Her strongest childhood memory was of her mother getting ready to go out on Saturday nights. Her mother would run around from the bathroom to the bedroom to the laundry in her high heels and stockings and bra. She would spray her hair and paint her nails in the laundry. Then she would make the last-minute adjustments to her make-up and put on her perfume in the bathroom. Finally, she would get dressed in the bedroom. The whole house seemed to float with the scent of her.

Ella decided that she would call her mother when she got to the office. She began singing again. "In olden days a glimpse of stocking." She had been singing this song for days now. She sang it in the car. She hummed it while she worked at the keyboard in her small cubicle at Newsource Limited. The whole chorus had suddenly slipped out of her at an editorial meeting. She had been so embarrassed. She was a terrible singer. She couldn't carry a tune. She sounded OK to herself but she knew that she was bad because people always laughed if they overheard her singing.

As soon as she got to her desk she tried to ring her mother. But it was too late. Her mother's line was engaged. Her mother would be on to the second or third of the twenty or thirty phone calls she made every day. She said the same thing to each of the people that she spoke to, and they probably gave her the same replies. She always complained about her husband. She had several complaints about Ella's father. The chief complaint was that he hadn't made enough money. Most of their friends were wealthy, and although the Tennenbaums were not poor, they were not wealthy. Another standard complaint was about Ella, and her failed marriages, and her current lack of a husband. These complaints kept her mother happy.

Ella settled down in front of her computer. She logged in and headed up her piece. She was writing up an interview she had done last week with the film-maker, Robert Celine. She had felt too complicated to write the piece before now, and today was the deadline.

She had interviewed Celine at his home. And she had done something that she had known that she would regret. She had allowed him to seduce her. She squirmed at the memory. After making love for about two minutes, he had shouted: "Make me come, make me come." She had been startled, and hadn't known what to do. Why did he want to come already, and how was she supposed to make him? She had felt embarrassed, and had tried to fuck faster. She should have just stopped, got dressed and gone home, she realised later. Instead they had both become sweaty and dank. Finally Robert Celine had said "It's no use," and rolled over and picked up a magazine.

Ella had wondered how Robert Celine could have got it so wrong. Didn't he know that a good lover was supposed to last some distance? Still, she had felt inadequate for not knowing how to make him come. She had resolved never again to have sex with someone she wasn't yet comfortable talking to. Fucking was such a fragile thing. One minute it could feel so urgent and all-encompassing, and the next minute it could dissolve into something squalid.

She decided that she would call Celine "stout" in the opening paragraph of the article. But first she would try to get through to her mother again. She dialled her parents' number. The phone was still engaged. She felt agitated. One way or another she had always had trouble communicating with her parents. After forty-five years in Australia, their English was still poor and heavily accented. They lacked all subtlety in English. Their English was a stub of a language. And Ella couldn't speak Polish or Yiddish. While Ella pondered the difference between mellifluous and melodious, her parents voiced everything in terms of this sort of stuff and that sort of stuff. They could summarise any event with either of those two phrases.

Her parents never read anything that she wrote. Sometimes her mother would call her to tell her about a message on a greeting card she had bought. She would read the card out loud to Ella as an example of a moving piece of prose. The last two cards she had read out were an anniversary card she had bought that said "Happy Anniversary to a couple who has created an exemplary marriage based on true love and total commitment", and a bereavement card that read:

For each thorn there's a rose-bud . . .
for each twilight . . . a dawn
for each trial . . . strength
to carry on.

Ella had agreed with her mother that these messages were beautiful. Ten years ago, she would have said something like, "Would it ruin this moment if I vomit?" and her mother would have clasped her head and said, "What did I do to deserve a daughter like this?"

She knew that her parents were ashamed of her. They were ashamed of her for not having any children and for having had too many husbands. Ella was one of the few Jewish women of her generation who had always supported herself. Her parents saw this as an embarrassment rather than an accomplishment.

Ella finished her piece on Robert Celine, and was reading it through on the screen when Paul Sunderland, who had been working across the aisle from her, swivelled his chair up beside hers. "Don't ever invite Paul Sunderland to your place," Jean Stafford, the Arts Editor, had warned Ella when she had joined Newsource ten years ago. "He's appalling. Two minutes after he's walked into your front door, he tries to get his head into your pants." To Ella, that had been a revolting prospect. Paul Sunderland had yellow teeth and a wet mouth.

Sunderland must have been bright and fresh once, Ella thought. Occasionally, when he spoke about one of his favourite authors or a new magazine that was coming out, you could see his former youthfulness and enthusiasm. But he was fifty now, with four wives and six children behind him. He looked worn and used. He looked discarded. He reminded Ella of a cigarette butt.

He was still witty, and sometimes good to talk to. He presented himself well enough. His clothes were contemporary and slightly flamboyant. But he had a stale aura which even the gel gleaming in his hair couldn't cover. When Ella was feeling low, she felt in danger of being contaminated by his decay.

"Now that you're a single woman again," he said to her with a flourish, "would you do me the honour of having dinner with me one night?"

"Thanks, Paul," she said, "but you know that I'm working on my novel at night, and I'm not going out at all."

"How is it coming along?"

"Not bad. I just have to keep plugging away at it."

The truth was that she had wanted to write a novel for years. She had had several ideas for storylines. They had seemed full of potential when she was lying in the garden or walking along the street, but when she sat down to write them out, she came to a full stop. She thought that maybe she just liked the notion of writing a novel, or maybe it was the prospect of acclaim as a writer that appealed her.

"Well, if you want to take a break one night, just call me," said Paul Sunderland.

Ella was peeling off her leotards after the aerobics class. She felt satisfyingly sweaty. She had worked hard, yet with a greater ease than she had had up until now. She must be getting fitter, she thought. When Ruthie Brot had first asked her if she would like to do aerobics once a week at Ruthie's house, Ella had opened her mouth to say no. She hardly knew Ruthie. They had talked on the beach in Surfers Paradise when they were teenagers. Ruthie had been a brunette then. Now her head and shoulders were covered with a blanket of blonde curls.

Ruthie Brot looked like exactly the sort of person that Ella had dreaded becoming. Ruthie was co-ordinated from one end of her slim figure to the other. That day she had been a symphony of creams and greys, with a dash of bright yellow. She had sparkling teeth, polished nails and a seamless tan.

Ella's mouth had been open, ready to form an excuse, when she had paused and surprised herself by accepting the invitation.

Now that she knew Ruthie better, Ella felt ashamed of the snap judgments she had made about her. There was a warmth and a generosity about Ruthie that Ella had rarely experienced in anyone. She felt mothered by her. Ruthie always had clean towels, shampoo and a spare hairdryer ready in the bathroom. She often sliced and peeled a piece of fruit or buttered a bread roll for Ella to eat in the car on her way to work.

At the first couple of aerobics classes, Ella had seen herself as the outsider in a group of good Jewish girls. She knew that this was ridiculous: there were only four of them, and Zoe wasn't Jewish, and Golda battled with her weight and her mother.

Ella looked down at herself in the shower. Her stomach was distended. She looked at least four months pregnant. She knew that it was a premenstrual swelling. Sometimes when she was swollen like this she would arch her back and push her stomach out further. She would pretend that she was pregnant. She would stand the way she had seen pregnant women stand, with both hands on the back of her hips. It was always a nice feeling.

Ruthie and Zoe were sharing the other shower. Ella could hear them laughing. She knew they had been friends for years. She listened to their laughter. She felt envious of their intimacy.

Ella's phone was ringing when she arrived at work. It was Robert Celine. The call took her by surprise. "Could you hold on for a minute?" she said to him. She composed herself and picked up the telephone.

"I'm calling to see if you'd like to come over to my place after work," Robert Celine said. "I've got a rough cut of my new film and I thought we could watch it and then go out and grab a bite to eat."

"I'm pleased that you called," she said to him, "because it's broken the ice and I won't feel so embarrassed when I see you, but I felt awful the other night and it's not something that I'd care to repeat."

"The other night was a mistake," he said. "I was tired and I was a bit impatient. I'll be more patient next time."

"Patient?" she said. "You need to be a lot more than patient, Robert. I've got to get back to my work. Goodbye."

"Nobody else thinks I'm stout," he said.

She squirmed when she hung up the phone. How could someone get to be his age, with two wives behind him, and be so inept? What had he been like with his wives? Had he shouted at them to "make me come"? She then remembered that both of his wives had been very young, and they had both left him.

She decided to call her lawyer. Then all of the business to do with men would be over with early in the day. Husband Number 2's demand for a greater share of her house had been hovering uneasily at the back of her mind.

"Hello, George," she said to her lawyer. "I got your letter yesterday. You can tell that arsehole to go and fuck himself. He's not going to fuck me around any longer."

"I'm glad to hear that you're in good form this morning," said George. "I've already given his lawyer that message. I told him that his client's got no chance. We'll go to court if necessary, and we'll make mincemeat of him. Don't worry about it, Ella, the guy's got no case."

Ella liked George. She liked his decisiveness. It seemed to her that men were becoming more and more wimpish. They wore their long hair in pony tails and suffered from anxiety symptoms. They had sensitive stomachs and sensitive psyches. Where were all the solidly male men? They were probably driving trucks up the Hume

Highway, she thought. They certainly weren't to be seen among the intelligentsia.

She was anxious and fearful enough herself; she didn't need a nervous man. She didn't want a man she had to placate and pacify. She wanted a robust man. God, she sounded like someone she didn't recognise, she thought. She used to be drawn towards sensitive men. As soon as she spotted a set of complexities she knew that there was the man for her. Maybe she was ready for a truck driver.

She went to the toilet. A bit of stress was good for the bowels. She was pulling her tights up when she saw the water level in the toilet rising and rising. She was panic-stricken. Big pieces of shit were floating within an inch of the top of the bowl. She gathered her skirt up and grabbed her handbag from the floor. She thought that at any moment the shit would spill out and flow out into the offices. And everyone would see her shit.

The water stopped rising just as it reached the top of the bowl. She felt a terrible humiliation. She couldn't call the janitor. She would have to find something to unblock the toilet with.

This had happened to her once before, when she was thirteen. The whole family had been at Joey Feinblatt's barmitzvah at the Dayenu Reception Centre. Luckily her stepsister, Yvette, had been in the bathroom with her at the time. Yvette had found a coat hanger in the cloak room and unblocked the toilet. Ella remembered watching Yvette prod the shit down. She had felt as though Yvette was touching her insides.

Ella had felt that same feeling of being fundamentally in touch with another person only one other time in her life. She and her first husband were staying in a country motel. He had had too much to drink, and had vomited all over the carpet. Ella had been too embarrassed to call the porter. She had cleaned the vomit up, one teaspoonful at a time.

Yvette wasn't officially Ella's stepsister, as Ella's parents hadn't completed the formal adoption procedures. Ella's parents had brought Yvette to Australia from Paris when Ella was six years old.

Ella still remembered Yvette's arrival clearly. Yvette had been fourteen, a small girl with large pale blue eyes. She was a Jewish orphan. She had been hidden in a convent in Grenoble during the war. After the war, the nuns found out that both of Yvette's parents had perished and they had sent her to an orphanage in Paris. Ella's parents told her that she was not to ask Yvette any questions.

For her first two weeks in Australia Yvette had slept in Ella's bed. She hadn't wanted to sleep alone. She later told Ella that Ella's small body pressed up tight against her had stopped her from shaking at night. She told Ella that every time she had cried during the night, Ella had thrown her arms around her. Ella had no memory of it.

Ella did remember an awful scene at school about a year later. The English teacher had read Yvette's homework out to the class as an example of how not to write a composition. Yvette had started crying and had not been able to stop. The teacher had called in the assistant principal and the principal, but none of them could pacify her. Yvette was lying on the floor, uttering a hoarse cry like that of a wounded animal. Someone called Ella. Ella ran up three flights of steps. She could still remember her panic. She ran into the classroom and threw herself down next to Yvette. She held her until Yvette stopped crying.

Years later, Yvette said to her that she felt that day as though Ella had saved her life. "We must have looked so strange," Yvette had said. "A seven-year-old girl lying on the floor holding a fifteen-year-old. You know, you lay there next to me for at least an hour. It took the headmaster about six months to get over that episode. He used to smile at me nervously every day. And none of the other teachers ever said a sharp word to me again. I think they were terrified."

"What were you crying about?" Ella had asked her.

"I started crying because I felt so humiliated by the English teacher, but then it became like all my crying, just a mixed-up big sadness. Sometimes the sadness was so strong that I wouldn't be able to breathe. Your mother used to think I was putting it on."

Ella's mother hadn't particularly liked Yvette. Ella thought that it was because Yvette was so pretty and not compliant enough. Ella had never understood what had made her mother bring Yvette to Australia in the first place. She thought that maybe it had been an attempt to assuage the guilt that she had felt at getting out of Europe before the war.

When Ella was seventeen Yvette left Australia to live in Israel. She married an Israeli doctor and had four children in quick succession. Last year Yvette had had her first grandchild. Ella couldn't imagine her as a grandmother.

Ella had felt bereft when Yvette had left for Israel. She had flung herself into a series of boyfriends and outings and parties, and she had still felt terrible. Yvette used to write to her once a week, but Ella never wrote back. She thought now that she had been too furious with Yvette to write to her. Yvette still wrote to her three or four times a year.

Ella stepped out into the corridor to see if she could see a maintenance man. There was no-one around. When she came back, the toilet had begun to drain. She heaved a sigh of relief. She waited another few minutes. It was definitely draining. She flushed the toilet again. It worked. Everything drained away and a new swill of fresh water appeared.

Ella sat at her desk. She felt dogged by a sense of loss. "I always feel lost after my divorces," Paul Sunderland had said to her. She had glared at him. She didn't want to be associated with his failed marriages. And she didn't want to be identified as a much-married person, even though she was amply qualified.

She didn't know why she felt this sense of loss. She didn't miss any of her husbands. She savoured the space they left behind them. She had indulged in a small ritual each time one of her marriages had ended. She had bought herself new sheets. Expensive, smooth, white linen sheets.

It was already dark when Ella came home from work. She had been interviewing a young American concert pianist. The pianist was a gorgeous-looking young girl. All creamy skin and dark curls. She was twenty-six and had played with many famous orchestras and conductors. "The most exciting thing that I could envisage," she had said to Ella, "would be to play with someone that I was in love with."

"It would be like sharing arteries," Ella had agreed.

Driving home, she had thought about what romantics women were. Regardless of their age or their accomplishments, they were suckers for romance. Ella thought that this was one of the nicest things about women.

She drove into her garage. Her house looked lovely. She had known that she would be late home and she had left the lights on. She hated coming home to a dark house.

There were messages on her answering service from Robert Celine, Paul Sunderland and Ruthie. Robert Celine must be a masochist, she thought. He must be turned on by rejection. She rang Ruthie.

"Ella, darling," said Ruthie, "you were in Esther Schenkler's class at Academy High, weren't you?"

"Yes," said Ella. "I was in her form right through high school."

"Ella, I'm sorry to tell you this," Ruthie said. "I don't know how well you knew Esther Schenkler, but I thought that I should tell you rather than have you read it in the paper tomorrow. My father just told me. Esther committed suicide yesterday. She took an overdose of tranquillisers or sedatives or something, and she locked herself in one of the lockers in the shelter sheds at Academy High. They found her there last night. Isn't it awful?"

Ella felt stunned. She hadn't known Esther particularly well, but she had liked her. Esther had been one of the brightest girls in the A form. She had had extraordinarily thick hair and beautiful green eyes.

"Why did she do it?" Ella asked Ruthie.

"No-one knows," said Ruthie. "I don't know anyone who knew

her well, but an old friend of my dad's is a friend of Esther's parents. Apparently they're devastated."

"She was such a bright girl," said Ella. "We were all such bright girls." She started to cry.

"I'm sorry I'm crying, Ruthie, it's just a big shock," she said. "What could have happened to Esther to make her life that unbearable? Didn't she have two children?"

"Yes, she's got a son and a daughter," said Ruthie. "My dad said that the daughter is almost hysterical."

"Poor Esther," said Ella. "Ruthie, I think I'll go now. Thanks a lot for telling me. You were right, it would have given me an awful shock to read about it in the paper."

Ella sat on the end of her bed and wept. They had all been so clever, so promising. Esther had been captain of the debating team. No-one had stood a chance against her. What went wrong with her life? Ella wondered. Ella sat on the bed for a long time. She felt very low.

The next day she called her mother. "I heard about Esther Schenkler," said her mother. "What a thing to do to her parents."

"Her parents?" Ella said. "What about poor Esther?"

"Of course, she was poor," said her mother. "She didn't have a husband, and I heard that she had let herself go. But she shouldn't have done it. After all, she had two children and her parents to think of."

"Maybe she needed more than her children or her parents to think about."

"Of course. She needed a husband."

Paul Sunderland dropped Ella's mail on to her desk. "I picked it up with mine," he whispered. She nodded thank you. She noticed a letter from Yvette. "Mum, I'll say goodbye now. I've just got a letter from Yvette, and I haven't heard from her for ages, so I'll read the letter and ring you and give you her news later."

"That's Yvette," said Ella's mother. "She writes to you and not to me. Who brought her here from an orphanage? Was it you or was it me?"

Ella said goodbye and opened Yvette's letter. She could see that it was only a short letter. She started to read it. "I have been missing you," Yvette wrote. "I have been missing you very much. I have been dreaming about you. I love you. I need to see you. Love and kisses, Yvette."

Ella started crying. Her eyes were still swollen from last night. She went to the bathroom to be by herself. In the bathroom she went on crying.

She rang Yvette in Israel. When Yvette answered the phone, just hearing her familiar French accent made Ella feel tearful.

"Ella, my Ella," Yvette shouted. "How are you, my darling?"

"I'm fine," said Ella. "I got your letter today. It made me very happy."

"Ella, darling," said Yvette, "I was thinking a few weeks ago about how I had lost so many people in my life. And of course I have new people. I have my husband and the children and now a beautiful grandchild. But Ella, you are the only one who knew me when I was a poor skinny orphan. And I felt that you loved me from the day that I arrived in Melbourne. I was thinking, Ella, why do we have to live so far away from people that we love? Isn't that what we are living for? For love? I can't move to you because I would have to move so many people, but you can move to me. You can live with us, Ella. We've got a beautiful house. Are you with a man at the moment?"

"No," said Ella.

"Well that makes it easier to leave, doesn't it?"

"What about my job?"

"You have been complaining about your job for years," said Yvette. "We will help you to get a job here."

"But I can't speak Hebrew."

"Of course you can. Remember, it's your sister you are talking to. Remember I used to help you with your Hebrew homework from Bialik. I knew that one day we would both be grateful to your mother for forcing us to go to Bialik."

"Yvette, that was years ago."

"Darling, after a few weeks in Israel it will all come back to you. Also, I've got a very nice man to introduce you to. He is forty, divorced with no children. He is a physicist, and he plays the cello."

"Yvette," said Ella, "I'm giving up men. Four marriages would seem positively seedy."

"This one could be Mr Right," said Yvette.

"I think I'd be too nervous to even try living in Israel. I mean there are so many Jews there. Everyone is a Jew. I've never mixed much with Jews."

"You'll get used to it. You know, darling, there are some very nice Jews. Just think about it, Ella darling, please."

"What about your job?" Ruthie said when Ella told her about Yvette's proposal. "You couldn't leave your job, could you?"

"Why not?" asked Ella.

"Because you're an A-grade journalist on a top newspaper, and that's a major achievement," said Ruthie.

"It's not such a major achievement."

"Well I think it is. Look at me. What have I achieved? I have never earned a penny in my life. I was supported by my father, and then Eddie took over and supported me. I've never had a career."

"You've got two gorgeous boys," said Ella. "And a career isn't all that it's cracked up to be. And some big career I've got. No woman ever gets to be an editor here. So what I've got to look forward to is more of what I have already got. What I've got is not bad, but it's important not to get it out of perspective."

"Do you think you'll go to Israel?"

"I think I might," said Ella. "It's not something that I ever thought I'd do, but I think I might. If I don't like it I can always come back."

Ella could hardly believe what she had just heard herself say.

"She's going to Israel to be closer to her sister," Ella's mother told all her friends. "I am giving up both my daughters to Israel. I am losing a daughter, but her sister is gaining a sister, and Israel is getting an A-grade journalist."

"I'm so proud of you, Ella," her mother said. "You have made me the happiest mother in Melbourne."

Ella was bewildered by her mother's pride and happiness. She decided not to question it. She thought she might as well enjoy it.

It was a week before she was due to leave. Everything was done and in place. Her suitcase was packed, and her house was spotless. She was renting the house out to a visiting academic for six months. She had decided only to take one suitcase with her. That way it seemed like a less permanent move.

She was using Yvette's old suitcase. The one Yvette had arrived with. It was made out of board covered with worn brown leather, and had large brass locks. The suitcase was the only thing that she had taken from her parents' house when she had left home twenty-two years ago.

In that last week she had a round of farewell dinners and parties. It was funny, she thought, how much nicer people were to you when you were leaving.

Ruthie drove her to the airport. "I'll miss you," she said.

"I'll miss you too, Ruthie," said Ella. "I'm so glad that I said yes when you asked me to come to the aerobics class. I almost said no. I was so arrogant. I imagined that I knew all about your life, and I would have nothing in common with you. I've learnt a lot from you, Ruthie."

"That's nice of you to say that. I'll start crying in a minute," said Ruthie. "I'm glad you said yes too. I almost didn't ask you. I was scared of you. I was intimidated by you."

"Why are human beings so stupid?" asked Ella.

"Bye, bye," said Ruthie. "Write to me."

Ella moved her suitcase along beside her in the check-in queue. It was so old and battered. She felt nervous. She felt like a cross between a refugee and an escapee. What was she doing? She wasn't sure. But she felt that it wasn't going to be a disaster. Suddenly, she felt as though all her disasters were behind her.

She was almost at the check-in counter. The cello-playing physicist, she thought, had probably been hearing about the brilliant and gifted journalist for weeks.

A Hormonal Imbalance

It was 9:20 a.m. when Rosa Cohen left her analyst. After five years, she shut the door of the small, dimly lit room for the last time. She walked down the familiar path. She got into the car and drove off. Tears were streaming down her face.

At every red light she took a handful of Kleenex and blew her nose and wiped her eyes. At the last red light she put some blemish concealer on her nose and some eyeliner under her eyes.

Rosa arrived home at 9:50. Allan was waiting for her. The suitcases, which she had locked and labelled before she left for her session, were standing in a row by the front door. Allan began to pack them into the car.

"Are you all right, my love?" he asked.

"Yes, I'm fine. I'll just have a quick piss and ring my dad up for one second, and then I'll be ready," she answered.

At 10:30 they were at Tullamarine airport. At 11:45 Continental Flight 16 to New York took off. In her hand luggage, Rosa had the seventeen-volume diary of her analysis, the manuscript of a play she was working on, two books of Marina Tsvetayeva's poems, and eight large reference books on the Holocaust. This took up all their hand luggage allowance; it was heavier than any of their suitcases.

Allan had carried the books while they did some duty-free shopping at the airport, and then onto the plane. He hadn't complained, although last night he had pointed out to Rosa that New York was the bookshop capital of the English-speaking world and he was sure that she would be able to buy any book she wanted there. But Rosa had said that some of the books were out of print and others were hard to get, and she didn't want to be without them.

Before her analysis, when she was heavier, she used to take packets of pantyhose with her in her hand luggage. She used to take enough pantyhose to last for however long they were away. She always overestimated how many she would need, as the emergencies that she had made allowances for rarely eventuated. In those days, it was hard for her to find pantyhose that fitted her. She had a horror of being left without pantyhose. Especially in winter.

When Rosa was at her largest she used to take her entire wardrobe on board with her. She had been too nervous to let her clothes go in the cargo hold in case they got lost.

Allan handed Rosa new issues of *Vanity Fair, Atlantic Monthly* and *Esquire*. He had searched the plane for good magazines and was pleased with his find. Kim Basinger was on the cover of *Vanity Fair*. Rosa wondered whether Kim Basinger would have anything interesting to say.

Rosa was looking forward to seeing the children. Zeke, Poppy and Kira had already been in New York for two weeks with Allan's studio assistant. Rosa put a packet of peppermint-flavoured toffees and a copy of *Hitler's Death Camps* into the pocket of the seat in front of her, and settled down for the flight.

In her first week in New York, Rosa furnished the apartment they had rented. Allan was having an exhibition of his paintings in Soho in November. While he set up his studio, Rosa organised a home. She bought a lounge suite, a dining suite, three beds, four desks, three standard lamps and four desktop lamps, two armchairs, two television sets and a computer. She bought a dinner service, a set of cutlery, saucepans, sieves, wooden spoons and a potato peeler. She bought sheets and towels and face washers. She bought eiderdowns and tea towels. She bought a blender, a toaster and a waffle iron.

At the end of the week she was exhausted. Standing in Macy's, wondering whether she should buy a round or a square grater, Rosa felt like a pitiful Polish refugee. Except, Rosa realised with a jolt, most refugees weren't in Macy's with three credit cards.

When all the furniture and all the appliances and all the accoutrements had been delivered and put in the right place, Rosa had expected to feel pleased. And she did feel pleased. But on the outer edge of that pleasure was a space. It hovered around her.

It wasn't a fear. Rosa was used to feeling fear. She often woke up in fear, and couldn't shake it off until she'd showered. Some mornings she could see the fear wash away with the warm water.

No, this gap, this absence, that Rosa felt was something new. She tried to busy herself. She knew from her analysis that she spent too much time thinking about herself and too little time thinking about others. She fussed around Kira.

"How was school today?" she'd ask. "Are the other children nice?" "Do you like your new teacher?" "Who do you have lunch with?" "What are you eating for lunch?" "Were you warm enough?" But Kira was fine. At school she was the new girl from Australia, and everyone wanted to know her.

Rosa started to think about her mother. Three or four times a day she found herself thinking about her mother. She felt her mother's presence vividly, and then just as vividly she would remember that her mother was dead. Her mother had died three years ago. She had shrivelled up like an old woman, and quietly, without admitting defeat, and without saying goodbye, she had died.

But for Rosa her mother hadn't died. Her mother had remained strong and iron-willed. Rosa had continued to have the same battles, the same arguments, the same conversations with her mother as she had had before her mother's death. Rosa's mother was so alive in Rosa that Rosa hardly grieved for her. Hardly felt her absence. Now, three years later, Rosa began to miss her mother.

She wanted to talk to her mother. Why did her mother have to die? Rosa thought. Why couldn't she have lived a bit longer? It was such a pathetic, plaintive plea, and so late in coming, that Rosa felt too ashamed to voice it to anyone. Things had been much better between Rosa and her mother in the last two years of Mania Cohen's life, but when Mania's cancer was diagnosed Rosa suffered a massive regression. She went back to the old Rosa. She thought her mother was perpetually angry with her. And she felt responsible.

Sometimes the thoughts about her mother felt so painful that Rosa tried to blink them out of her head. But she could no longer blink thoughts out of her head. Why did she have to die? A small squeaky voice in Rosa asked this question ten times a day.

She spoke to her father in Melbourne. She pictured him on the telephone surrounded by a large emptiness. An emptiness with a pull of its own. An emptiness that threatened to suck him into its centre. But her father was fine. He had mourned and wept for his beloved Mania many times, and he was all right. Speaking to her father anchored Rosa more firmly into her own life. She was in New York with a husband she adored. Her children were with her. Everything was all right. There was no reason to feel miserable.

Rosa had never needed a reason to feel miserable. She had mostly felt very miserable with very little reason. Well, that was in the past, she thought. That was all behind her. She had sorted things out now. Her parents had been the victims, not her. They had been in Auschwitz, not her. They had suffered, not her. She had created her own suffering. It had been a sort of equalising manoeuvre, a redistribution of the pain in the Cohen household.

At night, on the island of Manhattan, Rosa dreamt about her mother. In one dream, Rosa felt joyful. Her mother was in a state of remission. Rosa looked carefully at her mother to see if there was any sign of the cancer, and no, there was not. Rosa was so happy. In the dream she went back to that happiness again and again, and each time it was intact. She checked her mother over and over again, and her mother was fine. Mania looked robust, strong-armed and healthy.

In another dream, Mania was in her garden. She was standing

near the apple tree that she had planted. She looked strong and tanned.

One night, in one of the dreams, Rosa kissed her mother. She was surprised at how easy it was to kiss her mother. The next night Rosa kissed her mother again in her dreams. But this time Mania was ill with the cancer. She was lying in bed, frail and jaundiced. Rosa patted her head and held her hand. By the end of the dream Mania didn't look so sick. When Rosa woke up she wondered why in real life it had been so hard for her to kiss her mother.

Rosa ordered her days. She wrote in the morning, and again in the afternoon. In the middle of the day Rosa and Allan went for a long walk. They walked the streets of Manhattan and they talked. Allan liked to explore a new area every day. He loved New York. He had been waiting for Rosa to finish her analysis so that they could live in New York. He told Rosa that he felt a complete sense of contentment being in New York.

Rosa wasn't scared in Manhattan. She had been worried that she would be. Rosa and Allan were usually there in the American winter, which was when Rosa's analyst took her summer break. But now it was autumn and the city looked more mellow, more languorous, less threatening.

Rosa was relieved that she wasn't frightened in New York. She was looking for signs of progress in herself, signs that she was a different person after this analysis. In the last few months of the analysis she felt that she had been given back her life. She laughed with a freedom and a girlishness that she hadn't felt since she was sixteen. She was curious again. She felt lucky.

From her bedroom window, Rosa could see Stuyvesant Park. She could see squirrels darting across the grass. Doves and pigeons nuzzled and mated on her window sill. The sun was shining. Manhattan looked positively bucolic. To her surprise, Rosa realised that she felt happy. She loved living in an apartment. She loved the feeling of other people living above her and below her and on both sides of her. The building had a doorman. Rosa felt a deep peacefulness knowing that there was someone on guard all night. In Melbourne Rosa had lived with a monitored security system and deadlocks on the doors and windows. In Manhattan, in her sixth-floor apartment, Rosa slept with the windows wide open.

Some evenings, when she and Allan walked through Greenwich Village or Soho, Rosa felt an enormous happiness. She felt the life inside her, and she felt joined to the life around her.

She had to watch herself, though. She had a terrible tendency to slip into the old Rosa. Old Rosa loved to complain. Old Rosa couldn't resist detailing every fleeting moment of misery to Allan. Old Rosa was a misery-guts, Rosa thought. She wondered how Allan had put up with old Rosa. She was grateful that he had.

Rosa had to watch herself because she no longer had KJ to keep an eye on her. Rosa called her analyst KJ. Those were her initials. Rosa hadn't actually had an occasion to call Katherine Jamieson KJ, but she always referred to her as KJ.

For five years Rosa had found it difficult to feel attached to KJ. Rosa had been contemptuous and arrogant, a condescending, competitive daughter to this new mother. But she had never missed a session, and she was never late. KJ said that Rosa's attendance and punctuality were due more to a sense of not wanting to miss out than of wanting to learn.

During the analysis Rosa had had trouble remembering what KJ looked like. She walked past KJ on her way to the couch every day, and again on her way out. Five minutes after Rosa left the session she couldn't picture KJ's face.

Sometimes she wondered if she would recognise KJ if she bumped into her in the outside world. What did KJ look like? Rosa had no idea. Some days Rosa thought that KJ looked thin, haggard and old, and some days Rosa saw her as slim, elegant and beautiful. How old was KJ? Thirty-eight? Forty-two? Fifty-four? Rosa couldn't tell. Her expression and age changed according to how Rosa felt.

Now, Rosa missed KJ. Here, on the other side of the world, Rosa felt connected to her analyst. She felt part of KJ's life. Before, although Rosa's link with KJ was sometimes so brittle it could have snapped, Rosa wanted to be the only person in KJ's life. She used to be obsessed with wondering who else was part of KJ's life. Rosa used to come to the sessions early to catch a glimpse of the patient before her, and delay her departure to see who came after her.

She looked for other signs. Did the Volvo that was always parked outside belong to KJ? Or was KJ's car the Jaguar that was parked across the road? Rosa didn't know. One day Rosa examined a pile of newspapers that had been put outside KJ's house to see if she could learn anything from them. She didn't. Rosa knew that there was a Mr KJ and a small KJ. She had spoken to a child the one time that she had phoned KJ at home. It had been when her mother was first diagnosed as having cancer.

Rosa carried KJ around New York with her. If she felt herself becoming scrappy, KJ's voice would interject and point out that this was Princess Rosa we were seeing. Rosa knew that Princess Rosa was not someone she wanted to be close to. She had once pasted a large sign above her desk: "Princess Rosa . Death. Normal Rosa . Life."

On the whole, Rosa was fine. She didn't panic in crowds, she went to art functions without complaining, and she attended dinner parties where she was seated far away from Allan without feeling anxious. Things were looking OK, she thought.

Their apartment, which was off Third Avenue, had three bathrooms. Each bathroom had mirrors on three of its walls. In the mornings Rosa was often startled when she looked at herself. She was looking more and more like her mother. She had had her hair cut before she left Melbourne. It must be the shorter hair, she thought. But it unnerved her to see the similarity. The same shaped face, the same shoulders, the same hands. The same worried expression. It was the expression that most upset Rosa. She wondered whether her mother would have been proud of her. She didn't know.

In her tenth week in New York, Rosa started weeping.

Everything made her cry. She couldn't listen to snatches of sentimental songs coming from the radios in taxi cabs without crying. Andy Williams singing "Moon River" in a newspaper kiosk made her cry. If Allan looked tired, she cried. And she couldn't stop. She cried three or four times a day. She had never cried like this.

People walking their dogs cheered her up a bit. In Rosa's neighbourhood it seemed everyone had a dog. Allan called their area the canine capital of Manhattan. There were poodles, pugs, pekinese, whippets, dalmations, spaniels and samoyeds. There were dogs with hats and coats, there were dogs with jumpers and ear muffs.

A photographer in their building had offered Kira borrowing rights to his basset hound, Rosa. Rosa the dog was on her last legs. Her idea of going for a walk was to sit in the lift. She was pathetically eager for attention. She rolled over when anyone approached her. Rosa the human tried not to identify with Rosa the dog.

When Rosa stopped crying long enough to think, she wondered if this crying could be hormonal, a hormonal imbalance. She wasn't premenstrual, but maybe she was premenopausal. She wished she had read the book that she had bought on menopause. She had so many gaps in her knowledge. She didn't really know much about how her body worked. And now she had no idea whether weeping was a premenopausal symptom or not. That was something else she had learned about herself in the analysis. That she had a lot to learn. Well it was no use knowing that without doing anything about it, she thought. But she felt too fragile to go out and look for a book on menopause.

She had no-one she could ask about menopause. She contemplated asking her Puerto Rican cleaning lady. Maria was forty-two, the same age as Rosa, but Maria had trouble understanding Rosa's accent and Rosa felt horrified at the thought of a confused conversation about menopause.

Rosa had two older women friends. She corresponded with a seventy-four-year-old woman in Los Angeles, and a fifty-two-year-old woman in New York. She adored them both. Sometimes she felt overcome by the fierce attachment she felt to these two women. Until last year she'd never been close to anyone older than herself. But she felt unable to ask either of them about her weeping.

She felt a bit nauseous too. Maybe she was pregnant. She had wept through the first months of all her pregnancies. She decided she couldn't be pregnant. She and Allan hadn't made love since her last period.

Certain smells made her nausea worse. One afternoon somebody in another apartment was boiling chicken soup. The smell filled the hallway. Rosa felt bilious. She hadn't been able to eat boiled chicken for years. When she was twenty-five, she had had a stall in the Carlton flea market. She had had new clothes made up from old crepes and satins. She advertised regularly for dress materials. A Mr Borenstazn had rung in reply to one of her advertisements.

Mr Borenstazn had opened the door of his flat, in St Kilda, holding an artificial leg in his hand. He waved the leg at Rosa and shouted: "Come in, come in." The flat was very dark and smelled of chicken. Rosa was frightened. Mr Borenstazn had hobbled around looking for the parcel he had put aside for Rosa. "Sit down, sit down," he shouted at her. "Why are you so quiet? I lost this leg in the war. Haven't you ever seen somebody without a leg?"

Rosa sat down and looked around her. In the middle of the dining room table was an enormous bowl of boiled chicken bones. It looked like the site of a mass burial. Rosa felt sick.

"I think I'll go now," she'd said to Mr Borenstazn. "I'll come back another time."

"Why are you such an impatient girl?" he shouted, prodding her with the plastic leg. He finally found his parcel. It contained two men's suits.

"I don't need men's suits," said Rosa.

"Your advertisement said 'old clothes wanted'," said Mr Borenstazn.

"No, it said old dress materials."

"Well, you can make a dress from these suits." Mr Borenstazn wanted twenty dollars. Rosa gave him thirty and fled.

Rosa hadn't cried very much at all in her life. Maybe this was the weeping that she had neglected to do earlier, she thought. Allan was distressed by her tears. He felt responsible for bringing her to New York. "If we'd stayed in Melbourne, you could have stayed with KJ," he said.

"I had to leave some time," she said.

On the seventh day of the tenth week, Rosa and Allan were walking around the East Village. A battered-looking middle-aged black woman was shouting at a battered-looking middle-aged black man.

"The Queen of England don't owe you a piece of shit," she shouted.

Rosa laughed and laughed.

"I'm sorry for this awful week," she said to Allan. "I think I'm going to be all right now."

In a bookshop Rosa saw a photograph of a Kalabari ancestry screen. These screens were also called "foreheads of the dead". They were three dimensional screens with sculptures of relatives who had died. Rosa was mesmerised. The screens looked beautiful. Not at all morbid. The people who were carved in them looked as though they were still alive. Rosa found the screens comforting. She thought she might ask Allan if he could make an ancestral screen for her.

Allan had asked her earlier in the week if she would like to go to the country for the day. He wanted to go to Westchester. He said the Westchester landscape in autumn was supposed to be spectacular. Rosa had hedged around, not answering him, even though she knew how much he wanted to go.

"Shall we go to Westchester on Sunday?" she said to Allan now. "I'm sorry I was so half-hearted when you suggested it." She thought she would buy some bagels for the trip, and some smoked salmon, and cream cheese, and a salad. Maybe she'd buy a thermos and they could take coffee.

Allan laughed at her. "The only reason you're leaving the city is because it gives you a chance to plan a picnic."

Rosa and Allan walked arm in arm, as they always did. They walked along First Avenue. Rosa thought about her mother. She thought about KJ. She thought of a line from a poem by Marina Tsvetayeva: "I kiss you — across hundreds of separating years."

Rosa thought it was a beautiful line.

The Alpha-Jerk Field

Rosa Cohen moved her legs across the bed until they touched her husband's legs. She moved closer to him and rubbed her legs against his. Even when he was asleep his legs felt strong. Allan Richards was very strong. He had strong arms and legs. He could lift Rosa easily.

Once, when her feet had been sore, he had carried her for three blocks along the Boulevard St Germain in Paris. She had laughed uncontrollably all the way. She had felt like a small child. She couldn't remember being carried as a child. Even as a child she had felt too big to be carried.

She pressed herself into the curve of Allan's back. He was still asleep. She had often wondered how hairy legs could feel so smooth and soft. She put her face on his back. He stirred slightly. She closed her eyes and inhaled his smell. She loved the smell of him.

She lay there for several minutes. Her body felt light. She felt as though everything inside her was working properly. As though her arteries and lungs and veins were doing a good job. Cleansing, sorting and recycling. A symphony of harmonies. She felt very peaceful. She wished that she didn't ever have to move.

But she had to have a piss. She always woke up dying to have a piss. She slipped quietly out of bed and went to the bathroom. When she got back, Allan was lying in the middle of the bed. She warmed herself against him. She rested her hand on his stomach. His stomach felt so nice. She patted him, making small circles around and around his navel.

She looked at her watch. It was 7:28 a.m. In two minutes the alarm clock radio would turn itself on. They both had a lot to do today. Allan had two exhibitions of his paintings opening simultaneously in New York and Chicago next month. Some of the paintings weren't signed, some weren't even stretched yet, and the works on paper still hadn't come back from the framers.

She knew that she shouldn't do anything that would delay the start of the day. But she felt so good. And Allan felt so good. She leaned down and put her mouth around his penis.

When she came up for air, Allan was smiling. "This is the most perfect way to wake up," he said. He moved over on top of her, and slipped himself inside her. He put his mouth around her left breast, and pushed what felt like several fingers of his right hand, high inside her bum.

She felt filled and plugged and gripped. He fucked her slowly. She felt almost giddy with pleasure. She knew that she wouldn't last long. She tried to think of something distracting to stop herself from coming.

She wondered how many other people in New York were fucking at this very moment. Here, in New York, people were always talking about fucking. Yesterday, in De Roberti's Cafe on First Avenue, two men in their thirties were discussing someone who fucked apples. "Yeah, he loved to put his cock into an apple," the blonder of the two men kept repeating. Three elderly women at the next booth seemed oblivious to the conversation. Rosa asked Allan if he thought that the apple would be raw or cooked. "Who knows?" Allan replied. One of the women leaned over to Rosa. "I think it was probably a baked apple," she said.

Just as Rosa thought that she couldn't hold out any longer, Allan's pace quickened and he began to fuck her with short stabbing strokes. They came together. Rosa had more intense and longer orgasms when she and Allan came at the same time. She loved to feel him spurting into her.

They lay there, damply joined together. She held his head. "I love you," she said. It was a miracle to her that, after twenty years of marriage, she still lusted after him. She wasn't so much surprised at the fact that she still loved him. She'd expected to always love him. What astonished her was how feverishly she could want him. She still felt that it was a luxury to watch him get dressed in the morning. She often felt aroused just watching him walk across a room. It really was a miracle.

It felt like a miracle to other people too. Some of them were irritated. "Stop walking so close together!" Susan White, a Melbourne literary editor they hardly knew, had shouted at them when she'd walked past them in Lygon Street a few years ago. "You two make me sick," she had said.

Julian Sandhurst had told half the Melbourne art world how he'd come across Allan and Rosa kissing in a small Algerian restaurant in Paris. "I didn't even know they were in Paris," he said, "and there they were, engrossed in a kiss so long and so deep I thought it must have been a couple of Parisians. What's wrong with them?"

What was wrong with them? In the Caffe Dante, on MacDougal Street, where Allan and Rosa often ate lunch, a quiver of disbelief went through the three Maltese waitresses the day Zeke, Poppy and Kira joined them for lunch. "Are these your children?" asked the youngest waitress. "They are so big."

"Yes," said Rosa, "Zeke is at law school, Poppy is doing fine arts, and Kira is still at high school."

"We thought you two had only just met," said the waitress. "He always looks at you so nicely. It's not normal to be like that when you've got children."

Rosa made the bed briskly, but with care. By the time she finished, the bed looked beautiful. It was covered with a hand-woven Ming blue raw silk bedspread. Four black tapestry bolsters sat on each end of the bed, and six large aqua-shot silk cushions and six small white Swiss cotton cushions were placed across the head of the bed. It was what Americans called a dressed bed.

Rosa had always made her beds up beautifully. She wrote

sitting on the bed. Sitting on her various beds, she had written four plays, a Masters thesis, a trunk-full of diaries and endless letters. Letters to Allan, letters to the children. When the children were small she'd written a letter addressed to them once a week. In these letters she had described herself. She described her feelings about them, she wrote about the events of the week, the children's activities, and their development. "I'm doing this," she had explained to Allan, "in case anything happens to me." In a letter attached to her will, she had asked that the children not read any of the letters until they were at least eighteen.

Zeke was now nineteen, Poppy was eighteen and Kira was sixteen. The letters were stored in Melbourne, in four boxes on top of the trunk that held her early diaries and her notebooks.

All the stretching and smoothing and tucking and fluffing of the pillows and sheets had activated Rosa's bowels. She sat on the toilet. Allan came in looking for his painting overalls. "I'm enveloped in a sea of chopped liver fumes," she said to him. "I'm farting chopped liver."

"I know," he said. "I can smell it."

"I'm sorry," she said. "It's worse for me than it is for you. You can get away. We shouldn't have eaten at the Second Avenue Deli last night. My body is obviously in a state of shock. No meat comes through for months and months, and then in one night it has to deal with a mountain of chopped liver."

"I'm going upstairs to have some coffee," said Allan. "Do you want some?"

"No, thanks."

She turned on the shower. Every morning she left the shower running for five minutes while she prepared her work for the day. She knew that it was a waste of water, but it was a luxury she felt she couldn't give up yet. By the time she'd set out the right pens, the right notebooks and the right folders, the bathroom was hot and steamy. She loved the feeling of walking into the wet warmth.

After the shower, she rubbed Fracas body lotion on her arms, breasts and legs. She dried her hair and got dressed. She felt a bit constipated. She'd done nothing but fart when she was on the toilet. She decided to have some pineapple. She thought that the fibre in the pineapple might speed the chopped liver through her system. She visualised the pineapple wriggling through her intestines, unblocking solid lumps of chopped liver.

She went upstairs and cut herself three slices of pineapple. The pineapple was not quite ripe. She felt a bit sick. Why was she so fixated with what went in and out of her, that she tried to counterbalance chopped liver with pineapple? It was a Jewish trait, she decided. Jews spent an inordinate amount of time thinking about what they had eaten, and what they hadn't eaten, what they should have eaten, and what they should not have eaten.

Despite this, Jews didn't look any healthier or happier than anyone else. On the whole, Rosa thought, Jews were fatter than non-Jews, and they looked sadder. They ate more, and spent more time thinking about the repercussions of that eating.

With all this emphasis on eating, it was no wonder that Jews didn't run, or play tennis, or build cupboards, fix cars or repair leaks. There wasn't enough time.

Rosa wondered if God was punishing her for eating so much chopped liver. She realised that she thought of God only in the most banal terms. Her generation was so fucked up about religion. She thought of her cousin, David Greenblatt. He wasn't really her cousin. When her parents had come out of Auschwitz, they'd had no relatives left, but Rosa had called Mr and Mrs Greenblatt "Aunty" and "Uncle". David Greenblatt was in Israel at the moment. She'd got a letter from him yesterday.

Before he'd discovered religion, David Greenblatt had been exceptionally good-looking. He was tall, dark-haired and long-limbed. He had a sensuous mouth and a disarming smile. Then he began to go to synagogue. After that, every time Rosa saw him he had added another orthodox accoutrement to his dress. Now he wore a thick, wide beard and a large, black hat. Various threads and thongs either dangled or were wound around him. His sexuality seemed to have dissolved into the folds of his long black coat.

Before David Greenblatt had become an orthodox Jew, he'd had tempestuous affairs with two of the tallest, blondest shikses in Melbourne. He had almost married the last one. Two days before the wedding she had told him that she was in love with someone else. Another Jew.

Mrs Greenblatt went to synagogue for the first time in twenty years when she heard that the wedding was off.

"Dear God," she had said, tears rolling down her face, "dear God, thank God you listened to my prayers."

"I forgot to tell you," Rosa called out to Allan, "we got a letter from David Greenblatt. He said he was having a good time in Israel, although he seems to have spent most of his time avoiding the endless matchmakers who have been chasing him with lists of eligible, attractive, intelligent, sensitive, creative, religious young women. Why do you think he doesn't want to meet these young women? They sound perfect for him."

"I think that David Greenblatt likes being the pious one," said Allan. "That way he feels superior. If he were with a religious woman, he wouldn't feel so special."

Rosa thought that maybe Allan was right. People were strange. Rosa knew that. She knew how strange she herself was. She didn't seem all that strange. And she was much better than she used to be. But she knew what a struggle it had been to iron out all the kinks and chinks in her thinking.

She and Allan had been living in New York for over a year. Six months ago, she had sent a checklist of her progress to her analyst in Australia.

Dear KJ, [she had written]
This is how things are going.

1. I haven't lost any more weight.
2. I have hardly felt dizzy.
3. I am thinking more about others. Not enough, but more.
4. I am working. I might even earn some money soon.
5. When *Paradise Palace* won the B.B. Harrington Drama Prize, I kept it in perspective and didn't think I was fabulous.

6. I have wept, in mourning, for you and for my mother.
7. I think that *Drowning the Victim* has been nominated for the Victorian Play of the Year Award.
8. I haven't been out alone.

KJ had said that if Rosa felt that she needed to have some more analysis, she would help her to find an analyst in New York. Rosa knew that finding an analyst in New York shouldn't be too hard.

One day when she felt a bit shaky she had looked up psychoanalysts in the New York phone book. There were so many of them. She rang up New York University Psychoanalytic Department. She wanted to know the average cost of a session.

"It's very expensive, honey," said the woman who answered the phone. "But we offer a low-cost analysis here," she said. "We have analysts in training. They're really very good. Would you like an appointment?"

"No, thank you," said Rosa.

The one aspect of her life that she really wanted to fix up was the fact that she never went anywhere on her own. She worked from home and only went out with Allan, or Allan and the kids.

In Melbourne she used to go to KJ's five times a week on her own. In the last couple of years of her analysis she had started going out by herself. But here, in New York, she hadn't even left the apartment building without Allan.

Nobody seemed to notice that she never went out on her own. She blurred her impediment by saying "I went to the supermarket" instead of "we went to the supermarket."

Sometimes the prospect of going out alone didn't seem too daunting. Several times she had made plans to walk down Second Avenue. Maybe four blocks down and four blocks back — something easy to start with. But she hadn't done anything more than think about it.

She wished that she knew why such a simple thing seemed so difficult. People often told her what a courageous writer she was, yet she was incapable of doing something so basic as walking down a street alone. Small children and old ladies went out on their own every day.

Yesterday morning she and Allan had gone to the Metropolitan Museum to see the Velasquez exhibition. It had snowed overnight, the first snow of the season. The streets and avenues looked smooth. Snow had filled the potholes and given the city a cover of cleanliness and purity. A fresh start. A new beginning.

Snow blanketed the parked cars and public parks. Outside the New York Public Library, the stone lions looked benign, blinded by masks of snow. A cluster of birch trees with left-over patches of autumn leaves looked as though they were sprouting snow blossoms. In Gramercy Park, two boys in T-shirts tumbled over and over together in the snow. There was a peaceful feeling in the air.

The panhandler on the corner of Second Avenue and Thirty-Fourth Street was wearing a maroon knitted tea cosy on top of his red wig. Rosa wasn't scared of him any more. She'd been terrified of him when they'd first arrived in New York. "He's a sober, hard-working man," Allan had explained to her. "He's on this corner every day. He works long hours. I've seen him early in the morning and late at night. He never takes a day off."

Yesterday morning when they passed him he had said, "Kids, this snow is good for the soul."

"It sure is," Allan had answered.

"I like being called a kid," said Rosa. "Nobody else calls us kids. It makes me feel so young."

They had arrived at the Metropolitan just as it was opening. At the top of the steps, in front of the entrance, a young Senegalese man was standing behind a box of umbrellas. As people walked by he called out "Hamburgers, hamburgers." Rosa turned away from him and laughed. It did look very funny.

"Poor thing," said Allan. "Somebody has given him the wrong word."

Rosa walked up to the man and said, "These are called umbrellas."

"Five dollars," he said.

"This is an umbrella, not a hamburger," she said.

"Five dollars," he repeated.

She bought an umbrella.

Now, as she was clearing her desk before settling down to work on the final scene of a play she had been writing for over a year and a half, she thought of the umbrella man. There he was, on his own, at the top of those vast museum steps, in a strange country, with no English. Why wasn't he scared? she wondered.

She straightened the photograph of her mother and father which she kept at the back of the desk. She had had the photograph in a drawer until recently. It had been taken after the war. Rosa was in it. She was about two months old, huge-eyed and fat-cheeked. She looked a bit bewildered even then. She was perched in between Mania and Moniek Cohen. One year after being liberated from Auschwitz, Mania Cohen looked chubby. Her face was round and her shoulders and arms were thick.

"All the women were fat that year," she had told Rosa. "None of us could stop eating. We went from looking like skeletons — you know I weighed sixty-eight pounds after the war — to looking like fatties. We could hardly recognise ourselves. We had so many changes in the way we looked. When they first shaved our hair in the camp, even though we were so frightened, we were laughing because we looked so funny and we didn't recognise each other. When I saw myself in a mirror, I didn't know I was looking at me. After a few months at Auschwitz, I did get a glimpse of myself in a piece of glass, and I was sure it was not me. I was twenty-two and I looked like a seventy-year-old woman. After the war, I got so fat. I couldn't stop eating. Even when I felt so full that I felt like vomiting, I did keep on eating. And you know what, Rosala darling, when I was such a fatty, I still felt very thin. I thought I was so thin I would die. I had to let out my two dresses and they were both a very big size. Your dad said to me that I had to stop eating because he was risking his life selling coffee on the black market, and all his profits he had to spend on buying bigger skirts and blouses for me. He said we would never get enough money to go to Australia."

Rosa's phone rang. "Hi, it's Paula from Saks Fifth Avenue. Sweetheart, where have you been? I've called you a few times. I've felt concerned, because I know that you work from home. Have you been OK, honey? Is everything all right?" Rosa felt lulled by the motherliness in Paula's voice.

"Everything is fine," she said. "I've just been out quite a bit lately." She tried to remember who Paula was. What had she bought at Saks recently? She remember that she had phoned through an order for Fracas perfume. Saks was the only department store in Manhattan that always had Fracas. Rosa had worn Fracas for years. Allan was amused by the name. "Only my wife", he used to say, "would wear a perfume that suggests chaos." He would pronounce Fracas with a broad Australian accent and emphasise the S.

"Do you need any more Fracas?" Paula asked.

"No, I've got plenty," Rosa answered.

"Well what about some Estee Lauder Eyezone Repair Gel? Have you run out of that yet?"

"No, I've still got some," said Rosa.

"And how are you going with the Micro-Targeted Skin Gel, and the Firming Eye Creme?"

Jesus, thought Rosa, they obviously kept track of what you bought on a computer. She thought about it and decided that keeping this sort of information about people wasn't really harmful.

"We've got a marvellous new face lotion, honey," said Paula. "It will make your skin look five years younger."

"With all the age-reducing creams I use, I should look like a four-year-old," said Rosa.

"Oh, that's funny," said Paula.

Rosa relented. She ordered eye gel, face gel, face firming cream, eye firming cream, and the new wrinkle-dissolving lotion.

"I'll ship these things to you today," said Paula, "and you'll have them tomorrow. You look after yourself now. Take care. Goodbye, sweetheart."

Rosa put down the phone. She felt very calm. For an outlay of just over $135, she had had twenty minutes of maternal concern. Twenty minutes of mothering.

She was about to put the answering machine on when Priscilla Burns rang. Priscilla was a journalist Rosa had vaguely known in Melbourne. The common bond of being far away from home often turned acquaintances into close friends. Priscilla called Rosa almost every day.

"Hi, Rosa," said Priscilla. "Have I caught you before you begin work for the day, or have you already started?"

"Well, I'm just about to start, so I won't chat for long," said Rosa.

"Did you know that Victoria Jones is getting married?" Priscilla asked.

"Really?" said Rosa.

"Yes," said Priscilla. "She thought that travelling on the Concorde might be a good way to meet someone, so she bought herself a return trip from New York to London. It cost her ten grand, but you wouldn't believe, she met someone. She met this guy on the way from New York to London. She stayed with him at the Dorchester in London, and now they're getting married. The wedding's next month. He's loaded, and quite respectable looking. She said that being on the Concorde was like belonging to an exclusive club. Everyone is very nice to everyone else because they assume you're one of them. Victoria said that I should buy myself a ticket. She said there were at least four very interesting guys on her flights. And maybe I will. Ten grand is quite a small investment if it results in a really good husband."

"It's not such a bad idea," said Rosa.

"I'll think about it," said Priscilla. "Frankly, I'm getting a bit sick of looking for a man. Most of the nice ones I meet are married, and if they're not married they're gay. Maybe I'll become a lesbian.

It wouldn't be that bad being with a woman. Really, I was thinking about it seriously until last night. I was thinking that rather than go out and get screwed by someone you know very little about, and have to worry about AIDS, it'd be much safer to have sex with a woman. You'd probably get used to it. But, before I had a chance to experiment with being a lesbian, this guy I met at Gerry's place rang up and asked me out. We went to a bar, and then we went to his place for coffee. He isn't everything I want in a man. For a start he votes Republican and wears flared trousers. It's not that he's really voguish, it's that he's only just caught up with the sixties. And I think he was wearing a toupee or that woven false hair."

"This doesn't sound very promising," said Rosa.

"You're right," said Priscilla. "But he had the biggest cock I've ever seen on a man. It felt just fabulous. I've never been fucked by a man with such a big cock. I had the best orgasms. Three in one evening. I wasn't even disconcerted when I thought I felt his hair slipping to one side."

Rosa started to laugh. "That sounds gruesome."

"I can tell you, Rosa," said Priscilla "the toupee was irrelevant next to the size of his cock."

"Was it really that big?" said Rosa.

"It was huge. I was almost coming from the moment he put it inside me."

"The size really made a difference, did it?" Rosa asked. "I thought it wasn't supposed to. I thought that when they were erect they were all more or less the same size."

"Well, let me tell you, after this experience I'd always go for the more rather than the less. I think that myth about all cocks being the same size when they're erect must have been started by men with small pricks. I can tell you that this guy's huge cock made a big difference. I guess you've been married for so long you can hardly remember being fucked by anybody else. Have you ever been fucked by anybody else?"

"Of course I have," said Rosa. "And I can still remember."

"Have you got a lot of work on at the moment?" Rosa asked Priscilla.

"Yes, I have," said Priscilla. "I've got three speeches and two letters to finish by tomorrow."

Priscilla had been in New York for two years. For the first six months she had worked as the New York correspondent for *Australian Women's Wear Weekly*. She earned $A310 a week, which translated into US$230. It was not even enough to pay for the 350-square-foot cupboard she lived in on East Twelfth Street.

One day, in desperation, she had put an ad in the *Village Voice:* "Speeches and Letters written for all occasions. Multi-Qualified English Graduate. Eight hundred words for $300 plus delivery." The multiple qualifications she had been referring to were a Bachelor of Arts from the University of Melbourne and a Diploma of Shorthand and Typing from Scott's Business College.

From that ad Priscilla had received four requests for speeches and six orders for letters. Three speeches were for weddings and the fourth one was for a funeral. All the letters were love letters. Now Priscilla averaged three jobs a day. She spent twenty minutes on the phone interviewing each client. She had set lists of questions for weddings, engagements, birthdays, barmitzvahs, funerals and births. She had thirty-five prototypes of love letters into which she interspersed individual clients' names and other details. She employed a secretary three days a week, and cleared $4,000 most weeks. She could easily afford a trip on the Concorde.

Rosa was impressed with Priscilla's speeches and letters. Priscilla had shown her a speech for a funeral last week.

"Andrew Jackson," Priscilla had written, "was in his short life more of a father to Darren and Jodie than those fathers who live until their children themselves are middle-aged. Andrew adored Darren and Jodie. And he knew them. He spent time with them. He made a point of not working late more than two nights a week so that he could be with his children. He had his priorities. He gave his children his time, his knowledge, his guidance and his love.

And Andrew was more of a husband to Phyllis than ten husbands put together who lived with their wives into old age.

"Although he died at forty, what Andrew gave Phyllis, Darren and Jodie cannot be measured in years. It must be measured in love. And, in these terms of accounting, Andrew gave Phyllis, Darren and Jodie several lifetimes of love. So, although today is a very tragic day because we have lost someone so dear to us, someone so special, we must not overlook what Andrew has left behind, and how enriched we are by that. Andrew's presence will live on in his children. It will live on inside Phyllis, who will never stop loving him. And his presence will live on the hearts of his many friends. We keep people alive in many ways. Andrew's spirit will not be extinguished."

The speech had gone on for another page and a half. Rosa had felt tearful when she had finished reading it.

"Maybe if this stupid play doesn't work out, I might come and work for you," said Rosa. "Do you think you could train me? I probably wouldn't be all that good. I tried to write romances for Mills and Boon about ten years ago, and I was really hopeless."

"I don't think you should compare that Mills and Boon shit with my letters and speeches," said Priscilla.

"Oh, sorry," said Rosa. "I didn't mean to."

"My speeches have reduced whole halls of people to tears," said Priscilla. "I don't know why you had to try and put me down. Maybe you're jealous because I got fucked by a guy with a great cock."

Rosa contemplated retorting that Allan had a great cock, and she had no need to be jealous, but she took a breath and said, "Look, Priscilla, it's a sign of what a good friendship we have that we can have these minor skirmishes and hurts and get over them quickly. I'm sorry if I was inadvertently offensive. OK?"

"OK," said Priscilla. "And I'm sure that Allan has a great cock too. Speak to you tomorrow."

Rosa hung up. How come, at forty-something, women could still sound so adolescent? Maybe it wasn't just women? Maybe men were like that too? Maybe that was the curse of their generation. They were finding it hard to grow up.

She worked for two hours on the play. It was called *The Circle of Contempt*. She wrote and rewrote dialogue. She made Esther die of cancer, and then she saved her life. She killed Joe off, and then she brought him back to life. She had him leave his wife and move in with Sophie and live happily ever after. None of her moves worked. She contemplated awarding Joe an OBE for services to the arts, but she didn't think he was involved enough in the community. She was getting a headache.

She rang Allan in his studio to see if he was ready for lunch. He said he would be up in ten minutes. She put out a platter of sliced tomatoes, baby mozzarella cheeses, some marinated artichoke hearts and some olives. She sliced a loaf of particularly chewy Italian bread and put the kettle on for coffee.

Allan kissed her hello. "Did you work well this morning?" he asked.

"Not really," she said.

"I'm sorry," he said. "Don't worry, you'll get there. I think that this play is going to be brilliant. It's much more complicated than your other ones. You're trying to do something very difficult, and you'll do it. You're the most naturally fluent writer I know."

"I think you're a bit biased," said Rosa.

"I've worked quite well," he said. "You know that large canvas I've been struggling with for weeks, the one I was almost going to leave out of the New York show? Well, I think I've pulled it together. I'll sit and look at it this afternoon, but I think it's a good painting now."

"Good. I'm pleased. I'll come down and see it."

"This mozzarella is fabulous," said Allan. "It's so light. It's better than the mozzarellas we bought at Balduccis. They look like little white breasts sitting on the plate. See, they've even got the tremulousness of breasts. I wonder what mozzarellas made out of breast milk would taste like?"

"Sounds awful to me," said Rosa. "Maybe it's a reflection of my relationship with my mother that I find the thought of mozzarellas made out of breast milk so revolting.

"I've been thinking about going for a short walk today," she said. "On my own. Most of the time it doesn't bother me, the fact that I can't go out by myself, but every now and then I think this is a mad way to live. This isn't a great way to emerge from five years of psychotherapy, two years of group therapy and five years of analysis. And it bothers me that you have to come everywhere with me. Sometimes it's an appalling waste of your time. I know it's not much fun sitting in the waiting room while I see the dentist. Not to mention the hairdresser, or the endless times you've waited while I buy underwear or shoes or bathers."

"You know that I don't mind at all," said Allan.

"I know that," said Rosa. "But sometimes I remember the terrific feeling of freedom I had just driving to KJ's on my own, or visiting Inara or Anna. I used to feel so independent. They're pathetic examples of independence, aren't they?"

"There are other ways of being independent," said Allan.

"Well, I'm not interested in independence as a theory. I just want to live a better life. I want to stop shackling myself. I want to stop paying a price for whatever freedom I have. Whatever I mean by that. All that shit I struggled with in my analysis about separating from my parents. Knowing that it was they who had been in Auschwitz, not me. Knowing that I hadn't suffered that damage. All I'd had were damaged parents. Well, I think I left the analysis too early. I think I haven't really separated their experience from mine. I think that may be why I can still get so scared out in the world. I do know that I was never in Auschwitz. And I can go to the theatre now, and sit in the middle of a crowd without imagining that Nazis are going to appear and round me up. But when I think of walking down a street by myself, I feel I might be swept away. I might just float off, and blend into the air. I might disappear.

"You know, I think I understand for the first time why I never had Jewish boyfriends, or didn't marry a Jewish husband. I used to think it was because I wanted to dement my parents, and I think that it was partly that, but I think it was also because I knew I would feel much safer with a non-Jew. I think I might have thought that it would be too dangerous to marry a Jew; we would be too Jewish."

"I thought you married me because of my good looks," said Allan.

"I did," said Rosa, "but your not being Jewish clinched the deal."

"You publicly identify yourself as a Jew," said Allan. "You write under your maiden name. You couldn't get a more Jewish name than Rosa Cohen. And you write about Jewish themes. Remember how anxious your mother was that you would provoke anti-Semitism by being so obviously Jewish? Remember, she suggested that you write under your married name. She wanted you to write as Rosa Richards. Then she suggested Rosemary Richards. Remember how furious you were with her?"

"I remember," said Rosa. She found it hard not to think of her mother without crying. This crying had come very late. It had begun three years after her mother had died. It was now more than four years since her mother had died.

"I think I'll walk down Second Avenue to Cafe Orlin," she said. "I'll have a coffee, and then I'll walk home. That will be ten blocks there and ten blocks back."

"That sounds like a perfect first walk," Allan said. "I've got to go back to the studio. The framer is meeting me there in five minutes, but I'll be by the phone all afternoon. I love you. You'll be all right if you go for a walk and all right if you don't."

He kissed her half a dozen times. On her forehead, on her cheeks, on her lips.

Rosa thought about KJ saying that Rosa didn't like to suffer any discomfort. That she wanted someone else to make the effort, to make the changes. "You would like me to wave a magic wand and fix you up without you having to do any work," she used to say. It had seemed not too bad a proposition to Rosa.

She would do it now, she decided. She would go out. She packed away her work. She hated to leave it lying around, even though she knew that no-one else would be coming into the room. Somehow the notebooks and papers looked exposed and vulnerable left on the bed.

She put on two scarves and her black woollen overcoat. She grabbed her sunglasses because the snow looked very bright. They were new sunglasses. They had four hearts, a pair of red and white dice, and a plastic giraffe glued to the frames.

She checked her handbag. She had money, credit cards, peppermints, two pens, a small notebook, several Valium and two Inderal. Rosa had swallowed an Inderal tablet on the two occasions that she had had to speak in public. The Inderal had stopped her from shaking. She had carried Valium and Inderal in her handbag for years. Every year or so she got a new prescription, and changed the pills in her handbag. She carried the tablets in case of an emergency. She wasn't sure exactly what sort of emergency she was expecting.

She went down in the lift. So far so good. She said "Hi" to the doorman. She wondered if he noticed that she was on her own. He seemed unmoved.

Outside the apartment block a small group of people were gathered at the side of the road. Rosa walked over to see what was happening. A squirrel was lying on its back in the road. Its heart was pounding violently. Its white chest was heaving up and down. Every now and then it tried to raise its head. Just then, a city van pulled up. Two men got out and put the squirrel in a plastic garbage bin. Rosa felt upset. What had she expected? she wondered. Had she thought that an animal ambulance would come along and carry the squirrel off on a miniature stretcher?

She wondered what had happened to the squirrel. It hadn't looked injured. Maybe it had had a stroke? Did squirrels have strokes? She didn't know. A young man standing next to her said, "That squirrel fell into the Alpha-Jerk Field. Just like Jimi Hendrix."

Rosa walked down Second Avenue. She felt a bit upset about the squirrel, but she didn't feel too bad within herself. The sun was shining. It wasn't too cold. And she had walked two blocks already.

She was crossing Fourteenth Street when a tall, young black man came up from behind her, and fell into step with her. She walked a bit faster. He kept up with her. She took a quick sidewards glance at him. He was well-dressed. He was wearing a grey Sara Sturgeon suit. Rosa recognised the style. Allan had two Sara Sturgeon suits. She decided that this man wasn't someone to worry about. She kept walking.

"Excuse me, miss," he said, "you may be wondering what a good-looking young black guy like me is doing asking for money. You may be a bit suspicious. But I'm not ashamed to ask for money. I'd be ashamed to steal your car or your wallet. I'd be ashamed to sell drugs to your kids. I'd be ashamed to sell crack to your brother. I'd be ashamed to sell my body like some two-bit gay prostitute."

"I don't have a car or a brother," Rosa said, and tried to walk ahead of him.

"Hey, come on man, just one dollar. You can give me one dollar," he said.

She fumbled around in her bag for a dollar.

"Thank you," he said. "Take care, and don't look so worried."

She was almost at Eighth Street. Another half a block and she would be at Cafe Orlin. She had almost made it. Her heart was racing slightly and a hint of dizziness hovered about her, but she wasn't feeling too bad.

She chose a table at the back of the cafe. She left her umbrella on the table while she went to the phone and phoned Allan. "Hi, it's me," she said. "I'm in Cafe Orlin. I've survived ten blocks of those streets out of hell." That was a private joke between them. An Australian friend had asked them how they could possibly live in downtown Manhattan. "Those streets are straight out of hell," he had said. Rosa and Allan had often laughed about the streets straight out of hell as they watched young children playing in the parks, people walking their dogs, mothers with babies, old couples.

"How are you feeling?" Allan asked.

"I'm OK," she said. "I'm feeling a bit dizzy, but I've got that nice table in the far corner, and I'm going to have an expresso and two almond biscuits. I'll call you before I leave here. I love you."

"I love you too. Take your time. Stay as long as you want to. I'll be here, in the studio," Allan said.

Pinned up on the wall next to the telephone was a sign. It said, "Good home wanted for 8-inch ferret. Eats cat food." Someone had crossed out the "8" and replaced it with "16". Clearly the owner had not had a lot of luck placing his ferret. Rosa thought that in order to make the ferret look more desirable they really should have written out a new sign. It was a bit demeaning to the ferret, too.

A man at the table next to Rosa's was talking in a very loud voice. He was drowning out the two young girls that Rosa had been listening to. One of the girls had been saying that the best sort of sex was casual sex. Rosa felt as though she should interject some motherly advice, but she was too nervous.

"Our co-op board president," the man's voice boomed, "had a meeting with the local cocaine dealers. We want to work hand in hand with them to keep the crack dealers off the block. The cocaine addicts are a much better class of addict than the crack addicts." Rosa could see how you could think that these streets were streets out of hell.

She sugared her coffee. It smelt good. She leaned over and picked up a copy of *New York* magazine from an empty table. She read an article about prostitutes. It was commonly assumed, the article said, that prostitutes faked orgasms when they were with clients. However, whether they faked their orgasms or not was not something that they ever discussed among themselves, despite the fact that they were very frank with each other. There would be something humiliating, Rosa thought, about responding to a grubby client with an orgasm.

Rosa turned the pages to the personal ads. A successful Wall Street executive who was also a singer/songwriter, and who had Woody Allen's demeanour and Tom Cruise's looks, was looking for a dark-haired green-eyed healthy non-smoking thirty-two-year-old woman with an athletic build.

A svelte 5-foot-8 single white twenty-eight-year-old female with a PhD was hoping to spend some time with an articulate emotionally secure non-smoking professional. An attractive exciting and successful white Jewish couple with good bodies were seeking an attractive female, from twenty to thirty-eight, for fun nights.

There were four Jewish doctors looking for wives this week.

Page after page of attractive, slender people were seeking equally attractive partners. Rosa wondered how they would fare if they advertised themselves as having varicose veins and being prone to constipation.

Rosa had been sitting in Cafe Orlin for three-quarters of an hour. She had had two coffees and four almond biscuits. She called Allan again. "Well, I'm past the half-way mark," she said. "I'm leaving now. I might stop and pick up a roast chicken on my way home. See how carefree and adventurous I've become. If I feel too anxious, I won't bother with the chicken. So I'll either be home in fifteen or twenty-five minutes."

At Rego's Roosters Rosa had to wait five minutes for the fresh batch of chickens to come out of the ovens. A young Hispanic woman was feeding her kids, two girls and a boy, at one of the three tables. The children were immaculately dressed. One of the woman's daughters, a dark-eyed, long-haired girl of about six, was wearing a white satin and lace dress. It had puffed sleeves and three tiers of lace frills around the waist and the hemline. The outfit was at odds with the faded laminex decor of Rego's Roosters. Rosa decided that the family must be on their way out to a formal function.

"What gorgeous children," Rosa said to the woman.

"Thank you," the woman replied.

"That's such a beautiful white dress. Is she going to a party?" Rosa asked.

"No," the woman said. "She used to be a very sick girl. She used to have convulsions. So I promised her that if she got better, I would buy her the prettiest white dresses, and dress her in them every day for a whole year. So she got better. And I dress her in a white dress every day."

The boy, who was only a toddler, was sitting on top of the table. He was dipping his chips into a plate of tomato sauce. The woman leaned over and peered into the back of his trousers. "Yeah," she said to Rosa, "he's still got the diarrhoea. I got to take him to the hospital. That's where we're going."

Rosa picked up her chicken. She tried to dissociate the chicken from the kid's diarrhoea. She walked back up Second Avenue. She wondered whether she should buy herself a white dress.

Moving Meals

Dora Lipshitz was angry. Her sister was already twenty minutes late. Why couldn't Golda do anything right? She didn't work. What did she do all day except sit around on the phone?

Dora checked her anger. She had asked Golda to lunch because she wanted to feel closer to her. Being furious with Golda wouldn't be the best way to begin this reconciliation. Well, it wasn't exactly a reconciliation, Dora thought. They hadn't fallen out. They had never been in.

What had gone wrong? There was nothing specific. They probably had much the same values in life. They were both left-wing politically. They were both married with two children. They were both in good marriages. They shared the same parents. They should have a great deal in common.

So why weren't they close? Fighting wasn't the problem. They spoke to each other over the phone once or twice a week, but it was mostly perfunctory. "Hi, how are you?" that sort of thing. Afterwards Dora sometimes wondered why they both kept making the phone calls. So little was said. There seemed to be no point. Maybe the point was that they didn't become estranged.

Their children didn't see much of each other. They saw each other at birthdays, anniversaries and barmitzvahs, but that was all. Her Vivian and Anna were two years older than Golda's Danielle and Simone. When the children were smaller they used to play together, but now the age difference seemed too great.

Dora paced up and down the pavement outside the Spotted Zebra Bar and Grill. She didn't like sitting in restaurants by herself. Golda was now half an hour late. Dora felt agitated. Maybe Golda had forgotten about the lunch.

She heard a screech of brakes. Golda had arrived. Golda wound down her car window. She looked flushed.

"I'll just park the car," she shouted. "I'm so sorry I'm late. Bloody Bella Fleker rang me just as I was leaving, and I couldn't get off the phone." She drove off to park the car.

When she came back Dora was still standing in the street. "You weren't capable of telling Bella Fleker that you had to get off the phone?" Dora said. "I've been standing here in Chapel Street for half an hour. Do you think I've got nothing better to do with my time?"

"Do you have to start lunch by telling me how much busier you are than me?" said Golda.

"That's not how the lunch is starting. The lunch started with me standing in the street, in my uncomfortable new shoes."

"Why didn't you wait inside?"

"I didn't want to. Why should I be waiting for you, anyway? Do we have lunch together so often that you can treat it in a cavalier fashion?"

"I didn't treat it in a cavalier fashion," said Golda. "You're talking as though this lunch was a summit meeting or something."

"Firstly," said Dora, "you shouldn't keep anyone, anywhere, waiting for half an hour. And, secondly, the lunch may not have seemed important to you but it was important to me."

"I'm sorry I'm being aggressive," said Golda. "I think I was expecting you to be aggressive, so I got in first."

"Anyone would be aggressive if they had been waiting for half an hour. I'm not aggressive to you."

"How can you say that?" said Golda. "You put me down all the time. You're always making references to the fact that I don't work, and when I did that interview with Rosa Cohen about being the child of concentration camp survivors you very smartly let me know that I was stupid for thinking that Mum and Dad's past had anything to do with me."

"Look at us," said Dora. "We haven't even got inside the restaurant yet, and we're arguing. Do you think we could go inside and have something to eat?"

"Yes," said Golda. "Let's go inside."

The restaurant was almost empty. "Where shall we sit?" asked Golda.

"Anywhere," said Dora. "The place is empty. We won't sit near that window, because it is next to the Ladies, and some days you can smell the toilets."

"I'd like to sit against a wall," said Golda.

"OK, let's sit here," said Dora.

"Could we sit against the other wall? It's closer to the door. I like to be close to the door," said Golda.

"All right," said Dora. "Here's a table that's against a wall and close to the door. Will that do?"

"Yes."

"Nobody else has to hold a seminar on where to sit," said Dora. "We've taken so long choosing a table they've probably stopped serving lunch."

"No they haven't," said Golda.

"I was only joking."

"Do you mind if I sit in this chair?"

"No, not at all."

"I have to sit in a certain position," said Golda. "It's not a specific position, like, say, facing north, south, east or west. In fact I don't even know my norths souths easts and wests. It's just that there is a particular direction that is the right way for me to be facing at each table. I don't know which direction that is until I see the table. If I sit facing the wrong way I feel very anxious."

"What is wrong with you? What difference does it make which direction you sit facing? You just get a different view."

"No, if I sit in the right direction I feel safe," said Golda. "If I sit in the wrong direction I feel really on edge. When there are lots of people at a table, I have to sit at one end of the table. I can't sit in the middle. I get the creeps in the middle."

"Oh, no, Golda," said Dora. "Why do you have to be so crackers?"

"I'm not crackers," said Golda. "I'm just fussy about where I sit. I thought you weren't going to be mean to me today. I thought this lunch was supposed to be friendly."

"I'm not mean to you," said Dora. "I'd just like you to be more normal."

"Speaking of normal," said Golda. "Bella Fleker told me that her mother told her that Pola and Jack Newman have split up. Bella's mother, who knows everything, said that the children are staying on in the family home, and Pola and Jack are taking it in turns to live there. She does a fortnight, and then he does a fortnight. Jack lives at his surgery the rest of the time, and Pola has got a small flat in Carlton. Isn't that mad?"

"Is that what you and Bella were talking about while I was standing in the street?" said Dora.

"Yes," said Golda. "I couldn't believe that Jack and Pola had broken up. I used to feel so intimidated at their dinner parties. Pola always seemed so together. After all, she's a psychologist. Some psychologist she must be to think of this solution to a marriage breakdown."

"You were talking about Pola and Jack Newman, while your sister was standing in Chapel Street waiting for you for half an hour?"

"There was something about the crazy nature of the Newmans' solution that made me feel good. I may not have a successful psychology practice, and I may not put on elegant dinner parties, but I'd never, ever subject my kids to the circus of one parent or the other constantly moving in and out."

"What's so wrong with that?"

"What do you mean, what's so wrong with that?" said Golda. "Everything is wrong with that. The Newman kids are going to feel like lunatics. People coming and going all the time. Who should they expect at home this week, and who should they expect to be at home next week? They're going to feel as though they're living in Flinders Street Station. And what are Pola and Jack going to do? Are they going to put away all their personal items when the other one is there? I mean they'll be able to read each other's mail, look at each other's purchases. That's all right when you're married, but not when you're divorced. Bella said they're definitely getting divorced. They've been married for fifteen years. Apparently they've been having trouble for a long time. You couldn't tell. I guess you mostly can't tell."

"It still doesn't seem so crazy to me," said Dora.

"What will they do about the bedding?" said Golda. "Will they sleep on the same sheets? I mean, if you can't bear being married to someone, how could you bear to be sleeping on the same sheets? And will they look in the bed for evidence of each other's lovers? It sounds very messy to me."

"Sheets are sheets," said Dora. "What does it matter who slept on them?"

"How can you say that? Would you like to sleep in a stranger's sheets?"

"They're not strangers. They've known each other for fifteen years."

"They may have known each other for fifteen years," said Golda, "but they are strangers now. They don't speak to each other. They hate each other. You can be a stranger to someone you've known for a long time. Strangers don't necessarily not have to know each other."

"All right, they're strangers," said Dora. "I don't want to fight about Pola and Jack Newman. I don't even know them. Why should we fight about Pola and Jack Newman?"

"We're not fighting about them," said Golda. "We're fighting about lifestyles and values."

"I don't want to fight about anything," said Dora. "Let's order some food."

"I think I'll have the squid salad," said Golda. "I've been back on a diet for two weeks. I've lost two pounds."

"You look OK to me," said Dora. "You're not too overweight. Maybe you shouldn't worry so much about dieting. I've read that some people are naturally bigger than others. It's such a short life. Why waste it not eating the food you love?"

"That's nice of you to say that," said Golda. "I'm lighter than I was last year. I'm ten stone. But everyone else my height is eight stone."

"Maybe they're the wrong weight," said Dora.

"Ha, ha. That's funny," said Golda. "I think I'll stick to the squid salad. It's actually what I feel like."

"I'll have it too."

"I used to be so jealous of the fact that you weren't fat," said Golda. "I used to wish I was you. I used to wish I was anybody else in the world other than me. I used to wish I was one of the drunken old men I would see in the street, or a ragged old lady. I used to wish I was anybody who was thin."

"It makes me feel very sad to hear you say that."

"Oh good," said Golda. "I'm glad you can feel something other than anger and hostility towards me."

"I don't feel anger and hostility towards you."

"I think you do," said Golda. "You're like Mum and Dad. They're always telling me how much they love me, yet almost everything that they say to me is a complaint or a criticism."

"I don't think that's fair of you. They do love you," said Dora.

"You don't have to defend Mum and Dad. You always agree with them, that's bad enough."

"I want us to be close," said Dora. "That's why I organised this lunch. I want to be able to share things with you. I'd like to be able to share tips with you. Do you know that if you light a match in the bathroom after you've been to the toilet, the lighted match extinguishes any smell? A nurse at the Rosenthal Homes told me that. I tried it, and it works. It's amazing. I thought you might like to know that."

"That's very interesting," said Golda. "I think if I lit a match after Charlie had been to the toilet, the whole house might go up in flames. Thanks for telling me that."

"Are you being sarcastic?"

"No, I mean it," said Golda.

"I don't know why we're not closer," said Dora.

"We never were, were we?" said Golda. "Mum told me that when I was two you tried to feed me a cup of dissolved aspirins."

"Mum has told me that aspirin story about a hundred times," said Dora. "She loves that story. She always laughs when she tells it. I'm not sure who the laughter is for. Whether it is at the thought of how wicked I was, or at the thought of you nearly dying. Why do you think she thinks it is so funny?"

"I don't know."

"I don't think that I had murderous intentions towards you, although I can't remember," said Dora. "What would a shrink make of it?"

"A shrink would say that you tried to kill me."

"And what would a shrink say about Mum finding it all so funny?"

"He'd say that Mum had a good sense of humour," said Golda.

"What a joke!" said Dora. "Mum has no sense of humour. There's a malicious pleasure in her voice when she tells the aspirin story, but I can't work out what is pleasurable to her, and who the malice is directed at."

"You know that Mum tried to have an abortion when she found out she was pregnant with you?" said Golda.

"What?" said Dora.

"Didn't you know?" said Golda. "She felt that she wasn't in a position to have a child. They had no money. They were refugees, remember? She felt humiliated being pregnant. She soaked herself in endless hot baths. She drank red wine and walked up and down the stairs, but nothing happened. Luckily for you, you were as stubborn then as you are now."

"You're making all of this up, aren't you?" said Dora. "You're trying to upset me."

"Of course I'm not making this up. Mum told me years ago."

"She's never said anything to me," said Dora.

"It's not something that you tell the would-be abortee."

"You can be very cruel," said Dora. "I read that children whose mothers tried to abort them always felt uncomfortable in the world. They knew that they were not wanted."

"Where did you read that? In the *Women's Weekly*?" said Golda. "It's garbage."

"You've really upset me," said Dora.

"How can I have upset you?" said Golda. "You're the one who thinks that Mum and Dad have been perfect parents. Nothing could upset that."

"I wonder why she didn't want me."

"I don't think it was you in particular that she didn't want," said Golda. "It was just that she didn't want a child."

"You're right," said Dora. "It was nothing against me personally. I'm not going to be upset about it. Jesus, I'm very lucky that I made it."

The waiter brought the squid salads.

"I can't believe this," said Golda. "Salad servers in the shape of a giraffe's head."

"Look at the bowl. It's got black and white stripes," said Dora. "Like a zebra. Get it? We're at the Spotted Zebra."

"Oh no," said Golda. "That explains the lion-shaped salt and pepper shakers. They want us to think we're on a safari."

"It's hilarious, isn't it?" said Dora. "It makes the aspirin and the abortion seem quite sane."

"Oh, God, look who's just walked in," said Golda. "It's Diane Burnett and her boyfriend. Wasn't she in your year at school?"

"No," said Dora. "She was in the year below me. I didn't really know her. She looks good, doesn't she? I think all the Jewish girls in my year wanted to be blonde and blue-eyed like her."

"See the guy she's with?" said Golda. "He's eighteen. He's her lover."

"How do you know?"

"Bella told me."

"Do Bella and her mother know everything about everybody?"

"I think they do," said Golda. "Apparently Diane had an affair with Harry Silver, Ruthie Brot's husband's sister's husband. The affair is over now. Harry Silver and his wife are in therapy to sort out what went wrong. Apparently Diane Burnett took the break-up very badly. I think she really loved Harry."

"Ruthie Brot's husband's sister's husband?" said Dora. "Is this what you think about all day?"

"It doesn't take all day," said Golda. "Bella said that this guy is so young that Diane Burnett is probably breastfeeding him. He does look very young, doesn't he? He only looks about fifteen. Bella said he is definitely eighteen."

"Breastfeeding him?" said Dora. "That's sickening."

"Why is it sickening?"

"I don't know. Breastfeeding is for babies. I loved feeding the girls. I enjoyed it so much that I felt there must be something wrong with me. I can still remember exactly what it felt like. I was almost in a trance while I was breastfeeding. God, that was over twenty years ago.

"I hated breastfeeding," said Golda. "It made me squirm. I just couldn't bear the feeling of anyone sucking my nipples. I really couldn't bear it. It set my teeth on edge. Like that awful feeling you get when someone scrapes chalk on a blackboard. I felt such a failure. All these years later, I still feel a failure talking about it. I tried to breastfeed Simone. I was determined that I wouldn't be as miserable a failure at it as I was with Danielle. I joined the Nursing Mothers Association. I rubbed lanolin into my nipples for months. I even asked Charlie to practise on me. I grimaced and got through the practice runs with Charlie. I thought that the baby wouldn't feel as bad as Charlie. After the birth, I drank masses of water so I'd have lots of milk. A volunteer from the Nursing Mothers Association came in to see me every day. Every day she massaged my nipples. That felt all right. But as soon as they put

Simone on my breast, I wanted to scream. It was obviously some deeply embedded neurosis, connected to my childhood."

"Don't be silly," said Dora. "It just didn't feel right to you."

"Do you remember Mr Rigaro, the next-door neighbour?" said Golda. "He used to masturbate me when I was about ten. He used to sit me on his knee and give me one of those viewers that you look into and see different stories. I used to look at the Leaning Tower of Pisa and the Mona Lisa, and he used to masturbate me. It felt wonderful. I knew it was wrong, but I went back to him day after day. Mum thought that I was watching television there. I've never told anyone about it. Not even Charlie. I don't think about it much, but when I do, I feel such a deep sense of shame. Mr Rigaro must have been about fifty. Actually he could have been any age from twenty to fifty, I couldn't tell."

"How could you let him do that to you?" said Dora.

"I don't know," said Golda. "In the beginning, I just sat on his lap and looked at the viewer, and then gradually he started masturbating me. I don't even remember the first time it happened. I remember we used to sit facing a corner of the room. No-one else seemed to be home at the time."

"I still don't understand how you could let him do it," said Dora.

"I don't know why I let him," said Golda. "It felt good. And maybe I enjoyed the attention. I think, Dora, maybe you could see me as being exploited by Mr Rigaro rather than worry about my moral stand at the age of ten."

"I do feel sorry for you," said Dora. "I just can't believe that you let him do it."

"The really sad thing," said Golda, "is that I have never let anyone do it to me since."

"Why is that sad?"

"Dora, how can you be so thick? Of course it's very sad to be an adult and never allow yourself to be masturbated, and never even masturbate yourself."

"I don't think that's such a big tragedy," said Dora. "It's not a matter of life and death."

"You sound just like Dad," said Golda. "You reduce life down to its lowest common denominator, we are alive if we are breathing and we will stay alive as long as we eat. Well that's not life. That's more like death."

"I'm sorry," said Dora. "I've never been masturbated, and I've never masturbated myself."

"I'm sorry," said Golda.

"Why should you be sorry?" said Dora. "It's not your fault."

"You know why I stopped going to the Rigaros' place?" said Golda. "I stopped going there because Mum told me that they ate my pet rabbit for Easter."

"They didn't fry the onions before putting them into this salad," said Dora. "It takes just a few minutes and makes all the difference. You fry them in a little butter with parsley and spring onions, and it changes the flavour of the whole dish. What they've probably done is throw the onions into some wine with half a dozen bouillon cubes. Bouillon cubes cover any short cuts. Except all the food tastes the same. It doesn't matter if you're eating fish or brains or chicken, it all tastes the same. I'm disappointed, I thought this was supposed to be a really good place."

"The squid did have a bit of an indiscernible flavour," said Golda. "You've always been interested in cooking, haven't you?"

"Yes, I really enjoy cooking," said Dora. "Do you think that enjoying cooking might make up for never being masturbated?"

"Are you laughing at me?" said Golda.

"No, I think I'm feeling sorry for myself," said Dora. "I haven't experienced anything even slightly sleazy like you did. No-one approached me, no-one wanted me to show them anything. And I was supposed to be the pretty one. Probably even then you could tell that I wasn't a very sexy person. Sex isn't all that important to me. I've heard women say that they feel sexually frustrated. I can't imagine what that feels like. Maybe I've felt it and I don't know. I can't even imagine what it feels like to be masturbated."

"I think you have to distinguish between sleazy and not sleazy," said Golda. "It was sleazy with Mr Rigaro, but masturbation in general is not sleazy."

"Is this a sex education lecture?"

"No, I'm just trying to be helpful."

"I'm sorry, I think I'm feeling sensitive about what I've missed out on," said Dora.

"I've been thinking about what I've missed out on too," said Golda. "I've never worked. I've never held down a job. Maybe never having worked is worse than never being masturbated? Anyway, I've missed out on the masturbation too. The times with Mr Rigaro don't count."

"Maybe we should change the subject," said Dora.

"Yes. Talking about what you've missed out on is depressing," said Golda. "Especially when you're getting old."

"I don't think the subject of how old we're getting is the one to replace what we've missed out on," said Dora.

"Well, we are getting old," said Golda. "There's not a lot of time left to get our shit together."

"I've got my shit together. Anyway, I don't like that phrase."

"There's not a lot of time left to get our act together. Is that better?"

"Mine is together," said Dora. "I've got Abe and Vivian and Anna. That's my life. That's my act. I've also got my work at the Rosenthal Homes."

"You don't get paid for any of that," said Golda.

"That doesn't matter. Why should money be the way in which you value what you are doing? Anyway, how much money do I need? I've got enough. What would I do with the extra money? Drive two cars at once? I'm already thinking of selling the Mercedes. Mr Zelig at the Homes needles me all the time about driving a German car. I wonder if Mr Zelig has got anything against the Japanese? Maybe I'll buy a nice Toyota."

"I don't agree with any Jew driving a German car," said Golda. "If all Jews boycotted all German products, then the German economy would feel it."

"I don't think it would make any difference to the Germans."

"Of course it would make a difference. Jews are big spenders."

"Not big enough to make a difference to the German economy."

"So, now you're an expert in economic theory?"

"You don't have to be sarcastic," said Dora. "I think it's very bad for you to think about the Germans. You've got to stop living in the past. The past is over with. It's got nothing to do with the present."

"The present is starting to depress me," said Golda. "You know what the high point of my year was last year? Don't laugh. It was the aerobics class I went to at Ruthie Brot's house. I loved being part of a group. There were only four of us. I never worried about what I looked like leaping around the floor. I felt completely unselfconscious. I've spent my whole life holding my stomach in, and covering myself up from head to foot. At Ruthie's, I used to wear leotards and share a shower with Ella Tennenbaum. The classes fizzled out when Ella went to live in Israel. Ruthie went back to university, and I guess she didn't have time for aerobics any more. I saw her last week. She wasn't very friendly. I don't know why. I thought she was a nice person. Shall we have a cake?"

"Yes. Let's have a cake," said Dora.

"I hardly touched my bread roll, and I didn't eat the avocado in the salad, so I can afford to have a piece of cake," said Golda. "I think I'll have the cheesecake with the rugelach and chocolate sauce."

"I'll have the sacher torte," said Dora.

"Do you like working at the Rosenthal Homes?" said Golda.

"I do," said Dora. "I really do. I've grown to love quite a few of the inmates. I shouldn't call them inmates. They're residents. Some of them are so sweet. They've all got their own groups, their own friends in the Homes. It's funny, you'd think that they would all mix together, but the Polish Jews hang around with the Polish Jews, and the Hungarian Jews hang around with the Hungarian Jews, and the German Jews still think they are superior to all the other Jews. Even the most ardent atheists go to the synagogue at the centre, because that's where the social life is. In so many ways they're like kids. They can earn pocket money by filling sausages in the kitchen. It sometimes makes me feel like crying to see a group of old men filling sausages in the kitchen."

"That would make me feel like crying too."

"Some days," said Dora, "some of the residents drive me crazy, but I can see that they get a lot of pleasure out of driving me crazy. Mr Zelig, who often really torments me, last week reduced me to tears by asking me if I would come to his funeral. He said he didn't mind if not too many people came to his funeral, as long as he knew that I would be there."

"Isn't that touching," said Golda. "I'll come with you if you like. Is Mr Zelig ill?"

"No," said Dora. "He's ancient, but he's as strong as a horse. He's always yelling at me about rich Jews who don't do enough for Israel. I'm not sure if he thinks I'm one of them. A couple of days ago he said to me that there was a resurgence of anti-Semitism in the air. He says it's been allowed to surface because Jews are now a divided people, and a divided people can't defend themselves adequately."

"Does he mean divided about the Intifada?" Golda asked.

"Yes," said Dora. "He says that those smart left-wing liberals are going to get the shock of their lives when they wake up one morning and see that they've become second-class citizens again. He says they're going to feel sick when they see how they've contributed to their own demise."

"He sounds like a very smart old man," said Golda.

"He's really smart," said Dora. "He reads all the newspapers. He gets the *Washington Post* and the *Economist* airmailed to him. It's a gift from his old boss, Mr Goldman. Mr Zelig worked for Mr Goldman for fifty-three years. He says he doesn't mind that

Mr Goldman never visits him because he feels Mr Goldman's gratitude, for all the work he did for him, every day when he opens up his newspapers."

"What a nice thing of Mr Goldman to do," said Golda. "I've heard that he's an incredibly nice man. I must tell Dad. Dad's always railing about how the rich Jews only care about making more money."

"Don't bother telling Dad," said Dora. "I don't think he'd be very impressed by newspaper subscriptions. He's not really into newspapers."

"You're right," said Golda.

"Do you want to hear a joke that old Mrs Berner told me yesterday?" said Dora.

"Yes, I could do with a joke," said Golda.

"What does a woman do if a pit bull terrier tries to fuck her leg?" said Dora.

"What's a pit bull terrier?" said Golda.

"You're spoiling the joke," said Dora. "A pit bull terrier is one of those killer dogs. I'll start again. What does a woman do if a pit bull terrier tries to fuck her leg?"

"I don't know," said Golda.

"She fakes an orgasm," said Dora.

Golda laughed. "Mrs Berner told you that? How old is she?"

"About eighty," said Dora. "Being with older people has been good for me. We didn't grow up with anyone old around us, did we?"

"No, they were all killed off by the Nazis," said Golda.

"I know that," said Dora. "I don't need you to tell me that. I may not want to dwell on it, but I do know about it."

"Of course you know about it," said Golda. "I wasn't telling you about it. I was merely stating it as a fact. Don't be so sensitive."

"Watching old people has been very reassuring for me," said Dora. "It's made me feel younger, and it's also made me aware of what's in store for me."

"You should touch wood when you say 'what's in store for me' or you'll invoke the evil eye. You have to touch wood or spit three times in mid-air," said Golda.

"Golda, you're a lunatic," said Dora. "All right, I'll touch wood. Watching people coping with their old age has made it seem less frightening to me."

"Old age has never seemed frightening to me," said Golda. "I've never thought I'd reach it. I don't think of people dying of old age. I think of them being killed in car accidents or plane crashes, or else they have heart attacks. I've never seen myself as living until I'm old. I'm surprised that Mum and Dad are still alive. They were always threatening to drop dead. This was going to kill them, and that was going to kill them — mostly something I'd done."

"I remember those conversations about you doing a better job than Hitler. What was it that you were doing that was so terrible?" said Dora.

"I don't know," said Golda. "I wouldn't keep my room tidy. I didn't lose weight, and I wasn't very pretty. Then I wouldn't study law. That nearly killed them. They were furious. Well, I've paid the price for that too. I wish I'd done law. I'd be somebody today."

"I don't think university graduates are better somebodies than other people," said Dora.

"Well, that's nice of you, but you know what I mean. I would have accomplished more than I have, and I would have felt better, I think," said Golda.

"A university education isn't the prestigious thing it used to be," said Dora. "Mr Zelig boasted to me that his grandson had dropped out of law to begin a paper recycling business. He collects waste paper from offices and recycles it. He's making more money than Abe, and he's half his age. I heard Mr Zelig tell someone that his grandson was a garbage collector. At least Mum and Dad wanted you to go to university. They didn't care if I went or not. They were really pleased when I got married so young. I think they thought I was too stupid to bother with an education."

"No," said Golda, "the reason they didn't plague you to go to university was that they thought you were pretty enough to survive without it. With my looks they thought I definitely needed a degree or two."

"It all sounds so sad, doesn't it?"

"It does," said Golda. "At least this cheesecake with the chocolate sauce is really good. I wouldn't have thought of putting chocolate sauce on top of cheesecake."

"Did I tell you," said Dora, "that I've been organising literary readings at the Rosenthal Homes? I organise people, mostly young actors and actresses, to come in and read to the residents twice a week. We had a fabulous morning last week. This young actor, Gerald Floor — you've probably never heard of him, but he's really good — read from Morris Lurie's *Whole Life*. Well, Mrs Blatkin was up in arms. 'How can this Lurie write such things about his father?' she kept shouting. But Mr Zelig defended Lurie to the hilt. He railed at Mrs Blatkin, 'Lurie doesn't say his father was not a nice man, he just writes about some of his not-so-nice qualities. But he writes about his father's life, and that's a big honour, a big mitzvah.' Mrs Blatkin didn't agree that it was a big honour, but they got over it. They've had Patrick White read to them and Kurt Vonnegut and Raymond Carver and Fay Weldon. These old-timers, my Mr Roth, and Mr Zelig and Mrs Blatkin and Mrs Rose and all the others, they're the literati of St Kilda. Would you like to come to one of the readings?"

"I'd love to," said Golda. "Maybe I could read? I used to love reading to the kids when they were little."

"You've always had a nice speaking voice," said Dora. "I think Dad's dream was that his daughter with the beautiful voice and the perfect English would out-argue all the other lawyers and win every case."

"Do you think so?" said Golda. "I didn't catch a hint of that dream. I only saw the nightmare in which he always had to let me know exactly how plain and unattractive I was."

"He was hard on you, wasn't he? I wonder why?" said Dora.

"I don't know," said Golda. "He was punishing me for something, I'm just not sure what. Sometimes I think he was punishing me for not having been in Auschwitz like him. I think he would have preferred one of his sisters to have survived and lived with him in Australia, instead of me. He definitely doesn't think I'm grateful enough for growing up in Australia. Maybe if I'd seen Lodz I'd be grateful to be living in Melbourne. Melbourne's OK, but it's nothing to get down on your bended knees about. Anyway, I'll never know what he was angry about. Dad himself, I'm sure, doesn't know. What will I read? Do you think the residents would like Isaac Bashevis Singer?"

"They would love Isaac Bashevis Singer. That's a perfect choice," said Dora.

"What about Proust, Dostoyevsky, Salman Rushdie? What about *Love in the Time of Cholera*?"

"Let's start with Isaac Bashevis Singer," said Dora.

"OK. I'll read them *Enemies, A Love Story.* That's a wonderful book."

"Look at the time," said Dora. "It's three-thirty. I guess we should get a move on."

"I guess we should," said Golda.

"How is Abe?" said Golda. "I haven't seen him for ages."

"I haven't seen too much of him myself," said Dora. "He always seems to be working. The less I see him, the less I miss him. It's funny, that, isn't it? Maybe that's human nature. You make the best of what you've got. If you've got a husband who's around a lot, you like having him around, and if you've got one who's not around, you don't miss him as much as you thought you would. You probably don't think very highly of that as a piece of psychological insight, do you?"

"It sounds quite sound to me," said Golda.

"Don't be mistaken," said Dora, "Abe and I are very close. He showers while I'm having a shit. He strains on the toilet in front of me. You have to be very close to a person to be able to strain on the toilet in front of them. Wouldn't you agree?"

"It's not my area of expertise, but I would tend to agree with you," said Golda.

"Oh, no, look who's coming over to say hello," said Dora. "It's Mrs Hoffman."

"Hello, Golda, hello, Dora," said Mrs Hoffman. "How nice to see two sisters having lunch together. Shvesters, shvesters, nothing in the world can be as close as sisters. May your parents have nothing but naches from you. Give my best regards to your mother and father."

"That old bitch took her brother to court," said Dora. "She claimed that her brother diddled her out of some of her cousin's will. The brother and his wife had looked after the cousin for years. The brother's not a wealthy man, and sweet Mrs Hoffman is loaded. So much for all this shvesters, shvesters. I don't think family togetherness is Mrs Hoffman's forte."

"How do you know all of this?" said Golda.

"I hear it at the Homes," said Dora. "I know who's doing business with whom, who's buying who out, who paid too much and who got a bargain. I'm sure my knowledge could be valuable to someone."

"You could write a gossip column for the *Jewish News*," said Golda.

"I could. I hear a lot of things," said Dora. "Some of the things you hear you have to ignore. Last year someone told me that Abe was having an affair."

"What?"

"Yes, you heard it right," said Dora. "Mrs Berner thought she should warn me that she had heard that Abe was shtooping someone else. But I said to her that Abe wasn't all that interested in shtooping."

"That's what I would have thought," said Golda.

"How can you say that?" said Dora. "You'd have no idea whether Abe was interested in shtooping or not."

"Why is it OK for you to say it but not for me?"

"Because you don't know and I do. Because it's insulting when it comes from you. When I say it I'm being understanding and tolerant."

"I'm sorry," said Golda. "It's not that I think Abe is unattractive, it's just that I can't imagine him being a sensual person."

"I think you should stop because you're becoming very insulting again," said Dora.

"I like Abe very much," said Golda.

"I like him very much too," said Dora. "I love him. I think the reason I've forced myself not to miss him since he's been working these long hours is that I don't want to nag him or upset him. I don't want to complain all the time either. So, if he wants to work hard, then that's the way it's going to have to be."

"Why are you crying? What's wrong?"

"I don't know what's wrong," said Dora. "Sometimes I get very frightened. I can't imagine my life without Abe."

"But why should you imagine your life without Abe?"

"I don't know."

"Abe's always been a good husband and a good father," said Golda.

"He has," said Dora.

"You don't think there was any truth in what Mrs What's-her-name said?"

"I think I'm too frightened to think about it. I can't imagine Abe having sex with someone else. Or touching someone else. Or kissing someone else. I think of Abe partly as a very private part of myself. And it feels impossible to think of him joined to someone else."

"I'm sure he's not."

"I think it's much better that I believe that he's just working very long hours," said Dora. "He's always been a hard worker. A very hard worker. And he's done a lot of good for a lot of people."

"You're absolutely right," said Golda. "Abe is a very good human being. And a very hard worker. Please stop crying. I'm sure that there's nothing wrong. Abe loves you. He's loved you for years. Everyone can see that. The two of you have grown up together. He loves you and he loves Vivian and Anna. He's so nice he even loves Mum and Dad. Charlie doesn't love Mum and Dad, but Abe does. And he loves his parents too. A man like that would never leave his wife."

"That's what I'm more scared of than anything else," said Dora. "That he'll leave. I don't mind what he is doing as long as he doesn't decide that whatever it is is better than being my husband. I really do love him."

"Of course you love him," said Golda. "In all the years you've been together I've never heard you say a mean word to him or about him. I've complained about Charlie, but I've never heard you complain about Abe. You've cooked him beautiful meals, and you've been a fabulous mother to the girls."

"That's nice of you to say that," said Dora. "I haven't really had anything to complain about. That's why I haven't complained. Abe's got a very good heart. You don't meet many people who are such good human beings. I've always been proud of him."

"I'm sure he is very proud of you," said Golda.

"Whatever he's doing or whatever he's not doing, I am going to be his wife," said Dora. "I'm not going to ask questions or make phone calls or check up on him. I'm going to keep acting like my normal self. And my normal self is Abe's wife. I'm Mrs Abe Lipshitz."

"Of course you are Mrs Abe Lipshitz," said Golda.

"I think that Mrs Abe Lipshitz might go out and buy herself a really sexy black negligee. I saw one in Georges," said Dora. "I might get my legs waxed too. I've never had that done. I think this might be a good time to try a few new things. You never know, I might get to know about masturbation yet."

"Do you think we should go halves in a copy of *The Joy of Sex* if it's still in print?" said Golda.

"Golda, you've been really good to listen to me talking like this," said Dora. "I've always kept my worries to myself. It's been very good for me talking to you, because I was in a muddle. I thought that I didn't know what I was doing. But I can see that I know exactly what I am doing. I'm staying married to Abe. I think I'll go and buy a nice salmon. He's coming home for dinner tonight. He loves baked salmon. And I can cook a beautiful baked salmon."

"I know you can," said Golda. "I've had your baked salmon."

"The secret," said Dora, "is to seal the salmon in silver foil, while it is baking, and be sure not to overcook it. I take it out of the oven when I test it to see if it's cooked. If you leave it in the oven while you test it it can overcook."

"I'll remember that," said Golda.

"I love you, Golda," said Dora. "I know I don't always show it, but I do feel it."

"I love you too," said Golda. "I'm really sorry I talked about Mum trying to abort you. I know she never would have tried if she'd known what you were going to be like. You're the daughter she's really pleased with."

"I don't mind knowing about the abortion, or the would-be abortion," said Dora. "I do love you. I used to have fantasies about being really close to you. I used to daydream about it. I daydream about a lot of things. One of my daydreams was that you and I went into business together. We set up a catering service that delivered ready-to-heat meals for new mothers. It was called Moving Meals. We delivered elegant meals for the parents, and fun meals for any children they already had. The only person the mother then had to feed was the new baby. Moving Meals was a roaring success. Mothers all over Melbourne were grateful to us. 'Those Gotberg girls are so clever,' people used to say in my daydream."

"No-one has called us the Gotberg girls for years," said Golda. "I like the sound of Moving Meals. Maybe we should think about that seriously?"

"Maybe we should."

"Let's go and do our shopping together. You can tell me exactly how to bake the salmon. I might start swotting up for Moving

Meals. Let's go in the one car. We can go in my car, and I'll drop you back to your car when we've finished shopping."

"That would be nice," said Dora. "I haven't been shopping with you since we were kids."

"This has been a really nice lunch," said Golda.

"Do you want to hear another one of Mrs Berner's jokes?" said Dora.

"Tell me when we're in the car," said Golda.

All Kinds of Things

Rosa Cohen
203 East Fifteenth Street
New York, N.Y. 10003
22 May

Dear Ella,

I can't remember why we're not speaking to each other. We were such good friends. What happened? I don't know. Maybe you know? All the things that went wrong seem so small. I think that things started to disintegrate when you lost weight and I didn't. Why does that sound so shallow?

I've missed you. I've thought about you a lot. I knew you were in Israel. Paul Sunderland came through New York and told me. We had dinner together. He's still a real sleaze. When Allan went to the bathroom, Paul gripped my wrist, stared into my eyes and asked me if I'd like him to come around to the apartment the next day. I didn't know whether to be furious or grateful. I felt premenstrually crazy and ugly that day.

Paul told me that you had a Russian boyfriend. A violinist, he said. That sounds good.

It is strange that we have both uprooted ourselves and left Australia, the country our parents struggled to get us to.

How are you managing? Managing is such a sad little word, isn't it? Since I have been here, I have often felt lost. And I have often felt loss. A generalised loss. Loss of friends, acquaintances, local shopkeepers. God, I have even felt the loss of people I didn't like much.

The loss hangs around me. It hangs low in the air, and if I'm not careful I bang into it. Once I do, I'm done for. I weep. I weep for my mother, I weep for my analyst, I weep for our house in Melbourne, I weep for our garden, I weep at the memory of the children walking around with bare feet. The truth is, I hardly spent any time in the garden, and didn't like the children to wear no shoes.

We sold our house in Melbourne. Three truckloads of saucepans and cutlery and china and electrical appliances and furniture went off to the auction rooms. It was all sold off as junk. I felt as though my past and present were being dispersed into tiny particles. As though my life was made up of the three truckloads of knives and forks and spoons and toasters and blenders.

I saw the receipt from the auction rooms. Do you know that I had three electric fruit juicers and four toasters? We never juiced fruit, and we toasted bread under the griller. I had forty-three wooden spoons, four graters, and thirty egg cups. No-one in the family liked eggs.

And I had seven rolling pins. I never baked anything. Why did I need rolling pins? This receipt was really a social document of our times. No-one is going to be buying rolling pins in the future. I must have imagined myself rolling out doughs and pastries. The right rolling pin must have seemed to be something that every mother needed. I can remember buying them. I had them sitting in a stoneware jar in the kitchen. Maybe I had them there to create the right ambience in the kitchen. Do you remember my rolling pins?

I think I've been a really good mother. You would think so, too, if you'd read the list of stuff that went off to be auctioned. Pizza trays, a pasta maker, cookie cutters, one hundred and eighteen pairs of scissors. What was I cutting?

One hundred and sixteen boxes of books and photographs are being shipped over to us. Even that makes me sad. I feel awful thinking that your life can be so neatly wrapped and packaged. Right now all those boxes are probably bobbing up and down on some strange ship in the Pacific Ocean. Years and years of reading, years and years of photographs, years and years of diaries. In Melbourne I never looked at my diaries. I don't know why I'm having them shipped here. But what else could I do with them? I couldn't leave them with anyone.

I miss you. I miss talking on the phone to you. I don't have long phone conversations any more. I had a telephone dream the other day. There were six telephones in a row. Press-button phones, dial-phones and credit-card phones. And none of them worked. I thought the dream was a symbol of how I have regressed. Towards the end of my analysis I had a dream in which I dialled a number and got straight through. Now I'm back to all the phones being broken, and I can't get through, no matter what buttons I press or what numbers I dial.

I didn't mean to veer off on a depressing tangent. Really, things are OK. They are even more OK. More than OK. What a pathetic expression.

I think I always used to feel that it was dangerous to feel happy. It still doesn't come naturally. When I talk to Allan about living in New York I slip into a list of complaints and worries. And then I have to remind myself that it's OK to feel the joy of living here. Actually, just that it is OK to feel the joy of living. I think I thought that if my life didn't mean all that much to me, then it wouldn't feel so bad if someone took it away from me. Not that I knew that I felt all of this. It took me thousands and thousands of dollars worth of psychoanalysis to find this out. Or, more accurately, it took Allan thousands and thousands of dollars for me to find all this out. What an expensive wife I turned out to be!

I'm trying to write a cheerful letter, but it's not working. By now you're probably thinking that you're glad you haven't spoken to me for three years.

Let me tell you about New York. It really is wonderful. It is a very provocative city. Something assaults your senses all the time. You can't drift your way through. Because we live downtown, we don't see much of the elegant, ultra-thin, ultrarefined, rich New

York. We see the incredible confluence of intellect and argument, youth and old age, drug abuse and hustling and love and joy and passion that makes up downtown.

We walk three or four miles every lunchtime. On days when I feel a bit flat, as soon as I step out into the street I feel better. It's as though the city corrects your perspective. It might be because you are forced to see a larger view of the world, so your own problems appear less pressing.

And it also might be because you see such poignant and funny things. A few days ago there was a man standing on the corner of Second Avenue and Twelfth Street, which is close to where we live. He was about sixty, shabbily dressed in a grubby black three-piece suit. He had thick grey curly hair and a thick grey beard. He had fourteen short-haired black dogs (I counted them) on half a dozen black leashes. While they were waiting for the lights to change, the biggest black dog was going for his life, fucking the shit out of one of the medium-sized black dogs.

Right behind this man, a young woman of about thirty was saying to her friend: "He loves me much more now than he did when we were having sex." And on the same corner an assortment of small girls were filing into a doorway which had a sign on it saying, "Snow White Rehearsal".

We often have lunch at a vegetarian restaurant which boasts that they use no animal products, not even honey. They take allergies and the resultant anxieties so seriously. All the customers seem to ask a million questions about the contents of each dish. Perfectly healthy looking young men make enquiries worthy of someone who is terminally ill. In this company I feel casual and carefree.

I have gone back into analysis. This is my third analyst. You've had three husbands and I've had three analysts. I see this as being just a short bit of analysis to finish off what I didn't quite sort out in Melbourne.

I went to the Upper West Side to see an analyst who my analyst in Melbourne said couldn't see me herself but would refer me to another New York analyst. Did you understand that? There were a few too many analysts for one sentence. Anyway, I saw this analyst on the Upper West Side. Her name was Dr Grace. I talked flat out for fifty minutes. By the time I finished explaining my parents' past, my understanding of their past, my reaction to their past and my reaction to them, then their fears and my fears, and their nightmares and my nightmares, I could see that I was the perfect analysis candidate. Completely fucked.

I told her that I was much better than I used to be. That I was successful in my working life, that I was happily married, that I had really good kids. I tried to explain casually how in the last few years I'd been unable to go anywhere without Allan. That explanation stripped me of all the dignity I'd managed to muster.

I'd arrived at the session in a tailored black suit, with my lips perfectly outlined and dark red lipstick on them. By the end of the session, I was in a sweat. My face was purple and puffy, I'd smudged my lipstick across my chin, and my chest was covered in red blotches. And when I went to leave I couldn't find my way out of her consulting rooms. I walked through the waiting room and out the wrong door. I spent twenty minutes wandering around her apartment. I couldn't find my way out. I was in her lounge room, her dining room, her bathroom. I was in a panic. I couldn't believe I'd done it. I felt like a thief, an intruder, a criminal. I thought I'd never get out. Finally I found my way back to the waiting room, and left through the correct door.

Dr Grace referred me to Dr Silver, who has rooms downtown in Greenwich Village. Dr Silver, as though you couldn't tell, is Jewish. Two out of my three analysts have been Jewish.

After two weeks with Dr Silver I can now go to the sessions on my own. I can now walk the streets on my own. I'm so independent. I hail taxis. I've become an expert taxi hailer. The first time I went to the session and back on my own, I was so anxious to flag down an empty taxi that I ran into a young boy and knocked him over. Poor kid, he was all right, but I think he'll be suspicious of middle-aged Jewish women for the rest of his life.

I keep calling myself middle-aged, and then wanting to deny it.

It sounds so old. If I'm middle-aged, then you're middle-aged too. Or almost. You're only three years younger than I am. Do you feel middle-aged? There's a part of me that feels that middle age is a state much older than the state I've reached. Maybe I'm talking about emotional middle age. Emotionally I'm still fighting my way out of adolescence. The rest of me is heading towards menopause. You're probably not thinking about menopause yet. I don't want to depress you, but I've been thinking about it a lot.

Dr Silver is on the twelfth floor. There's no telephone in the lift, just a small emergency button. But I'm fine. I travel up and down in it with ease. I smile and nod at fellow passengers.

I even say hello to the young man who has the session before me. In the beginning, I used to look away when he came out. I thought it wasn't the correct thing to do, to acknowledge seeing someone in an analyst's rooms. But he always said a very bright hello to me. And then I realised this is New York. Everybody has an analyst.

This young man wears smart, contemporary suits, and always looks composed when he comes out of his sessions. I'm sure I emerge looking either frantic or lobotomised. Come to think of it, though, his grin did look a bit queasy this morning.

This morning I was telling Dr Silver that yesterday I had tried to find out the phone number of the Museum of Fine Art in Boston. I rang enquiries and the telephonist asked me which Boston I wanted. I said, just Boston. She said there were about fifty Bostons. I said I wanted the big Boston. She said how could she tell which was the big Boston. She said did I want Boston New York, Boston Massachusetts, Boston New Jersey, and a string of other Bostons. I said I wanted the main Boston. She said she didn't know which one was the main Boston. When he came up from his studio, Allan told me that Boston is in Massachusetts. I'm sure you know that.

Dr Silver suggested that my lack of geography may be related to my parents' past. And that I really didn't want to take in what was where because that was one way of keeping their past more blurred to me. One more way of pretending it didn't happen. I have often been bewildered by how, no matter how many maps Allan draws for me, I have no sense of what country is where.

I went straight home and studied a map of Australia. The kids have always been appalled by the fact that I didn't know where Melbourne and Sydney were on the map, let alone Victoria and New South Wales. Well, I do now. And I haven't forgotten. Next I'm going to tackle a map of Europe.

My last play, *Drowning the Victim*, got good reviews everywhere. There was only one bad review. Before I'd had anything published, I used to think that acclaim was what I was aiming for. Now, I know it's not. The praise and the prizes are so transient. They make you feel good for half an hour. The real achievement in life is to be a good human being. That sounds a bit sickly, doesn't it? A bit trite. But it's so hard to be a good human being. To be good to those who love you and those whom you love. Just to be good. And not to squander your life.

Someone, reviewing *Drowning the Victim*, wrote that I had become aware that time was our only true commodity, and it was a finite one at that. I wish I really understood that.

Now that I'm back in analysis I have to make sure that I don't get pregnant. Probably I'm too premenopausal to get pregnant anyway. As soon as I'm in analysis, I want to have a baby. It's so that I don't have to look at the baby within myself. It's hard looking at the baby within yourself when you're feeling almost menopausal, if not geriatric.

I had Kira because my first analyst went away for two months. When he came back I was pregnant. Instead of feeling his absence I had filled myself up. I wouldn't have not had Kira for anything. She is the one who will still hug me and cuddle me. She still thinks it's great to come out to lunch with us. The other two kids say that we should enjoy this aspect of her while it lasts, as it will be over very soon.

Kids today are so smart. They know everything. When I looked moon-eyed over a baby that a friend of ours has adopted, Zeke said to me that obstetrics today was so highly refined that it would be quite safe for me to have a baby. Then he warned me about the lack of freedom that having another child would bring us. "You would be trapped for at least another seventeen or eighteen years," he said.

Can you imagine talking to your parents like that? I couldn't have even let my parents know that I knew how babies were conceived when I was already the mother of three.

Do you still feel ambivalent about having children? I've been a mother for so long that I can't imagine being an adult and not being a mother. I'm always touched by mothers. They do so much mothering. They're always pushing arms and legs into clothes, pushing pushers and prams, spooning food into mouths, cooking food, cleaning. It's non-stop. Then they go off to work to give their kids more opportunities.

Two days after my friend adopted the baby, she said to me that she would now recognise him in a room full of babies. It made me cry.

You must have still been in Melbourne when Esther Schenkler committed suicide. You were in her year, weren't you? What happened, Ella? What went wrong with her life? Remember her shiny hair and her high cheekbones? And she was so clever. She was friends with Susan Link from my year, so she sometimes walked to the tram stop with us. She had a certainty and a purposefulness that I never had. I still remember how passionately she led the school debating team on "Should Aboriginals Be Allowed To Drink?"

What does it mean when a kid who has so much energy and optimism ends up killing herself at forty? What has happened to her kids? They were quite old, weren't they? Why didn't they notice that something was wrong? And what about her friends?

What happened to Esther Schenkler's cleverness? What happened to her shiny hair, and her curiosity and her conviction? What happened to Esther Schenkler?

It gave me the creeps when I heard that she had been found in a locker in the shelter sheds at Academy High. It must have felt like a safe place to her. It made me cry to think that that old locker room was where she chose to end her life. As though she was going back to a place of happiness.

A friend of mine just called. Her name is Barbara. She is the only real friend I have here. I met her two years ago — in Israel, actually. Five minutes after I had met her I felt as though I knew her. I still remember every word of that first conversation, and every nuance of her expression. She has a Southern lilt to her accent, and the loveliest face. She is fifty-three. She is a New Yorker. I wrote to her regularly before we moved here.

Anyway, she just rang to say that her eighty-four-year-old mother and her husband's cousin's eighty-one-year-old mother were celebrating their birthdays together tonight at the Shabbat dinner. I envied her having all those family members around her. I know that families have so many cracks and crevices and pits that you can fall into, and get trapped and buried in. But families are also places of learning. You have different generations, different perceptions, different foolishnesses, different wisdoms. And you have love. So what if the love is messy. We all love each other messily.

I never thought that I would have come around to this view. I guess that's what happens with age. All the things your parents shouted at you and you shrugged off now come to be your own truths.

I think about all the times in Australia when I complained about having to go to lunch at Mrs Kinder's or Mrs Bloom's. But I miss that now. I miss being with them. I miss learning from them.

I miss my mother. I've had terrible moments of missing my mother. It's been four years since she died, and I still can't believe that she's dead. Sometimes I have such a strong longing for her. And when I realise that all the longing in the world won't help, I feel terrible. I think that the sadness must stay with you forever.

Some days odd images of her come in to my head. I see her peeling apples. I remember her peeling a Granny Smith apple a few weeks before she died. For a few minutes her hands looked firm again. She peeled the apple slowly. The peel came off in one piece, like it always did. She looked so happy when she had finished. Over the years I'd watched her peel hundreds of apples. She'd peeled apples for me, apples for compote, apples for fruit salad, and she peeled apples for my children. I'd give anything to watch her peel an apple now.

Sometimes I catch glimpses of her that I never allowed myself to see when she was alive. I knew that she was seventeen when she went into the ghetto, and then on to Auschwitz. But it was only recently that I felt what she tried so hard to tell me. That she was only a baby. She was just a child. Only a year older than Kira is now.

I also knew that she was raped in Auschwitz. But I've also known that without feeling it. I've known it intellectually. Last week I was in a taxi when a picture of my mother being raped came into my head. I sat in the taxi, travelling up Third Avenue, weeping. Why did she have to be raped? Weren't the other horrors that she'd endured enough? It was as though nothing was enough. You would think that once you'd lost your mother and father and your brothers and sisters, and watched children dying in the streets, and babies being smashed against walls or used as footballs, that would be enough. God obviously didn't think so. No wonder my parents no longer believed in God.

I wish that I could have told her that I understood why she was the way she was. Remember how distracted she was? Jesus, I'm distracted, and nothing calamitous has happened to me. My mother's death is the worst thing that has ever happened to me. With all the thoughts of death, and all the dead relatives floating around our lives, I still never thought that my mother would die. I thought I had forever to fix things up with her.

All this missing my mother and feeling regretful hasn't really made me a nicer person. I was watching a TV program the other day, a half-hour documentary program of interviews with Holocaust survivors. An old man, a survivor of Bergen-Belsen, was talking. He was myopic and bent, and he spoke with a lisp. He was talking about Bergen-Belsen. "We saw all kinds of things. All kinds of things," he said. All kinds of things. I felt a fury. Why couldn't he say more? Why couldn't they have chosen someone more articulate? "All kinds of things" must be a phrase that translates directly from the Polish. My father uses it to describe everything. All my kindness left me, all my understanding, all my tolerance. I wanted to shake this man and tell him to speak properly.

I think I was having a bad week. The same night I got a call from Mrs Birnbaum, who went to school with my mother and was in the Lodz ghetto with her. She rings me from time to time. Mostly I'm pleased to hear from her. She just says hello, talks for a few minutes and then hangs up. I'm not sure why she keeps in touch. That night, I felt dismayed when I heard her voice. I felt tired of the thick accent and the ever-present anxiety.

When Mrs Birnbaum first contacted me, I felt so excited to meet someone who knew my mother when she was a young girl. I've had lunch with Mrs Birnbaum a few times now, and I've never asked her one question about my mother.

My dad is lonely in Melbourne. He misses us. He doesn't see many people. I don't know what happened to the large group of friends my parents had. My mother was always entertaining, always having dinners and lunches. Remember the beautiful dinners she made? My mother looked after so many people, and look at what happened when she died. Nobody rushed over to repay that hospitality and friendship. My father was left quite alone by that group of friends who'd known each other for over thirty years. No-one visits him. Few people invite him out. And he's such a nice man.

I think of Mr and Mrs Menski, and Mr and Mrs Diksteen, and Mr and Mrs Jablonski, and all the others. I thought they were family. When I was a kid they always seemed to be there. I would have sworn at least Mrs Menski loved me. All those sighs, and pinching of my cheeks. What did that mean? Not much, that's for sure. She still smiles when she sees me, but basically she couldn't give a shit.

Allan says that that is just life. People care about their own families, and that's it. He says we are like that too. But I don't think we are.

The mistake was to think that Mr and Mrs This and Mr and Mrs That were our family. They weren't. I guess they were a temporary family. Maybe we were all family to each other when we needed family. Later everyone built up their own real families.

Allan is on the verge of converting to Judaism. I have done everything I can to delay it. I have delayed it for years. The thought of it bothered me, and I wasn't clear why. I think it was partly out of a sense of loyalty to my parents. Is that perverse? I nearly broke their hearts when I married a non-Jew. But marrying a non-Jew is a different matter from forming an allegiance to God. There was no God, as far as they were concerned, and I didn't want to be disloyal.

Poor Allan. He's been interested in Judaism since he was sixteen, and he had to go and marry the only Jewish girl in Melbourne who knew nothing about Judaism, and who feels worried about stepping into a synagogue. What I know about Judaism I've learnt from Allan.

I think I was frightened of having a Jewish husband. I felt as though I would be much safer with a non-Jewish husband. I thought I wouldn't be so Jewish if I didn't have a Jewish husband. And I worry about him. I worry that he'll be in danger if he's Jewish. I can't get the feeling that it's dangerous to be a Jew out of my head. It's not a thought that occupies a lot of my time, but it's there.

I sound so potty, don't I? And this is the new, mature, come-to-terms-with-myself, over-analysed me. Sometimes I feel so tired of carrying all this baggage. Suitcases of dead relatives and Nazis. Remember when I had that dress made with about eighty dolls' faces sewn into it? I stitched little flowers and glass beads next to each face. One way or another, I carried my own entourage, my own family, on me. And do you remember when I hung those yellow plastic skeletons on a black lurex dress. We were oblivious to the significance of it all, weren't we? I thought I was just an idiosyncratic dresser.

My cleaning lady just came downstairs to my study. She's my age, Puerto Rican, and a grandmother. She seemed a bit flat. I asked her what was wrong, and she said, "You don't know what it is to be poor." And I knew that she was right. I didn't know. I know that our financial struggles look pale next to hers.

My parents always told me that I didn't know what real suffering was. The cleaning lady tells me I don't know what it is to be poor. You always used to say that I didn't know what it was like to have an unfaithful husband. Zelda Tishler, who's still unmarried, says that I don't know what it's like to be single. Even Allan sometimes says, when I feel furious with one of the kids, that I don't know what it's like to have kids with real problems. All in all, I've come to the conclusion that I don't know much.

This morning, on my way home from my analysis session, I walked past a group of homeless women. They're always on the corner of Twelfth Street and Broadway. They sit together in a doorway, four of them. Somehow they seem to make a homely space out of that doorway. They have an old portable radio on the ground in between them. They listen to music and they talk. Sometimes they share a bottle of Coca-Cola. They sit on their boxes and bags and they talk. They talk and talk. They are always talking. Women always have something to say to each other.

Will you write to me and let me know how you are, and what you are doing? Tell me what your life in Israel is like. Tell me about you and Yvette. And about your mother and father. Paul Sunderland said that he thought that you had applied for a job on the *Jerusalem Post*. I hope you got the job; it's a fabulous newspaper.

Can we be friends again? I'm tired of not being friends. I'm tired of being apart.

Love,
Rosa

On Different Fronts

Rosa rolled the hand towels into sausage shapes. She put them into a cane basket on the floor. She folded the face washers. She had put four face washers, six hand towels and four bath towels into the spare bathroom, or the guest bathroom, as some people would call it.

Rosa had read in the *New York Times Magazine* that week that it was essential to put an alarm clock into the guest room. She didn't have a spare alarm clock. Maybe she would go out and buy one later.

The *New York Times Magazine* also suggested having reading lamps, extra pillows and blankets in the guest room, as well as an interesting assortment of books. Above all, the magazine said, it was important not to clutter the guest room by dumping unwanted objects and spare furniture in there.

Rosa checked the room for unwanted objects. She wondered exactly what constituted an unwanted object. There was a fax machine in the guest room. That definitely wasn't an unwanted object. She and Allan loved their fax machine. Allan's desk was also in the guest room. That was because the guest room doubled as Allan's office.

"If you have the space, an actual reading area is always nice," said the *New York Times Magazine*. They also advised readers that "a tiny chair next to the bath tub is always a nice touch".

Rosa wondered how tiny this chair should be. She also wondered why it should be tiny. Maybe a large chair next to a bath tub would be aesthetically displeasing? Maybe it would just be in the way?

"My favourite guest rooms," said another decorator in the same article, "are the ones where you really get a feeling of your hosts, which is why I always put family photographs in my guest room."

Rosa decided she would put her newly framed photograph of her father on the window sill. She thought the *New York Times* was right. A photograph of her father would make Ella fell at home.

Ella was arriving in New York this afternoon. Two weeks after Rosa had written to Ella, Ella had phoned her from Jerusalem. Three years of not speaking to each other were erased in the first hello.

"Hello, hello, Rosa. It's me," Ella had shouted. "I'm coming over to see you. I found out yesterday that I got that job with the *Jerusalem Post*. I don't start work until the first of July, so I'm going to come and spend two weeks with you. If that's all right, that is."

"Of course that's all right," said Rosa. "It's more than all right. It's fabulous. I'm thrilled. It's wonderful. Congratulations on getting the job. That's fabulous. When are you coming?"

"Next Thursday."

"I'll have everything ready for you. Oh, Ella, I'm so happy to hear from you."

"I was elated to get your letter," said Ella. "I walked around all day singing. My singing hasn't improved, but I sang and sang. I went through my whole repertoire."

"That makes me feel like crying," said Rosa.

"I cried and I sang when I got the letter," said Ella. "Don't rush around preparing things for me. I can sleep anywhere. Living in Israel makes you very flexible. You get used to roughing it a bit. Although I've got a gorgeous apartment. I was very lucky to get it. It's in the Yemin Moshe area. Next to that beautiful windmill. Do you know that area?"

"Yes, I do," said Rosa. "It's so beautiful. It's where I'd like to live if I lived in Jerusalem."

"I live about two minutes' walk from the windmill," said Ella. "I walk past it every day. I'm very fond of it. You know why it was built? Montefiore built it. He built a whole row of cottages here in the middle of the nineteenth century. They were the first dwellings built outside the old city. Montefiore was trying to get Jews to move out of the old city, because it was overcrowded and unsanitary. But the Jews wouldn't leave. They were worried about crossing the hills every day to go to work, because the hills were infested with bandits. So Montefiore built the windmill, so that the Jews would have an industry there. But it was a Jewish windmill. They built it with the blades facing the wrong way. It's never worked."

"That's hilarious," said Rosa. "Ella, who would ever believe that you and I would be talking about Montefiore, when we were two of the least Jewish Jewish girls in Melbourne?"

"I certainly feel a Jew now," said Ella. "I'm surrounded by Jews. The chemist, the podiatrist, the hairdresser, the librarian, even the car mechanic, they're all Jews. Everyone is Jewish. I can't get used to everybody being Jewish. There are even Jewish hookers. Would you have believed that? And, in the middle of all these Jews, I can see myself. I see myself in so many of them. I see my mother and father. I see so many Jewish faces of my childhood. And I see that I fit in."

"Life is very strange, isn't it?" said Rosa.

"It's actually very good," said Ella. "Can I give you another shock? I'm getting married again. In August."

"Oh, Ella, who to?"

"To that violinist," said Ella. "He's just divine. His name is Andrei."

"Congratulations. Mazeltov," said Rosa.

"I know it's a bit hard to say congratulations wholeheartedly when it's a fourth marriage," said Ella. "But this time it's really going to work. I really love him. I like being with him. I like talking to him, listening to music with him, going to the pictures with him and fucking with him. I've never liked being with anyone as much as I like being with him. He's just got a position with the Israeli Symphony Orchestra, so between us we'll be quite comfortably off. He's only been out of Russia for a year. He's younger than I am. Much younger. He's only twenty-eight. But he's cleverer than I am, much cleverer. Living in Russia really sorts out your priorities. You don't dwell on the trifling irritations. You've got larger concerns. And he loves me. I think he's quite dotty about me."

"I did mean my congratulations," said Rosa. "I think you've had a rotten run of husbands. And Andrei does sound wonderful."

"Thanks," said Ella. "I can't wait to see you. I'll be there on Thursday week."

"I can't wait to see you, either," said Rosa.

In the bathroom, Rosa arranged bars of pink Herbal Bouquet lanolin-enriched bath soap in groups of two. Two bars on one end of the bath, and two bars on the other end of the bath. Two on the basin, and two on the shelf above the mirror. She put a new tube of pink and white striped toothpaste and a dark red toothbrush into a ceramic maroon toothbrush holder attached to the wall. She arranged bottles of shampoo, conditioner, bath oil, bath salts and a large jar of talcum powder on a small side table. She put a packet of aspirins, a packet of emery boards, a box of tissues, a shower-cap and a clothes brush inside the bathroom cupboard.

She stood back and admired the bathroom. She thought that the *New York Times* would approve of this bathroom. All she had to do now was to straighten the papers on Allan's desk and arrange the flowers she had bought.

She had chosen a mixture of yellow roses and yellow lilies. She looked for the cream glass vase. She had put it aside yesterday. Maria must have moved it. Maria had a will of her own. It seemed to Rosa that Maria, like all Rosa's previous cleaning ladies, ignored most of what she said to her. Every week she asked Maria not to move the papers on her desk, and every week Maria rearranged the papers into neat piles. Maria put household accounts together with drafts of dialogue, she put correspondence that had yet to be answered with bills that were already paid. Every week Rosa had to undo Maria's neatening and straightening.

Rosa had a bad history with household help. She had hired people for reasons other than their ability to clean. One year she had had Yolanda, a Czechoslovakian barrister who'd escaped from Czechoslovakia. Yolanda wept a lot. One day, Rosa had arrived home to find Allan washing the dishes and Yolanda weeping at the kitchen table. "She's having a bad day, and I thought somebody had better do the dishes," Allan had said. Rosa had given Yolanda her old typewriter and asked her to leave.

Soon after Yolanda, Rosa had hired May Wu. May was twenty-seven and came from a remote, rural part of South China. The trip to Australia was the first time she had been on an aeroplane. She had come to Australia to learn secretarial skills. In China, May Wu had taught English. An employment agency had sent May Wu to Rosa. They said she was willing to do all kinds of household work to put herself through secretarial school. May Wu couldn't clean. She couldn't iron. She took three hours to iron one shirt. She was a tiny woman, with thin ankles. She wore over-sized white high-heeled shoes. She could cook, she volunteered. Rosa hired her.

For three months, three nights a week, May Wu cooked for them. She used recipes titled "Real Chinese Food" from the back of a 1950s *Australian Women's Weekly* that someone had given her. Nothing Rosa could say could persuade May Wu that they would like her to cook authentic Chinese food. May did branch out, however. She looked in the front of the magazine and learned how to make schnitzels, lamb chops and chicken casserole.

She chopped chicken for her always-undercooked chicken casseroles on a a chopping board on the floor, and balanced dishes of string beans and pumpkin pieces on the lid of the rubbish bin.

Allan was the one who said they shouldn't fire May Wu. "This job is keeping her going, and it's not too much for us to endure," he said to Rosa.

"But I hate lamb chops and I've never liked schnitzel," Rosa replied.

May ate with the family. Rosa and Allan praised her cooking every night. "This is good for us," Rosa said to the children when they complained about the raw chicken. "Think of how much we're learning about Chinese culture."

"It won't do us much good when we're dead from botulism," said Zeke.

One day May Wu met an American serviceman. Two weeks later he asked her to marry him. She said yes. May and the American serviceman moved to Tokyo. The day before May left Melbourne, she came to say goodbye to Rosa. "I have been so happy with you and your husband," she said. Rosa felt terrible. She wished she coud take back every insensitive thought she had had about May Wu.

"I don't know anything about marriage," May Wu had said to her. Rosa hadn't known what to say.

"It'll be all right," she had said.

Rosa found the vase. Maria had put it back with all the other vases. She arranged the roses and the lilies. They looked beautiful together.

She hummed with pleasure as she surveyed the guest room. She had put a Spirex shorthand notebook and a new disposable fountain pen next to the bed. "Summertime, and the living is easy," she hummed to herself. She had been humming that tune all morning.

A group of musicians had played "Summertime" at a function they'd been to a few nights ago at the Jewish Museum. It was Rosa's first experience of a Jewish function in New York. She was surprised at how New York Jews looked just like Melbourne Jews. There were the same faces and the same expressions on different people. There was the group that talked their way through the guided tour, and through the speeches. There was Mr Bloom, who clapped loudly and vigorously to show his appreciation of the music. There was Mr Rosenthal, heatedly arguing a point with Mrs Adelson. Only Mr Bloom and Mr Rosenthal and Mrs Adelson were not Mr Bloom and Mr Rosenthal and Mrs Adelson of Melbourne, they were Mr, Mr and Mrs Someone Else of New York.

"Fish are jumpin' and the cotton is high," she sang. She smiled to herself as she thought of Ella, always singing some song or other. Ella had often said that whatever song she was singing could be interpreted as a barometer or a metaphor for what was happening in her life.

During her second divorce, Ella had sung "Killing Me Softly With His Song" over and over again. Rosa thought that the prospect of Ella's imminent arrival must be the cause of her own humming and singing today. She began to sing again. "Summertime," she sang, dragging the melody out slowly.

A noise like that of an animal in distress sounded through the apartment. This meant that the doorman had a message for her. Rosa pressed the antiquated intercom system. "I have a parcel for you," the doorman said. "Shall someone bring it up?"

"Yes, please."

Gretel Strand had left the parcel downstairs for her. Gretel had told her that she would drop off the electric kettle, some mugs and cutlery and other odds and ends that Rosa had lent her when she and her husband had first arrived in New York. They were here for a six month sabbatical, and were now moving into a furnished apartment.

Rosa didn't know Gretel very well, but she liked her. She smiled as she unwrapped the parcel. Gretel was a wrapper and packager after her own heart. The parcel was sealed with at least two rolls of masking tape. Rosa cut through the tape and unwrapped the brown paper. Underneath, was a layer of plastic. Around the plastic was more masking tape. Four layers of paper and tissues later, Rosa got to the contents.

Rosa understood the need to wrap securely. She was always trying to avoid leakage and loss. To have everything intact and in place. Sealed and safe.

When Rosa sent letters, her envelopes were always sticky-taped shut. She licked them down first, but never felt that they were secure enough without the sticky tape. She felt as though her neurosis were very visible in these tightly taped envelopes, but no-one had ever said anything.

Rosa also usually stamped her letters with double the postage that was required. As though twice the postage would guarantee the letter's safe arrival. She knew that this was irrational.

Rosa looked at her watch. It was three o'clock. Ella would be arriving in about an hour. She rang El Al to see if Ella's flight had arrived on time. She had called the airline two hours ago, and the flight was still on schedule then. A recording now told her that Ella's flight had landed seven minutes ago, three minutes early.

She looked around the apartment to see if there was anything else she should do. She decided to put a bowl of fruit in Ella's room. She chose three apples, two mandarins, two bananas and a mango, and arranged them artfully in a shallow turquoise basket of plaited straw. She contemplated putting a small bowl of Rademaker's Koffie Hopjes sweets in Ella's room, but she felt worried that she might have overdone things already. She knew that there was a fine line between preparing the guest room according to the guidelines in the *New York Times Magazine* and behaving like a lunatic.

She sat down with the *Jewish Forward*. It was the first time she had bought a copy of the weekly paper. She had read half of it last night, and was very impressed with it. This week had been quite a Jewish week, she thought. Last night she and Allan had gone to a screening of a film about the Lodz Ghetto. They had been introduced to the producer of the film at a buffet dinner beforehand. He had asked Rosa what work detail her mother had been on in the ghetto. Rosa told him that her mother had made straw shoes for the German army.

"Oh, yes," he had said, "the soldiers wore those straw shoes on top of their boots. I think you might see your mother in the film. We've got some footage of women making straw shoes." Rosa had felt the blood rush to her face. Her skin had turned bright red, and she had thought that she was going to pass out. Allan took her hand and they sat down in the theatre.

She had searched the screen for her mother. But all the women looked like her mother and all the men looked like her father. Much of the old footage and many of the still photographs had been taken in the last year or two of the ghetto's existence. By then most of the Jews had been transported to concentration camps. But Rosa's family, her mother's family and her father's family, had lasted out in the ghetto until well into 1944. So it was quite possible, Rosa thought, that the people who looked like her family were her family.

When Rosa's parents were transported to Auschwitz from the ghetto in June 1944, there were still 114 members of their families alive. Only her mother and father survived.

Rosa felt tired. She had had a 7:30 a.m. analysis session this morning. Three mornings a week she had an 8:30 a.m. session, and one morning a week her session was at 7:30. To make that session, she had to get up at 6 a.m. This gave her time to shower, dry her hair, get dressed, have a glass of seltzer, take her iron and vitamin C tablets, and make the bed before she left the house.

She always made the bed at the last minute. She couldn't go out without making the bed. Leaving the bed unmade made her feel uneasy. It made her feel scattered and untidy. If she worked at top speed, she could make the bed in ten minutes. There were so many bolsters and cushions and pillows to arrange. And the stripes of lace in the middle of the white duvet cover had to be right in the centre of the bed. At that hour of the morning it wasn't always easy for Rosa to ascertain the exact centre of the bed.

Most mornings she tried to let Allan sleep as late as possible. On her early mornings she could only let him sleep until 6:50 a.m.

She was grateful to Allan for understanding that she had to make the bed before she could leave the house. She wished she knew why she had to make the bed. Intellectually she thought that it was because she worked in the bedroom, and liked the room to be ready for her to begin work when she got back. But she was sure that there was a more profound and complex reason behind her need to make the bed.

She was tired of searching for the meaning behind every one of her actions. But she guessed that, until her actions looked more normal, she would have to keep searching.

She was tired, though, and she was often humiliated. It was humiliating and undignified to keep crying about what her mother had done to her as a child. Lying on the couch, she sometimes wondered how old she would have to be before she stopped crying about her childhood. Obviously older than she was now.

This morning she had been telling Dr Silver about her mother's perfect figure. "She was a perfect SSW," she had said. Then, realising that the American sizing system was probably different, she had explained the range of sizes to Dr Silver. SSW was Small Small Women, she had explained. SW was Small Women, XSSW was Extra Small Small Women. Lying on the couch differentiating between all the Smalls had made Rosa feel even larger.

At fifteen Rosa wore a size W. Size W was Women's size. But it wasn't really considered suitable for women to be a Women's size. Size W was considered large. The next size up was OS. OS stood for exactly what it looked as though it stood for, Outsized. By the time she was seventeen, Rosa was outsized. She had wept at the memory of her outsized youth.

In the lift on the way out of Dr Silver's building, a young Puerto Rican maintenance man, who'd got in on the tenth floor, had looked at her and said, "What's wrong with you? You look so sad, like you are praying. Is it the weather?"

"No, no. I'm fine," she had said. His question had made her laugh. She thought that she came out of her sessions looking quite collected. She usually stopped in front of the mirror in the waiting room and wiped away any smudges of eyeliner from under her eyes, and straightened her hair up a bit.

"It's going to clear up later today, it's going to get better," the young man had said.

"That's good," she had answered.

Rosa liked Dr Silver. She was surprised at how quickly she'd felt comfortable with her. She'd thought it would be much harder to get used to a new analyst. It should have been. It was like finding another mother, and good mothers weren't all that easy to find. Good mothers and fathers were as difficult to find as good lovers. If it was so hard to find the right lover, it should have been just as hard to find the right mother.

But she felt safe with Dr Silver. She trusted her. She felt close to her. Sometimes this not only surprised Rosa but worried her. She decided that she wouldn't worry about it at the moment. Ella should be arriving any minute.

She felt nervous. She hadn't seen Ella for over three years. She hoped that she would be able to be as affectionate towards Ella as she felt. She hoped she'd be able to show Ella how happy she was to see her.

She wondered if Ella was still very slim. She chided herself for that thought. What difference did Ella's size make? Why should she even think about Ella's size?

The doorman buzzed Rosa. Ella was here. She was on her way upstairs. Rosa ducked into the bathroom. She looked at herself in the bathroom mirror, patted her hair into place and walked to her front door.

Ella and Rosa hugged each other tightly.

"I made it," said Ella.

Tears came into Rosa's eyes. "You made it," she said.

"I made it," said Ella. "On time and without a hitch."

"You look wonderful," said Rosa.

"I was just going to say the same to you," said Ella. "You look gorgeous."

"We've made it, haven't we?" said Rosa. "We've pulled through. We're back together again, aren't we?"

"We're back together again," said Ella.

Still hugging each other, they walked up the stairs.

"Allan will bring your suitcase upstairs later," said Rosa. "Would you like a cup of tea?"

"I'd love a cup of tea. I feel quite dehydrated from the flight," said Ella. "The lady next to me was almost lying on top of me to talk to a man on the other side of the aisle. She was having the most animated conversation with him and gesturing left right and centre, which made me feel nervous and ill at ease. I didn't drink anything or eat anything. It's the only airline in the world where the stewardess looks as though she's going to have a breakdown if you don't eat. Just before we took off they showed us a small promotional film extolling the virtues of flying El Al. The *piece de resistance* came when they showed us the advantages of flying first class. If you fly first class with El Al, the announcer said, you can eat any time you want to. No-one laughed. I'd love some tea. Are you still drinking that Red Zinger tea?"

"Yes, I am," said Rosa. "Some things don't change."

"You haven't changed at all," said Ella. "You look wonderful. You're as beautiful as ever. I think you've become even more beautiful."

"Thank you," said Rosa. "I don't feel beautiful, but I'm trying not to think too much about what I look like. I've wasted so much time, planning diets, being depressed about being overweight, being worried about not losing enough weight, then finally losing weight and feeling worried about losing too much weight, then putting it on again. Now I put some make-up on in the morning and try not to think too much about what I look like for the rest of the day."

"Well, you look beautiful," said Ella.

"You look lovely, too," said Rosa. "It's so nice to look at you again. Tell me about Andrei."

"Would it sound too lascivious if I said that he's got a lovely body?" said Ella. "He's not a pale, poetic violinist. He's dark, with very strong shoulders. He's got the most beautiful hands. Big, wide, muscular hands. He's very emotional. He cried when I left.

Actually, I feel very loved. Andrei cried when I left, and you cried when I arrived. Where is Allan?"

"He's downstairs in his studio. He said he'd leave us alone to say a proper hello to each other before he came up."

"I'm really looking forward to seeing him," said Ella.

"Are you worried about the age difference between you and Andrei?" Rosa asked.

"Everyone asks me that," said Ella. "I wonder why people are so fascinated by it? They don't question the age difference between an older man and a younger woman. But everyone wants to know if it's a huge problem with Andrei and me. There's twelve and a half years' difference in our ages. Why is that such a big deal?"

"I'm not saying that it's a big deal," said Rosa.

"I told my parents that I was getting married," said Ella. "They didn't sound all that excited. They seemed even less excited when I told them that Andrei was twenty-eight. I thought that the fact that he was Jewish would outweigh any other considerations, but it hasn't seemed to. I guess they've had this news before. They probably would have preferred me to remain single, so that they could have had a daughter who had been married three times instead of a daughter who will have been married four times. I thought that they might come over to Israel for the wedding, but my mother said that they are too old to shlep themselves over to the other side of the world for yet another wedding. That was the way she phrased it, yet another wedding. She said to me: 'How many weddings can you go to for the same daughter? We were there for the first one and the second one and even the third one. You can manage on your own this time. You're very experienced at the whole marriage business. You don't need our help.' I got off the phone and howled like a child. I felt as though she'd sullied my love for Andrei. I wept for hours.

"When I told Andrei, he said my mother sounded like a prize arsehole. He quoted a line from Catullus's poem 97. It went something like this: 'As God is my witness where is the difference between/the smell of Aemilius's mouth and that of his arse?' I felt much better after that."

"Andrei sounds fabulous," said Rosa.

"He's pretty good," said Ella. "I'm very happy with him. I have the feeling that I'm going to be with him forever. I didn't feel that with any of the other three. God, it sounds so appalling and sleazy, already having had three husbands, doesn't it?"

"I think that it stops sounding sleazy after three," said Rosa. "It begins to sound exotic. Up to three is sleazy. More than that and it becomes interesting. Having a fourth husband sounds sophisticated."

"You're funny," said Ella. "We're going to have a small wedding. His parents and his brother are still waiting to get out of Russia, and my parents won't budge out of their lounge-room. I don't really mind that my parents aren't coming. Maybe I do mind. I don't know whether I mind or not. I think I'll stop thinking about my mother."

"Do you think I'm looking like my mother?" said Rosa.

"Yes, I think you are. Quite strikingly so. I noticed it as soon as I looked at you."

"I knew it. I knew it," said Rosa. "I knew that I was looking more like her. I've always looked like her, but I thought I might be imagining that I've become more and more like her."

"You do look more like her. But that's OK. Your mother was so beautiful," said Ella.

"I'm not saying it's not OK," said Rosa.

"Well, you look as though it's not OK at all."

"I think that the part of my mother I see in myself is the worried, distressed face that greets me in the bathroom mirror in the morning. It quite freaks me."

"You resemble your mother, but you look like yourself," said Ella.

"Sometimes it takes me until the afternoon to look like myself."

"I remember your mother's nerves and tension."

"If I make an effort, I can remember her laughing and smiling," said Rosa. "That's what I've achieved after half a lifetime of lying on an analyst's couch."

"I think I'm looking like my mother too," said Ella. "And that really is a problem. I mean, she's got a good figure, but she's got a face like a battle-axe. She'd die if she heard that. I have been feeling much fonder of my mother since we've been separated by a few oceans and continents."

"I'm so happy to see you," said Rosa. "I feel quite weepy at how happy I am to see you. I'm so glad you came."

"I'll start crying in a minute if you're not careful," said Ella. "I've missed you. A lot. It was a big chunk out of my life, the fact that we weren't speaking. At first I didn't care, I was so furious with you. Then I started wondering what you were doing, and who you were talking to on the phone instead of me."

"You were furious? Why were you furious?"

"Let's not examine what went wrong," said Ella. "Who cares what went wrong, and who was more right or more wrong than whom? I don't."

"I don't either," said Rosa.

Rosa brought out two mugs of Red Zinger tea and a bowl of almond and aniseed biscuits. "These biscuits are delicious," she said to Ella. "They're so light. I'm sure they couldn't have very many calories. Listen to me, I sound like my mother talking about her calorie-less sponge cake. Remember? It had no flour, no sugar, no butter. It was made of whisked air."

Ella laughed. "I know why you're laughing," said Rosa. "I laugh myself. I'm still preoccupied with calories. Three analysts and forty-three years into my life, and I'm still counting calories, or overlooking calories."

"I remember when you wrote to the Life Savers Company to enquire about the calorie value of a Life Saver," said Ella.

"That's right," said Rosa. "And they wrote back to me saying that I was the first person in Australia to make that enquiry."

"Each Life Saver was seven calories, wasn't it?" said Ella.

"Yeah. Seven calories. That's not bad, is it? You can eat a whole packet of Life Savers for roughly the same number of calories as an apple."

"You're mad, Rosa," said Ella. "After twenty-something years of marriage, three children and three analysts, you still think about the comparative value of a packet of Life Savers as opposed to an apple. Oh well, I guess I think about some pretty stupid things too. This tea is delicious. Since I've been living in Israel I've been hooked on Turkish coffee. I haven't had tea for ages."

"Was it hard for you when you first moved to Israel?" Rosa asked.

"It was much easier than I thought it would be. The fact that I lived with Yvette and her family made me feel very safe. I only moved into my own place last month. And Yvette's husband has paid my first twelve months' rent. They've been so good to me. I feel I'm one of them. One of their family. I certainly never felt part of my own family. I often think of the irony of my mother bringing little orphaned Yvette to Australia so that Yvette would have a family, when having a family wasn't something my mother was great at. You know, Yvette's got four kids. We all get on amazingly well. Her eldest daughter, Yael, has got two kids already, so I'm a grand-auntie. A grand-auntie who's just about to marry her twenty-eight-year-old fourth husband, and I feel pretty happy. It's a bit of a scary business, this feeling of happiness."

"I know exactly what you mean. I think I've given myself all these anxiety symptoms in my life in order to feel as bad as I can. When you've got masses of anxiety symptoms, you feel as though nothing worse could possibly happen. So you're safe. If you're feeling happy, all sorts of horrendous things can happen."

"This conversation is taking a morbid turn," said Ella. "I don't think we should descend into the pits of despair quite yet. We've got two weeks to go."

"Oh, we're not descending into despair," said Rosa. "We're talking about how happy we are."

"Oh, are we?" said Ella. "Would you mind if I had a shower

before we explored any more aspects of our happiness? I think I'll be able to recognise it more clearly when I feel clean."

"I don't know what to use first," Ella called out from the bathroom. "I haven't seen a display like this since I had that free make-over at the Elizabeth Arden Salon."

"I wanted you to feel welcome," Rosa called back.

"Well, I hope you never learn moderation," Ella shouted.

Rosa sat on the couch in the lounge-room. She could hear Ella singing in the shower. "You got nothing I want. You got nothing I need," Ella was singing. Rosa wondered who Ella was referring to.

The sound of Ella's out-of-tune tones made Rosa smile. Every note Ella sang was either flat or sharp. According to the law of averages, Ella should have managed to hit the right note every now and then, but she never seemed to. "You got nothing I want. You got nothing I need," came from the bathroom again. Ella was reaching a crescendo.

Rosa felt happy. Just looking at Ella had made her happy. Ella hadn't changed. She looked prettier, if anything, Rosa thought. Her large grey eyes were lighter, more blue, as though they had absorbed some of the Israeli sky.

Rosa looked around the lounge-room. The apartment looked like a real home now. There were paintings on the wall. There were bookshelves and books. There were books on the shelves, books on the tables, books lining the window sills. She wondered why books made a home look so homely.

She leaned back on the couch. It was very comfortable. She rarely sat on the couch. She usually sat at the kitchen table. She ate at the kitchen table. She read the newspapers at the kitchen table. She entertained friends at the kitchen table. She always sat perched on the edge of her chair, as though she was about to get up and leave. Just like her mother. Rosa couldn't remember her mother ever reclining in an armchair or relaxing on a couch.

Ella came out of the bathroom. She was wearing the white towelling robe that Rosa had put out for her. She looked clean and scrubbed and young. She sat down next to Rosa. "I used the cleansing cream shampoo, the after-bath revitaliser, the talcum powder and the foot scrub. I feel terrific."

Rosa leaned against her. Ella's body still felt warm from the shower. Ella put her arm around Rosa's shoulder. "I'm so glad I'm here," she said.

"So am I," said Rosa.

"You've got so many books on the Holocaust," said Ella. "Did you bring them from Australia?"

"No," said Rosa. "My books from Australia are still on their way here. They're supposed to arrive this week. I bought these books here. I can't stop buying them. I found four new books on the Lodz ghetto last week. I was overjoyed. It's strange to be overjoyed about books on the Lodz ghetto. Maybe it's not so strange. We saw a film on the Lodz ghetto last night. The audience was mostly Jewish. After the film the producer of the film gave a talk. Someone stood up and said: 'Why didn't the Jews resist?' No-one had an answer. The audience was silent. I felt furious. I had an answer. My answer was that that was the most appalling question. I couldn't stand up and say anything because I felt too shaky. But I wanted to shout at the audience that the Jews couldn't resist. They'd been systematically degraded and deprived of all their rights, their dignity and their health. How the hell could they resist? I wanted to stand up and shout some statistics at the audience. I wanted to ask them if they knew that in the Lodz ghetto the Germans had allocated 5.8 people to every room. And some of the rooms were minuscule. I wanted to ask them if they knew that out of 31,721 apartments in the ghetto, only 725 had running water. They had very limited use of electricity, hardly any medical supplies and the most appalling shortage of food. Everyone was sick or starving or dead. Under those conditions they were supposed to resist? We can't resist society's pressure to diet. We capitulate to pressure all the time. But the Jews were supposed to resist submachine guns, and the most unimaginable brutalities. Not to mention the awesome indifference or complicity of half of

Europe. Under those squalid and inhuman conditions Jews still taught their children music and Hebrew and maths. Wasn't that the highest form of resistance?

"I'm sorry I'm so riled up about it. It's a question I've heard so many times, and I can't understand how Jews can ask that question. I know the question is asked out of ignorance, but it makes me feel crazy. I feel crazy just talking about it. And I feel hot. I think I'll open the window. In New York no-one opens their windows. It's one of the few Australian habits I'm retaining."

Rosa opened the window. New York noises floated in. Noise of air-conditioners, sirens, car horns. Rosa loved the sound of the car horns. She loved the feeling that whatever time of day or night it was there was always a steady stream of traffic making its way up and down the avenues.

"Look at the view," she said to Ella. "You can see all the way down to Wall Street from here."

"There's so much traffic," said Ella. "Is it always jammed like this?"

"This isn't a jam. The traffic's moving. It's flowing, it's making its way. It may get stuck in a knot every now and then, but it soon unravels and continues on its way again. And you always get to where you want to go. You never grind to a halt in New York. It may look chaotic out there, but it isn't. Traffic here doesn't go by a set of traffic rules. It moves according to a higher law. An organic law, like the movement of tides or flocks of birds or shoals of fish. When you get more used to it, you'll see that the tooting and honking are quite benign. People honk their horns to participate, to say get a move on. They don't honk them in anger."

"That's the most poetic interpretation of urban traffic I've ever heard," said Ella. "I'm going to drag the conversation down a notch or two. Would you mind if I plucked my eyebrows? Don't laugh. The light in here's so good. I meant to pluck them on the plane, but the light was terrible."

Rosa laughed. "I'm glad you're still looking for the perfect light to pluck your eyebrows in. There's something reassuring about us all doing the same small things we always did, despite crossing continents. Do you still pluck your eyebrows while you're driving?"

"Yes, I do," said Ella. "And it's even more dangerous in Israel. The traffic is erratic. And people admonish me. They get out of their cars to give me sermons. Men and women. 'You should look where you're driving,' they say. I am looking. I only pluck my eyebrows at the lights, I don't pluck them while I'm actually driving. 'Be careful,' an old lady shouted to me. She was crossing the street with a withered arm and a walking frame, and she yells at me to be careful.

"This light is great. I can see hairs that I haven't noticed before. How are the kids? You're getting a reputation for having turned out fabulous kids. I heard that Mrs Bergman asked Susan Bergman, her daughter-in-law, why her kids weren't as good as Rosa Cohen's children."

"That's awful," said Rosa. "No wonder Susan Bergman hates her mother-in-law. And Mrs Bergman doesn't even know me."

"I know," said Ella, "but Acland Street is full of stories of how bright and good-looking your kids are."

"That's hilarious. I was the terrible child, the shocking child who wore the wrong clothes and went out with the wrong boys, and my children are held up as examples to others. They are good kids, though. I'm not sure why they turned out to be so nice, but I'm grateful. I'm grateful to them for turning out so well. Sometimes I'm astonished by their lack of fear, and their confidence, and their freedom to express a huge happiness. I never had that, and it still amazes me that they can be like that.

"Zeke was in a car accident here last year. When we moved to New York I thought that one of the advantages would be that I didn't have to worry about who my kids were driving with. No-one drives their car around Manhattan. The one thing I thought I wouldn't have to worry about in New York was car accidents. Two weeks after he got here, Zeke was involved in a head-on collision between two taxis. He was really lucky. He got a broken nose and some bad bruises, but that was all.

"Allan and I heard about it from a policeman from Bellevue Hospital, at two o'clock in the morning. Allan took the call, and I could tell something was wrong. I thought: this is it, this is one of those calls of your nightmares. I started to feel sick. I thought it was my father. I thought he must have died, or something pretty terrible must have happened to him. I felt so sick and shaky. And then after a couple of minutes I realised that it must be one of the kids, and I thought I was going to die. My heart was pounding so violently. I leapt out of bed and grabbed the phone. A nurse at the hospital was on the line now, but she wouldn't tell me exactly what was wrong with Zeke. I was hysterical. I shouted at her until she told me that he was conscious and could move. They hadn't X-rayed him yet, so they weren't sure of the extent of his injuries.

"Poor Zeke, when we arrived at the hospital he was still in the Emergency Room strapped to a trolley, waiting to be seen. He had blood all over his face, and his features were swollen and distorted. He was quite calm. He told me that the nurse had said that his mother seemed very anxious, and that he'd said to her, 'What a surprise.' I promised Zeke I'd never be mean to him again. I looked around in the middle of all my promises, and a guy with a gunshot wound in his shoulder was pissing himself laughing at me, and this spaced-out, derelict-looking man with a gash across his face was nodding his head and grinning.

"Afterwards, when we'd got Zeke home and I knew he was all right, I felt terrible for feeling that it was more of a catastrophe when I realised that something had happened to one of the kids, not to my father. I guess it's natural, though."

"Of course it's natural," said Ella. "You expect parents to die. You may dread it, but you expect it."

"I think the truth is that I love my kids more than I love my father," said Rosa. "I do love my father. I love him despite the fact that he doesn't listen to me. I wrote to him last week, because I wanted to tell him something. Nothing complicated. Just more than I'm fine, the kids are fine, Allan's fine. I felt that that was all we'd been saying to each other over the phone for months. I wanted to tell him that it hasn't been all that easy moving over here, but that on the whole I'm happy with what I've got in life. I wanted to feel connected to him in more ways than an endless chain of 'I'm fines.' I knew that if I went into any detail over the phone, he'd talk over the top of me. Even when we lived in the same city — or the same house, come to think of it — I found it very hard to get his attention. As long as I said I was fine everything was all right.

"Listen to me. Sometimes I sound pathetic, even to myself. I wonder if I'll still be talking about how my father wouldn't listen to me when I'm eighty. At a dinner party here I met a woman who was eighty-two. She was talking about her father, who was a very successful man, and she said: 'He had time for everybody except me.' And she looked so pained. It shocked me that it still mattered so much to her."

"That's sad, isn't it?" said Ella.

"What's sad about it isn't that she's still talking about her father, but that she still feels the hurt so acutely," said Rosa. "You'd think that even if you never worked things out with a shrink, time and age would dilute the pain."

"It's depressing," said Ella.

"Except she wasn't depressing," said Rosa. "She had lots of life in her, and she was really funny. When I told her that Poppy was going on a trip to Italy with a girlfriend, she said that Poppy should be very careful around Italian men. Then she stood up and mimicked a lecherous, arrogant Italian stud. She was strutting around, scratching her crotch. It was very funny.

"Poppy doesn't really need me to tell her to be careful," Rosa added. "She's so responsible. She's much more responsible than I was. And she's a much nicer daughter than I ever was. When I was a kid I could never understand why I couldn't make my mother happy. At least my kids know that they make me happy."

"I understand now that after what my mother went through it

would have been pretty hard for her to feel happy. I think my mother gave up on me when I became a teenager. It wasn't as though I'd been a fabulous daughter anyway. And I think maybe she didn't want me to have any more mothering than she'd had. You know, she was only seventeen when she went into the ghetto. God, it's complicated enough having children when you've come from a normal life! I know what it's like to watch young girls grow up and blossom. They're blossoming and blooming, while you're drooping and dropping and drying out. Now I sound like a horticulturalist."

"You're still upset by the thought of not having been a good daughter to your mother, aren't you?" said Ella.

"Yes, I am," said Rosa. "I think if I'd started with my second analyst earlier I might have been able to change earlier, and the new Rosa would have had more time with my mother before she died."

"I don't remember that you were such a terrible daughter."

"Oh, I think I was," said Rosa. "Maybe we should change the subject. You've only been in New York for two hours and the conversation has already become morose."

"It's not morose. It's life," said Ella.

"Well, the rest of your trip is not going to be morose," said Rosa. "I want you to meet my friend Barbara. You'll love her, and she'll love you. Allan wants to take you for a walk around the East Village. He adores it. We'll walk down Avenue A, past Tompkins Square Park. We walked past it a few days ago, and the Hare Krishnas were having a training session for new recruits in the park. I always thought that Hare Krishnas looked a lost and dissolute group, despite the spiritual implications of their orange robes. But you should have seen the Krishnas-in-training. They were a disarrayed and disarranged bunch, in jeans and T-shirts. And they were hopelessly out of rhythm and unbearably out of step with the Krishna chant. God, it was sad.

"We're going to have a really good time in the next two weeks. There's so much I want us to do together. I want you to meet this woman called Gretel Strand. She's about sixty. Her mother was Jewish and her father Catholic. They were German. They lived in Berlin. In 1939 Gretel's father told all his Catholic relatives that he was moving to America with his wife and kids, and then they moved to a small town somewhere in Germany. For six years Gretel's mother stayed hidden inside the small house they moved to. She never went out. She never saw anyone. She walked up and down the stairs for exercise. Gretel and her sister went to school locally. They told everyone at school that their mother was dead. No-one knew they were Jewish.

"After the war her father took Gretel to visit Buchenwald. Gretel was about sixteen. This was literally within the first few days of the war ending. He said he wanted her to see the camp, because in years to come people would say that the whole thing hadn't happened. So they went to Buchenwald. She said that all the dead bodies had been cleared away, but all the prisoners were still there. This woman, Gretel, was telling me this at the bar in the Oak Room in the Plaza Hotel. I was having trouble keeping steady on my bar stool. When I'm anxious, I still get dizzy.

"Almost as an afterthought, Gretel told me that she and her father had missed the last bus home, and had had to spend the night at Buchenwald. She said that her father was a bit worried at first, because he knew that none of the men had seen a young girl for so long, but there had been nothing to worry about. The men were all so grateful that Gretel and her father were interested in what had happened to them. Gretel and her father slept in the bottom rung of a row of wooden bunks in the barracks.

"I couldn't stop thinking about her sleeping on those wooden bunks. I think you'll really like meeting her. Or does it all sound a bit grim?"

"No, I'd like to meet her," said Ella. "What a story!"

"I think the itinerary is sounding a bit grim," said Rosa.

"It doesn't sound grim," said Ella.

"It won't be grim. We'll go to Balduccis, the Carnegie Deli, the Russian Tea Room. We'll go to Rumpelmayer's for ice-cream sodas and chocolate sundaes. Or does that sound too fattening? Maybe grim is better than fattening?"

"It sounds fabulous," said Ella.

"We'll go to Central Park," said Rosa. "And we'll go to the opera. Allan got tickets for *Rigoletto* with Pavarotti. I can't wait to see Pavarotti. IIe's supposed to have lost lots of weight. I read that he eats on his own now, away from his family, because he's on a really restricted diet and he can't bear to see what they're eating. Poor Pavarotti. That's a big price to pay for losing a few pounds, although I've heard that he's lost more than a few pounds."

"My head is reeling," said Ella. "I've barely taken in your friend spending the night in Buchenwald, and now I've got to try and think about the effect on poor Pavarotti of not being able to eat with his family. I think I'm feeling my jetlag. Maybe I'll have a nap for an hour or two. I've usually got more stamina than this. The thought of Pavarotti eating in a room on his own shouldn't be making me feel faint."

"I'm sorry," said Rosa. "I should have talked about some more light-hearted things until you'd had time to recover from the trip."

"Don't be silly," said Ella. "I didn't come here to talk about light-hearted things."

"You know you look gorgeous, Ella," said Rosa. "You look strong and healthy. You look as slim as a sixteen-year-old. And you know, I don't mind the fact that you're slim, and I'm still battling to lose weight. Well, more or less battling. More like the odd skirmish than a concerted battle, really."

"You've won battles that I haven't even begun to tackle," said Ella.

"That's nice of you," said Rosa. "I think you're right. I think we've both been battling on different fronts."

"On different fronts, said Ella, "but on the same side."

"On the same side. Yes, definitely on the same side," said Rosa.

Wombat Lodge

Ruthie Brot was looking at the mole on the side of Abe Lipshitz's neck. It was squat and stout. It was shaped more like a wart than a mole, she thought. She wondered why she hadn't noticed it before.

"This apartment still doesn't feel homely, does it?" said Abe.

Ruthie looked around the room. Everything was elegant. Art deco chairs, leather couches, matching chrome and glass coffee tables. The television set and the music system were built into a lacquered and hand-painted Chinese sideboard. There were art books, cookbooks and novels on the bookshelves. Two wrought-iron magazine racks were filled with *Esquire, Atlantic Monthly, Vogue* and *Vanity Fair*. It had taken her two months to furnish the apartment. She had shopped and shopped until she never wanted to see the interior of a shop or a warehouse again.

"It doesn't look homely, does it?" said Ruthie. "I don't know why. Maybe it's because it's not a home. If you buy an apartment to have an affair in, maybe it always looks transient. Too temporary to be a home."

"We didn't buy this apartment to have an affair in," said Abe. "We were already having an affair. And why do you have to call it an affair? An affair sounds tawdry. We're in love."

"We are in love, Abe," said Ruthie, "but we are also both married to other people, and that makes our relationship an affair. I think we both thought that getting a place of our own would lessen Dora and Eddie's presence in our lives. But the opposite has happened. Somehow, it's made them more visible. More present.

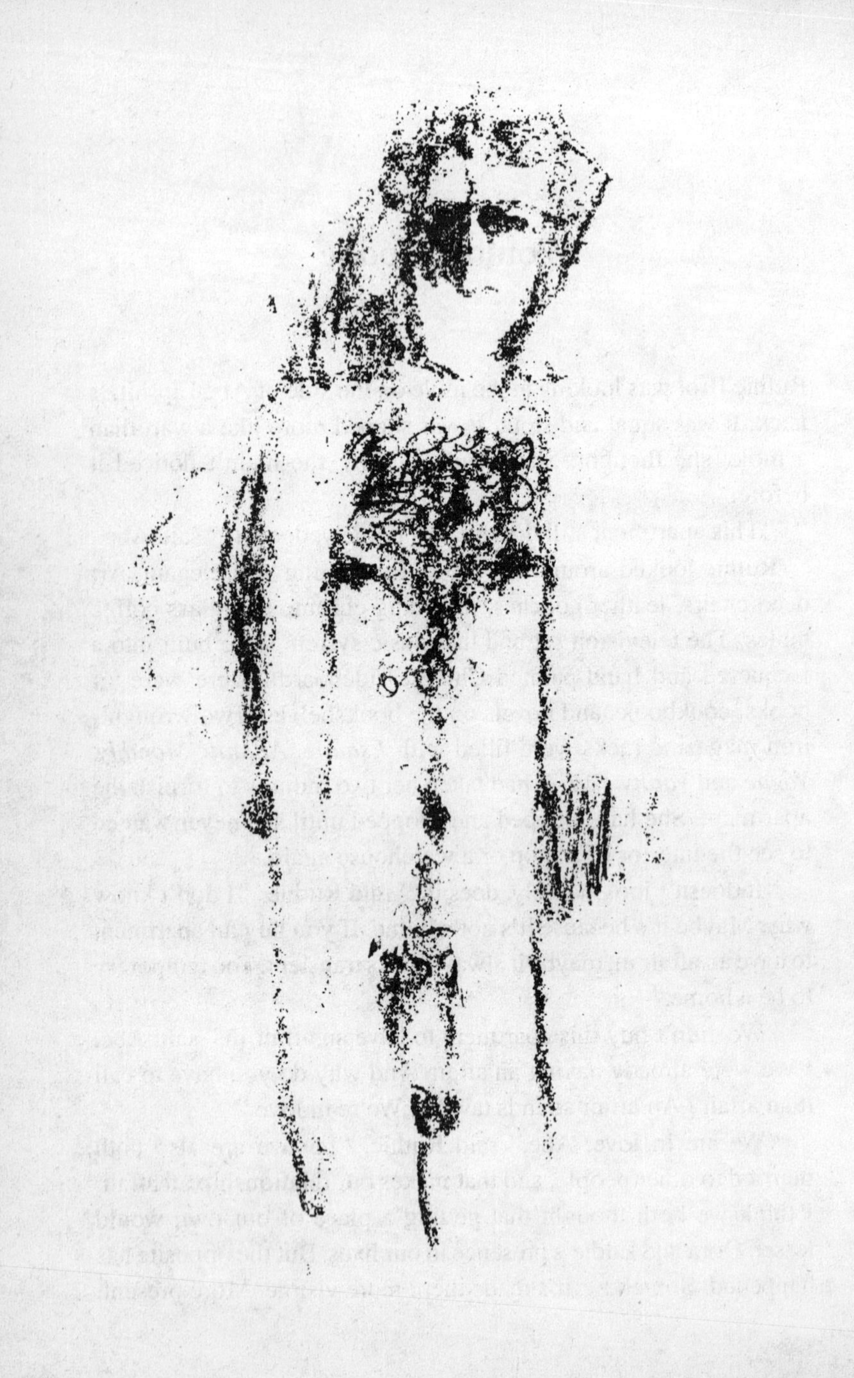

I mean, my own house is so full of life next to this barren apartment."

"Do you have to call it barren?" said Abe.

"That's how it feels to me," said Ruthie. "I know we've put in all the necessary ingredients. We've got saucepans, cutlery, towels, sheets. We've got a kettle. We've got a pantry full of food and a big bowl of nuts on the table. But it feels barren. Maybe you have to live in a house to make it feel lived in. This apartment smells unlived in. Last week I sprayed half a bottle of Chanel No. 5 around the place to give it a more lived-in smell, and it still smelt empty."

"I feel as though you're criticising me, not the apartment. I feel as though you're telling me that I smell, and that I'm empty," said Abe.

"I'm sorry," said Ruthie. She patted him on the head. "Of course I'm not talking about you. I'm talking about the apartment. Something is wrong."

"Maybe we should cook more meals here," said Abe. "The smell of cooking would be nice."

"Last time we cooked a meal here, we spent half our time shopping, separately, for the ingredients, and the other half of our time was spent washing the dishes. The ventilation in the kitchen wasn't working properly and I smelt of fried onions all night. Remember that? Has the ventilation been fixed yet?"

"No, it hasn't. Why are you so irritable?"

"I'm sorry, I know I'm being ratty. I think the strain of making sure we're never seen together, and all the lies I have to invent to come here, is getting to me. Being adulterers doesn't seem so sophisticated when you have to hide and lie all the time."

"So now we're adulterers."

"We've been adulterers since we met," said Ruthie. "When we went to motels the adultery seemed more normal. But here, in this domestic little setting, what we're doing seems aberrant."

"Do you know what this domestic little setting cost?" said Abe.

"I know," said Ruthie. "You've already told me. We're sounding just like an old married couple, aren't we? Well, we are part of an old married couple, it's just that our other parts are not each other."

"Ruthie, what's wrong? Why are you feeling like this now? We both made the decision to buy the apartment. You used to look so happy to see me."

"I don't know. When we were first together, I used to think of you all the time. I used to be able to close my eyes and imagine you fucking me. I didn't think past how wonderful I felt when I was with you. Everyone who saw me told me how good I was looking. Now everyone asks me what is wrong. Yesterday I went to Scheherezade with Minnie for lunch, and saw Mrs Buchbinder, who was also eating there. The first thing she said to me was 'Ruthie, you're so thin'. And about five other people said the same. All I could hear was a chorus of 'Too thin, too thin. Why is she so thin?' "

"You have lost weight, haven't you? I noticed too. But you still look very beautiful," said Abe. He knelt down beside her and stroked her legs. "You've got such beautiful legs, Ruthie." He reached up and slipped his hand inside her underpants. She shifted away from him.

"Ruthie, please don't be distant," he said. "I love you. I know it may seem crackers for us to be together like this. But what's the alternative? You won't leave Eddie, and I admit that leaving Dora wouldn't be easy. This way we can be together and not hurt all the people around us."

"How can you be such a smart barrister and believe that we're not hurting anyone? We're lying to everyone," said Ruthie.

"I love you, Ruthie. I'd leave Dora. I'd marry you. You're the one who can't leave Eddie," Abe said. He moved towards her again. He kissed her on the side of her neck. He unbuttoned her dress and undressed her. Ruthie sat limply on the couch. He put his fingers inside her. She clamped her legs together. "It doesn't feel good, Abe," she said.

"It feels wonderful to me."

"Well, that's not enough, is it?"

He tried to prise her legs open. "Let me lick you," he said.

"I don't want to be licked," she said. "I'm too tense. I can't relax. I think it's this apartment. It's made me very conscious of what we're doing. Before, what we were doing was blurred in the excitement of motel rooms. And what we were doing was what lots of people do in motel rooms. Apartments are supposed to have real lives lived out in them. The emptiness of this apartment makes our coupling seem empty."

"Our coupling? We don't couple, we make love," said Abe. "Look, why don't we go to a motel?"

"You can't go to a motel when you've paid $300,000 for an apartment," said Ruthie. She got dressed.

"If we had no money, we'd probably still be happy together," said Ruthie. "We'd probably be fucking each other stupid in parked cars, and feeling terrific."

"That's ridiculous," said Abe. "No-one was ever helped in life by having no money. And don't look down on my money. I've worked very hard to earn this money, just as Eddie has worked very hard for his money."

"Oh, so now you're befriending Eddie," said Ruthie. "Remember he's the shmuck you were ready to overthrow? Now suddenly he's your partner in money-earning. I noticed that you were careful to make the point that it's Eddie who earns the money, not me."

"I didn't make that point at all," said Abe. "Let's not fight. I'm tired. I've had a long day; I've been up since five. Can I take your clothes off again and just hold you?"

"No," said Ruthie. "I don't want to be undressed again. Let's clean the apartment. That would be a nice, normal thing to do. I think it would make me feel better. The place needs cleaning. We haven't cleaned it once since we got it. Look at the dust on the window sills. And there's fluff on the floor, underneath the couch. I'll get out the detergent and the rags. We'll clean the windows too. Clean windows make a big difference. Clean windows can make even a grubby place look clean."

"This place isn't grubby," said Abe.

"No," said Ruthie, "but it's going to look so much nicer when it's clean."

"OK," said Abe. "Tell me what you want me to do."

Ruthie was at home alone. She felt out of sorts. She had tried lying in the sun. Sunbaking always used to soothe her, but this morning, lying out on the lawn, she felt hot and prickly. She had given up and come inside.

She decided to ring Zoe. Zoe was in between men. Zoe was much calmer and more level-headed when she wasn't connected to a man. It was funny, Ruthie thought, how Zoe, who was the creative director of a large advertising agency, could manage a complicated job with ease, yet always had the most fucked-up relationships with men. You could almost pick who Zoe would go for, thought Ruthie. If he had a certain meanness on his face, a quick temper and was decidedly detached, Zoe would find him attractive. Ruthie wondered if Zoe could sum up what was wrong with Ruthie's life as succinctly. It was so easy to see where other people went wrong.

"Hi, Zoe," she said. "Have I caught you at a bad moment? Can you speak?"

"Yes I can, if you can just hold on for one minute," said Zoe.

Zoe came back on the line. "Hello, Ruthie darling. I had someone in the office with me. I just got rid of them. How are you?"

"I'm so-so," said Ruthie. "How are you?"

"I'm much better. I'm feeling better than I have in months. I haven't seen Mike for three weeks and I'm starting to feel human again. Next time I look as though I'm falling in love with a tight-arsed arsehole, do you think you could give me a shove?"

"I'd have to knock you out cold for it to have any effect," said Ruthie. "I told you I thought he was really aggressive to you the first time I saw you together. Remember you said that when I got to know him I'd see that Mike was reserved and shy, not mean?"

"Don't remind me," said Zoe. "I know, I must be mad. My life got so fucked up when I was with Mike. I spent my time running between his house and my house. I carted face creams and hair driers and underwear and cocktail dresses in the car with me every day. I didn't sleep in my own house for weeks on end. Everything ran down. Plants died, globes burnt out, food rotted. The place started to look like part of a deceased estate. And I did all this for a shmuck who was probably fucking someone else anyway."

"Oh, no, you don't think Mike was fucking someone else while he was with you, do you?" said Ruthie.

"Yeah, I think he was," said Zoe. "I was a bit suspicious of him anyway, and then a kid in the office told me that she saw him at the Metro twice, on a Friday night, and he was with a very young blonde girl. Friday was the night he couldn't see me. He said he always spent it with his mother. With his mother! What a jerk. And what an idiot I am. Now I'm driving myself berserk worrying about AIDS. I think I might go and have a blood test."

"You used condoms, didn't you?"

"I know it's pathetic, but we didn't. The first time we slept together he used a condom, but he hated using them. I felt it was churlish of me to insist. It's crazy, isn't it? Here I am, mature, educated, middle-class, and I feel as though it's prudish to ask a man to wear a condom. He said there was no evidence of AIDS in the heterosexual population of Australia. That's not even true. I wanted to ask him if he'd ever had any homosexual experiences, but I was too embarrassed. I'd obviously rather die of AIDS than ask an embarrassing question."

"Oh, Zoe, what a fabulous couple we make. Please go and have a blood test. It'll put your mind at ease."

"I think I will," said Zoe. "What's happening with you and Abe? Eddie doesn't suspect anything, does he?"

"No, I'm sure he doesn't," said Ruthie.

"That's good."

"Well, things aren't that good. I used to feel such an enormous freedom when I was with Abe. A real freedom to be as sexual as

I'd ever fantasised I could be, to be coquettish, to be young. I felt as though he'd freed something in me. But that feeling is disappearing. Things are a bit edgy between us. It started when he bought that apartment. He paid $300,000 for it, but we'd be better off without it. Before that, I really thought I loved him. I couldn't wait to see him. My heart would leap and I'd feel weak at the knees. Real movie-scene stuff. Now, we sit in this chic apartment and pretend that we're partners in more than a few furtive, subversive moments."

"Furtive, subversive moments. That's no way to speak about a lover. Things don't sound too good to me," said Zoe.

"Well they're not," said Ruthie. "We sit in this apartment like Ma and Pa Kettle. We pretend we're Mr and Mrs Normal. Mr and Mrs Normal! Mr Normal is married to someone else and Mrs Normal is married to someone else. Mrs Normal has told her husband that she's taking art appreciation classes with the Council of Adult Education, and Mr Normal tells his wife he is working. The telephone calls to his office are re-routed to the phone in our apartment, in case Mr Normal's wife calls. But Mr Normal's wife has never called. I sound like such a bitch, don't I? I don't know why. I really do like Abe. I think I've been happier since I've been with him. Maybe Abe and I should have counselling. Why don't people know how to live their lives any more? Why do we all have to be counselled? And how come these counsellors are so smart? Are they running their own lives really well? Eddie's sister and her husband, you know Susan and Harry Silver, are having counselling. They go to special classes. The class is called 'How To Get Over A Partner's Infidelity'. Everyone in the class is in the same position. Probably most of Melbourne would qualify for that class. Maybe Abe and I could go to a class for Adulterers Who Can't Decide What To Do?"

"Did the apartment cost $300,000?" said Zoe.

"Yes," said Ruthie, "but don't tell anyone."

"Of course I wouldn't."

"I know you wouldn't. I'm just sensitive about it, because it's such a lot of money to shell out for two people to spend three hours together twice a week. I worry about people saying, 'Only a rich Jew would do something like that.' Well, Abe did it out of the best intentions. He wanted us to have a chance to do more normal things together. But it hasn't worked. We can't do normal things. We can't watch a video or television because we don't want to waste the time. We don't read for the same reason. I cooked a couple of weeks ago, but by the time I finished cooking, we had to bolt the meal down, because it had taken me longer than I'd expected and it was almost time to go home. So what's left for us? Fucking. And even the fucking isn't fabulous any more."

"But why would you want to cook or watch television with Abe?" said Zoe. "You can cook and read and watch television any time."

"It's not that I'm desperate to watch television with Abe," said Ruthie. "It's just that all we do together is fuck. When we were going to motels it seemed more appropriate for our relationship to revolve round fucking."

"Ruthie, you'd be the only one in your Adulterers Who Can't Decide What To Do class complaining about too much sex," said Zoe. "All over town women are shaving their legs, trimming their pubic hair and perfuming their armpits in order to entice men into bed, and you want to watch television with Abe."

"You don't understand," Ruthie gulped. "That's all right. I don't understand either."

"I think I understand," said Zoe, "but someone's just arrived for me. I have to go. Call you back later. Bye, bye."

"Bye, bye," said Ruthie.

She walked around the house. The house looked calm and peaceful. Everything was in its place. Dolores, who had been cleaning and cooking for Ruthie for fifteen years, came every morning. This morning Dolores had put a large vase of freesias in Ruthie's bedroom. Freesias were Ruthie's favourite flowers. She breathed in their scent.

Dolores had put new navy sheets on the bed. Ruthie

remembered when she and Eddie had bought the bed. It was a beautiful bed. It had soft yellow lights built into the bedhead. Ruthie remembered thinking that it would be very romantic to have only those lights on in the bedroom. That was eighteen years ago.

She felt edgy and restless. How had she got herself into this position? What was she doing with Abe? Did she love him? What was love? The questions circled around and around her head. There were no answers in sight. Why wasn't she happy? She wasn't happy because she was married and lying to her husband. But she hadn't been happy before she met Abe, because she and Eddie had a dismal sex life. Happy. Unhappy. What was this god-awful preoccupation with happiness? Was happiness being fucked well? She didn't think so. What was happiness? Why wasn't she happy? She didn't have cancer. Why wasn't that enough to make her happy? She had Eddie, and she had Jonathan and Jason, and her father and Esmeralda. How many people did she need to love in order to feel happy?

The phone rang. It was Moishe. "Hi, Dad, how are you?" Ruthie said.

"Hello, darling," said Moishe Zimmerman. "I rang to see how you are. You didn't look so happy to me the last few times I did see you. Is something wrong?"

"No, Dad, there's nothing wrong. I've just been a bit tired," she said.

"Is it maybe too much to study law, even a part-time study, and to be a mother and have such a big house to look after?" he asked.

"No, Dad," she said. "Going back to uni was the best decision I've made in years. And Dolores does everything around the house. Uni is on holidays at the moment. I'm missing the two days a week I spend there. I'm sorry if I looked flat. There's nothing wrong. How is Esmeralda?"

"She is such a good girl," said Moishe. "She has got a heart of gold. I can see sometimes that people look at her and me in the street, and they probably think that I did buy her from a mail-order firm. It doesn't upset me. I would probably think the same if I saw an old Jew walking with a young Filipino wife. But it upsets Esmeralda. She is very Jewish. She gets upset at small things. She gets upset at the same things that used to make Mum upset. And she is a worrier just like Mum."

"Tell Esmeralda not to feel bad. There's always some imbecile somewhere who stares at you because you're the wrong colour, or the wrong height, or the wrong size."

"That's what I said to her. Ruthie, I'm going to another funeral this afternoon."

"Who died?"

"Mr Levinson," said Moishe. "He died in the middle of our card game. Last night. It was lucky Esmeralda wasn't there. She usually comes to the games, but she had an upset stomach, so she stayed home. We were at Mrs Dunov's house. Mr Levinson stood up. He said he didn't feel good. And then he fell down. Dead."

"Poor Mrs Levinson," said Ruthie.

"She was very calm," said Moishe. "All her life she was so nervous. Her husband falls down dead and she is quiet and calm. You never know how people are going to act. I called an ambulance. I knew Mr Levinson was dead, but I thought it was better to give us all a few more moments of hope. And I thought that maybe they could bring him back with that mouth-to-mouth resuscitation. But he was dead. He was only seventy-two. You know, Ruthie, I've been to ten funerals this year. I counted them this morning."

"Ten!" said Ruthie. "That's terrible."

"I didn't mean to upset you with all this talk about people dropping dead and funerals. I rang you really because Esmeralda said that you are losing weight."

"Esmeralda must be Jewish, Dad. She's as bad as Mum was. She notices everything. Tell her not to worry. I've lost a few pounds because I've been rushing around. I'm not dying. While I'm a few pounds lighter, I'll be able to eat chulent and cheesecake with you at Scheherezade with a free conscience. Tell Esmeralda I'm fine. I love you, Dad. I'll speak to you tomorrow."

"I've been thinking about things," said Abe. "What you and I need is a holiday. We need to get away from everything and relax together. I think a holiday will ease the tensions that have built up between us. I can tell Dora that I've got to go away for a few days on business, and maybe you could tell Eddie that you just want a quiet couple of days away with Zoe. Eddie will have noticed how tired you're looking. I'm sure he won't be fussed."

"How do you know what Eddie will feel?" said Ruthie. "You don't know him."

"Well I've heard you talking about him so much that I do feel as though I know him. Don't be so snappy. What about my idea? What do you think of it?"

"Where would we go?"

"It wasn't easy to think of a place where we wouldn't bump into half the Jewish community of Melbourne, but I've thought of somewhere where I'm sure there are no Jews, or at least no Jews we know. Tasmania."

"Tasmania?"

"It's not on Mars. It's still part of the same planet," said Abe. "And it really is very beautiful. I've been there before. I thought we'd go to Launceston. If there are any Jews they'll be in Hobart, at the casino."

"I don't know," said Ruthie. "Do you really think it's a good idea to go away?"

"I think it's a fabulous idea," said Abe.

"I guess I have been feeling very tired lately," she said. "Maybe it is a good idea. Okay, let's go to Tasmania."

"You won't regret it, Ruthie," said Abe. "We'll have a wonderful time. I'll book us on separate flights, and we'll meet at the hotel. There's a hotel called Wombat Lodge. It's slightly out of town. Apparently it's set in a spectacularly landscaped English garden. I'll book us in there."

"Why do you think it's called Wombat Lodge?" said Ruthie.

"Maybe it's owned by a Mr and Mrs Wombat," said Abe.

Ruthie laughed. "You're a lovely man," she said.

"Shall we jump into bed, Ruthie?" he said, smiling.

"I really do feel tired," she said. "I think I'll go home and have an early night. I'm sick of people telling me that I look thin or pale. And it will be nice for Dora to have you home early for a change. She can't have seen much of you lately. At least on the nights when I'm not with you, I'm at home with Eddie, but when you're not with me you're at the office, working."

Ruthie walked to her car. She and Abe always left the apartment separately. There was never anyone else around. The building was new, and most of the apartments were still empty, but Ruthie was always on edge, arriving and leaving. She expected to bump into one of her father's friends, or her old kindergarten teacher, or the butcher. When she was sixteen she had climbed out of her bedroom window and gone for a walk with a boy from her school. Before she'd arrived home, one hour later, two people had phoned Mr and Mrs Zimmerman to ask them if they knew that Ruthie was walking down Alma Road, in the middle of the night, with a strange boy.

Ruthie wondered why she was leaving early tonight. She had told Eddie that she would be home later than usual. She'd said she was having coffee with Zoe after class. Earlier in the day she had thought that maybe if she and Abe had some extra time together they might sort out what was going wrong between them. So why was she going home early? She didn't know. She backed the car out of the garage. If she took the freeway, she would be home in six and a half minutes.

"Tasmania is a friendly island. We call it the Apple Isle," the airline brochure said. Apples and friendly people, that was about as much as Ruthie felt she could cope with. She was sitting in the very back row of the plane. She'd arrived at the airport too late to get a better seat. Zoe had picked her up and driven her there. It had been partly to avoid Eddie offering to drive her to the airport, and partly to reinforce her alibi for the weekend. Having Zoe as a witness to the deceit had made her feel worse. She and Zoe had waved goodbye to Eddie until he was out of sight. She had felt sick, and Zoe had been very quiet.

The man sitting next to Ruthie was very large. Ruthie felt sorry for him. His face was florid and he was sweating. He looked as though he was jammed into his seat. She offered to lift up the armrest between them so that he would have a bit more room. He was grateful. As soon as the armrest was removed his body spread out and occupied three-quarters of Ruthie's seat.

"Do you eat airline food?" he asked Ruthie.

"Yes, I usually do," she answered.

"Let me give you a piece of advice," he said. "Never ever eat fricassee of anything. I was in hospital last year. Every night they had fricassee of something. Fricassee of lamb, fricassee of chicken, fricassee of beef. Even the porridge looked like it was fricasseed. Bloody awful it was."

"I'm sorry," said Ruthie.

"The fricassee of fish was the worst," he said. "You couldn't tell the fricassee from the fish. Lucky I was only there for ten days. I had gallstones. Ever had gallstones?"

Ruthie started to feel sick again. Finally, they landed in Launceston.

She caught a taxi to Wombat Lodge. Abe was waiting outside the front entrance. He looked thin and vulnerable. He ran up to the taxi. "Hello, Ruthie darling," he said. "You look so beautiful. I thought you'd never get here. I had this awful feeling that you wouldn't come. I imagined myself standing outside Wombat Lodge all weekend waiting for you. I'm so happy to see you."

"I'm happy to see you too, Abe," she said. She kissed him.

"Mmm, what a delicious kiss," he said. "I know it's going to be a good weekend. Did you have any trouble with Eddie?"

"No," said Ruthie. "Eddie was happy for me to have a weekend away with Zoe. I think I was hoping that he'd be difficult about it, so I could resent him. Zoe drove me to the airport to add some authenticity."

Abe took Ruthie's overnight bag. "Come and I'll show you the room," he said. "It's Cabin 28. It overlooks the rose garden. It's very sweet."

"How was Dora?" Ruthie asked.

"Dora wasn't home when I left," said Abe. "She's been doing more and more work at the Rosenthal Homes for the Aged. She's not just helping with the cooking. She's organised reading groups two mornings a week. She gets young actors and actresses to read poems, short stories and plays to the residents. It's been a real success. The first week about twenty people turned up, now they're getting ninety to a hundred people to each session. Dora chooses the work to be read. She pays the actors. They get fifty dollars for reading. She raised the money for it herself. She went to old Mr Goldman and suggested that he fund it, and he said yes."

"You're proud of her, aren't you?"

"Yes, I am. She's making a difference to a lot of people's lives with the work she does at the Homes. And it's all on a voluntary basis, which doesn't bring her any kudos in life. When people ask her what she does, and she says she does charity work, you can see their eyes glaze over with boredom."

Abe unlocked the door to Cabin 28. In the middle of Cabin 28 was a four-poster brass bed. It was covered with an ornately worked patchwork quilt. It took up most of the room. White candles in silver candlestick holders stood on the bedside tables. A large bowl of potpourri was in the centre of a small Edwardian table. "This room is just gorgeous," said Ruthie. "And it smells so nice. What is that scent?"

"That smell is rose petal oil," said Abe. "They sprinkle it on the potpourri. It comes from their own garden. The receptionist told me all of this. I chatted to her all morning. The place isn't doing very well. It's too far out of town. We're the only ones here this weekend. We definitely won't be bumping into anyone we know at Wombat Lodge."

"I'm going to get changed," said Ruthie. "It really is lovely here. I think we're going to have a good weekend." She unpacked her clothes, and put on a pair of shorts and a T-shirt.

"You look so sexy in your shorts," said Abe. "I've never seen you in shorts. Can I jump on you?"

"Let's have lunch first. I'm starving."

"I ordered a picnic lunch for us outside. I ordered salmon, cheese and cucumber sandwiches."

"That sounds fabulous," said Ruthie. "I'm famished. I haven't eaten anything today. I couldn't even drink my coffee on the plane because the man sitting next to me kept talking about fricassee of fish. I thought I was going to throw up."

"Fricassee of fish?" said Abe.

"Yes," said Ruthie. "Let's not talk about it or I'll feel sick again."

Ruthie and Abe walked through the gardens of Wombat Lodge. There were terraces of flowers and shrubs. The air was almost too sweet. They walked through the rose garden and past a large, oblong pond full of speckled trout. Next to the pond was a white gazebo. Lunch was set out for them on a wicker table inside the gazebo.

"This is almost unbearably picturesque," said Ruthie. "How did you find this place?"

"I rang the Tasmanian Tourist Bureau and said I wanted somewhere really romantic. They said Wombat Lodge would be the place for me," said Abe.

"These sandwiches are delicious," said Ruthie.

"It's doing my heart the world of good to see you looking so relaxed. I feel as though your unhappiness is my fault."

"Of course it's not your fault, and I'm not really unhappy."

"Intellectually I know that it's not my fault, but I still feel as though it is. I feel that if it hadn't been for me, you would have been happy."

"That's not true," said Ruthie. "If I hadn't met you, I wouldn't have gone back to law school. I wouldn't have known what it was like to feel really fucked. Fucked well. Physically connected to someone. That would have been a lot to have missed out on."

"Is that all it is, fucking? Not making love? It sounds so brutal when you say it. You never used to refer to our lovemaking like that. It feels ominous to me," said Abe.

"I think you're being hypersensitive," said Ruthie. "I've always said fucking. To me, fucking is making love. Anyway, let's not argue about it. Can't you see how much you've given me?"

"No, I can only see that you're unhappy. And I want you to be happy. I feel as though I've been trying to make a woman happy, one way or another, since I was a small kid. My mother always looked so miserable. It didn't matter what I did, she always looked sad. When I'd come top of the class, which I think I did every bloody year of my life, she'd look happy for one minute. And then the old sadness would come back. Now I understand. I know that when you've been through Auschwitz, nothing can take away that sadness. Now that I'm older, I understand that the tragedy was part of her. It wasn't something that could be taken away. And what does one kid coming top of the class mean compared to having all your family die? No amount of scholarships and honours could bring back her mother or father, or her two brothers. But when I was a kid, I couldn't understand why I couldn't make her happy. I thought it was my fault that they were both unhappy.

"Maybe when Dora and I had Vivian and Anna it took away some of my parents' pain. They really love the girls. The girls give them a happiness that I never could. And it's funny, because Vivian and Anna don't even try. They are just themselves. I tried so hard. I don't think I ever sat an exam that I didn't get honours in."

"I remember when you topped the state in the HSC," said Ruthie. "No kid had ever had a higher aggregate. It was on the front page of the *Jewish News*, wasn't it?"

"Yeah, it was," said Abe. "And you know what my mother said when people rang to congratulate her? She said, 'Yes, Abe is a clever boy. But it's easy for him. He doesn't have to work to help support the family. He doesn't even have to wash the dishes at home. It's not like it was in Poland.' She would hang up and sit down and cry. And then she'd tell me about how brilliant her younger brother was. How he worked before and after school, and still came dux of the school. This brother took her place in a shipment of Jews from the ghetto to Auschwitz. He told her to hide. But no-one would hide her, and she was put on the next train. As soon as she arrived in Auschwitz, someone told her that her brother had been bludgeoned to death on the railway platform for answering back to a kapo. Her brother's name was Shimek. I used to hate Shimek, because she cried every time she mentioned his name. I used to hate Shimek, and feel sorry for my mother. I felt sorry for my mother, I felt sorry for my father, I felt sorry for myself. Now, I feel sorry for you, sorry for Dora, sorry for the criminals I have as clients, sorry for their victims, sorry for myself. Sorry, sorry, sorry. When I was a kid, I used to watch Zorro on TV. I used to imagine myself playing his sidekick called Sorrow. Zorro and Sorrow. I thought we'd make a terrific team."

"Oh, Abe, I'm so sorry," said Ruthie. "I'm sorry that I'm upsetting you. I think that whatever it was that made you feel responsible for your parents' happiness is the same thing that keeps creeping between us. I don't know what it is. Guilt. Responsibility. I can't name it. It's a feeling in me that what I'm doing, breaking up two families, is against the essence of Jewishness. And it was because of that same Jewishness that so many people were murdered. And what is that Jewishness? It's not going to synagogue, or being religious. It's raising a Jewish family. Why would we be breaking our families up, Abe? For love? I love Eddie, I love the children. You love Dora, you love your girls. For lust? That's not enough. For lust with love? I do love you, Abe, but I've been in such a muddle about what we're doing. Now I think I can see that my unconscious has been making the decisions for me."

"What do you mean?" said Abe.

"I mean," said Ruthie, "that it is all over between us. I can't go on. And you can't go on like this. You've spent enough of your life feeling guilty. And you know, no matter how hard I tried, no matter how many times I told myself that lots of people have affairs, that lots of marriages break up, that it's no big deal, my unconscious was telling me something else. My unconscious has been giving me messages."

"What are you talking about?" said Abe.

"When we first got together," said Ruthie. "I used to think you were elegantly slender. I loved the thinness and tallness of you. Now, when I look at you I think your head looks too small and your shoulders too narrow. I try not to see you like that, but I can't stop myself. I think my unconscious has distorted the way I look at you. Sometimes I make your neck so long, it looks ridiculous. I hate myself for doing it. And something else. I've hardly been able to look up when you eat. A few weeks ago I noticed how you don't close your mouth properly when you eat, so while you're chewing your food little bits of food slip to the sides of your mouth. I remember Zoe once saying to me that when you are irritated by the way a man eats it's a definite sign that the relationship is on the way out. And I've been more than irritated. Sometimes I've felt sick. I'm not usually put off by things like that. I remember when my dad used to have little clumps of food stuck to his lower dentures, it didn't bother me. Esmeralda must have said something about that to my dad, because since he married Esmeralda his teeth have been fine. I'm sorry I'm talking about my father's false teeth, but I'm a bit shocked at what I've just said."

"What are you shocked about?" said Abe. He was crying.

"Please don't cry," said Ruthie. "I feel awful enough anyway. I really didn't mean to hurt you. I didn't know I was going to say this. I didn't even know I felt most of this. I'm shocked that it's suddenly clear to me."

"It's lucky that I ate my sandwiches before you told me how repulsive my eating was," said Abe.

"I'm sorry I said that," said Ruthie. "I know it's really hurtful. I don't think there's anything really unattractive about the way you eat. I just think that I didn't want to leave Eddie, and so your eating looked awful to me." She started to cry.

"Why didn't you tell me my eating was repulsive?" said Abe.

"Because I knew it would be very hurtful."

"Well, it's certainly very effective. I feel as attractive as an old sock. You can't make love to someone who can't stand the way you eat. Maybe Zoe was right. Maybe it's a very simple measure of love." He wiped his eyes.

"Shall we go home?" he said. "I feel sick now, and that's without anyone mentioning fricassee of fish."

"Maybe we shouldn't say fricassee of fish in front of the trout," said Ruthie. "They may be sensitive."

"Let's see if we can get a flight back to Melbourne tonight," said Abe.

"That's a good idea," said Ruthie. They packed up their picnic.

Ruthie looked around her. In the pond the fish were weaving in and out of each other's way. Frogs croaked. Birds sang. A large brown dog was scratching itself against a carved wooden sign that said "Welcome To Wombat Lodge".

We Are All Brothers and Sisters

Minnie Brot put the walnuts into a bowl. She had bought them in the health food shop. They definitely weren't as good as the walnuts from Mandel's delicatessen, she thought. They were pale and dry. Pale walnuts were usually fresh and sweet, but these were dry.

The customers in the health food shop looked pale too. Everyone was enquiring about whether this was organically grown, and whether that had any chemicals in it. Minnie wondered why people so preoccupied with being healthy should look so unhealthy. In Mandel's the customers might be a bit on the fat side, but they certainly didn't look as though their life was draining out of them.

Sadie Greenfield was arranging dried apricots, muscatel raisins and scorched almonds on a platter. Sadie had arrived an hour early for the card game. Minnie knew that this meant that Sadie had something that she wanted to talk about. Fania Frishman and Fela Plotkin always arrived together, at 8 p.m. sharp. The girls, as they called themselves, played gin rummy every Thursday. They began at 8 p.m. and finished at 11 p.m..

"I think I won't put out too many scorched almonds," said Sadie. "After all, I am on a diet, and Fania and Fela are on a diet."

"Sadie, put out all the scorched almonds," said Minnie. "You three are always on a diet. I put out this amount every week, and there are never any left, so scorched almonds must be part of your diet. I think that when you are over seventy you are allowed to eat scorched almonds."

"I'm not over seventy," said Sadie. "I'm sixty-eight."

"Well, the rest of us are over seventy," said Minnie.

"I'm upset, Minnie," said Sadie. "That's why I came early. I wanted to talk to you. You know that my Rachel and her husband, John, haven't got a lot of money. Leon has always felt bad that he didn't make enough money to be able to buy his only daughter a house. But, to tell you the truth, Rachel was never interested in owning a house. And the same with John. They liked to live simply, which was a good thing because the two of them they don't bring in a lot of money. How much can two social workers earn?

"Rachel said that one of the advantages of not being able to have children was that she and John could take the jobs they were most interested in. They didn't have to worry about climbing up the public service ladder because they had to support children. Anyway, then we had the miracle, this year, of Rachel getting pregnant.

"As soon as Leon heard about the pregnancy, he wanted Rachel and John to buy a house. Leon said that if a child grows up in Australia he should have a garden. If they'd bought one when they first got married, they would have had no trouble, but now everything is so expensive. So, Leon went to Adek Jablonski. You know Adek Jablonski?"

"Yes, I know Adek Jablonski," said Minnie.

"When Adek Jablonski came to Australia," said Sadie, "Leon was working in Mr Brajtstajn's factory in Flinders Lane. To help Abe get a start, Leon went into the factory every morning two hours before everyone else, and he cut out garments for Adek Jablonski. That's how Adek Jablonski began his business in 1950. With dresses that Leon cut out for him in the mornings. Leon lent Adek money, many many times. We didn't have too much ourselves. We were still living in one room.

"My Leon has never asked anyone for anything in his life. He used to say to Rachel, 'Never expect anything from anybody and you will never be disappointed.' But he always helped people. He helped Adek so many times. And I helped Mania Jablonski. When they had their first child, I was there every night for the first three months. Mania was so nervous, she didn't know what to do with the baby. Even Rachel used to help with the baby. Mania and Adek Jablonski were our closest friends.

"Anyway, to cut a long story short, Leon asked Adek to lend him some money so Rachel and John would have a deposit on a house. Do you know what Adek said? He said he was sorry but he had to pay one million dollars in tax this year and he was short of money himself. Leon was crying when he came home. It was the first time, in forty-four years of marriage, that I ever saw Leon cry. Two weeks later, we heard that Adek's daughter had bought herself a Mercedes for $250,000.

"What does it mean, Minnie? Do you think Adek didn't know how hard it was for Leon to ask him? What does the friendship mean if you can say no so easily? I would understand if Adek didn't have enough money to look after his own family, but he's got so much he couldn't use it up in ten lifetimes. Leon still cries when he thinks about it. We still see Mania and Adek, and I don't want to cause any trouble, but nothing is the same. The baby is due next month. Adek hasn't even asked how Rachel and John are managing. Is that what you end up with after all those years of friendship? After all those years of birthdays and barmitzvahs and engagements and anniversaries? Is this what you are left with?"

"I don't know how Adek Jablonski can forget that Leon cut out the dresses for him and lent him money," said Minnie.

"I thought that Mania was a real friend," said Sadie. "I told her things that I didn't tell other people. She used to cry with me because I couldn't have any more children."

"I didn't know that you couldn't have any more after Rachel," said Minnie.

"It was a miracle that I had Rachel," said Sadie. "Mengele operated on me in Auschwitz. He cut out one of my fallopian tubes and did a few other things. I was one of the lucky ones. Most of the girls died. And the really unlucky ones lived with half of themselves cut up and cut out."

"Oh God, Sadie. I'm so sorry," said Minnie. "I didn't know about that. I knew you were in the camps, but I didn't know about Mengele."

"When I went to doctors here, because I wanted another child, they said it was a miracle that I had had Rachel," said Sadie. "When Rachel couldn't get pregnant, I thought it was my fault. I thought that because I was in such bad condition when I was pregnant with Rachel, something in her must have not formed properly. Rachel said to me last week that she thought maybe she couldn't get pregnant out of sympathy with me.

"You know how many times Mania Jablonski cried when I told her that I would probably never be a grandmother? She cried and cried. I thought it was out of sympathy for me, but now I think she just likes to cry. Maybe she thinks that if she cries a lot it means that she is a very sensitive person."

"I think Fania and Fela are here," said Minnie.

"How do you know?"

"Because I can hear Fela's car. She always does a U-turn, and drives over my neighbour's lawn and up on my footpath. I had a tree that the city council planted outside my house. Fela knocked it over every week. The council replaced the tree three times. I asked Fela to be more careful, but she said she was very careful. I'm the only one in the street without a tree in front of their house."

"Hello, hello, hello," said Fania. "I am in a lucky mood tonight. I said to Fela, I can feel it in my bones that I am going to win tonight."

"Minnie, can I make a quick phone call?" asked Fela. "You all go and sit down. I will be at the table in a minute."

"Fela, are you ringing Shlomo again?" said Fania. "What did you forget to tell him tonight?"

"I didn't tell Shlomo that there is a nice piece of honey cake in the fridge," said Fela. "You go. Go and sit down. I'll join you in one minute."

"She treats that Shlomo Plotkin as though he was two years old," said Fania. "And Shlomo enjoys it."

"Well, if she enjoys it and he enjoys it, what's wrong with it?" asked Minnie.

"What's wrong with it is that Shlomo is seventy-four. He knows where the cake is, and he can get it himself," said Fania.

"Was Shlomo happy to hear about the honey cake?" Fania asked Fela.

"As a matter of fact, he was. He said honey cake was just what he wanted," said Fela.

"Good," said Fania. "Now we are all happy. Deal out the cards, Minnie."

"Are you being sarcastic, Fania?" said Fela.

"No," said Fania. "I am serious. I am happy that Shlomo is happy. I am, altogether, feeling very happy tonight. I am wearing the new stockings that my daughter-in-law bought me from America."

"They are not stockings, Fania," said Fela. "They are pantyhose."

"OK, they are pantyhose," said Fania. "It's the same thing. These pantyhose are a brand called Opal. They are so comfortable. On the packet it says: 'Opal for the Ample'. That's a good way of putting it, isn't it?"

"Opal for the Ample. That's very clever," said Minnie.

"Opal for the Ampule?" said Fela. "What does it mean?"

"Ample, not Ampule," said Fania.

"I thought it was ampules, like the Elizabeth Arden ampules I put on my face," said Fela.

"Ample means large," said Fania. "Well, maybe not large, but bigger than medium. Yes, bigger than average, that's what ample means. And these Opal for the Ample are wonderful. They fit me just right around the tuches. That's where I am ample. I'm not so big in the waist, as a matter of fact I've got a small waist, and still very slim legs, but it's my tuches that is the problem."

"That was nice of Jack to buy you the ample pantyhose," said Fela.

"I told you it wasn't Jack," said Fania. "It was Christine. I tell you, she is a shikse, but she is a very good daughter-in-law. I can't complain about her. When I think about how upset Joseph and I were when Jack told us he was going to marry her. She is more of a mensch than Jack is. He is lucky to have her. She sends the boys to Bialik to learn Hebrew and to learn about their Jewishness? You think Jack would do this? Never. What does he care about his Jewishness? When the boys were little Christine said to me that she wanted them to grow up with some knowledge of religion, and that as the Jewish religion was acted out in the home, mainly, not in some church, and was based around the family, she would prefer the boys to know about Judaism."

"What use will it be to the boys to know about Judaism?" said Fela. "According to the Jewish religion they can never be Jewish because their mother is not Jewish."

"That is typical of you, Fela Plotkin," said Fania. "You always try to spoil things. Well, let me tell you, you don't know everything. You don't travel, you don't know what goes on anywhere in the world apart from Caulfield. So how can you be so confident that you know what the Jewish religion accepts and doesn't accept?"

"The Jewish religion says that the mother has to be Jewish. It has always been like this," said Fela.

"Well, Fela Plotkin, the world is changing. It may be not be changing so quickly in Caulfield, Australia, but it is changing. Christine told me that in America they are accepting children whose fathers are Jewish, as Jews. It's the Reform synagogue. If they are doing it in America, they will be doing it here in a few years."

"Jack must have been happy to hear that," said Fela.

"Jack? Pheh!" said Fania. "Do you think he cares about his

Jewishness? He doesn't care. Do you think he cares about his mother? Of course not. He is a big shot. A doctor. A gynaecologist. He belongs to the South Yarra Tennis Club. He plays tennis, my Jack. He is more interested in his tennis than in his mother. A big gynaecologist he is! I told him that I have got a problem, right down there, in his area. Does he listen? No. He says, 'You're fine, Mum.' Fine, I could be so fine that I could drop dead. I had to go to my GP. He referred me to a gynaecologist."

"I remember Jack was such a sweet boy," said Fela.

"He was a sweet boy," said Fania. "But he's not such a sweet boy now. I don't know what happened. And my Miriam, she is not much better. She used to be sweet too. Now, she talks to me in the same voice that she talks to her children. Like I am an idiot. I wanted to give her something special for her birthday. She has got enough money to buy herself whatever she likes. So I thought I would give her something of mine. Something from my own home. After all, it's the home she grew up in. I showed her all my beautiful silver, and my crystal. I showed her the gold and white coffee service, the silver salad bowls, the Czechoslovakian china fish platters. Nothing interested my beloved daughter. 'It's not to my taste,' she said. 'It's not to my taste.' She said this to everything. And what is this very special taste that she managed to get? It is a snob's taste. And how did she get this snob's taste? She got it because both of her parents worked like dogs so that she could study and be educated. She got so educated that now she knows exactly what is to her taste and what is not. But she didn't get educated enough to know that it is better to have something from your mother than something that is to your taste.

"Pheh! When I think of how hard Joseph and I worked to give her this good taste. I asked her if she would like to come to the Victoria Market with me to see where Joseph and I had our first stall. She said she never goes to markets. She doesn't like to be in crowds. She doesn't like to be in crowds! When you are a princess, like my Miriam, you can know what you like and what you don't like, and what is to your taste and what is not to your taste. She learnt all of this while Joseph and I were selling socks and underpants in the Victoria Market."

"That makes me very sad," said Fela. "I remember when they were small. They had such happy little children's faces. They were so nice."

"Yes, they were nice," said Fania. "Anyhow, enough of this talking. I'm not concentrating on the game. No wonder you are winning, Fela. Have you picked up your card yet, Sadie?"

"Yes, but this card is no good to me. No good at all," said Sadie.

"Maybe I can use it. Maybe I can," said Fania.

"Everybody has got problems with their children," said Fela. "When all the children were small, everybody said how their Johnny was so clever, and their Esther was the best in the class, and nobody could play the piano like little Hymie. And now it's trouble, trouble, trouble. Maybe it's not so bad that Shlomo and I didn't have children. I heard, Minnie, about your Susan and her Harry."

"That's all fixed up now," said Minnie.

"I heard about it quite a while ago, but I didn't want to say anything," said Fela.

"I heard too," said Fania.

"Me, too," said Sadie.

"Everybody heard," said Minnie. "When you paint 'My husband is shtooping a shikse' on the front of your house, everybody knows."

"I think it was a call for help," said Fela.

"A call for help?" said Fania. "I would say it was more a sign of madness."

"I think it was a call for help, too," said Sadie.

"Susan didn't really need to make this call for help," said Minnie. "By the time Harry saw the sign, he already knew he had made a big mistake. He already knew that his life was with Susan, not with the other woman. He said to Susan that it was almost a relief to him when he saw that big sign. He had been trying to think of how to explain himself to Susan. When he saw the sign, he started to laugh. He said to me that he wasn't sure why he started to laugh. But he sat on the front steps, and he laughed and he laughed until he nearly platzed. He said he deserved the sign. He thought it was the perfect thing for Susan to have done. He is an interesting man, my son-in-law."

"He sounds a bit of a pervert to me," said Fania.

"He's not a pervert," said Minnie. "He is an interesting, complicated man. He wanted to paint 'Your husband is sorry' underneath, but Susan wouldn't let him."

"Are they all right with each other now?" asked Sadie.

"Yes," said Minnie. "They are all right. I always knew he loved Susan. She knew too. And he knew."

"If everybody was so clever about knowing who they loved, why did he have to shtoop the shikse?" said Fania.

"Fania, darling," said Minnie, "we are only human beings. None of us knows, all the time, exactly what we want, and what we are feeling, and what is the right thing to do. Just as you did your best for your children, Harry did what he thought was the thing he had to do."

"Don't look so upset, Fania," said Sadie. "You asked for that."

"Minnie didn't say anything offensive to Fania, Sadie," said Fela. "Minnie was just explaining how you can do the things that you think are for the best, and they are not always for the best."

"I don't need your help, Fela," said Fania.

"Girls, girls, pay attention to the game," said Minnie.

"So Harry and Susan are happy together now?" asked Sadie.

"Yes," said Minnie. "They are happy together. They are in therapy together now. They are learning to understand each other more."

"They have been married for a very long time," said Fania. "How much more can you learn about someone?"

"You can always learn more," said Fela.

"Therapy?" said Fania. "Everybody is in therapy. You get a

headache and you go to headache therapy. What did people do before therapy?"

"They suffered," said Fela.

"They are still suffering," said Fania. "Only now they are suffering in therapy."

"Harry didn't have an easy life when he was a young boy," said Minnie. "You know he was in Europe during the war. He was in Buchenwald."

"Hitler, Shmitler," said Fania. "I don't want to talk about the Nazis."

"You never did want to talk about them," said Minnie. "You were lucky. You left Europe before the war. If you'd stayed, you may not have been able to avoid talking about them, or you may not have been here to talk about them."

"If I was so lucky to leave Europe, you were even luckier. You were born in Australia," said Fania.

"Fania, don't be so infantile," said Minnie. "My point was that you never wanted to talk about the war. Not now, and not in 1948. I remember you wouldn't come and help us at the Jewish Welfare."

"My Jack was very little and he needed me," said Fania.

"Well, look at what Jack says now, when you need him. He says you'll be fine," said Fela. "Maybe it would have been better for Jack to share you with the refugees."

"Fela Plotkin," said Fania, "you haven't got any children, so I don't think you are in a position to tell me how I could have been a better mother. Look at what is happening to me tonight. I am losing every game. I am losing all my money. I am just not playing my best. It is all the talk about Jack. I come here to forget Jack."

"Don't worry, Fania," said Sadie. "We all mixed our children up. We thought we could create a perfect world for them. We thought we could create new families for them. We asked them to call our friends Aunty and Uncle. Aunty This and Uncle That. Rachel had so many aunties and uncles. The truth was that she didn't have one aunty or uncle. And all the pretend aunties and uncles didn't turn out to care about her at all. We gave her so many relatives, and not one of them felt related to her. They all cared about their own children and their real relatives. And I guess that is fair enough.

"I wanted Rachel to have a big family, like the families that Leon and I grew up in, but what I learnt was that you can't create families, you have to be born into them. And Rachel was born into a family that were all murdered. I'm sorry, Fania, to upset you by mentioning the war again."

"How can you say that Rachel has got no family apart from you and Leon?" said Fania. "Where you have got Jews, you have got family."

"How can you be so hypocritical, Fania?" said Minnie. "You wouldn't even help with the Jewish Welfare. Was that in the spirit of family feeling?"

"Are you trying to make me feel bad?" said Fania.

"Maybe," said Minnie.

"Well, you can't make me feel bad," said Fania. "I've won this round."

"You've won the card game, but not the argument," said Minnie.

"I've also won ten dollars," said Fania.

"I used to think that Jews stuck together," said Sadie. "Looked after each other. They do stick together, but only when it suits them. When it doesn't suit them, they turn away. Jews use Jewish lawyers and doctors and accountants. If there were Jewish hairdressers, they would use them too. But they use the Jewish lawyers, doctors and accountants only because they trust them more, not because they want to help them by giving them the business."

"I'm sorry, you are wrong," said Fania. "We had a Jewish plumber, here in Caulfield. He was from South Africa. He had to go back to South Africa. He was very good, but the Jews didn't use him."

"Of course they didn't use him," said Minnie. "Jews know that Jews know nothing about plumbing."

"But he was a good plumber," said Fania.

"How were we supposed to know that he was a good plumber?" asked Fela.

"We should have given him a chance," said Fania. "He was one of us. A brother."

"That's what the women from the Jewish Welfare said to Leon and me when we arrived in Australia," said Sadie. "She came on to the boat to meet us, and she said, 'We are all brothers and sisters working together to make a new world.' I remember, I kissed her. I was so happy to have a new sister. Well, it turned out that no-one was anyone else's brother, and all the sisters were someone else's sister. And Leon and me, we stayed as sisterless and brotherless as we arrived."

"I'm your sister, Sadie," said Fela.

"And you've got me," said Minnie.

"I know," said Sadie. "I'm sorry."

"I have lost again," said Fania. "It's Sadie's fault. All that talk about brothers and sisters. It upset me."

"You are losing, Fania, because you are not playing very well," said Fela.

"That is what I said, Fela. I am too upset about the brothers and the sisters to play well," said Fania.

"Is that the telephone I can hear?" said Sadie.

"Yes, it is," said Minnie. "I didn't hear it. I'll go and answer it. I'll sit this round out, girls. I'll go to the bathroom while I'm up. You go ahead and play."

"Hello?" said Minnie.

"Mum," said Gloria, "I know you're probably in the middle of your card evening, but Mrs Berner's daughter just told me that Ruthie is having an affair with Abe Lipshitz. Mum, this can't be true. First Susan and Harry, and now Ruthie. What is happening to our family? Have you heard anything?"

"Gloria, calm down," said Minnie.

"Calm down?" said Gloria. "First I'm the laughing stock of all Melbourne because my sister paints 'My husband is shtooping a shikse' on the front of her house. Then, just when I explain to people that Harry was very disturbed by the war, he lost his parents and his brothers, and this year he forgot for a moment that he really loves Susan, Mrs Berner's daughter calls me to say that Ruthie is shtooping with Abe Lipshitz. Tell me it's not true, Mum."

"It's not true," said Minnie.

"Are you sure it's not true?" said Gloria.

"I'm sure it's not true," said Minnie.

"How can you be so sure?" said Gloria.

"I can be so sure," said Minnie, "because I know that it is all over now."

"All over *now*?" screamed Gloria. "So she was shtooping with Abe Lipshitz, the little bitch. What is wrong with Eddie? Wasn't one man enough for Ruthie?"

"I think that when she was shtooping with Abe she wasn't shtooping with Eddie, so probably one man was enough," said Minnie.

"Are you trying to be funny? How come you are sounding like one of those radical feminist, left-wing communists? 'Oh, my daughter-in-law can shtoop this one as long as she's not shtooping that one.' When did you become such a women's libber?"

"Calm down, Gloria. I said, it is all over."

"How do you know it is all over?"

"Because Ruthie told me," said Minnie.

"Ruthie told you about it?" screamed Gloria. "How could you let her talk to you about it? You're Eddie's mother."

"Could you stop screaming, Gloria? Ruthie told me about it when it was all over. She thought that I suspected something, and she wanted the air to be clear between us."

"If she wanted to have clear air around her she should have

stayed clear of Abe Lipshitz. I think it's pathetic. It's disloyalty of the first order. Disloyalty to Eddie, and to Susan and Harry, and to me and Manny, and to you. Did you suspect anything?"

"Yes, I did."

"You suspected something and you did nothing about it?"

"What should I have done?" asked Minnie.

"Punish her," said Gloria.

"I didn't do anything, because I trusted Ruthie," said Minnie.

"And what did she do? She betrayed your trust."

"No, she didn't betray my trust in her. I thought, and I still do think, that she is a very good human being. And I can see that she loves Eddie."

"She loves Eddie so much that she had to shtoop with Abe Lipshitz, is that it?"

"She loves Eddie so much that she didn't leave him for Abe Lipshitz," said Minnie. "She didn't leave him, even though the boys were old enough to understand."

"Children are never old enough to understand," said Gloria.

"You may well be right, Gloria. That may be the cleverest thing you've said tonight."

"What do you expect me to say? 'Oh, how liberating and exciting it is that my sister-in-law can cheat on my brother'?"

"There are worse ways to cheat and belittle your spouse than to shtoop with someone else," said Minnie. "There are men and women all over Melbourne who have cheated their wives and husbands, and have never once shtooped with someone else."

"I have never shtooped with anyone else in my life," said Gloria.

"And you are also a very good wife to Manny," said Minnie.

"Thank you," said Gloria.

"And Ruthie is, and has always been, a very good wife to Eddie," said Minnie.

"And it's definitely over between Ruthie and Abe?"

"Definitely, that I can tell you for sure. In fact, Abe and his wife just left for a month in Europe together. Dora's sister, Golda, told

Ruthie. She said it is Abe and Dora's first trip away together without their children. Golda said that Dora was as excited as a child. She said that Abe didn't even tell his secretary where they were going. It's going to be a real holiday for them, Golda said."

"You let Ruthie talk to you about Abe Lipshitz and his wife holidaying in Europe?" said Gloria.

"Why shouldn't I?"

"I don't think you should have been encouraging Ruthie to talk about Abe Lipshitz."

"But she was talking about Abe's trip to Europe with his wife. She was saying, that according to Dora's sister, it looks as though Abe and Dora are definitely trying to fix things up between themselves."

"I still think Ruthie should be talking about Eddie," said Gloria.

"She talks about Eddie, Gloria darling. She talks about Eddie. But I better stop talking to you, or the girls will have eaten all the scorched almonds."

"Did Eddie know?"

"I don't know if Eddie knew," said Minnie. "And I think that maybe Ruthie is not sure if Eddie knew or not. But what I do know is that Eddie knows that Ruthie loves him. It wouldn't surprise me if Eddie knew about Abe. But Eddie's always been a very smart boy. And not just smart at making money. He knows what he's got in Ruthie."

"I think I'll ring Eddie and ask him and the boys to dinner this Friday," said Gloria.

"You mean that you will invite Eddie and Ruthie and the boys," said Minnie.

"Yes, Mum, of course that's what I mean."

"Well, it's not what you said."

"Maybe I'll invite Susan and Harry too."

"That's a very good idea," said Minnie. "And what about me?"

"You always come on Fridays," said Gloria.

"I was joking," said Minnie.

"What a family table it will be," said Gloria. "Do Susan and Harry know about Abe and Ruthie?"

"I don't know," said Minnie. "But please don't say anything."

"What do you think I'll say? 'Hey, Susan, you and Eddie have got more in common than you know'?"

"Gloria, are you trying to make me nervous?"

"No. Go back to your card players. I hope there are some scorched almonds left. I feel like some myself after this conversation. Goodbye, Mum."

"Gloria, before you go, I forgot, I wanted to ask you something," said Minnie. "Can you lend me fifty thousand dollars? Just for a few years. Four or five years?"

"Of course," said Gloria. "What do you want it for?"

"For something."

"You're not going to Europe for a special holiday with someone, are you?" said Gloria.

"Me?" said Minnie. "I'm very happy in Caulfield."

"So you're not going to tell me what the money is for?"

"No."

"OK. Don't tell me. I don't care. When do you want it by?"

"As soon as possible."

"I'll drop in a cheque to you tomorrow," said Gloria.

"You're a good girl, Gloria," said Minnie. "You were a good sister to Susan and Eddie when they were small, and you are a good daughter to me."

"Oh, Mum, you'll make me cry," said Gloria. "Go and have a scorched almond, and I will too."

"I thought I was going to be lucky tonight," said Fania. "Some luck. I have lost thirty dollars, and I have got an upset stomach. Maybe it was the walnuts? Where did you get those walnuts from, Minnie?"

"From the health food shop," said Minnie.

"They don't look too healthy," said Fania. "I thought you always bought your nuts from Mandel's?"

"I usually do," said Minnie. "But Sofia Ritman came to visit me this morning, and we talked so much that I didn't have time to go to Mandel's. Next time, for sure, I'll go to Mandel's."

"Good," said Fania. "I don't want to make you feel bad, but I don't feel too good after these walnuts."

"How is Sofia Ritman?" said Fela. "I haven't seen her for a couple of years. Did she find another husband?"

"No, not yet," said Minnie. "But she's trying."

"I heard that she almost got Moishe Zimmerman before that Filipino girl grabbed him," said Fania.

"Fania, I've had enough from you tonight," said Minnie. "First, the walnuts, now Moishe Zimmerman. Moishe is my mechatunim. Remember? He is Ruthie's father, and he is a very fine person. And so is his wife, Esmeralda."

"I still think he would have been happier if he'd had a Jewish wife," said Fania.

"How happy do you want him to be?" said Fela. "He looks very happy to me."

"He looks happy to me, too," said Sadie.

"Fania, I saw your own dear husband yesterday," said Fela, "and he didn't look so happy."

"Fela, Joseph had an upset stomach yesterday, and that's why he didn't look too happy," said Fania. "I myself hope that Moishe Zimmerman is happy because everyone says that second marriages among the older generations don't work. And I can understand that. You can't get used to a new husband or wife after you have had your old one for thirty or forty years. It's different for young people. They are married for a few years and then they get divorced. By the time they marry the second husband, they can't remember what the first husband looked like."

"I don't think it is quite like that, Fania," said Sadie.

"It's like that. It's like that. Believe me. I know," said Fania. "All the young are divorcing. The *Jewish News* should have a divorce notices page. They could put it after the barmitzvahs and engagements. Or it could go in between the births and deaths."

"There's something in what Fania says," said Fela.

"Yes, a divorces page might not be such a bad idea," said Minnie. "All the young people could see who is eligible again."

"I wasn't talking about the divorce page," said Fela. "I was talking about second marriages being harder for people our age. You have extra problems. Like, who inherits the money, your children or their children?"

"Fela's right," said Fania. "Mrs Rose divorced Mr Frenkel because he wanted to leave all his money to his children and not to hers. I understood her point of view. His children were already wealthy. He had given them money all his life. Her children were not wealthy. And, if he really loved her, surely he would have wanted to look after her children, not to just keep giving his own spoiled children more and more."

"It is eleven o'clock," said Sadie. "Time to go."

"You played very well, Sadie," said Fela.

"I wasn't too bad tonight, was I?" said Sadie.

"I wasn't in my usual form," said Fania. "I am sure it was the walnuts."

"Fania, I'll clear the table up quickly, while you use the bathroom," said Fela. "I went to the bathroom before."

"Thank you, Fela," said Fania.

"I won sixty dollars tonight," said Sadie.

"I think that's a record, isn't it?" said Minnie.

"I think so," said Fela. "We will ask Fania. She always knows what everyone wins and loses."

"I think maybe we shouldn't mention to Fania how much I won," said Sadie. "She is in a bad enough mood from not winning herself."

"Fania will be all right," said Fela.

"Are we ready?" said Fania.

"Yes, we are ready," said Fela.

"How much did you win, Sadie?" said Fania.

"Sixty dollars," said Sadie.

"Sixty dollars," said Fania. "None of us has ever won sixty dollars in one night. Some people have all the luck."

Minnie walked Sadie, Fania and Fela to their cars. Fania and Fela got into Fela's car. "Sadie," said Minnie, "about that problem with Adek Jablonski. I think I can help you."

"Don't say anything to Adek Jablonski, please," said Sadie.

"Of course not," said Minnie.

"I don't care about Adek Jablonski knowing that you know," said Sadie. "It's just that Leon would be so ashamed if people knew that he had asked Adek Jablonski for fifty thousand dollars and Adek Jablonski had said no."

"I wouldn't dream of saying anything to anybody," said Minnie.

"I know you wouldn't, Minnie," said Sadie.

"I think I've got a solution to the problem, anyway," said Minnie. "I'll call you in the morning."

"Minnie, you're a mensch and a half, and not just because you are looking for a solution to my problems," said Sadie. "Goodnight."

Minnie watched Fela reverse over the curb and drive on to the neighbour's lawn. Fela waved to Minnie. Fania waved from the passenger's seat. Minnie waved goodbye to them.

She walked back into the house. She had noticed that there were a few scorched almonds left. She was pleased.

What God Wants

Every second Sunday Moishe and Esmeralda Zimmerman visited Bluma Zimmerman at the Springvale Cemetery. Moishe always wore a suit and Esmeralda wore her dark green hat and matching jacket. They cleared the stray leaves and odd bits of stone and earth from Bluma's tombstone. Even though Springvale Cemetery was well maintained, the graves always needed extra cleaning. Moishe paid Mr Arbat, who looked after a lot of people's tombstones, thirty dollars a week to make sure that Bluma's grave was neat and tidy, but Mr Arbat, Moishe decided, had too many clients to give the graves the attention they deserved.

Every second Sunday Esmeralda would polish the marble headstone and remove the dead heads from the azalea, which was growing vigorously in its concrete pot. Then Esmeralda would go for a walk while Moishe talked to his wife.

Moishe no longer felt Bluma's absence so painfully. For the first two years after her death he had felt as though he had a large hole in his chest. He could feel himself leaking from this hole. Every day he had woken up surprised that there was still some of him left.

Moishe wasn't sure when this had changed, but one day he had caught himself talking to Bluma. He was telling her about Sofia Ritman's attempt to seduce him with her almond biscuits. And Moishe had realised that he had Bluma back. She was there, inside him, intact, and he could again share the details of his daily life with her.

Moishe told Bluma everything. He told her about his boss,

Harry King, and how the business was going. He told her what the takings from the shop were each week, and which fabrics were currently most popular. He told her about Ruthie. Ruthie had looked after him very well since Bluma's death. She rang him every morning, and again every night. He knew that Bluma would have been proud of her daughter.

When he had decided to marry Esmeralda, the first person he told was Bluma. He knew that Bluma would have been surprised by the news. Neither of them would have expected that Moishe would marry again, but then neither of them had expected that Bluma, who had been eight years younger than Moishe, would have died before him.

Since Bluma was taken away from him so unexpectedly he had become wiser, and knew more about the surprises of life. And he knew that Bluma, in her death, would have learnt things that were difficult to learn in life. Moishe now knew that it didn't matter if people were Jewish or not Jewish. He knew that Bluma would now know that too.

He knew that there had been a lot of gossip about him and Esmeralda. Not many Jews in Melbourne had Filipino wives who were almost half their age. Moishe didn't mind what people said. As long as Bluma understood, he was happy. And he had explained enough to Bluma for her to understand that Esmeralda was as much of a refugee as any Jew. She had suffered hunger, persecution, war. And as for her age, in terms of what she had experienced, Esmeralda was as old as any of them.

Esmeralda hadn't taken over Bluma's house. She had quietly found a few spare spaces, and squeezed herself in. Bluma's presence was everywhere in the house. Bluma's creams and lotions were still in the bathroom. Her clothes were in the cupboards, and the bedroom drawers were still filled with her bras and girdles. Two of her clean, unironed blouses were in the laundry.

The Bluma who was present was not the sick Bluma who had wasted away with cancer. Esmeralda had put away all the medications, all the vitamins, the tubes and clamps and pumps, the disposable syringes, the special cushions and all the other accoutrements of illness.

The Bluma who was there was the healthy Bluma. The Bluma before the cancer. Photographs of her and Moishe at barmitzvahs and engagements and weddings were on the sideboard in the lounge-room. On the television there was a photograph of her at the beach with Ruthie when Ruthie was small. And in the bedroom, in the middle of the dressing table, framed in an ornate silver frame, was a photograph of Bluma when she was sixteen. It was Moishe's favourite photograph. You could see Bluma's quiet exuberance. It was a characteristic Ruthie had inherited, thought Moishe. Neither Bluma nor Ruthie had found it easy to express outright joy. And Moishe could understand why. They were Jews. And Jews knew that no matter how happy they were, a disaster could come and hit them at any moment. Esmeralda knew that too. If the phone rang late at night, she jumped. If there was an unexpected knock at the front door, she retreated.

When Moishe stood next to Bluma's grave, he felt very close to her. As he talked to her, he could almost smell her. He could almost touch her. Often Esmeralda interrupted Moishe to remind him of something that she felt Bluma should know. This morning she had come up to him twice. "Did you tell Bluma that Ruthie got an honour in Contract Law?" she had asked.

"No, I forgot," he had answered. "I'll tell Bluma straight away."

"And tell her how pretty Ruthie is looking," said Esmeralda. "Tell her that Ruthie looks more pretty every day."

Five minutes later Esmeralda came back. "I want you to mention to Bluma that I keep the house very clean for her."

"I think Bluma knows this," Moishe said.

"I want to make sure," said Esmeralda.

Once they had driven all the way back to the cemetery when Esmeralda had discovered that Moishe hadn't told Bluma that they had found Brownie, Bluma's old cocker spaniel, who had gone missing for four weeks. "Bluma will be very happy," was the first thing Esmeralda had said when Brownie had reappeared.

On Sundays, when Moishe finished talking to Bluma, he and Esmeralda usually went for a walk around the cemetery. Every fortnight there were new graves. The cemetery was almost full. Moishe could remember when it was opened. He could remember Morry Glatt's builders finishing off the red brick fence that circled the cemetery. Now there were very few empty plots left.

The cemetery was like a village. The gold and black lettering on the headstones looked like calling cards. Announcements of each particular resident, and their place in the universe.

"Look, Esmeralda," said Moishe. "There's Sarah Green's grave. Poor Sarah, she wasn't even cold yet when someone was trying to get her husband. Minnie Brot told me that at the minyan there were three widows with such low-cut dresses that nearly everything was falling out."

Most Sundays there was a funeral taking place. Today the rabbi had just finished the prayers and the mourners were shovelling spadefuls of earth over the coffin. Moishe explained to Esmeralda that this custom was partly to guard against the ghost of the departed one returning to harm an old enemy. Thinking about some of the people who were buried there, Moishe felt that it was a good custom to continue.

Moishe and Esmeralda saw Sofia Ritman.

"I wish you a long life," said Esmeralda.

"I wish you a long life," said Sofia Ritman.

"I wish you a long life," said Moishe.

"You see, she is already a Jew," said Sofia Ritman to the woman standing next to her. "First she took a Jewish husband, and now she is taking on the Jewish religion. She knows the right thing to say on every occasion. At Pesach she wished me 'Shana Tova'. And somebody told me that she can play a good gin rummy. It is shocking."

"Which part is shocking?" the woman asked.

"All of it," Sofia Ritman replied.

* *

Springvale Cemetery was a place where, sooner or later, you met most of the Jews in Melbourne. The community was made up largely of postwar migrants who were now being buried by their children and their grandchildren. Death was indiscriminate. The rich were dying and the poor were dying. And here at Springvale they lay one next to the other. Tied to each other, in the end, not by their donations to Israel or their mansions in Toorak or their positions on the board, but by their faith. Even the ones with no faith claimed their Jewishness in death.

Moishe and Esmeralda walked past Herschel Bodsky's grave. "It's a shame that you didn't know Herschel," said Moishe. "He was a simple man. He didn't make big money, but he would have given me and Bluma the shirt from his back. Whenever Bluma and I were in trouble we rang Herschel. He was like a father to us, which is a funny thing because he was only a few years older than me. He had a heart of gold."

"I wish I had known Herschel. I'll bring some flowers for him next time," said Esmeralda.

"Next to Herschel is Mr Schneider," said Moishe. "He is a big shot. Well, he's not a big shot any more, he is dead, but he used to be such a big shot. He owned nine factories. He came to Australia before the war. I worked for him for a few months. He paid me half the wages he should have. He did that to all the Jews he employed. He was such a stingy man. He shouldn't be buried next to Herschel. Herschel is too good a man to be a neighbour of Sol Schneider."

They had reached the section of the cemetery where only Cohens were buried. "Cohens are supposed to be the highest order of Jews," said Moishe. "They are supposed to be responsible for religious teaching. They can't even go to a funeral unless it is the funeral of one of their family. If they want to go to a funeral they have to stand far away from where it is being conducted. You should see some of the Cohens. If they are higher people then God must know something that the rest of us don't know. There is

Shimek Steinberg. He was a Cohen. He was a shmuck. He cheated everybody, even his poor wife. Some higher person he was! Henry Baume, who killed himself, was a Cohen, but he can't be buried there. People who have committed suicide have to be buried far away on the edge of the cemetery. They have to be at least six feet away from any other dead Jew. People said that Henry Baume lost the will to live after his wife died, and now he is not even buried next to his wife."

"That's terrible," said Esmeralda.

"That's what God wants," said Moishe. "It's a funny business, this business of what God wants. It would be better if the things that God wanted were a bit closer to the things that we all want."

"Maybe there would be more things wrong if God listened to all of us," said Esmeralda.

Ruthie knew that something was wrong when Moishe arrived at her place at lunchtime on Wednesday. He still worked five and a half days a week, and never took a day off work.

She watched him walk up her driveway. He looked pale. She had a terrible sinking feeling in her stomach. She ran downstairs and opened the front door.

"Hello, Dad," she said. "What's wrong?"

"You can see straight away that something is wrong?" he said.

"You don't look well. Come inside and sit down."

Moishe sat down in the middle of the cream leather sofa. He sank into the overstuffed sofa and nearly disappeared. Suddenly he looked small.

"Ruthie, I don't know how to tell you this," he said. "To tell you the truth, it is not something that I ever dreamed I would have to tell you."

"What is it, Dad?"

"I don't know how to tell you, darling," he said. He looked down at the floor, and when he looked up again his eyes were full of tears. Ruthie looked at her father and started crying.

"Dad, please tell me," she said. She put her arms around him.

"Ruthie," he said, "Esmeralda is pregnant."

Ruthie felt herself go limp with relief. "Oh, Dad," she said, "I thought you were dying, or someone was dying. I'm so relieved."

"Ruthie, darling, I feel ashamed of myself. I feel ashamed that Esmeralda is pregnant. Esmeralda thought that she was sterile, that she couldn't have any children. Ruthie, it is not that that part of our lives is a very big part, but we are two normal people and every now and then we did what normal people do, and now Esmeralda is pregnant. And now I feel like I'm going to bring shame on Mum's name, and people will talk even more than they are already talking. Ruthie, I am seventy-six."

"How does Esmeralda feel?" asked Ruthie.

"She was very shocked when the doctor told her. She was sure he had made a mistake. She went to him because her stomach was swollen. She thought it was constipation."

"Her stomach is already swollen?"

"The doctor told her she is six months pregnant."

"Six months and she didn't suspect anything?"

"Well I think that's because she has never been pregnant, so how could she know what it feels like?" said Moishe.

"And how does she feel now?" said Ruthie.

"I think that really she is very excited," said Moishe. "Except that she knows that I am feeling very mixed up and she is such a good person that she doesn't want to look too excited in front of such a mixed-up person."

Ruthie felt stunned. She didn't know how she felt. "Dad, I'm so glad there's nothing wrong with you," she said.

"Nothing wrong with me?" Moishe said. "I am seventy-six and my forty-four-year-old wife is having a baby. What else should be wrong with me to have something wrong?"

"I don't think it is such a disaster," said Eddie when he came home. "We can be grandparents while we're very young, without most of the hassle."

"Eddie," said Ruthie, "we won't be grandparents. This child will be my brother or sister, and your brother or sister-in-law."

"I don't think it's going to be a calamity," said Eddie. "Esmeralda is pretty calm. I think she'll manage well."

"It was a pretty strange feeling to have my father confessing to a pregnancy," said Ruthie. "My dad had tears in his eyes. I remember when I was young, the worst thing in the world that my girlfriends and I could imagine happening to us was having to tell our parents that we were pregnant. The abortion didn't seem to be the insurmountable problem. It was telling your parents. I was one of the few girls who never ended up having an abortion. Remember how I wanted to have an abortion when I was pregnant with Jonathan? And you insisted that I have the baby. I remember feeling so miserable about leaving uni. I've never really told you, but I'm very glad that you didn't let me have an abortion."

"I knew it. I didn't need a formal acknowledgment," said Eddie.

"This afternoon," said Ruthie, "when I was talking to my father, I had the oddest feeling of roles being reversed. It felt very topsy-turvy."

"Ruthie," said Eddie, "let's buy a beautiful nursery for this baby. We'll buy a cot and a pram and a bassinet and some toys and whatever else it is that babies need."

"You really are unbelievable," said Ruthie. "You support me and the boys. You looked after my mother and father, and you still look after my father. He has no idea how much you paid for his new car. And now you're going to look after the new baby."

"We've only got one family, haven't we, Ruthie?"

"Moishe Zimmerman is a pig," said Sofia Ritman to Minnie Brot. "At his age to shtoop so that that shikse gets pregnant."

"For a start, she isn't 'that shikse', she is his wife. And secondly, pardon me if I'm ignorant about this, and I could be because I myself haven't shtooped with anybody for a long time, but isn't it the same if you shtoop to get pregnant or not to get pregnant?"

said Minnie. "And after Bluma Zimmerman died, weren't you yourself hoping to be the next Mrs Zimmerman, if I remember correctly? I may have forgotten about shtooping, but I still remember how much you were trying to impress Moishe Zimmerman."

"Yes," said Sofia Ritman, "but with Moishe and me, shtooping would have been like holding hands, not like what he did with the shikse."

"I wish you wouldn't call her the shikse. Her name is Esmeralda," said Minnie.

"Well, to tell you the truth, Minnie," said Sofia, "I noticed at the cemetery that this Mrs Esmeralda Zimmerman was looking a bit fat. I thought to myself, thank God it is not just the Jewish wives who become fatties. So, your daughter-in-law, Ruthie, is going to have a brother or sister over forty years younger than her?"

"It's not the worst thing in the world that could happen, Sofia," said Minnie.

"Nothing escapes Sofia Ritman," Minnie said to Ruthie. "None of us noticed anything at all, and she had already noticed that Esmeralda had gained weight."

"Sofia knew more than Esmeralda did," said Ruthie.

"How do you feel about the baby?" Minnie asked Ruthie.

"Well, it gave me a terrific shock," said Ruthie. "And, actually the thought of Dad and Esmeralda making love made me feel a bit uncomfortable. I know it's naive to think that they wouldn't have been making love, but somehow I imagined that they were with each other for comfort."

"And you think that sex isn't part of comfort?"

"I guess it is. I've been thinking about babies myself lately. For the first time since I had my tubes tied, I've been feeling clucky. It's probably part of getting older and seeing my childbearing years coming to an end. I don't want any more children, I just don't like the thought of not being able to have any. I think this will be a good time for me to be a grandmother to Esmeralda's baby."

"You'll be the best-looking grandmother in Melbourne," said Minnie.

Ruthie rang her father. "Dad," she said, "I just want you to know that I am very happy for Esmeralda that she is pregnant. It was a shock at first, but now I've got used to it. Every woman should have a child. And Esmeralda's got no family except for us. So now we'll all have a bit more family. Dad, I want you to know that I'll always be here for Esmeralda and the baby. Eddie and I and the boys. We are your family and her family."

"Darling, you have made me more happy than you could know," said Moishe.

"Can I speak to Esmeralda?" said Ruthie. "I just want to say the same to her."

"I'll get her," said Moishe.

On 17 December, after a two-hour labour, Esmeralda Zimmerman gave birth to an eight-pound baby boy. Ruthie took the birth announcements to the *Jewish News*. She gave the woman in the office her announcement. It said:

> We wish to announce, with great joy, the safe arrival of Adam Zimmerman. Brother, brother-in-law, and uncle of Ruthie, Eddie, Jonathan and Jason Brot.

Moishe had written his own notice. It read:

> Moishe Zimmerman, widower of the late Bluma Zimmerman, and his wife Esmeralda Zimmerman, stepmother of Ruthie and Eddie Brot, and grandparents of Jonathan and Jason Brot, wish to announce the birth of Adam Zimmerman. Son, brother, brother-in-law and uncle.